ABUNDANCE

Also by Sena Jeter Naslund

Ice Skating at the North Pole

Sherlock in Love

The Animal Way to Love

The Disobedience of Water

Ahab's Wife; or, The Star-Gazer

Four Spirits

ABUNDANCE

A Novel of

Marie Antoinette

Sena Jeter Naslund

wm

WILLIAM MORROW

An Imprint of HarperCollins*Publishers*

This book is a work of fiction. References to real people, events, establishments, organizations, or locales are intended only to provide a sense of authenticity and are used fictitiously. All other characters, and all incidents and dialogue, are drawn from the author's imagination and are not to be construed as real.

Designed by Betty Lew

ISBN-13: 978-0-7394-8378-7

For my beloved daughter

Flora Kathryn Naslund

Oh, you women of all countries, of all classes of society, listen to me with all the emotion I am feeling in telling you: the Fate of Marie Antoinette contains everything that is relevant to your own heart. If you are happy, so was she.... If you have known unhappiness, if you have needed pity, if the future for you raises in your thoughts any sort of fear, unite as human beings, all of you, to save her!

—Germaine de Staël, from *Réflexions sur le procès de la reine* ("Reflections on the Trial of the Queen"), 1793

ACT THREE

Contents

ACT FIVE

Author's Note

History, like fiction, is in many cases a matter of interpretation, especially when one tries to understand motivations or to link causes and effects. My readers may well wonder how accurate a historical portrait is presented in these fictive pages. Relying primarily on contemporary scholarship, I have tried to imagine the Marie Antoinette story accurately and to achieve a degree of understanding of this traditionally misunderstood and often maligned queen. Often, I have tried to employ phrases, translated into English, available in the historical record—initially recorded in memoirs by those who heard her remarks or surviving in real letters exchanged between Marie Antoinette and her mother, the Empress of Austria.

Within this novel the reader will hear Marie Antoinette, when she first sets foot in France, spontaneously ask her hosts in Strasbourg, France, to speak to her only in French, not in German, implying how fully she wished to embrace her new identity as French; she actually did say the words given her in this novelistic rendering of the occasion. Likewise, at the end of this novel, when Marie Antoinette mounts the scaffold to the guillotine, the words she speaks were her actual words. Many readers will expect to meet in these pages the Marie Antoinette of tradition, a woman reputed to have said, when informed that the people of eighteenth-century France were starving, "If they have no bread, then let them eat cake." But that notorious retort will not be found here. Why? She never said it, and contemporary biographers, such as Antonia Fraser, have taken care to vindicate Marie Antoinette in this matter. That heartless sentence was the speech of another queen, the wife of Louis XIV, not Louis XVI, a hundred years before a very young and innocent Marie Antoinette traveled by horse-drawn coaches from Austria to France to marry the Dauphin destined to inherit the throne of France.

The fate of this charming, beautiful, extravagant princess is well known, but through imagination, based on research, the reader will experience her life as she lived it moment to moment. Full of human needs, fears, and talents, Marie Antoinette engaged life with an abundance of feeling and met death with heroic courage, during the Reign of Terror in the French Revolution. I have written this novel believing that her life, one often marked by compassion and gaiety, like all our lives, is a valuable one.

Act One

An Island in the Rhine River, May 1770

Like everyone, I am born naked.

I do not refer to my actual birth, mercifully hidden in the silk folds of memory, but to my birth as a citizen of France—*citoyenne,* they would say. Having shed all my clothing, I stand in a room on an island in the middle of the Rhine River—naked. My bare feet occupy for this moment a spot considered to be neutral between beloved Austria and France. The sky blue silk of my discarded skirt wreathes my ankles, and I fancy I am standing barefooted in a puddle of pretty water.

My chest is as flat as a shield, marked only by two pink rosebuds of nipples. I refuse to be afraid. In the months since I became fourteen, I've watched these pleasant rosebuds becoming a bit plump and pinker. Now the fingers and hands of my attendants are stretching toward my neck to remove a smooth circlet of Austrian pearls.

I try to picture the French boy, whom I have never seen, extending large hands toward me, beckoning. What is he doing this very moment, deep in the heart of France? At fifteen, a year older than myself, he must be tall and strong. There must be other words than *tall* and *strong* to think of—to describe him, to help me imagine and embody his reality.

My mother, Empress of Austria, has told me how to anticipate the meeting of our bodies and all the events of my life to come; I am always in her prayers. Every month I will write to her and she to me, and our private letters will travel by our own couriers between France and Austria. When I try to picture my future husband, Louis Auguste, standing in the forests of France with hands and arms outstretched to me, I can only envision my most dear mother, dressed in black, sitting behind me like a dark wedge at her desk; she awaits the courier bearing a white rectangular packet, the envelope that represents me.

After I am married at Versailles, when Louis Auguste and I are alone in bed, certain events will follow. We will copulate through the door at the bottom of my body; next, I become pregnant. Nine months after my marriage I give birth to a baby. There will be many witnesses when my body, then age fifteen, opens to produce a future king. Years from then, after my husband has died, this baby will be the seventeenth Louis, King of France. This is what I know.

While my ladies flutter like bright butterflies around me, I glance at my naked body, a slender worm. Louis Auguste and I must be much the same, as all humans are really much the same, except for the difference of sex. We all have two legs—mine are slender—supporting a torso; two arms sprout on either side of a bodily cabinet, which contains the guts and bladder in the lower compartment and the heaving lungs and heart in the upper section. In between, for women, is the chamber called the womb. From the trunk, a neck rises up like a small lookout tower whose finial is the head.

Mine is a graceful body—made strong by dancing and riding—and of a milky porcelain color. Recently a few curly threads emerged from the triangle between my legs. Squeezing my thighs together, I try to shelter this delicate garden because my new hair seems frail and flimsy.

The French word for him, the prince who will become my husband and king, is *Dauphin,* and the French word for me, who will be his bride, is the same, but with a small letter *e*, curled like a snail in its flinty house, at the end of the word: *Dauphine.* I have many French words to learn.

My darling Austrian ladies sail around me in their bright silk dresses—cerise, and emerald, deep blue-with-yellow-stripes; their throats and sleeves bedecked with frothy, drooping lace. Like dancers, they bend and swoop to gather the garments I've shed; other ladies, standing patiently, hold my new French clothing folded across their forearms, cloth of gold and filmy lavender.

A flock of goose bumps sweeps over my bare flesh.

Antonia, the pretty mouths of my ladies breathe, *Antonia.* Their eyes glisten with unshed tears, for I am about to abandon my old name.

The stern French require that I step forward, naked, with no ribbon, memento, ruby, or brooch of Austrian design. To my ladies, I display my open palms so they may witness and affirm that I leave empty-handed and am beholden in no way to my native Austria. Resplendent in rich colors, they draw near, in a solemn circle, to regard my vacant hands.

My nakedness complete, now I die as *Maria Antonia,* Archduchess of Austria, daughter of Maria Theresa, Empress of Austria.

To be her worthy daughter, I will that my chilled flesh unpucker itself and become all smooth and lovely. Clothed nobly in nothing but my own skin, described as *pearly* by some in its translucent sheen, I begin the donning of French clothes, no longer *Maria Antonia* but my French self, now named: *Marie Antoinette.*

I GASP—my first damp breath of French air on this small island embraced by the arms of the rushing Rhine—and remember the admonition of my mother: *Do so much good to the French people that they can say that I have sent them an angel.*

So said my mother, Empress of Austria, and I *will* love them, and they will love me, and I will love my husband, who is shy, they say, and the old King, Louis XV, who is not my future husband's father (that Dauphin having died without his ever having become king) but his grandfather; and I will love the maiden aunts of my future husband, Louis Auguste, who will become Louis XVI, God willing (but not soon, not soon I hope and pray, for in fact I know that not only my unformed body but also my spirit is still that of a child), and I will love the Duc de Choiseul, the great foreign minister of France, who has made my happiness come about by mating me with Louis Auguste, whom I have never seen yet—and I will love the Count Mercy d'Argenteau, for he is Austrian—*Austrian!*—and my mother's friend and our—no, not "our" but "the"—Austrian ambassador to France. I will love them all, especially Choiseul the foreign minister and Mercy the Austrian ambassador, even as I have been instructed always to love those who further our cause—the peace of Europe. And I will find new friends, my very own friends, to love as though they were sisters.

But now they say Mops is not to accompany me. Mops! More precious than any ornament of silver or gold because Mops is a living being who scampers across my heart with all four of his fast little feet! My loyal companion, Mops is not a *thing* to be abandoned! Mops has tender feelings. But it is this very loyalty, and mine to him, that disqualifies him for passage.

I place the heels of my hands, like broad stoppers, against my closed eyelids, behind which hot tears are collecting. Unfortunately, when I press inward, tears gush out and track my cheeks. Someone is pulling my hands away from my face. I must present a cheerful countenance to the French—no one needs to remind me. Making myself cheerful is my own chore, a task I must spare these kind souls around me. Because I hold no handkerchief or possess not so much as a sleeve with which to dry my tears, I hunch up the round of my bare shoulders, on each side, to wipe my eyes and cheeks.

Then *Mops, Mops!* I cry again, while my imploring hands beseech the empty air. He lifts his darling black-button pug nose and howls and yaps. Tossing his forelock from his brown eyes, he struggles to leap from the vise-grip of strong female hands. He cannot prevail, so he wags his tail like a little plumy flag, the best flag, the flag of my own heart to try to cheer me. *Au revoir*, Mops.

The bare ends of my toes yet touch the blue silk of Austria, puddled on the floor around my feet. Blue, blue as the Danube swirling through Vienna on a bright blue day. I believe silk and water *do* have something of the same fluid slipperiness.

My ladies would have me to step forth. It is the littlest toenail of the most little toe on the left foot that lastly brushes the fabric of the House of Hapsburg. All my being rushes into this insignificant toenail, not so big as a shiny sequin or a flake of trout skin. My toenail is like the loop on the letter *e* at the end of a word: *Dauphine.*

Auf Wiedersehen—my little toenail whispers to the silk. To think, that it is the tiniest toenail so honored, the last part of me tangent to home!

"She's like Venus rising from the sea," my Austrian attendant exclaims, to make me feel clothed in beauty. But I am rising from the Rhine and am the Daughter of the Danube.

"Like Flora, goddess of flowers, and a goddess herself," another murmurs, so that I lift my chin, to be worthy, and I suck the air through my nostrils as though, indeed, I were smelling flowers, as though I were among lilacs in some enchanted garden—yes, a theatrical garden, on a floral stage. Trained by the best dramatic coaches of Europe, I raise my eyes and inhabit my role.

"You make too much of me," I say gently and smile.

"How prettily she speaks."

"They will adore her," they say.

Emotion plays within their words as fragrance lives in flowers; their sympathy for me is fringed with fear.

Suppose the French do not adore me, neither the King, the Dauphin, nor the people?

"My sorrow is to leave you behind," I say, performing serenity, but, lo, now I myself experience that feeling I have invented for their dear sakes.

Turning to embrace them once more—how strange to embrace someone who wears clothes, when you yourself wear none! Their skirts rustle and creep against my bare thighs, while their own firm legs are veiled in layers of fabric. My skin brushes against their silk ribbons, a stripe of velvet, hard jewels sewn against the colors of their skirts.

Unclothed, I feel less human than they, in their finery.

From outside this chamber, Mops barks once, distantly, in his high, sharp voice. *Punctuation!* my mother, the Empress, humorously used to say of such unexpected assaults on the ear.

Quickly, quickly, my darling Austrian attendants dress me in a chemise of creamy French silk, then come the sterner, scratchier petticoats from Paris. The soft stockings, they say, were knit in Lyons (but where is that?), and tapered-toe shoes made at their court—Versailles, and next the lilac skirt and bodice of gold, laced tight, and oh, snowy lace, half made of airy nothing, settles around my throat. Tenderly, I touch my neck and feel my skin, more delicate than swan's down.

Does Mops still wear his blue silk collar, the silver buckle that I fastened this morning with my own fingers? They've carried him away.

In the place of furry Mops comes the stately Prince Starhemberg. Perhaps he is really Mops in disguise, transformed by fairies! If my sister, my best and dearest sister and also dearest friend, if my Charlotte were with me, she would smile at my fancy. Her sensibility is with me: they can never pry it from my soul! The Empress has selected Prince Starhemberg—short, sturdy, wrinkled of face—to be my trusted escort all the way to the depth of France, but I feel alone.

Clenching my fingernails into the heels of my hands, I wish again for my sister Maria Carolina, whom I call affectionately Charlotte, who loved just my own favorite card games and music and theatricals and sleighing and fun. I miss my Charlotte, already married and become the Queen of Naples, but I carry her in my heart. *Have your fun, daughters*, the Empress used to say, *before there are marriages and deaths, and alliances to be made.* She spoke to all of us, not necessarily to me, mostly forgotten, being the daughter in tenth place in the chain of diplomatic marriages, hence, tenth in my mother's hopes—and love. *Have your fun*, she would say, exhaling a long slow breath that reminded me of the north wind, *for life is not all play*.

I look at the prince whose eyes are like my mother's—direct, knowing, discreet. Then, can I trust him? I must, for I am clothed and named now in the French manner, and it is time to cross over, my hand in the crook of his arm.

When I hear the waters of the Rhine swirling around this island, I hear the sound of panic, even through the walls. Or is it the rushing of my blood through the vessels of my heart? Here the walls are smothered in tapestries; I gaze at myths of ancient, woven worlds, crowded spectacles that Prince Starhemberg and I must walk past. I see a feast table surrounded by flowers, lilies and roses. In a wedding scene, the banquet table is heavily laden; there, in a blue bowl, threaded apples sit beautifully round and red.

Dressed in the lavender loveliness of France, laced up with golden cord,

I progress in my new silk shoes, which fit strangely and tip my body at an unfamiliar angle. I must move forward. The angle itself propels me. Does Louis Auguste try to visualize me? By chance, is he walking toward me at this moment? Does he reach out his hand—but pause, instead, to pick up a book bound in red leather and stamped with gold? I fear he may prefer reading to conversation, no matter how polished the phrases or how musical the tone of voice. I do not like to read. I prefer the garden—*mille fleurs*—to the library and its myriad, unfathomable books.

At home, my mother must be conferring with her ministers. In Vienna, brilliant men lend the suppleness of their minds to that of majesty, but I fear both women and men who are too bright and knowing. My older sister Marie Christine was very clever—and cruel—to us little ones, but she is the daughter most loved by our mother. Marie Christine wanted us to feel that we didn't count. Perhaps my mother regrets that she could not make Marie Christine the Dauphine. Yet Fate, as well as my mother, has dealt me a card of Importance that far outweighs what marriage brought Christine. My hand on Prince Starhemberg's velvet arm, I will myself not to tremble as we walk forward, my curved French heels sinking into the deep rug.

Through a short hall, twenty steps traverse this conduit, and I am delivered to a room the twin of the Austrian one, left behind. Again, the walls are covered with tapestries.

A red velvet cloth cloaks a table, which, I have been told, represents the boundary of France, where stand her emissaries, waiting. My womb lurches within me, and I think of my disgrace should my blood flow now—at this moment. It is too soon, far too soon! Let it be my stomach, not my womb, that seizes itself! The boundary velvet is a hue exactly like that produced by my own body at the monthly visitation of our "Générale Krottendorf." *You may think of me and of home*, my mother told me, *when there are moments of special difficulty.* In France, I have faith, my buds of breasts will surely begin to swell and blossom, and I am not to doubt that this ripening will occur any more than I could doubt that the spirit of my mother the Empress, when it is her time to die, will join my beloved papa, who was her true companion, in heaven.

The maturation of my bosom is as sure as the resurrection of the body.

It is my stomach and not my womb that lurches, because my womb renews itself with its red tides *later* than it should but never *earlier.* Or is it earlier, and never later? Charlotte says the moon is a perfect clock for the arrival of her Générale, but my clock is erratic, and in what phase is the moon tonight? My mother does not like this irregularity about me, though she agrees it is beyond my controlling. Not me, but Générale Krottendorf commands the blood red tides, which some call the *curse* and my mother terms the *blessing*.

When my body ripens, inadequacy will be replaced by abundance. My breasts—my mother lifted two crystal goblets toward me, showing me the size and shape of their clear, capacious bowls—will fill such cups. Nonetheless, at this moment my lungs have become monstrous hands to wring my heart as I pass round the end of their table.

I CANNOT SPEAK! But my body, rushing forward, speaks for me.

I fling myself into the arms of Her, the French Comtesse de Noailles, who is to become my Maternal Guide—my mother, as I grow in France to womanhood.

In the very moment of flinging myself forward, I have remembered the flight of a cherub, a genius, a tiny body, surely winged, who did not hesitate but flew across a stately room. Mozart! age six, just my age, his astonishing performance at the keyboard completed, hurled himself to his destination, my mother's lap, where he was kissed and welcomed. "Now do you love me?" he not so much asked as demanded. Led by the fluttering wings of infant genius, I hurl myself spontaneously, only fourteen! without restraint, toward Her, the Unknown.

I am not welcome. No arms encircle me. From such blank rigidity, I rebound. The Comtesse de Noailles stands straight as a column, a body animated by no spirit. My eyes seek her face, a nose squeezed between two large circles of rouge. Her tiny mouth is moving.

Her words plank down like dead notes: there is no music in her speaking. She rebukes me for my impulsiveness: "You breach etiquette." I must loosen my embrace, step back, give the appropriate ceremonial embrace *first* to the Comte de Noailles. "To my husband, first," she instructs, "not because of his French noble rank but because he is a Grandee of Spain as well." True, I have forgotten his rank, though in the past, in Vienna, all their lineages have been memorized.

With perfect grace, though perhaps I blush, I comply with her request. Madame Etiquette, I dub her, secretly.

I meet all the new ladies-in-waiting. Yes, etiquette, plus formality, is their concern, but I will speak from my heart, in spite of them, with my own lightness. *How kind of you.... Enchanté.* My curtsies are as sure as a series of dance steps, a theme with slight variations, each nuanced, perfectly graceful. I twinkle and charm; my rosy blush, my lifted chin, my cherub cheeks, all partake most exquisitely in the minuet of manners. They cannot resist.

And now, I am French.

But one who will be Queen.

LIKE EVERYONE, I am alone inside this pearly flesh—and I am afraid.

Strasbourg

The hooves of the horses clatter over the bridge that joins the neutral island to the land beyond.

"To France," I remark conversationally to my companions within the crimson coach.

The Comtesse de Noailles clears her throat. The eyes of all the others merely look straight ahead, avoiding my gaze.

"More exactly," Madame Particular says, "the horses' heads are turned toward Strasbourg, which despite its Germanic name, we know to be thoroughly French."

I smile at her with utmost friendliness. "Yes," I say, being very careful of my French accent, "to my great delight, we shall soon be in Strasbourg."

"Not so very soon," she replies.

"I believe they are prepared to greet us most ceremoniously," I add. "Even the children of the city will bring me flowers and extend their warm best wishes."

"It is a nice enough town, I'm sure," she replies.

Perhaps she would like a little silence now. The Empress has told me to beware of too much curiosity and of chattering.

As in Adam all die, so in Christ are all made alive, my mother said devoutly. She slid off her chair to her knees and made the sign of the cross. Her black-clad arm swept across the dark widow's fabric covering her ample breasts. To think that I am her fourteenth child! God has made her a fountain spilling children instead of waters. I have not yet made a bosom companion of Jesus, but the Empress promises that he will come to me and help me whenever I truly call on him or any of the saints.

Mortality is a cause for humility, she said to me. *None of us knows when he might be taken, as your blessed father was taken. Death, like birth, comes to us all, regardless of rank or station in life.*

Yes, I understood and do understand how this idea is true. It could be the will of God suddenly to strike the Comtesse de Noailles dead, though that would be terrible, and I by no means wish for such an event. God could also strike me dead. At any moment my heart might stop beating. I press my fingertips against my breastbone. Very faintly, I feel the thumping behind the bone.

And yet, you were born to become a queen, my mother the Empress went on. *We believe in the divine right of kings and queens to rule, just as we believe in the right of God to do with us as He wills. People are born to their station in life, still you must take instruction now, and by letter, when you are away in France, as how best to prepare yourself for the day when God will take His Majesty Louis XV to heaven, and you and the Dauphin will become the King and Queen.*

She told me that she had counseled Amalia and Charlotte before their marriages, just as she was advising me. She told Amalia that because she would be a foreigner in Parma she must conform to the wishes of her husband, or she would be greatly disliked. *You, too, will be a stranger and a subject,* she told me, drawing me to sit on her knee. Because her stomach is so large, her knee was a small perch, and I feared I might slip right off the black satin.

The Empress said she also had told Charlotte not to draw comparisons between Austrian customs and those of Naples. *Charlotte, like yourself, has been chosen as a queen, not a mere duchess, like Amalia*, she said to me, and I could tell that she loved Charlotte more, though she loves Marie Christine most of all and let her marry somebody she knew—Albert. When Amalia wanted to marry Charles of Zweibrücken, whom she truly loved, our mother told her she must marry otherwise, for the peace of Europe and the good of Austria. Fortunately for me, I do not love anybody else.

I hope France's Louis Auguste is nicer than Charlotte's Ferdinand, King of Naples. Even though Ferdinand is seventeen, we learned through our ambassador to Naples, Ferdinand likes to play tricks on the courtiers and make them trip and fall. Once he even chased somebody with his chamber pot, full of stinking discharge.

The Comtesse de Noailles says, "The Archduchess, Madame la Dauphine, has thought of something amusing. Do share it with us, if you please."

"Pardon me," I reply. "It is only a family memory. I feel that I should devote my thoughts to the future, rather than the past."

Loyal Prince Starhemberg says in his mild way, "Of course you are quite correct about that, Madame la Dauphine." He looks out his coach window to signify that the matter is closed.

Charlotte says that King Ferdinand himself does not stink, though he is quite ugly. I hope he has nice eyes. We cannot control what kind of head our eyes are stuck into, but eyes themselves convey expression, and that reflects the soul.

Because my mother has spies everywhere, she sees or learns about everything important that occurs all over Europe. I overheard somebody tell her that King Ferdinand of Naples said the morning after his wedding night that our beloved Charlotte slept like a dead woman and sweated like a pig. I hate him for that crude speech, uttered so carelessly that it made its way back to Vienna. And what did he do to Charlotte to make her sweat?

In France, I shall find a friend whom I can love as much as Charlotte.

A FRIGHTFUL BOOM shakes the air.

They are firing the cannon in Strasbourg, this first of the French cities that I will someday rule as queen. Looking out the coach window and over the tops of the chestnut trees, I see a church tower and a joyfully swinging bell. All around our coach, bells are ringing. Their clappers are almost knocking themselves through the iron sides of the bells to express the excitement of the people. The exuberance of it all!

And here they parade! A troop of Strasbourg children in white, in the costumes of shepherds and shepherdesses come from fairyland, to greet my carriage. These children dressed like shepherds and shepherdesses seem like little lambs in all their natural innocence.

The coach stops; the door is opened; they crowd forward, holding up baskets of flowers to me, and I bend to put my nose into their sweet colors. When I look into their faces, I smile with all my heart at these lovely children. They are neither French nor Austrian, but simply children. In response to my smiles, their faces brighten from within. Like the sun, I can shine upon them and make them happy.

I know a truth: my greatest pleasure will always be to give my subjects pleasure.

I step down to stand among them. It is the impulse of my body that instructs me, and Prince Starhemberg murmurs approval. To express majesty, I stand tall, but my backbone remains supple like that of a good dancer, never stiff. As I walk beside the slowly moving coach, the children frolic ahead to strew my path with flower petals, pink, white, red, mauve, and yellow. Here are young maidens in their best dresses to toss before me small bouquets, the stems of the flowers bound together with thread or a prized ribbon, which sometimes I stoop to gather.

All these fair young people are intoxicated with happiness. In reassuring them with smiles and a pleasant countenance, I reassure myself.

I gasp: their fountains are gushing red! But the liquid is only wine.

In the square, whole oxen are roasting, and they perfume the air with their hearty aroma of crisping fat. From huge baskets members of the town council are handing small loaves of bread to the poor. In the trees hang glass balls, colorful as overblown fruit. All around me are the matrons and tradesmen and ancients of the city, with dark blue dresses and yellow shirts, and some still in their brown leather aprons, and white blouses edged in red thread. With my heart clapping against my ribs as hard as those iron tongues against their bells, I stand in the middle of it all, radiating love to the good people of my new country.

Waiting for me on a high platform are the nobles and clerics and the civic *dignitaires*, all of them dressed in silks with colors as rich as emeralds, sapphires, rubies, and topaz, and these gleaming fabrics are further adorned by wide lace collars and starched lace cuffs. Most splendid is the Prince

Louis de Rohan, whose lace collar is a wondrous web of intricate white threads. Though he is destined to become a prince of the church, like his uncle, he smiles at me as though he would like to invite me to dance. Demurely, I lower my gaze.

The *dignitaires* request me to climb the steps to their platform, where I can be seen by those even at the edges of the vast, joyful crowd. The people's pleasure in me and my pleasure in these simple folk of France form a true alliance. When speeches of welcome begin, in the German language, I gently interrupt and say to the gracious orator, "Don't speak to me in German. From now on I want to hear no other language but French."

The people howl with pleasure, so much do they approve of my gentle statement. The mayor and *dignitaires* are surprised by the firmness of my direction, and so am I. All their mouths stretch wide, smiling at my request for the French language. So delectable is the moment that I think *They would like to eat me up, as though I were sugared fruit.*

Prince Starhemberg, my knowing escort, whispers in my ear, "Well done, Madame la Dauphine." I know he speaks for my mother, the Empress. Behind me, someone remarks under his breath to a friend, "She shines as naturally as ripe cherries." It is the Prince Louis de Rohan.

Flowers perfume the air. Some of the matrons wear peonies in their hair, and maidens have threaded white lilies in their tresses. For the men and lads, *boutonnières*—bright yellow jonquils—trumpet their goodwill and stud their shirts like medals.

Clear and fresh, their speeches of welcome ring out in the spring air. At the end, I speak a few words of thanks and of appreciation for the beauty of the city and of the celebration. My words carry for some distance into the crowd, and then I see people turning around to tell those behind them what I have said, and those, in turn, turn around and tell the people behind them, so that like a ripple the content of my sentences is conveyed outward, as far as my eye can see.

DO SO MUCH GOOD to the French people that they can say that I have sent them an angel, my mother, through her maternal tears, bade me. I have begun.

Already, with much naturalness—for it is also my own desire—I have loved them.

With the nobility, I feel somewhat less at ease. Though entertained quite regally at the episcopal palace of the Cardinal Louis Constantin de Rohan, uncle to the young prince who dared to compare me to a bunch of cherries within my hearing, I am shocked by the lavishness of this family. They use the resources of the church as though its income were their own. In the morning I find myself more exhausted than refreshed by their tireless conversation about the importance of the de Rohan family, but I ask to hear Mass before continuing my travels. Prince Starhemberg armed me against their pretensions by whispering to me privately that Prince Louis, the nephew who is in his thirties, has already established a reputation for profligacy.

At the door of the great cathedral of Strasbourg, I am greeted not by the cardinal but by his nephew preening in his purple clerical robes as the coadjutor of the diocese. He is an ambitious young man. I hope he never inherits his uncle's position as cardinal. Although he makes a flowing speech to welcome me, I do not believe in his sincerity. I can tell he knows that I doubt him, for he ends his address by complimenting my mother, believing that I cannot fail to be won over by his praise of her: "You will become for the French the living image of the beloved Empress, admired by all of Europe for many years and whose reputation will continue to be venerated forever. Because of you, the spirit of Maria Theresa of Austria will become united with that of the Bourbons of France."

I bow my head with gracious gravity, but the gesture is calculated to hide the incredulity that must be registered on my face. Once inside the cathedral, I can barely see my way in the dim light. The prince takes my hand to guide me toward the altar to receive the sacraments. I can feel the jeweled rings on his soft fingers. It is the hand of hypocrisy and immorality, and I feel besmirched by it.

Nonetheless, before entering again the coach that is to bear me away, I experience a reluctance to leave this most hospitable town of Strasbourg. As I mount the step into the coach, upholstered this time in blue, my smile is steady; my heart quakes and trembles only a little. When I have seated myself, I close my eyes and burrow my nose into a pink bouquet of tiny early roses. I kiss the tiny faces of the roses.

We begin to move. The whip crackles in the air to make the horses step more smartly. Last fall, when I was still only thirteen, I shed tears for a rose beside my bed that had died in the night. In the morning, the pretty thing had turned from pink to tan, and its head drooped down on its stem as though it were embarrassed by its mortality. I sympathize with the fragility of flowers.

Sometimes I prefer to have about me flowers fashioned by thread, like these embroidered into the blue velvet upholstering the coach. And I love morning glories carved in marble mantels or sunflowers cast in metal, or blue iris represented in paint by skillful human fingers. The flowers of artifice are *safe* in all their prettiness.

The lovely lives of real flowers are short.

Inside the Blue Coach

We set off again on a journey that I am told will continue many days before we arrive at our destination. I am to meet my husband in the forest near Compiègne, deep within France, but still a day's ride from the Court of Versailles. Then I shall be presented for the first time, in my person, to His Majesty Louis XV, and his grandson, the Dauphin, said to be quiet and awkward, but fair-haired like myself and very pleasing in his portrait.

Because it showed him plowing, the first portrait of my Dauphin was rejected by the Empress. I, however, was charmed by the image of a king, like a farmer, at his plow. Perhaps he was only playing at plowing. I myself quite love to pretend, for it is the very best kind of diverting play. And pretending is so portable. One can pretend anywhere.

When the Empress and I first saw the portrait of the Dauphin, his ambassador also presented me a diamond brooch, which I promptly pinned to my dress, just outside my heart, to show my willingness to be wed with Louis Auguste. I said, "Already he is close to my heart," and my mother was surprised and most pleased with the appropriateness of my comment, which we both knew would be repeated when the ambassador returned to the Court of Versailles.

As this coach sways and rocks forward, I ask my companions about the pleasures of the Dauphin, and they say he likes to pick locks and to fashion new locks. And he likes to hunt. I myself love to ride.

When Charlotte left Vienna for her wedding trip, she stopped the coach to leap out and embrace me and to cry over me because she was leaving. At home, when one of us got sick, so would the other, to keep her company. In our portraits, one can scarcely tell Charlotte and me apart, though people say I am a little prettier. I don't think so, nor do I want to be. She is my darling, and my mother says I may still write to her, but our letters should be channeled through Vienna.

When I was married at home, ceremonially, in a gown of glittering silver that spread behind me like a wing, my brother, the graceful Ferdinand, substituted for Louis Auguste and represented the groom. I represented myself. At the altar in the Church of the Augustine Friars, when I knelt with Ferdinand, most seriously, I hoped he would wink, or at least smile. A little round of gold slid down the knuckles of my finger. I rolled the ring over and over like a tiny wheel on the axle of my finger.

In the old days, custom required that witnesses watch as the bride and proxy groom climbed into bed together. And then! Then! Yes, he was required to cock his knee and place it between her thighs! I would have laughed out loud to have brother Ferdinand nudge his knee against me, but this charade is not required in modern times. It is comforting to think that sometimes ridiculous practices are abandoned, but by what means? Perhaps there is a gradual *erosion*. I know that water can wear away a stone.

My mother has schooled me about the marriage art, and I know well what organ is represented by a knee between the thighs of a bride. But I cannot imagine what that organ resembles. Certainly not a *knee*, even a small one, or I would have noticed such a shape in men's trousers. My mother said, *His part will become like a finger—somewhat enlarged, surprisingly firm, straight and rigid.*

All depends on the wife, on her being willing, sweet, and amusing. The Empress herself has instructed me.

What of the Light?

This carriage takes me farther and farther from home. When on the island in the Rhine, I threw myself into the arms of the Comtesse de Noailles, the result was only a lecture on etiquette.

I feel only sorrow that I have failed to please. Sorrow—and not resentment—for my mother says that resentment is the most readily visible of all the sinful emotions, but sorrow can enhance one's sweetness and appeal. Resentment, the Empress says, is like a snake that nests in the bosom, and it can turn and strike her who harbors it.

Outside the carriage window, beyond the veil of dust rising up from our wheels, the countryside is full of fields of green-growing grain. I too would like to stretch and feel green. In the fields, I see a million *Marie Antoinettes* spread around me, like loyal subjects basking and stretching in the golden sun. When we roll into the shadowy forest again, the dark green leaves reflect spots and glances of brightness as though coated here and there with silver.

Is light more silvery or gold?

THE MAP TO MARRIAGE

Behind us, in a long and jointed tail, are dozens of carriages, all part of the procession to Versailles. I'm sorry that they must breathe our dust. I sigh. Sometimes, as we go round a curve, I see the lead horses, their great flanks and flowing manes and tails. Because they are changed frequently, I have no favorites, but I especially enjoy a large, dappled gray pulling us forward with his easy strength. For countless hours at home, I could study Clara the dangerous rhinoceros or watch Hilda the innocent hippopotamus lolling in our menagerie that our father populated with the most exotic animals from distant continents.

To see a creature so rare as slick, wet Hilda makes the whole scalp crinkle with pleasure, as though the brain is about to sneeze. To best give delight, my dear Papa used to tell me, one forgets who she is and simply floats and shines, like Hilda in her element.

Inside, this blue box is always the same, and I can scarcely enjoy the nobility of the trees for Madame de Noailles's droning away like a musette, or as we would say in German, like a *Dudelsack.* It makes me miserable to think that she is my most honored lady-in-waiting and yet so ordinary, so tedious. Yes, she is a *Dudelsack.* I doubt if she has any talents to enliven her soul.

The landscape seems to my eye more French at every turn of the wheels of this blue upholstered coach. The carriage wheels will roll down many days, with stops along the way, before I meet the Dauphin and the King. It is the King above all others whom I must please (but my husband, Monsieur le Dauphin, as well, of course), so says my mother, for the King has the right to send me back if he chooses.

As we jiggle along, I draw from a soft red morocco case all tooled with gold a map of the entire route from Schönbrunn to the heart of France. I carefully spread the map across my lap and study those places marked for me to note. I am to meet the King and his grandson, my husband, at a place where a far end of this very road crosses a river, at the Bridge of Berne, in the forest of Compiègne where the King and the Dauphin like to hunt.

I put my right finger on the map to keep my real place and my left finger on the Bridge of Berne, far ahead. I practice moving my right finger along the road drawn on the map till the right finger meets the left one. It appears that such a distance *can* be traversed and such a meeting *can* occur.

But will they love me?

The Nunnery

On our journey, we stop to visit Madame Louise, a nun, and the youngest of the Dauphin's aunts; the other three aunts (all daughters of Louis XV, all unmarried) await me. But Madame Louise, like myself, has herself changed her name—to become Sister Thérèse Augustine. She too has been born anew, but as a nun living in a Carmelite convent.

I like her face, framed with starched linen of the whitest white. She has kind eyes.

But I feel sorry for her locked away from the world. I speak to her of our journey, of the beauty of the chestnut trees in bloom and how the creamy panicles stand among the leaves like candelabra. I wonder if she ever considers her life to be a mistake.

When I am about to leave the convent, escorted by Count Starhemberg, Sister Thérèse suddenly draws me back to her. She smooths my cheek with her holy hand and then whispers in my ear, "You are the most perfect princess as to face and figure." She bends her face yet more closely to me, and I hear her wetting her lips with her tongue.

"You have an air," she breathes into my ear so softly that her words are like a pleasant dream, "all at once, of possessing grandeur, modesty, and sweetness."

In a swirl of black, she turns and floats down the crimson corridor.

Those words, more precious than any diamond brooch, I pin to the inside of my heart.

Inside the coach again, I vow, by the heavenly blue of the curtains that surround me, to try to be worthy of her terms: *grandeur*, which I owe my origins, my own royal blood, the gift of the Hapsburg dynasty, six hundred years old; *modesty*, which I owe my gender, as the descendant of Eve and as a mere human child of God; *sweetness*, which I owe to myself, because it is my true nature.

Surely her three sisters, those aunts of the Dauphin who remain in the world and live at the Court of Versailles, will guide and love me. With new dedication to obedience, I remember my mother's instruction to spend much time with Madame Adelaide, Madame Victoire, and Madame Sophie. *These princesses,* the Empress said, *possess many virtues and talents; you are fortunate to have them; I hope you will behave so as to deserve their friendship.*

My mother also wrote the King a letter about me, already anticipating that I shall make many errors. *Her intentions are excellent, but given her age, I pray you to exercise indulgence for any careless mistake.*

But I shall make no mistakes.

In the Forest of Compiègne

The horns of our entourage have sounded, and through the forest of Compiègne come the answering calls of France. I hear them again! *They* are present someplace in this wood. We rush forward, and so must they be rushing forward under the trees. Again and again the horns call to one another. Louder and louder as we grow closer, and it seems my heart is sitting on my tongue thumping away like a drum. I love to feel my beating heart, the excitement—the *life* of life! But oh, in what golden voices the trumpets speak!

Their royal coach, the first coach—all magnificence—containing I am told the King of France, his grandson, and his three aunts rushes into view! Behind them follow a great spectacle of colors, coaches, the guards, the light horsemen, musketeers, all with drums, trumpets, timbale, and oboes with their nasal bleat.

Suddenly we stop. We have arrived.

A long, ceremonial carpet is stretched over the forest floor from their carriage to ours. At my coach door stands the Duc de Choiseul, who has arranged my marriage, and will be presented to me by Prince Starhemberg, whose honest eyes I have failed to appreciate adequately, despite the length of our journey together.

My hand shakes as I balance my body, so richly clad, in the open door and gather my skirts about me. Prince Starhemberg's face is all seriousness (perhaps he is sad our journey is almost ended and now he must hand me over). I must not fling myself into the arms of anyone; I must preserve my poise and dignity.

To Choiseul, whose smooth face is proud and pleased, I promptly speak my gratitude: "I shall never forget that you are responsible for my happiness!" My speech is not planned, but there it is: the exact truth of my heart emanating from my lips.

"And your presence is the cause of the happiness of France," he replies, and I smile at his pretty compliment.

At the other end of the carpet, the King steps from his carriage, and others, but my gaze is all for him, said to be not only the most powerful but also the most handsome man in Europe and surely he is (how can he be sixty years of age?), with large but piercing eyes of passionate blackness and a large majestic nose. His eye is pleased with my face and figure. He likes me.

Now I fly to him, fling myself upon my knees before him, my brother in royalty, my dear grandfather, who will be my papa, the King. Confused by his greatness, I cannot move, but quickly he takes me in his arms, raising me up and kissing me again and again on both cheeks. I can scarcely contain my joy at his fatherly proximity and the strong sincerity of his welcome. Modestly, I look down, but I have seen his eyes, his approval! To think, it is my own self, arrived, that he holds between his hands. I am encompassed by and have my being within the circle of his arms. With kindness that touches me to the quick, he calls me his dear daughter.

In the forest, he stands as natural as any tree but gloriously majestic.

Because I can scarcely embrace this moment as real, my spirit soars aloft and looks down on us from above; from up there I view throngs of people and carriages, banners and musical instruments—tiny, all of us—dabs of bright colors intermingled throughout the green of a woodsy tableau.

The skin of the King is brushing my own cheek. It is I myself standing in the forest, and his kind kisses are claiming me as daughter, as Dauphine, and the hope of his kingdom for its future peace and prosperity. The honor and joy of this meeting! The distinction of his person and yet his friendliness!

And here beside the King stands my future, the Dauphin. He *is* shy and clumsy. I see the truth of that characterization at once. The lids of his eyes are heavy, and he seems drugged with sleep. He lacks the courage to enter this moment; but, never mind, I give him the trust of my uplifted face—for he is quite tall—and in a moment he is reassured. He leans forward and kisses me on both cheeks. His lips are large but tender and careful. He straightens up and is all awkwardness again.

He can find no words to say to me. His eyes lift to the forest: how he wishes he were *there* in reckless pursuit; yes, hunting is his passion, as I have been told.

These woods must be full of game, I murmur and see the surprise in his eyes. I have no fear. I shall win his heart by proving that I would be his friend, and to him, above all others, I wish that my presence will bring pleasure. I am for him.

Next are introduced the three graces, the daughters of the King and the aunts of the Dauphin, who also stand beside the carriage. Madame Adelaide, they say, is a devotee of music, as I myself have always been, but she is not graceful, and I am surprised at the heaviness of her body. (Louis Auguste, too, is much heavier than his miniature suggested; his eyebrows are fiercely hairy and dark, and his countenance suggests nothing of the liveliness in the King's dark and luminous eyes.)

Madame Victoire, even more musical and one who plays the harp, as I do, might well have been pretty once, but I look at her and recall that her father's nickname for her is "Sow." Already the King calls me fairy and Flora. As his gaze passes quickly over these ladies to settle upon me, I realize the great advantage of possessing a light and graceful form: in it lies power.

Lastly is presented Madame Sophie, who carries her head tilted to one side and looks frightened, as though she might like to run away. To her, I give the reassurance of my most gracious smile: from me, she has nothing to fear. It is unkind that she was nicknamed "Grub" in her childhood, according to my sister Christine. My aunts look at me and think of me, I fear, as Austrian, foreign, but my mother has told me to rely on their guidance, and I shall nestle against them, as harmless as thistledown.

Quickly, the King begins to chat. He is much at ease, I see, with girls my age, glancing at me quickly but fully and then away. He is telling me of his own mother, who also came from far away to join the royal family, who died when His Majesty was only two, but, he says, that for a moment when he saw me, I reminded him of the goodness and charm of his own girlish mother. "I think she would have been as spontaneous as you," he tells me, and he is imagining and enjoying again how I glided straight to him and fell humbly upon my knees.

FROM THE FOREST near the bridge where the road crosses a small river, we progress to the Château de Compiègne for the evening. There, many of the Princes and Princesses of the Blood are presented to me, but the one whose fair countenance incites my instant admiration is the Princesse de Lamballe. When we traveled in the carriage, the Comtesse de Noailles said this young widow's face framed by shining hair shows a spiritual nature, and that she not only looks like an angel but also bears the nickname "the Good Angel." She is half German and half Italian, but the German side has lent her both a pure blondness and an air of melancholy, which clashes pleasantly with the fairness of her complexion. My mother wished me to be like an angel to the French, but when I compare myself to the Princesse de Lamballe, I seem more a sprite of green earth than she who is soulful as a sweet blue sky.

To his brothers, Louis Auguste presents himself just as he has to me: he has little to say. He stands ill at ease, with an almost sulky expression on his face.

Just as my sisters and I were all named Maria, several of them bear the first name Louis. Louis Xavier, the Comte de Provence, is my own age, but he would make three of me, he is so fat. Much fatter than Louis Auguste, Louis Xavier is as full of chatter as a magpie, and many lively expressions animate his face. His body is ponderous, but his mind and tongue are agile.

The third and youngest of the King's grandsons is dashingly handsome and resembles his grandfather Louis XV. This brother, who is only twelve, Charles Comte d'Artois, is slender and fair of face, but his eyes lack the darkly luminous warmth of Papa-Roi.

"You are so light," the Comte d'Artois says to me. "Someday we must have a race." When he smiles, he looks as ready for fun as one of my own brothers.

"I look forward to your friendship," I reply.

I guess that Artois would be a graceful dancer. His fair hair floats around his face; he nudges the Dauphin with his elbow and does not treat him with proper respect.

To the Dauphin, he says, "I imagine she is fleet as any doe. You'll have to pant to catch her." His pleasant smile makes me forgive his impudence, but the Dauphin jerks his head up, stares at the ceiling, and looks miserable.

I am the center of everything. Not having seen me in the flesh before, they are full of curiosity. There are too many of them for me to have the luxury of curiosity, but the color and splendor of their clothes makes me giddy with excitement. En masse, the spectacle of their dress, their jewelry, their dazzling bosoms, their heavily powdered hair, their style of gesturing, sings to me in a different key than that of the evening galas of Vienna. Nothing of the froth in my chest is manifest as frenzy in my manner; I give off only a quiet and gracious sparkle. Through a chain of whispers, the King's verdict is wafted close to my ear: "She is a most satisfying morsel." Eventually the King comes to me, and in his best fatherly manner Papa-Roi suggests that I have traveled long and far and should now take my rest.

Tonight I sleep by myself, of course, and my new ladies put me to bed with cheerful talk of dresses and bracelets and hairstyles and ribbons. My mother would call their quick French frivolous, but I like the lightness of their chatter. They speak of tomorrow when we go south to the lovely Château de La Muette for more festivities. La Muette lies closer, much closer, to Versailles, only a morning's drive from the site of my wedding.

When they have left me, I squeeze my eyes hard shut and think ahead: tomorrow night when I lay my head on the pillow of my chamber in the Château de La Muette, it will be my last night as my virgin self. The next morning after La Muette, which will be Wednesday, 16 May 1770, I arrive at Versailles, where my marriage will be signed again and the marriage ceremony enacted again, but that night I will share my bed for the first time.

My hands seek the cool blank spaces lying on either side of me. In which blank will he lie? Like two blind moles, my fingertips explore the low flatness between the sheets. I pretend it is a landscape all its own, where field and sky are scarcely separated. Perhaps Madame de Noailles will inform me there is a rule of etiquette that answers the question. What is etiquette and what is it for? It makes life orderly, the Empress once explained to all of us little ones at lesson time, for we had notions of etiquette in Austria too. But these people are conscious and proud in their etiquette in a way we were not. It is as though they are always dancing a minuet.

On which side of me will he lie? Nature, not etiquette, gives me an answer: the Dauphin will lie on the right side in our bed, for then he can, more comfortably, reach across his own body with his right hand to touch me. His hands and fingers are as big as a man's.

For my deportment so far, the Empress would be pleased with me. Tonight, I wish that she could know, now, in France, I have made no mistakes—at least I know of none. The King, who is of course the most important, likes me and I like him. With success and no mistakes, I have met the three aunts and treated them as my most dear mother has instructed. If I have not yet become an angel to the French, I have seen someone here who embodies the idea of goodness because of her beauty: the Princesse de Lamballe. I wish to know her better.

With wide-open eyes, I turn my head and press my cheek into the pillow to look to my right. The white wall reminds me of the pale side of the moon, as though she has come down and stands close to me, over there. The chamber walls are embellished with gilded arabesques; moonbeams make the gilding gleam like graceful curls and swirls of light. Ah, there is a high oval window, uncurtained, that admits the moonlight. Beyond this château, the endless trees of Compiègne lie all about us, and deer hide among the trees from hunters.

Just yesterday, I was riding, confined, in the glass coach through the forest.

I think of my three new aunts, like three good fairies, plump and perhaps soft, but I do not know, for they did not embrace me. My thoughts retract inward, like the sensitive eyestalks of snails. When I close my eyes to the visible world, immediately, the moon has gone back to the sky.

I think of Charlotte and how she made the coach stop. She was leaving Vienna to go to Naples and live a married life, but she stopped the coach so she could descend and hug me farewell once more. When we embraced, our bodies melted together, and I could not tell which was Charlotte and which was I.

To my surprise, behind our hats, she kissed me right on the lips and whispered *I will always love you best, my beautiful little sister.*

The Dauphin will close his eyes and I will close mine and then I will feel his lips covering mine.

To my sleepy mind, Sister Thérèse Augustine appears. She turns around, fluttering away from me like a raven down the corridor of the convent. That snowy Saint Nicholas's Day when I was only seven, half a lifetime away, I saw ravens walking on the snow, leaving their prints behind. With a rush of wings, they all rise up together and fly toward the western mountains. *Hold on tight, Marie*—the wintry mountains whisper. The sled rushes over the snow as I watch till the birds are mere black specks against the thin blue sky. I blink, and they are gone. *Hold on, Marie Antoinette.*

In the Depths

A woman with a hunched back stands under a tree; now she turns her face, ravaged with poverty, toward me. Is that Adelaide, Sow, or Grub, or Sister Thérèse Augustine standing beside a chestnut tree? Close to her cheek hangs a clear glass globe suspended from a branch. The globe transforms to glassy apple red and then to lemon yellow. Swiftly, the woman reaches for the fruit of the tree. "No!" I call out and know, in terror, that she is Mother Eve and not the Blessed Virgin. She snatches the globe from the tree and bites savagely into it. It shatters in her teeth, and yellow glass shards fall from her lips. Her mouth is full of blood.

When I gnash my teeth and cry out, some attendant, some stranger, as though she waited at my door for just this purpose, opens my chamber and rushes to hold me in her arms. *Fear not, little one,* she whispers. Do I only dream that comfort has come—is she too a dream?

Her face seems to be that of the Princesse de Lamballe.

But how could she ever have found me here?

When I awake, I am dressed, and I ride all day as though suspended inside a clear glass globe. The world surrounds me, but I am separate from it. No clocks tick, but I arrive at La Muette, am undressed, then dressed again for festivities.

A Mistake at the Château de La Muette

It is a supper party, and lightning glimmers around the edges of the drawn curtains. They are a heavy yellow damask, and no light passes through them, but around them leak the silver flashes of a storm, though it is far away. The thunder is a mere low growl, as though lions as far away as Africa were roaring.

Although I feel hungry, it seems impossible to do more than nibble from the edges of the elaborate dishes endlessly presented. I wish for two simple apples in a blue bowl. Too many eyes are upon me. At every moment, it is incumbent on me to appear engaged in pleasant conversation, else they may think I'm a dolt.

Silent and morose, across the table, sits Louis Auguste, but I know that he is only timid and perhaps resentful that he must endure another party that makes him feel caged and miserable. I smile at him encouragingly. He looks down, as though embarrassed. Still he could not fail to note my friendliness, and that with me, he may remain as silent as he pleases. Nothing will discourage me in my attempt to be amiable.

It is a kindness to me to let me gain familiarity with the Dauphin through these festivities so I do not feel I am marrying a total stranger.

ALL AROUND US is the clatter of conversation as pleasant as the faint rap of silver against porcelain. Still, I find it hard to eat. I ask the Comtesse de Noailles to tell me something of the beautiful widow Lamballe and her husband.

The Comtesse de Noailles informs me, "Her husband was not old."

"And was he as handsome as she is beautiful?" I ask.

"Handsome enough," she answers. "But given to vices. Unspeakable vices," she whispers. She glances around, unsure that the topic is appropriate for a supper party among the notables. How the dresses and frock coats gleam in the candlelight. The odor of powder from the wigs hangs heavy in the air. "We were all very sorry for her."

I say of the Princesse de Lamballe, "She has the special beauty that sadness leaves on a face."

"And how can Antoinette know anything of sadness?" The comtesse speaks to me from amid her thousand wrinkles, speaks lightly to me, as though she would encourage me in my happiness. Is there faint mockery in her tone?

I inquire if the Princesse de Lamballe might not marry again.

"Should she do so—" The Comtesse de Noailles speaks with a certain haughtiness and sits even straighter in her chair. "Should she do so, she might lose that standing she now enjoys at court."

When I ask for further explanation, the comtesse expounds: the rank of the princess springs from the family into which she married. "The Princesse de Lamballe devotes herself to her husband's father, the Duc de Penthièvre. His generosity toward her is well known, as is his generosity to the poor."

The story is interrupted as the Dauphin suddenly asks me if I have read the works of the English philosopher David Hume.

I reply that I have not had the pleasure, but I feel a flicker of irritation in my brain, for I am much more interested in the story of the Princesse de Lamballe.

"I met David Hume when I was but a child," the Dauphin tells me. "And I often read his work."

"My brother, the Emperor Joseph, advises that I spend two hours a day with books," I reply. "But so far, I have not had the time to do it."

"Hume writes with great insight about the plight of Charles I."

Suddenly the Dauphin's chubby brother, Louis Xavier, the Comte de Provence, rolls his eyes in his expressive face. "But, please, none of that bloody ax business at table."

The Dauphin bows his head, acquiescing, and says graciously to the comtesse, "Pray continue your account of the beautiful princess, whom my grandfather honors with his special esteem, as do we all."

Ah, my Dauphin does not lack social graces, if he chooses to employ them.

"The duc, her gracious father-in-law, is himself a grandson of Louis XIV." When the comtesse suddenly lowers her voice to a whisper, both the Dauphin and Louis Xavier courteously look away to either side. It is the gesture etiquette requires, I note, when someone in the conversation group whispers to the Dauphine—to myself. And perhaps to anyone?

Appreciating that she is among gentlemen, the comtesse confidently hisses on. "The duc's father was a bastard son. Louis took pity on this son, called the Comte de Toulouse, who possessed something of the goodness evident in his saintly and immensely wealthy progeny, and declared him legitimate." The Comtesse de Noailles seems as smug as though she herself has had the power to declare an immoral result "legitimate."

Inhaling, I enjoy the aroma of mushrooms in butter, of pheasant, of pork in cinnamon and stewed apples, of haricots in slivered almonds, of a puff pie stuffed with truffles and onions, chestnuts and hazelnuts, but for all their lovely fragrance, I merely nibble. I am too stuffed with information and with impressions to have room for real food.

ACROSS THE ROOM, I note a certain woman I but glimpsed from a distance at Compiègne. Not the Princesse de Lamballe, but another woman, less ethereal but perhaps even more enchanting. At the window curtains, the lightning flashes again and again so rapidly that several people pause for a moment in their conversation and appraise the curtained windows. The blond enchantress is one of them. She has very large blue eyes. If the

Princesse de Lamballe reminds me of the cool refinement of silver, then this woman reminds me of the warmer luster of gold. They both have blue eyes and blond hair, but the princess has feathery curls, and this woman has massively abundant golden hair. Her bosom is of the most ripe perfection, though her waist is small. A gentleman standing close to me is also looking at the enchantress.

"She but looks at the fabric of the curtained window," he says, "but even then her frank regard has a caress in it." I am shocked by the impropriety of his remark.

"I think she is looking at the lightning," I reply, "and she is afraid."

Now the woman who is the subject of his remark glances at me, as though she senses she has been the object of a comment. I ask the Comtesse de Noailles, still seated on my left, who the enchantress is, as she has not yet been presented to me.

The comtesse does not answer at once. She picks up her fork and plays with it, pressing the tines into the cloth of the table. Still, she hesitates, so I turn my face to her and see she is, indeed, at a loss for words and is searching for them. My curiosity grows, and I ask again *Who is she?*

Finally the comtesse says, "She is here to give the King pleasure."

I laugh and speak gaily, "Oh, in that case I shall be her rival, because I too wish to give pleasure to the King." I inquire of her lineage, for the comtesse is never at a loss on this subject: she must have ten thousand names crowded into her memory.

"Marie Jeanne Bécu. She has no lineage."

Suddenly the three aunts are leaning around my shoulders, speaking in disapproving whispers. They say she has no right to be here; they say her presence is a disgrace; they say that she is the staircase by means of which the King may descend into hell. Their righteousness and hatred bubbles around me as though risen from a cauldron.

Aunt Adelaide settles the matter. "But to answer your question, she is now known as Madame du Barry. Lately married to an obliging, legitimate count. Now he has conveniently absented himself from the court. You have no need to speak to her."

The other aunts agree, but the Comtesse de Noailles raises her chin and gives no sign. Mesdames les Tantes pat my shoulders and repeat that there is no need to acknowledge the woman across the room. When my skin crawls as though an insect has traversed my thigh, I understand *with my body* that the enchantress is little better than a harlot. Surely my mother knew of her existence. Why was I not prepared for her presence?

"We will protect you from her," Aunt Sophie says, leaning over my shoulder and tilting her head on one side, the better to look into my face.

"The English ambassador says she has the most wanton eyes he has ever seen," Victoire adds, just behind my ear.

"After the wedding," Aunt Adelaide says, "make it your habit, in the mornings, to come first to visit us. The King himself always comes, with his coffee cup in his hand, and you can see him there, without her."

Knowing that the King finds me charming, I wonder to myself if my own innocence might not help to save the King from the influence of such a seducer. And does he look at her with such kind, fatherly warmth as he looked at me?

I ask, "What does the King say of her? To excuse her presence?"

Adelaide replies, "He knows that she is nothing. He merely says that she's pretty, and she pleases him."

I resolve that I shall never speak to her and that gradually through sweet words I will help in guiding the King away from her. He will sense the sympathy of my soul for his soul. Again, she glances my way and takes note that the aunts are lending me their guidance. The woman half-smiles at me: as though to say she wishes me no harm. What a wanton charm she does possess. She is not afraid.

I wish that I had not inquired as to the identity of that beautiful woman. Looking at the bounty of her bosom, I feel flat and ignorant. I do not think Louis Auguste or any man would hesitate to melt into her lusciousness, but my future husband sits across from me, his heavy eyelids so lowered that he seems almost asleep. I realize that Madame du Barry is a person he would rather not discuss. Her existence hurts him. Along with the Comtesse de Noailles, he has absented himself from this conversation.

Perhaps it was a small mistake to ask about her; I must curb my curiosity. My mother has rightly identified curiosity as one of my failings. But all this is no more than a crumb on my shimmering green skirt. I flick my knuckles across the silk, as though to brush away a crumb. Perhaps an ant will find it on the floor tomorrow before the carpet is swept. And that ant will be grateful to me, the kind Dauphine who left her a crumb.

With this thought, I do break off with my fingernail the corner of a roll. I let my hand dangle beside me and drop a very real crumb on the floor. *Bonne chance!* I think, to the ants of the world.

"Do you not enjoy the food?" Louis Auguste suddenly asks me from across the table. He lifts his heavy, dark eyebrows as he speaks to try to make the whole eye open wider.

"He is so considerate," Aunt Adelaide announces.

"You look so very handsome tonight," says Aunt Sophie.

"The pastries are always our favorites, aren't they, dear nephew?" Victoire says happily, and again I recall that she in her great girth has been referred to as "the Sow" since the time when she was as young as my almost portly Dauphin.

"No meat can taste so sweet," I say to him and smile, "as that which yourself will someday offer me, after a successful hunt."

He blushes and looks down.

"And how was the last hunt?" Adelaide inquires hurriedly, "before you left Versailles?"

"Versailles began as a hunting lodge for Louis XIII," Sophie informs me.

"It's so much more today," Adelaide says, chuckling. "We have music and dancing, and theater, and cards. The wedding banquet is to be staged in the Opera House, finished just for the occasion."

"But how was your last hunting?" Victoire inquires again of the Dauphin, whom she rightly guesses to have little interest in conversing about the entertainments of Versailles.

"Nothing," he replies. He bows his head and blushes.

"Well then," I say cheerfully, "perhaps I may claim, after your next success, that I have brought you luck."

Louis Auguste raises his eyes to mine, "I most sincerely hope, Madame, that I shall bring good luck to you. And to our people."

The aunts straighten up, startled that he has spoken so felicitously. So, he is neither uncouth nor dull-witted. I never thought he was.

Suddenly the splendor of our candles, mirrors, diamonds, rubies, emeralds, and gleaming fabrics filling this large room at the Château de La Muette is washed to nothing with a fierce jittering of lightning. Everyone gasps but the Dauphin and myself.

Quite unafraid, I say across the table, as though shyly confiding just in him, "I think the lightning is lovely."

Versailles: A Royal Wedding, Wednesday, 16 May 1770

Versailles! Our carriage has paused on a small crest. Across the town, spread against another rise, is the Château de Versailles. In all her magnificence of gilded gates and roofs capped with gleaming gold, she holds out her arms to me.

The immense palace is organized by a series of three U-shaped courtyards, each flanked with stately stone buildings. Each opens into the next. Our coach will enter the largest courtyard first. The second courtyard, paved with cobblestones, is slightly smaller; the buildings of the royal courtyard on each side are less far apart than those flanking the Great Courtyard. The sides of the third courtyard come yet closer to one another; it is almost intimate in comparison to the others; called the Marble Courtyard, it is paved with black and white marble. In all her magnificence of gilded gates, walls, and teeming courtyards, with three pairs of arms, Versailles welcomes me. My new home!

As we regard from afar the spectacle of the palace, my heart flutters, excited and eager to fly to this realm of legend. Everyone about me stirs with excitement, and the coach is like a cage of fluttering birds in splendid plumage. Our three-week journey is soon to terminate in our release.

Unimpressed, our horses stamp their feet, and their tails swish at flies while they await the flick of the reins to signal that we progress. Comtesse de Noailles points to the distance with a long finger and instructs me to observe, in the center of the cobblestoned Royal Courtyard, a bronze equestrian statue of Louis XIV, whose architects drained a swamp to fashion this, the grandest court in Europe. The statue is too far away for me to see clearly, but I take, on faith, that it is not a large lump but indeed the Great Sun King, who so boldly proclaimed *L'état, c'est moi.* I am the state.

At the back of the smallest courtyard, paved with black and white marble, Count Starhemberg explains, is located the center of power: the bedroom of the present king, Louis XV. At one level elevated above the ground level, his tall windows rise directly as the back boundary of the Marble Courtyard. His chamber is at the center of everything, and all the arrangement of corridors, rooms, and buildings reaching outward and forward emanate from his bed. I realize that it is not here that he entertains the du Barry, but in some less stately boudoir.

I lick the roof of my mouth, that tiny room where the fleshy tongue must live. I moisten my lips, which are dry with the heat of awe.

I can only say aloud of Versailles spread before me in the distance, *It's magnificent.* Perhaps my tone conveys something of my reverence for the splendor and power of France. My companions in the coach are satisfied that I have scarcely breath enough to project only the shortest of sentences toward this assemblage of astounding wealth.

Our own palaces, the mighty Hofburg in the heart of Vienna and my beloved Schönbrunn, set some distance from Vienna, just as Versailles is some distance from Paris, do not compare in magnificence. But Schönbrunn is more beautiful, my heart reassures. Yes, at least to me. Its scale has remained fit for humans. Here, surely one must have wings and fly about like a god or goddess. Or a humble bird ignorant of the achievements of humans.

I nod, thus giving the simple signal, quickly conveyed to our postilion, that the horses are to move onward, toward my new home.

As we descend, the pattern of three courtyards of decreasing size, defined by the embracing buildings, loses its design and becomes a jumble, like a labyrinth. Yet, still rising above all the other buildings, though it is off to the right side, not so central as the bedroom of the King, the Royal Chapel remains distinct and defines itself most proudly. It is appropriate that

God's house should be highest. Under that highest roof, crowned with gold gleaming in the sunlight, we will be wed today.

I do not know where in all this array of mellow stone and brick, just where inside those long buildings, our bed lies. My body surges strangely at the thought, but in my clothing I sit still with no immodest stirrings.

A few months ago, when I was still a child, my mother drew me onto her lap to explain to me the marriage twins of duty and desire. She spoke of bliss, and of penetrant pain, of Générale Krottendorf, and of engulfing transports of wifely love. I squirmed with delight to hear of it, and she told me to sit still; she kept her arms tight around me as she talked.

Seated in this moving carriage, I allow no anticipatory squirming, only a slight turning of my head, as though some trifle had caught my attention. My mother said that I would feel desire, as all good wives should feel, but the feeling has come too soon. We are not yet wed. An impatience runs through my veins and nerves.

Ah, so soon, the carriage rumbles forward, toward the Court of Versailles through this small town, where the streets are full of happy people ready to celebrate the marriage of their Dauphin. The French are boisterous with gaiety for my sake. A woman reaches out to touch the coach as we pass. "Take care, take care!" The words spring from my lips, for I would not have this day marred by any accidental injury.

The coach slows, and I am glad. No one must be trampled! Not so much as a toe will be caught under my wheels.

How extravagantly joy is written on every face! I like their big sharp noses, and high cheekbones, and the high color in their cheeks. And there's a good round face! And the old people have tears in their eyes that they have lived to see their Dauphin's wedding day. I laugh aloud: a fishwife looks right in at me and pats her belly and gestures, her smile radiant, that I shall soon be made big.

I cannot help but laugh. She caught me so by surprise. Their joy joins with my own, and now we rattle through the tall, gilded gates, among the uniforms of guards and soldiers and the finer garments of less common people. How the ostrich plumes sway gently atop the ladies' heads. The hats look like so many small boats cocked upon dressed hair of strange height and width. A lovely sky blue handkerchief has been dropped on the cobblestones.

Now we arrive almost eye to eye with Louis XIV, cast in bronze, his horse vital with excess energy. The King's wonderful wig drapes his shoulders with curls, and I wish the style obtained today. Men's curls have become nothing but a sedate and orderly roll or two, a powdered wig, above their ears. Throughout his long reign, Louis XIV knew the glory of a flowing wig, dark and wildly curly. May we reign so long and well!

Every window of the flanking buildings is crowded with people who wish to see our arrival. Every window filled with the bright colors of the spectators!

And our carriage rolls up a wooden ramp over the steps onto the Marble Courtyard itself, gleaming black and white, like a giant game board. Now the wheels turn smoothly, and the horses' hooves clatter for a moment in a new key. Adorning the palace walls, the busts of austere gentlemen look down on us. Around the roof mythic figures sit. Here and there their marble legs and drapery hang over the edge of the roof. The gods are not confined by prescribed boundaries, but loll and take their ease. I much prefer their naturalness. I have never liked busts. Who wants to be depicted as only a part of one's body? Only half of oneself?

And now, since all journeys must eventually take their end, we stop.

I am handed out—I feel the hard marble under the soles of my slippers—and taken quickly, quickly—it is a swirl of confusion—to an apartment where I am to don my wedding dress. Versailles, Versailles—won't wait.

THEY HAVE BEEN preparing these private chambers for two years, though they are not quite ready and temporary at that. "Ah," my mother used to say, "are we ever really ready for anything?"

The ladies are displaying my wedding dress for me to see. It is enormous and stretches out like the sail for an iceboat. But the cloth is white silk brocade. It is so heavily worked with threads that it will be barely supportable by she who wears it. I am that she. There, someone holds the hoops that will hold out the wide skirt on both sides.

But here, the little sisters of the Dauphin: Clothilde, only nine. As I have been told, she is "round as a bell." What a merry face she has! Her good humor is writ large on her countenance. I believe she may be greater in circumference than in height.

I call her "my dear," and she curtsies very prettily, but then she seems stuck, as though she's forgotten what the next move might be. She nibbles the end of one finger. I walk to her and put my arms around her shoulders. I tell her that already I love her like a sister, and she smiles, becomes unstuck, curtsies again in a swift bob, and steps aside. When I invite her to watch me dress and say that she must make sure the dress hangs properly, Clothilde's round cheeks blush with pleasure.

Now the tiny, slight Elisabeth is presented, but six years old. She has been motherless since she was three. Ah, she has some of the family shyness. *How pretty you are*, I tell her, and now she looks into my eyes, smiles, and walks straight into my outstretched arms. My arms reach to her as the stone arms of Versailles reached out to me. *Do unto others*, I have been taught not so much by the priests, as by my mother, *as you would have them to do unto you.* Little Elisabeth forgets all about her curtsy, though various ladies whisper to her, from the sidelines. I bend and kiss her on top of the head, the way a mother would.

"I had a little doggie," I tell her, taking a step back to look into her eyes. "His name was Mops, and he had a little pug nose. Not nearly so pretty as yours." Slowly, so as not to startle her, I reach to touch her nose, most gently. "Mops and I used to romp and play together. Now you must be my pet and play with me. Will you?"

She replies solemnly that yes, she will.

Elisabeth is just a wisp of a child, so very slight. Then it occurs to me to remember that that is how many people regard me. My mother calls me "Little One." I smile at Elisabeth because she is a darling, and I can scarcely take my eyes off her. Almost I wish that I were she.

Suddenly she reaches up both arms to me again, and I bend to her so that her little hands may fit around my neck. These noble ladies do not expect me to bend, but I do as I please: it is my wedding day. When my cheek touches the soft cheek of Elisabeth, I feel a sudden sadness: yes, our fates are surely joined as one. We are of almost equal tenderness, inexperience, and softness.

"I wonder if I will someday marry?" she says.

"I do not know," I answer. And I feel aware of the three aunts standing by, watching us little chicks. *They* never married; marriage would have lowered their status as Daughters of France. It may be that Elisabeth too will decide to preserve her current rank, rather than step down for a mate. Or perhaps she will take the veil, like Louisa. But I try to fill my eyes with little Elisabeth only as she is now, a perfectly lovely child, in a simple dress, a pink ribbon around her waist. She, too, will have to be dressed in stiffer stuff for the wedding. I let my fingers touch and twine a strand of her soft, chestnut hair. I shall make sure that she never grows fat.

Now Clothilde has been patient enough. She returns for another hug, and I embrace them both again, and take them to touch the fabric of the dress—*if your hands are clean*—and tell them they may stay as long as their ladies think best, but they too have special clothes to don, and they too must sit for the hairdressers.

I look around and see that all the ladies, especially the aunts, are pleased with me, for my kindness to these natural little girls; truth is, my attentions to them cost me no effort: I had quite forgotten about anyone but the children.

A ladder is brought for a lady to stand on, to lower garments down on me. It feels as though they are building a room around me! But each piece is a joy to behold, so beautifully made, such tiny, strong stitches, such perfect surfaces. The fearful journey to France has been completed: this undressing and dressing is truly joyful in comparison to the event amid the rushing waters of the Rhine.

The hoops fit around me like a giant cage. And finally the great white wedding dress slides down, over all. I am like a pastry, and the dress is smoothed around me like fondant. It is a wonder to touch. The threads of the brocade serve to make the texture more interesting to the fingertips as well as to the eye; the fabric is a maze of intricacy.

Ah, they say that the jewels have arrived.

Bearing an enormous trunk, a troop of men enter, all bowing their heads and exclaiming. They cannot help themselves. They are stunned to see me in my wedding glory, but I will not become impressed by myself! I laugh and become more myself than ever. The casket they bear is a box almost large enough to hold not merely myself, but also someone as tall as Louis Auguste.

The casket is topped by an enormous crown lined with crimson velvet. When the first lid is opened, I nearly faint at the sight of the jewels nestled in azure silk. They represent the price paid for me, nothing but a slender and undeveloped girl of ordinary flesh and blood. I question my own worth. The crimson coach in which I traveled first flashes through my brain, and the crimson cloth that marked the boundary on the isle in the Rhine. Around my ears roars the redness of my own blood louder than river water.

"Does she faint?" someone asks, concerned.

"I am well." *No, I shall not faint for joy. I intend to inhabit this moment, like the best of actresses, and all the day to come.*

In this great chest are arrayed the diamonds and gems of Maria Josepha Leszczynska, valued at two million livres, that now come to me. More than the whole cabinet, I value a particular collar of pearls that I hold in both my hands. The pearls are bigger than my teeth and of a luster that makes me want to weep. Each pearl is a little globe of smoothness, pierced and strung with utmost skill, all linked together to form the fabric of the collar. This collar once settled round the neck and on the shoulders of Anne of Austria, a Hapsburg princess who married Louis XIII, and when this collar encircles my own neck, I will remember her, in all her courage and beauty.

Anne of Austria is a mutual ancestor of both myself and Louis Auguste. In her gift and by her blood, he and I are already united—kin. Her Versailles was little more than a hunting lodge, but she has bequeathed this collar to all the queens of France that follow her. Because Maria Josepha is dead, though I am only Dauphine and not yet Queen, the collar comes to me, through the wish of Louis XV, Papa-Roi, to honor me. When my fingers brush the smooth roundness of the pearls, I think of river stones magically transformed.

I hope that someday I will leave something of wondrous beauty to all the queens of France who are to follow me. To those who may come to

France from afar, as I have, and as Anne of Austria did, to marry my sons and grandsons and generations beyond. I think of those women as sisters; we join hands in a circle that grows larger and larger and look across time into one another's eyes.

And here are many gifts sent by the King. Drawer after drawer built into the sides of the immense cabinet is filled with dazzling gifts, but the one among them that I love most is a fan, crusted with diamonds. When I wave the glittering fan, heavy with gems, it twinkles and sparkles in the light as though it were fashioned in a sultan's fairyland. Its moving surface is all a ripple of light, but it wags heavy in my hand. I know I use a fortune merely to stir the air I breathe.

My breath catches to see my own cipher, an *M* imposed on an *A*—how beautifully those letters fit together—on the clasp of a diamond bracelet. This *M* and *A* stand as well for *Maria Antonia* as for my new self, *Marie Antoinette.* My diamond monogram is set in a clasp of deep blue enamel. This bracelet itself is a band of diamonds wide enough to warm my wrist. When I wear this bracelet, if I like, I can turn my hand over, and there at the wrist where the pulse beats closest to the surface, I have as my shield, the cipher of myself: *MA*, intertwined in one beautiful design that comprises, almost, a single *new* letter of the alphabet, uniquely mine.

Here is Elisabeth, a new little sister for me, nudging close to my body again, to look with me at the contents of the myriad drawers. I let her pull several of them open for me, and Clothilde does so as well. Clothilde says *Ooooo*, in a very practiced way, a parody of courtly exclaiming she's heard from older ladies. But Elisabeth merely sighs in her own childish voice when she sees some startlingly beautiful brooch or necklace.

The fairy Elisabeth leaves the room and returns with something, I think, held behind her tiny back.

"Toinette," she says, for so I have instructed her to call me, despite the glances of bored disapproval of my governess, Comtesse de Noailles. "Toinette." (The word fairly twirls off her tongue; she is the first at this court to use it.) "My brother the Dauphin has asked that I give you this."

From behind her back, she charmingly presents a pink rose, so perfect I think at first that it must be fashioned of silk or porcelain.

"Smell," Elisabeth says.

I bury my nose in the aroma, such as no jewel of any price can produce.

"My brother, the Dauphin, says there will be many more. To tell you so."

Quickly I glance at the door, where, yes, a large and lumbering figure passes, ignored by all, even on his wedding day.

Again I bend to the little princess.

"Please pass this gift to your brother, the Dauphin," I say, softly kissing her petal cheek. "Just like that."

I instruct her more minutely: "Ask him to bend over, so you can speak in his private ear. First the kiss, then whisper, 'She, too, says there will be many more.'"

Before she carries out her charge, Elisabeth steps back, then pauses, to look at me, and Clothilde joins her. Elisabeth is a bit puzzled by my promise of future kisses. I myself am a bit surprised; yesterday, I would not have thought of such an *amusant* message.

As though dancing, I turn from side to side to show them how the dress becomes me, though my hair is still loose. I would like to spin around and take their hands and truly dance, but I know I would become entangled in finery, so I merely look left and right, raising my arms accordingly in *port de bras,* as though I were about to leap, to throw, to toss myself across a lighted stage—*un grand jeté*.

"Your dress is very big," Clothilde says. "And beautiful," she tactfully adds.

"You look almost as small as myself," Elisabeth mentions, wonderingly.

"Are you really only twelve years old?" Clothilde asks. "I heard someone say so. 'Not above twelve,' he said."

Clothilde does not wait for an answer but goes on to inform me further of the gossip. "All of them, every single one of them says of you, 'Her bearing is superb!'"

THROUGHOUT THE ROYAL CHAPEL, the May sunshine, transformed by the stained glass edging the clear windows, illumines the two levels of the structure. People of astounding splendor fill the building. I am entering a Kingdom of Light and Joy, prepared for me by the Heavenly Father. Marble arches on the ground level, where I stand, lead toward the altar, where Christ lies dead, in golden bas-relief, taken from the cross.

I cross myself in reverence.

Borne atop the heavy pilasters of the white marble arches, on the second level, the fluted columns are of a simple white, crowned with Corinthian capitals. Those airy, fluted columns prepare the eye for the multitude of organ pipes hanging in glorious array above the altar. Like fingers stroking my racing heart, this splendor quiets me and fills me with joyful humility.

The floor on which I stand is a glory of colored marbles, rosy, gray, and cream, double circles in diamonds, a starburst in a circle. Soon my feet will pass over the length of them to the gleaming altar, where Christ lies slain.

On the high and vaulted ceiling is a vast painting containing all the colors imaginable in a tangle of human and angelic limbs, curved and bent like a great pinwheel, with Our Heavenly Father at its center. As the Almighty Father, Maker of Heaven and Earth, hovers in a patch of clear blue sky, I can see the sole of His naked foot.

The Heavenly Father's arms are open in blessing for all of us below; the dead body of golden Christ on the altar will rise again, so promises our Heavenly Father, and I see the risen Christ is depicted, too, on the ceiling. Now organ music begins, and sight is drenched by sound like a whirlwind, most rich, most elegant, most powerful.

Dizzied by the music of Couperin, I am floating forward while everyone watches me; I am gliding swanlike within my alabaster silk. I am here, with my feet barely touching the marble floor, and I am also up there, high above, among the confusion of colors of the vaulted ceiling, watching myself as though I were another stepping lightly forward to encounter her fate.

The Dauphin kneels with me before the slain Christ. Our knees sink into the velvet cushion. Here the music is so loud and grand that I feel, rather than hear, my heart beating in my ears. Whether he can experience it or not, I see that the Dauphin, too, *my husband, my love*, is enveloped in the grace of God, though to others he may appear at this moment to be a sulky boy. Grace succors his very bones, just as it does myself.

To him, I believe I resemble a solitary rose, pink and fragrant, standing in a crystal vase awaiting his touch. His clammy hands tremble as he himself, not my proxy brother but my true husband, slides the binding ring upon my finger. But I dare not look into his heavy, hooded eyes or behold his bold black eyebrows, though I can imagine them black as raven wings. I look higher than our foolish heads at a canopy of heavy silver brought forward on ornate poles and positioned above us like a cloud ushered cumbersomely indoors.

We kneel and kneel. After many words of blessing, we rise to our feet and turn.

Cradled by the Royal Chapel, bathed in holy light, swaddled in the polyphonic voice of God, we have been joined in marriage and go forth.

DURING THE SIGNING of the contract, I too tremble, and I let my husband see my nervousness, with the hope that he will pity me. As he signs the agreement, as the first of us, the King, my grandfather, looks at me, and his dark eyes glow with encouragement and pride. His signature is simple: he needs no further attributes or identifying words:

Louis

Secondly, my husband signs his name, with perfect control of his pen:

Louis Auguste

And it is my turn to write. If only I could dance my signature, then it would be all grace. But I have hardly ever signed this new name, and I must try hard to get the spelling right. I press down too hard, and the tip of the quill catches and stumbles. I blot the page, and then the last half of Antoinette, the new part, slopes suddenly downhill. But there it is, for posterity:

Marie Antoinette Josephe Jeanne

As though in a dream, I next awake to the royal banquet, for six thousand, filling the Opera House from one splendid wall to the other. I cannot eat, yet again. I am numbed by the thought that all of this array of wealth and power exists to celebrate my wedding. I have never felt so small, not even among the snowy mountains of home. How different it would all be if I were a simple peasant girl marrying a boy of my village whom I'd known all my life.

No, this celebration dinner in the just-completed Opera House of Versailles is not for me, I remind myself, but for the union of Austria and France, and these thousands represent uncounted hundreds of thousands, and the blessing of their lives to be lived without the shadow of war clouds.

For all their nobility and allegiance to protocol, the guests press to see me, the stranger who has come to make their Dauphin happy and to assure the future of the kingdom: Marie Antoinette Josephe Jeanne.

Like last night at La Muette, the lightning visits Versailles and begins to shake the sky behind the curtains, though I cannot hear the thunder, for an orchestra of sixty musicians is playing Lully's "Perseus." I can hear neither the rather dull music nor the more interesting thunder except in patches because of the roar of conversation. Part of the chatter comes from my own lips, for Louis Auguste says scarcely a word, and I must make up for his silence and bubble with delight. I play the role so well that I believe in it myself.

There will be no mistakes, or hesitations, no blots on the dinner, just laughter and smiling lips and fond eyes: grace for everyone.

The Duc de Croÿ returns to us to say that he has climbed up on the roof of the Opera. "It is from there that the view is most glorious. Ah, Madame la Dauphine, to see Versailles from the roof!" I ask him to describe the spectacle, and he does, saying torches and hidden lights glow throughout the gardens, and the fountains play with complete exuberance. The Grand Canal, which I have not yet seen, is filled with illuminated boats bobbing on the water. Because we approached the château from the east, the town side, I have seen nothing of the vast gardens and basins that lie to the west, beyond the palace. The garden walkways and bosquets are thickly packed with people. On the town side, as far as the eye can see beyond the gilded gates, the Duc de Croÿ reports, people fill the streets, rejoicing and waiting for the dark to fall and the fireworks to follow that will explode against the night. Many have walked here from Paris.

But, the duc adds, the wind is rising, and storm clouds are gathering in the west.

The King compliments me again and again (while the Dauphin is silent) and tells me and all the table that I look every inch a daughter of the Caesars. I think the King loves my high birth as much as he loves me, which, my mother the Empress would say, is as it should be. King Louis XV is pleased that to his grandson I bring the name of the rulers of the Holy Roman Empire, six hundred years old. With all my heart, I embrace and reflect the love of Papa-Roi, whatever its origin and basis may be.

An enormous clap of thunder, and then a torrential downpour.

There can be no fireworks. The King frowns.

To our table, the King remarks pleasantly, "I would think the heavens would be more cordial to the goddess of love." He tips his wineglass at me and says gallantly, "To Venus," and then to his grandson, jokingly, "To Vulcan too." But it is not a pretty comparison, for Vulcan was ugly and impaired—lame-footed.

"I fear the populace is disappointed," I say.

I know the people are soaking wet already and miserable, and it is three hours back to Paris. Here in the town of Versailles, the Parisians will know no one who might give them dry clothing.

"I'm afraid they're cold," I add.

"I'll send flagons of hot ale," the king says, "in your fair name."

Even we inside the château can feel the cooling breeze invading these rooms.

"To bed," says the King. He reaches out his arm to touch his grandson. "To bed, Monsieur le Dauphin."

My heart flitters into my throat and beats like vibrato.

I WALK BESIDE the Dauphin, who duly takes my hand. The passage leading through room after linked room to our chambers is long and damp. Far ahead, so far ahead they seem tiny, two members of the Royal Guard patrol. Each holds a leash against which two small spaniels lean. I think of Mops and say that I would like to pet those doggies. The Dauphin looks down at me fondly and explains that the dogs are at work.

"At work? Tonight? What is their work?" I ask.

The Dauphin very quietly explains that the palace is so vast, it is searched each night for any who might enter during the day and hide in its nooks and crannies. Though the spaniels are not fierce, they have excellent noses and are trained for this duty. Far ahead, the two men and the four dogs suddenly step out of our line of vision, which follows the aligned doors of stately rooms opening into stately rooms, their doorways framing a seemingly infinite regress of other doorways. By entering the rooms more deeply, the Guards and the spaniels are lost from our sight.

I hold the Dauphin's hand more firmly.

When I glance at his cheek and noble nose, my hand becomes warm and wet. In the backs of these public rooms, away from the windows beside which we walk, there are almost invisible small doors cut cunningly into the walls. These secret doors lead to other private rooms and secret staircases and hallways that form a labyrinth deep in the interior of the palace. The Empress has described that kingdom of hidden connections deep within the château and called it the Land of Intrigue, which I am to eschew, but I am curious and vow to go there someday.

Led by the King, we walk and walk. Our shadows, thrown by candlelight, move with us as we pass along the edges of the public rooms, named for the gods of antiquity. At our left, sometimes my elbow brushes the closed curtains of the high windows. The curtains hang like the drooping wings of doleful archangels. Sometimes a puff of storm air causes them to stir. Once, I fancy I see the toe of a boot—a worn and muddy shoe such as a peasant might be grateful to wear—protruding from the hem of a curtain. Ahead, I can see that doors have been closed; this walking will end.

We stop at an immense closed door, the one to our nuptial chamber.

Now will come the ritual of the royal bedding.

Here are no proxies. Here we play the roles of our own real selves. I myself must meet his expectations.

There is the broad bed and the high embroidered canopy that roofs it. Inside this room, it is the King himself who hands the Dauphin his nightshirt; the Duchesse de Chartres, the most newly married of all the noble ladies, places my folded nightdress in my hands. The Dauphin and I, with our attendants, step behind two screens and are helped into our nightclothes. Perhaps my life is but a series of moments of disrobing and robing again for the task at hand. Perhaps all lives could be measured in such terms. For me, it is a long process, for I have many layers to be removed. I am grateful for the helping hands that move like small animals around my body, unhooking, untying, tugging, and sliding my garments away from me. I could not emerge from this brocade chrysalis by myself.

When I stand naked, I feel as though I should ask them to shine and burnish my flesh so that I will gleam for him.

The nightgown tickles my skin like butterflies.

As has been orchestrated by our attendants, the Dauphin and I step shyly forward at the same instant from behind the screens.

How fragile, almost naked we seem, draped like ghosts in loose gauze. In the midst of all the court finery of the others, we alone seem simple and natural.

The bedcovers are pulled back, and the Archbishop of Rheims blesses the bed with holy water. I see water droplets spot and wet the bed linen here and there. Outside it is raining hard, and I think of the fireworks that lie dormant and are sadly wasted. The archbishop rapidly intones the Latin as the rain drones mournfully.

Now the King offers his hand to the Dauphin to lead him forward, to mount the bed.

And I wait my turn, standing in my simple nightgown, the lace knitted by nuns. *In face and form*, Sister Thérèse said, *you are a perfect princess*. I am helped into bed by the Duchesse de Chartres. Her hand is icy cold, and what has been the experience of her wedding night to leave such a chill? My mother spoke of rapture in one's joyful pain. But this hand is one of fear.

Have *courage*, my mother has instructed me, gently touching her own heart and then mine, as though to give some of what has been in her to me.

I refuse the portion of fear that nature would hand me.

No matter what happened in the nuptial bed of the Duchesse de Chartres, I *will* fill my heart with hope, but the duchesse is about my size—also slight and graceful—and for her, I feel pity.

"I thank you for your kind service," I say to her and smile with grave modesty.

Her eyes flicker recognition, but she does not smile.

All is done with utmost seriousness with all the attention of the State, for it is in our bed that France and Austria unite. No, even a peasant girl would greet her marriage bed with seriousness.

The court, the King, the most royal core of the vast court, turns in all its finery and makes its exit.

Vanished!

We are left alone, for the first time.

Our heads find the pillows.

Most soft and divinely comfortable, my pillow cradles my neck and head.

On his side of the bed, the Dauphin's head sinks like lead into the softness. Automatically, I half sit up again, to fluff the downy feathers a bit more, as I did as a girl. When I glance toward him, my eyes find his, gazing curiously, with strange calm, at me. His body in the horizontal posture, the Dauphin's jet eyebrows seem strongly handsome. Across the room, twelve candles long enough to burn all night are glowing. Settled again on my pillow, I turn my face toward him and wait. He stares now at the ceiling.

My mother said that he might first reach out his hand and take my hand in his. Perhaps my father did it so, on her wedding night. I wait.

His eyelids slide down. I listen to the rain drum and moan. As I wait, the rain falls steadily and beats against the glass of the windowpanes. I listen and wait. And wait.

Suddenly, the wind snorts. No, it is not the wind.

The Dauphin snores. The raucous rattle of air in his nostrils wakes him, for a moment. "Pray, excuse me," he says.

And he is asleep. Have I failed to please him?

I seem to hear the snuffing of a dog at the door.

I too drift toward sleep.

Whatever happens or doesn't happen, the Empress told me, *you are not to worry.*

WHEN I AWAKE to morning sunshine, 17 May 1770, a new day, I see my husband is already dressed. I notice the stubby row of dead candles with their tiny black wicks bent this way or that.

The draperies have been parted, and the sunshine streams in. Illuminated by a shaft of sunlight, the Dauphin sits at his desk and opens a book I know to be his diary, his hunting journal. He writes in it very briefly, the quill scratching into the paper.

Though I am still in the bed and I would never read his private accounts, I know what he has written; the word that he chooses to represent futility in a day of hunting is chosen now to represent the wedding ceremonies of yesterday and last night and our marriage bed.

He writes the word *Rien*, which means *Nothing.*

Later, to my mother, the Empress, I must tell the truth. I will *allow* myself to tell the truth, that he did not even do so much as to touch my hand.

The Next Night

Again, both our heads, at the very same moment, touch our pillows. But this time, his face is turned toward me, as mine is toward him, and we look more longingly at each other.

I am loving the caress of the cool linen against my cheek and hope his pillow gives his cheek the same smooth pleasure.

I feel my lips part, but no sound disturbs the air. Ever so slightly, the corners of my mouth suggest a slight smile.

"Your lips are the same shade as the flower so aptly named the rose," he says to me.

"Thank you," I say modestly. And nothing else, for every instinct tells me *Wait.*

I feel myself to be beautiful in his eyes. Pearly pink.

His hand is moving toward me. Slowly, palm first, the hand approaches the soft gathers that cover my chest. He has guessed the right place, and the palm presses against my slight mound of flesh and my small nipple.

He withdraws his hand.

"They will grow," I say shyly.

He only looks at me. His eyes, though sympathetic, are sleepy.

"I *am* a woman," I say. "Inside my body, I've changed already."

I would like to embrace him, but I dare not move. Steadily, I must present a docile manifestation of my charms. Waiting, barely breathing through parted lips, I slowly lick my lips, and then, with his flat palm, he touches my chest again, as though wondering if, before, his palm landed, perhaps, on the wrong quarter of my frame.

"They *will* grow"—I say with a slight smile—"as surely as the resurrection."

He throws back his head and howls with laughter.

"The resurrection?"

"The resurrection of the body and the life everlasting," I explain, for he has not understood my reference.

He controls his laughter for a moment, and then it squirts out of him again. He tries hard to tuck down the corners of his mouth into the proper seriousness for the congress of France with Austria.

"You are devout?" he says.

"I have no wish to be a nun," I reply.

Now he rolls away from his side onto his back. He stares at the ceiling. All mirth has left his body.

"I see you are a wit."

"Oh, no," I say sincerely. "That is something I have never wished to be, for wit is cruel, and my first wish is always to be kind."

"I believe you, Marie Antoinette."

Again, he turns onto his side, the better to look at me. He cocks his elbow and props his head up with one arm. I think he has a noble nose, very large, and powerfully arched.

"I like best to be called 'Toinette.'"

He places his hand on my waist, but he does not draw me to him. His fingertips amuse themselves by making small swirls in the fabric of my loose and mobile gown. He speaks slowly. "If you have not wit, most certainly, you have will. You tell me what you like."

"I like best to please you," I whisper, for I do not want to frighten him again.

"With saucy talk of resurrection?" he asks.

I remain silent, waiting.

"—when I have none to offer," he concludes.

I am puzzled and wonder at his meaning. Before I ask for explanation, I remember my mother's caution: I must curb my curiosity. A tear forms at the corner of my eye, and I feel ashamed. I am failing her. It is ever my duty to be light, cheerful, and encouraging. He sees the tear and touches it.

No, he *takes* it, on his finger.

The Dauphin of France puts his finger in his mouth to taste my tear.

"You need not cry," he says, and his voice is chilly and restrained. He sighs. "I would not have you cry, Little One."

It is my mother's pet phrase for me, her youngest daughter. But he must not think maternally of me. "I am . . . ," I begin, but as I unspool those words I remember the wanton, languishing look so openly displayed by Madame du Barry. Before my lips have completed the phrase ". . . the Dauphine," the sultry expression of the du Barry inhabits my own face, for I have been well taught the arts of the theater.

My husband plops down and rolls again onto his back. Staring at the ceiling, he says wearily, "You need not try to look like *her.*"

It is a shocking moment, for he has divined my thoughts.

"The fault does not lie with you," he says, but he speaks to the ceiling.

I think I see a tear forming at the corner of *his* eye.

I touch his shoulder gently. "Would you like to hold my hand?"

Without a word, he reaches toward me, and our hands find each other as though by magic. Like two magnets, our hands fly together. But he does not turn to me. I roll also onto my back, and our firm-clasped hands lie between us with fingers entwined in a pleasant knot. I think of the sarcophagus coverings of kings and queens who lie in marble majesty side by side. His large hand perspires against my flesh.

"Another night," he says.

"I am sorry for my awkwardness," I say.

There is silence, but then he replies, "And I for mine."

The Cup of Chocolate

When I awake, I am informed that the Dauphin has risen earlier to join the hunt, and the royal aunts, Adelaide, Victoire, and Sophie are hoping that I visit them in Madame Adelaide's apartment, before Mass.

Because the aunts are maidens, they cannot imagine anything about this pair of nights in the marriage bed, any more than *I* could have imagined a night sleeping in the same bed as a man when, while still at a distance from the Heart of France, my carriage paused on the crest of the hill, and I looked through the three courtyards of Versailles, each smaller and more focused than the one before it, to the windows of the King's bedchamber. At the heart of the heart of Versailles, I could only imagine some sort of bed. And that is all *they* can imagine. When they will see me, by all outward appearances, I will be the same, beautifully dressed—cheerful and hopeful.

But they will know, as everyone here knows, the conditions of the bridal linens the morning after the wedding. And again, this morning! There is no blood on the sheets. I am not yet truly made a wife. Most important, there is no hope of an heir. Now I long for that corporeal color—red! Perhaps when the Générale arrives, I will leave some of that blood on the sheets in order to trick them all.

But I have great and real hope that the Dauphin and I will very soon make true amends for this slow start. My spirits are not the least dismal in nature. I have slept so long and well, I am impatient to have my satin slippers put on my feet and to sail through these long corridors, across the rooms of state, as though pulled forward by silver strings. The Versailles "glide" they call it, and all my dancing at Schönbrunn, Laxenburg, and even the Hofburg assures that my graceful gliding will be the admiration of the court. It already is, according to precious, tubby Clothilde.

"MY DEAR AUNTS," I say and embrace them each in turn, from eldest to youngest. And then, oh horrible, I have failed to notice the King first, and to curtsy first before him. But he is not displeased—not much—I amuse him, and my apology is very pretty, for I make it more extravagant than it needs to be. I tell him the little comet of myself was so dazzled by the sun that I became confused and orbited by mistake the fair planets of my most beloved aunts instead of his august person.

He tells me that I have scarcely been introduced to the splendor of the château and not at all to the gardens and that I have much left yet to see of the glory of Versailles, and that he himself—like his own illustrious predecessor, the real Sun King, Louis XIV—will serve as my guide from time to time. "The Dauphin hopes to kill a fat goose for you," he adds. "Do you like goose?"

"I am myself a goose," I say, "and naturally admire my feathered cousins."

"But not a fatted goose," he says, his black eyes glowing. I know that he would like to pinch me, in play, to see if he could find an ounce of fat, but he is far too courteous and courtly to stoop to such.

Nonetheless, the aunts are alarmed, and they flutter around, truly like fowl in a barnyard, their having caught a whiff of fox.

"I do not know why you want the company of anyone outside the walls of this chamber," says Madame Adelaide, rather coquettishly to the King, "when you have such fine company here, and of the very best morals."

"I see I have not admired you often enough of late," the King replied. He is at ease with such banter, quite different from Louis Auguste. "There seems to be a new light, though, in the room"—he inclines his head toward me—"and everyone else basks in her glow."

"She is a darling," Madame Victoire chimes in.

"We love her already as though she were family," says Madame Sophie, somewhat infelicitously, with her head tilted to one side. I know she is not appraising me. It is just that her awkwardness of posture has become habitual.

"What a lovely painting," I remark, to move their attention to some subject more interesting than myself.

"It's known as *The Cup of Chocolate,*" Madame Adelaide explains. "By Jean-Baptiste Charpentier, painted only two years ago of the family of the Duc de Penthièvre."

"That much loved family, I believe, of Princesse de Lamballe?"

"So you remember!" Aunt Sophie says, in a congratulatory manner.

In the painting, which is indeed lovely and intimate, the composition is centered on a small table and is unified by the fact that each person holds a cup of chocolate. For most of the figures, one sees nothing of their legs, but the fourth man, the duc himself, is painted so that he is present from head to toe, and the way the light catches on his gleaming calves attracts the eye. Some of the figures are looking straight at the viewer, but one of them, the second man, the duc's son, gazes not outward, but to the side, in the direction of his wife, the Princesse de Lamballe.

"There are so many things to admire in this lovely painting," I say. But my focus has strayed to the round, plain face of young Prince de Lamballe, dead now from disease that came to him because of his licentious behavior. How could the princess bear to lie in the same bed with her husband?

"I always enjoy the little spaniel," Madame Victoire says in a genuine way, "and the fact that beautiful Princesse de Lamballe loves her little dog and reaches down to give him a tidbit of her affection."

Suddenly my heart is stirred, for I know that Madame Victoire, like myself, also values receiving affection from those around her, even as I do. I think of Mops.

"It's very clever of the painter," Madame Sophie puts in, "to position a mirror in the background so that one sees Princesse de Lamballe's coiffure from the back and the mirrored profile on the other lady. At first, I thought there were six people in the painting."

"When Madame de Lamballe's young husband died," Adelaide says, "the King himself called upon her."

"She is all purity and loveliness," the King says in a tone of genuine admiration.

"Not to any other living soul," Victoire says, "has the King ever paid a private call. It is the mark of his very highest esteem for a woman of the greatest purity in the face of incredible difficulty."

She alludes to the fact that the husband of the princess was a terrible debaucher. And I know also that she wishes to contrast the character of Madame de Lamballe with that of the du Barry, though she does not say so directly. Madame Adelaide is quite clever, and by just such subtle indirection would I too hope to loosen gradually the esteem and attachment that the King has allowed himself to feel toward that creature.

I remark, not looking at the King, "Nothing so becomes a lady, my mother says, as virtue."

"The Empress of Austria," the King replies, "will always outrank anyone in Europe for moral rectitude, and you must extend to your dear mother my most profound compliments when you write to her." Thus, he deflects the implication of my comment.

Still, I glow to hear my mother so praised. Because the King clearly wishes to discuss other less pressing subjects than female virtue, I compliment all the ladies on their appearances this morning, but privately I think Madame Adelaide is the most comely. She wears a court dress of blue velvet, with rows of white lace on the sleeves and one standing row across the bosom. After an expanse of lovely, smooth skin, a blue bow nestles directly under her chin. Madame Adelaide is rouged to a similar degree as myself, with large pink clouds on her cheeks, but not so large or dark as her sisters' unsubtle circles of rouge. Such defined spots of color could serve as an archer's target.

A number of small dogs lounge where they will on the floor, and I would like to play with them, but I restrain myself, for I must not untidy my clothing. On a table, a book of bound music lies open and spread wide. Madame Adelaide follows my gaze and tells me it is the music of Mozart.

Quickly I tell her that he and I are the same age and met as children at

Schönbrunn. (I note I have gone too far in saying aloud the name of my beloved Austrian home.) A bit flustered, I add prettily, but really I prefer the music of Christoph Gluck, who was my teacher at the keyboard, to that of Mozart.

"We shall have Maestro Gluck here," the King says gallantly, "if that is your wish."

I am truly overcome with gratitude, for Master Gluck is Austrian, and he likes me very much.

"He has," I say, "such mastery of the Italian idiom in his compositions."

Before we leave for Mass, I glance again at the apartment: it is a very pretty room, if somewhat underdecorated. One of the fireplaces is framed by a blue marble, or perhaps lapis lazuli, the exact shade of Madame Adelaide's blue velvet dress, and I suppose that she has had her dress made, in fact, to match, so that her movements in this setting would appear especially harmonious. The chairs here are white, and each has a medallion of pink flowers in its seat and on its back. The white skirt of Princesse de Lamballe in *The Cup of Chocolate* also has large sprays of pink flowers of the same lovely hue as the beautiful pink bodice that rises so gracefully from the skirt. I see that I was mistaken in thinking they all held cups of chocolate; the standing lady on the right holds a tiny bouquet of pink flowers.

To Madame Victoire, I add, as we exit, "It is the intimacy of the family portrait, is it not, that provides its ultimate charm?"

THE PROGRESS toward Mass is slow because we are often approached by others as we pass through the state rooms. Their doors line up to suggest a kind of passageway; instead of having a wall on our right side, the entire room, through which we pass along its edge, is visible to us. It seems to be the custom here that anyone may approach the King as he progresses toward Mass. In each room, we halt for a moment, then the King moves forward, chatting, with his petitioner keeping pace for a few steps. Apparently, it is a great honor if the King comes to an absolute halt to pursue the conversation in greater detail, but such a gesture causes its recipient to add many flattering curlicues to the substance of his request, thus clogging the delivery of the real message.

It is taking a very long time to pass through the Mars drawing room, as it is the largest of these state rooms so far. It is called the Mars room because the Roman god of war is featured in the central panel on the ceiling in an enormous painting called, Madame Adelaide explains, *Mars in a Chariot Drawn by Wolves*. Indeed, his chariot is pulled by wolves, a pictorial idea both fascinating and repugnant. I had not noticed these dogs of war—there is so very much to look at in these baroque paintings—and I politely thank Madame Adelaide for sharing her erudition with me. She names next a more reassuring painting: *Victory Supported by Hercules Followed by Plenty and Felicity*.

As we begin to move, my gaze fastens on a truly frightening painting. My entire body gives an involuntary shiver. Madame Sophie, hoping no doubt to be helpful and thus praised, as I praised her older sister, now supplies the awful words to accompany the painting: *Terror, Fury, and Horror Seizing the Earthly Powers.*

I am happy to see the King nod, which dismisses his petitioner and for us to leave these cerise walls to pass into the Diana Drawing Room. On the ceiling is a painting called *Diana in Her Chariot Presiding Over Hunting and Navigation*, and I cannot help but hope she is indeed watching over the safety of my husband as he rides to the hounds in this morning's hunt.

I am most enchanted, though, by a white marble bust of Louis XIV. As in the bronze equestrian statue in the Royal Courtyard, he is depicted with the most magnificent flowing hair. It billows like rushing water curling over stones upon his chest. His curls frame his noble face with vital complexity. His eyes possess great intelligence, and his nose is chiseled fine, as are his lips. Even the lace beneath his chin is rendered so finely as to suggest airy fabric instead of stone. Across the bottom of the bust is an arch of fabric, off center, like a windblown sash. The rush of that arch forcefully suggests the energy and the power of the man, though the statue is but a bust.

This bust of Louis XIV stands in marked contrast to the antique busts from Roman times, also displayed at intervals around the room, where their drapery hangs decorously but with no zest to it. Such baroque energy has made possible the magnificence of this entire palace.

When we enter the Venus drawing room, the King stops, reaches back, and takes my hand.

"You see on the ceiling, Madame la Dauphine, the image of yourself, prepared for you by the artist even before he knew of your existence."

I look upward with him. At first I can see only the heavy gilded frames of all the interlocking paintings on the ceiling. The golden frames are in bas-relief, and of such heavy and demanding intricacy that my gaze is almost overwhelmed and distracted from the more delicate paintings they contain.

Then I see her, bare breasted, and her chariot, drawn by doves in flight, resting on a cloud. Sharply, I draw a quick sip of breath. "And who is the painter?"

"Houasse," answers Madame Adelaide, who is clearly the most informed about music and the arts in the royal family.

The King himself supplies more information, and I can see that he has had a long and special attraction for this goddess who so nobly displays her classical body: "The painting is called *Venus Subjugating the Gods and Powers*."

All in a moment, the realization comes to me, more forcefully than ever, that preeminent men recognize not only the power in war and in the accumulation and display of great wealth: they are willing, at times, to bow to the power of beauty, and it is, indeed, a great power in this world for those who, through the gift of God, possess it. Viewing the appeal of Venus, half-unclothed, I cannot help but wonder if I must wait in inspiring the *puissance* of my husband till my body reaches greater maturity.

As though to read my very thoughts and allay my anxiety, the dear King says, "I cannot imagine anyone more like yourself in loveliness than Venus, the queen of Love and Beauty."

Above our heads, three lesser, bare-bosomed maidens are in the very act of crowning their queen with a wreath of pink and green, and a tiny winged Cupid, holding a darling arrow in one hand and his bow in another, hovers just above the crown. In a deep "U" a rope of flowers spills from her lap and the cloud whereon she sits down to the level of the subjugated Powers below.

Looking like Mars, or is it Apollo, or Achilles? standing in a deep marble alcove, a combination of hero and god, is a full-length white marble statue of Louis XIV. The King is as fascinated by this imperial figure as he was by Venus, who floats above us. Because the statue of Louis XIV stands on a high pedestal in his marble niche, all the lesser mortals, including Louis XV, must look up to his glory as we pass. I see the admiration, *involuntaire*, in the handsome eye of my king as he regards that of his fierce and despotic predecessor and great-grandfather.

"Papa-Roi," I say shyly, "there is no one with whom I would more happily lodge my trust and faith than you."

Now the King would tease. "You don't mean I am higher in your esteem than your dear mama, the Empress of Austria?"

"No, I mean, yes." Quickly I gather my scattering wits. "I mean no in the frame of natural affection, in terms of her maternity, which is hers alone to claim, and I mean yes in terms of my new status, where all my allegiance of every sort bends first of all to you."

"Madame la Dauphine's tongue is almost as nimble as her feet."

With that pretty compliment, he takes my arm and we hurry on through the Drawing Room of Plenty and beyond it, through the Hercules drawing room to arrive at the Royal Chapel for the celebration of Mass. For the ceremony of my marriage to Monsieur le Dauphin, I stood on the floor of the ground level, surrounded by the stout marble arches leaping toward the altar; now we enter on the higher level to inhabit the kingdom of the light and noble Corinthian colonnade.

IMMEDIATELY I AM engulfed by the organ music of Bach, as it issues in all its glory from the pipes hanging above the altar.

Like flights of golden bees, the music swarms around me and carries me to a realm beyond words.

Discreetly, at the corners of my eyes, unnoticed by anyone, appear those two pearls we believe are the distillants of blood called tears.

Versailles: The Bedchamber

Monsieur le Dauphin will arrive home from the hunt too late to dine with me, but I take my supper with my aunts, and they pet and pamper me as though I were their puppy. They have so many lovely puppies to play with—spaniels and pugs, white ones with tan spots, a tan one with white spots, one shaggy little gray thing with his fur parted down the middle of his back. I throw them balls and make them yap and lure them to dance on their hind legs and give a prize of candy to the one who dances longest. He spits it out on the carpet, but it is all very nice.

The aunts suggest that I ignore Madame du Barry as much as possible, and that, truly, this is the wish of the King and that it will raise me in his eyes to the status of the most virtuous Princesse de Lamballe, whom he respects so much.

But it troubles me that they are critical of the very Choiseul who arranged my marriage, and having achieved that union, how can they not regard him with the same affection with which they regard myself?

Perhaps the Count Mercy, the Austrian ambassador to the Court of Versailles, who represents the wisdom of my mother in all things, can explain these contradictions to me.

After playing well into the night with Mesdames a number of card games, which do not interest me at all, I return to our apartment, hoping that the Dauphin has arrived home. He has not returned. I send away my attendants, for I do not wish them to see me fretting, but now I am overwrought with anxiety about his safety. I think of last night and our intimate conversation, and I long once again to lie on the bed and lace our fingers together between us.

Eventually, I decide to undress and call for my ladies to help me.

They are embarrassed to be helping a Dauphine who has failed to arouse the interest of her new husband, but they try hard to be lightly encouraging. Their tinkling voices provide a divertimento, and I do not waste the opportunity to pay attention to them and appreciate them. Before they leave, each has received a compliment or a pleasantry genuinely appropriate to her unique charms, and they leave me feeling more happy in themselves than they were before they came into my chamber.

Alone again, I take out the diamond bracelet with the enamel and diamond clasp that the King gave me. I fit it around my wrist and admire again how my superimposed initials *M* and *A* overlap and fit together. And my own pulse beating beneath.

To delight my nose, I go to my dressing table and rub scent behind my ears. When I drop the bottle and spill the liquid across my lap, I burst into weeping. Now I smell like an overpowering harlot must smell, all boldness, when I should merely allure. I do not wish to send for another gown, but I don't know what to do. If I pour water on myself, I will be wet. I go to the window and pull aside the heavy drapery to look out.

The moon plays on the rows of geometrically shaped little trees marching away from the château. I think of the grand, unpruned chestnuts of the forests I traveled through, and how they seemed to hold up their panicles of flowers like torchères to light the passing of my carriage, as it rocked onward. What did I know then? I might as well have been a baby swinging in her cradle. But what do I know now? Not the pleasure of a husband's amorous embrace. Not the joyful pain the Empress anticipated for me.

Yet it is good to hold hands. Almost, it is enough.

Enough for me, but certainly not enough for the King, the court, and the whole of France, and not enough to please my most dear mother, the Empress, for there must be progeny to promote the peace and harmony of the two states.

These curtains framing the gardens and the deepening night are not what I would have chosen. Someday in the future I will decorate the rooms I inhabit to reflect my own spirit. Perhaps I would have flowers, pink ones flanked by ferns, in clusters on a silvery white field.

A sound at the door! The knob turns. I give thanks to God for his safety, but on a mischievous whim, suddenly, I duck to stand inside the folds of the curtain. He will not find me here, after all.

"Toinette," he calls. "Toinette."

Though he remembers how I wish to be addressed, I do not choose to reveal myself. *Petulance.* Yes, I am all playful petulance.

I hear the sound of his feet on the carpet. He drops something on the floor. I hear him fall heavily onto the bed. I am surprised that he cannot smell me, doused as I am in perfume. I hesitate and wonder what I should do next.

From within the shielding curtain, I look out the window and see the troop of trees, each pointing toward the sky. To the side is another display of the topiary art: the trees all consist of three balls, in graduated sizes, the smallest on the top and the largest on the bottom. They stand obediently still, and a cloud passes over the moon. Now the shadows are deeper and more ghostly. No human walks on the ground. An odor of wet copper, of blood, pervades the air of the room.

I decide to step from behind the curtain. Lying on the bed, the Dauphin sleeps in hunting garb. He has not even removed his feathered hat. He opens his mouth and snores. He has come to me unescorted by any valet. His clothing is splotched with blood from the hunt, and he has certainly besmirched the coverlet, which he has not bothered to pull aside. His boots are caked with mud.

Carefully, I stretch myself on the other side of the bed.

I do not speak to him, for it is clear that he is exhausted. His complexion is rough and ruddy from the day spent riding in the woods. There is a scratch across the back of his hand, with tiny beads of hardened blood dotting the line. He has taken no time to wash or to dine with his fellows after the hunt but hurried to our bed.

I do not close my eyes but spend many hours staring at the ceiling. I imagine the painting of Venus on her cloud, the wreath above her head, and little Cupid above that. I think of home, a fairyland, but I do not allow myself to weep. I remember Clara, the warlike rhinoceros, whose large splayed feet, plated hide, and mighty horn were often crusted with dried mud. I wonder if I now share my bed with some variety of heretofore unknown creature. Certainly, my husband's behavior is strange in comparison to what my mother has prepared me to expect.

In the night, he mumbles, "Forty birds. I killed them for you."

His voice seems to come from a distant room, and the walls between his room and mine seem very thick. The distance between us makes me want to leap high and to twirl fast, to play with such gaiety that he would wish to join me from his remote chamber. The loneliness and hope in his voice make me want to gain his attention.

I think of the glance between myself and the King today, before the marble incarnation of Louis XIV, *his* glorious great-grandfather and immediate predecessor on the throne of France. Of how, when I spoke to Papa-Roi of my gratitude and trust in him, *his* glance became one of gratitude, and some truth passed between us. Puzzled by the nature of that truth, I thought of lightning leaping. I thought of *inoculation* and a certain question about love.

Now I think of that dirty string that is used to protect royalty against the scourge of smallpox. My mother saw to it that her children were *inoculated*, and because I trusted her with all my heart, I was glad to allow the slit to be cut in my arm and for the string that had been dipped in the pus of a sick person to be laid inside my flesh. We do not understand how this practice protects, any more than we understand why bleeding helps to heal, but we trust what experience has taught us of their efficacy.

The stillness with which I lie straight and quiet in this bed offers protection from all my fears. But in the morning, I will twirl through the rooms of my life.

IN THE MORNING, I discover that my husband, who is not yet my husband, dropped his game bag just inside the door. The blood from the birds has seeped through the canvas bag onto the carpet, and of course the meat has spoiled.

Time Passes

Hours, days, weeks, even months have passed.

Phrases from my mother's letters haunt me. She writes that I have no duty but to please and obey my husband; she tells me that I must submit to him in all matters; she reminds me that the only true happiness to be obtained in this world is that of a happy marriage, and she reminds me of her own success in this matter—a success that gives her the freedom to advise me. For the success of the marriage, she lays all responsibility on "the wife, on her being willing, sweet, and amusing."

And always, always, she wants me to read more, to read books of religious devotion and of history, to discuss them with the Abbé Vermond, who has come to France from Austria to serve as my tutor and spiritual advisor, to send her lists of what I read, to annotate those lists. She wants to know of every illness and of the visits of Générale Krottendorf.

I write her that, since I have arrived in France, the Générale has failed to visit for four months, but I add that I am not missing my monthly for any desirable reason. She will know that the marriage remains unconsummated.

My body is so disappointed in its marriage that it retreats from womanhood. The red tides cease. I lose weight. I slip backward in time toward girlhood instead of progressing toward maturity.

FOR ALL HIS ASCETIC appearance, the Abbé Vermond has sparkling blue eyes, and his gaunt cheeks are creased with vertical lines because he smiles so often. I like his hooked nose, his shoulders slightly bent from poring over his books. And he is kind. As best he can, he ministers to both my spirit and my mind, yet I am not an apt pupil, but one too easily distracted. When I confess to him, he offers tender reassurance and promises that his little lectures will be brief. Just as I should rely on Count Mercy for advice on matters of state and politics, I must rely on the Abbé Vermond for more personal counsel.

The next day, over my lesson books, he speaks to me even more reassuringly.

"Your memory is excellent," he says approvingly. "You have excellent habits in listening. You listen quietly and forget nothing of what is said."

I tell him that I wish that I could pay more attention to the voices that come from the pages of books. "But I cannot. I struggle too hard to make sense of what is printed, while merely listening to real speaking makes a greater imprint on my mind."

"You are a musician, dear Dauphine. Spoken words are more like music."

"I will continue to try."

"Allow me to observe," he continues, "that you have an excellent influence on the Dauphin. Now he displays much more goodwill, and he is of a more agreeable nature than anyone thought him to possess. It is the influence of your sweetness."

In his desire to encourage me, he reaches forward and pats me on the knee.

BUT THE DAUPHIN comes to my bed only rarely. I express my joy at his company. He smiles. He says, he is tired tonight and would I hum a tune to him. With his head on the pillow, he looks at me with kind eyes, and his body becomes peaceful. He sleeps.

One night, he says to me, "You are so beautiful. Even your voice conveys your unique charm."

But he does not reach for me.

I smile. My eyelids lower. "I am so happy that I please you," I reply.

WHEN I TALK with Count Mercy, I ask him if he, like the abbé, believes I have been a good influence on the Dauphin.

"Without doubt," he replies, with crisp energy. Everything about the count is crisp and orderly. His mind and his clothing are cut from the same elegant cloth. Without flaw, his deportment and demeanor are full of subtle innuendo, which I do not understand, but I trust him.

"And the King likes me too," I say, with a slight question in my voice.

"Perhaps you have noticed, however, that the King is most expressive of his love when you go to his apartment *without* the companionship of Mesdames, your aunts?"

"They like to go everywhere with me."

"Like a herd of lapdogs," he lightly teases.

"I could not live without their devotion."

"But then you do much to further their causes," he replies.

I am silent.

"In the matter of the du Barry," he explains. "My advice would be to treat her with more civility. To speak to her, from time to time. The King will love you the more for it."

I cannot argue with the count; I am not clever enough. But the aunts have told me that I do well to keep the King reminded that the du Barry association is not respectable.

FOR MY FIFTEENTH BIRTHDAY, there is much celebrating. Both the Dauphin and the King shower me with gifts, though I neither need nor want anything. Best of all, the very next day, the Générale visits in the morning.

The Dauphin attends me and congratulates me, while I rest in bed.

To my surprise and pleasure, he begins to speak to me quite frankly.

"My dear friend, my dear Dauphine," he begins, "I wish to assure you, now that you are fifteen, that I do, indeed, understand everything about the marriage act. Quite deliberately I have refrained until we were both a little older."

I regard him with joyful amazement.

"I have been following a plan," he continues. "You know how I love the hunting at Compiègne. As does my grandfather. When we go next to Compiègne, there I shall act the part of a man with you."

My heart gives me my reply: "Nothing pleases me but to follow the will of my husband in the path that will lead to our happiness and that of France."

Most tenderly, he takes my hand and kisses it. "You are perfect in all ways," he says. "I promise it. At Compiègne, I will make you my true wife."

When he leaves my bedside and I dismiss my attendants, I pinch my nipples in the hope of stimulating their growth.

A Letter from the Empress

Rather to my amazement, my mother the Empress now wants me to be more careful not to offend Madame du Barry. The Empress admonishes me to take better care of my appearance. She has spies everywhere, and the Princess Windischgrätz, who visited here and then at Schönbrunn, has tattled on me. I sit at my desk, with the eyes of all my surrounding ladies glancing up in fluttering rhythms at me from their needlework to check my mood. While I wear a mask of perfect calm and equanimity, I read my letter from the Empress:

> *Because I asked her with my direct questions, the Princess was forced to admit that you are failing to take good care of yourself, even in the matter of keeping your teeth clean. Your teeth are a major aspect of making a good impression, and you will recall that before you left Austria, we spent much time with them in straightening wires, something that became necessary expressly because you suddenly became, by the Grace of God and the untimely deaths of others, in line to marry the throne of France. Finding that you could neither read nor write in any language, we immediately set out to correct that situation as well. When you left Austria, your appearance was entirely presentable, even charming, though that is due more to your manner than your natural endowments.*

Teeth are a key point in the pantheon of beauty, and even more so is your figure, which the Princess reported under my insistent questions she found to be worse than ever. Madame, my dear daughter for whom I pray every day, must recall that you are now developing your shape. If you send me your measurement, I will have proper corsets made here for you. I believe those made in Paris are too stiff. I will send new corsets by courier . . . And the princess reports you are badly dressed, sometimes your clothes are awry, as though you have been romping in an unseemly fashion, and because all eyes are upon you, I have also received other news that your waist is misshapen and that your right shoulder is out of alignment.

Now that you are fifteen, your body will change rapidly. You must always show the Dauphin good cheer. More caresses, my dear, more caresses!

You have blessed my life. For fifteen years, my dear daughter has given me nothing but satisfaction. Mercy writes to me that on the morning of my birthday, you celebrated the day on your knees, in prayer, and I am deeply affected by your charming thought and good action which was the very best way to celebrate my birthday and the way that can only please me most. I was surprised that in your letters you yourself did not mention this sweet remembrance of me. I kiss you with all maternal tenderness and bless you, my dear daughter.

Mercy's reports always praise you and say that you have every attribute of docility and sweetness which will make all people love you, especially the King and the Dauphin, who so much enjoys your company. You must always follow Mercy's advice, all of which is entirely for your own good, as is that of your faithful mother. But you must follow the advice of your new royal family, that is, of your virtuous aunts a little less closely and never express anything but neutrality to Mme. du Barry, certainly nothing negative. The royal French family do not appear to advantage in public; they do not know how to have fun in a proper way; their manners have done nothing but drive the King away and speed him down the path of straying because he does not find them entertaining or amusing, and therefore he must look for amusement elsewhere.

Do not withdraw from holding court but invite the great world in. You must set the tone at Versailles, and so far you have succeeded to perfection.

Remember that God has given you so many graces, special sweetness, and docility that you can play your role in a way that is sure to please. Always greet the King with enthusiasm and a willingness to oblige any line of conversation or diversion in which he appears interested. Do not be influenced by the approval of Mesdames in unpleasantness toward or negligence of those whom the King favors and certainly it is not your place to try to influence or mold His Royal Highness, from whom all favors and blessings flow. You must follow your own heart in its kind and pleasing impulses toward any person who is so fortunate as to be in your presence.

I am very eager to have before me a new painting of you, carefully dressed in appropriate court attire, not in a negligee or dressed as a man, but appearing as one who occupies the place that you do occupy. I kiss you.

You know that I am always
your faithful Mother

Hunting at Compiègne

The King, the Dauphin, and I make merry as our coach rolls through the deep forest, full of game. The postilion shouts that a stag is jumping across the road ahead, and we all stick our heads out the left window to watch him crashing through the brush of the woods to escape. His tail is held high, like a stiff flag, and his dainty heels flick up at us.

Then we realize that our heads are lined up, one above the other, the King on top, and under him the Dauphin, and then me, and we all giggle at ourselves, and the Dauphin seems happy and relaxed, and the King looks at me most fondly.

"Madame la Dauphine," he says, "must assure me again that she is in no danger riding to the hounds, for how should I ever face the Empress your mother if a mishap were to befall so rare and precious a person as yourself?"

How his dark eyes gleam! How comfortably he speaks! The phrases glide from his mouth like arabesques from the brush of a skilled painter.

"My mother the Empress wants me to be in the company of Your Majesty and to bring you delight with my presence, even in the hunt, though it is I and not Your Highness who finds the most pleasure in our conviviality." Ah, my utterance too rises in a curl and finishes in a graceful swoop. As long as it is speaking and not reading aloud, my words dance instead of trudge, and

I take pleasure in the rhythm of a sentence. Even writing is easier for me than reading because the pen only follows the sound of my voice in my mind.

The Dauphin only smiles at me; he cannot yet untie his tongue in the presence of his grandfather.

I chatter on. "Did Your Majesty know that last night, Monsieur le Dauphin and I held our own little ball in our rooms, just for the family, and by that I mean, our gaiety included mainly our brothers, the Comte de Provence and the Comte d'Artois?"

"Ah, you are a court of young people—and that is most appropriate. It pleases me to see you as friends."

"In everything the Dauphine does," my husband says, without shyness, "she acts with perfect grace."

The King reaches over and claps the Dauphin on the shoulder.

As I danced with the Comte d'Artois last night, my ladies reported to me that the Dauphin made just that exact comment as he watched. I knew that with only a little nudging here in the coach, he would remember, speak gallantly of me, and please the King.

Now it is for me to speak, as I always try to do, truly and from my heart while using the expressions appropriate to my station: "When the Dauphin smiles on me, I feel that I can fly."

"But not dangerously high," the King says. "You have not ridden this forest before, and you must take care."

"Papa-Roi, please tell me if in any way I give you anxiety, for that is not my intent. I want you to rejoice in all that I do. Give me but a glance, and I will slow my horse till he drops to his knees and crawls."

A postilion sounds a horn, and I see the now familiar facade of the Château de Compiègne appearing beyond the trees. Impulsively, I extend my hand to the Dauphin.

"This place will always make my heart beat fast," I say to him, "because it is here that we first saw each other."

"I love these woods like no other," he replies. "Here is the best hunting."

"Here, in this moment," the King amends, "is the person of the fairest princess not only in France but in all of Christendom."

"For my presence in France I always thank the minister Choiseul," I say, too quickly, for a shadow passes over the King's face. I know that Madame du Barry and her faction do not appreciate Choiseul. I smile brightly into Papa-Roi's clouded face. "I hope that soon I will dance not only with the King's grandsons," I add, "but also have the honor of accompanying the person to whom I most owe my happiness and most admire." I glance down submissively.

The shadow passes. The horn sounds triumphantly; the carriage horses' hooves clatter on the cobblestones of the courtyard, and the coach slows: we have arrived.

With merry eyes, I speak again to the King. "I hope that Your Majesty and the Dauphin do not mind that I ride astride?"

The King laughs. "Astride, my little princess? Astride and in command? Ride as you will. As you're accustomed to, in safety."

"In green pants."

The Dauphin surprises us by remarking that nature most often dresses in green. He adds, "Doubtlessly, that color, like everything else, will become you."

WHEN I DRESS for the hunt, I take some time before the mirror, adjusting the tilt of my hat. It must be just so: this accessory must make me look a bit different than usual so that I allure the Dauphin in a new way and add another charming impression for the King's mental portrait gallery. The tilt of the brim should be a bit daring, but one that emphasizes innocent youth. It must seem unplanned and spontaneous, for the King loves spontaneity, but a little more centered and balanced—there!—for too much spontaneity frightens the Dauphin.

It is my riding the Dauphin will admire, more than my hat. My lady offers me long black trousers to wear, but I say that none are necessary under my men's pants, cut to fit. She reminds me that Madame de Pompadour rode in long undertrousers and a skirt. To check her impertinence, I only smile and do not deign to speak.

I wonder what Madame du Barry wears in the hunt—probably something wanton, but everyone says she is inferior to Madame de Pompadour, whose position as the Favorite of the King she now fills. She must fasten the great bundle of her golden hair in a low snood at the nape of her neck. Though the King is thoroughly beguiled by the du Barry, I think his attention can yet be engaged in a modest and proper way that my mother would not only approve but applaud. I know his sometimes flirtatious manner with me is partly to instruct the Dauphin in how *he* should charm.

AH, I LOVE the way the hounds' tails lash about in eagerness above their backs in a hundred random motions, and how some of the hounds, mouths open and panting, seem to look up at us on horseback and smile. All around me, the horses' rounded haunches—like great hearts—a shape I love—jostle and gleam, while their large eyes glance wild and rolling. My horse is beautifully schooled and does everything at my slightest touch.

There is no need to modulate happiness and excitement here, and I understand better why the Dauphin loves this sport. His eyes have lost their sleepy cast, and like the horses, he looks about already in an excess of eagerness, though he does not look at me. More than two dozen of us are ready to be off!

When the King inquires if my seat is a comfortable one and my mount satisfactory, I reply, "As though we were born to ride together this day." The lace at my throat tickles my chin. "I thank Your Majesty who has mated me so well." Wishing I could tear away the irritating lace, I glance down at my well-behaved hands. The ring on my little finger is enhanced by the way my small hand lightly holds the rein. I must pull on my gloves. Now, I too am more than ready to ride to the hounds.

The Dauphin guides his mount closer. "Have no fear that you will outride the path," he tells me. "You could ride all day and not come to the end, here in Compiègne."

"I want to jump," I say.

"Then follow me," the King replies. He raises his hand, the horn sounds, and our horses spring into a gallop.

Behind a sea of hounds, we keep to the road a bit, the thud of hooves like muted thunder, the trees flying by on both sides, till we come beside an open field, one picked over for stones. The King leads us into the field, and I see a wide but shallow ditch lies ahead. I trust my mount to rise, and, glory! rising beside me is the Dauphin, and together we arc through the air, land safely to his cry of happiness as he urges his horse to take the lead.

Racing as much as hunting, we traverse the cleared field in a wink, and at the boundary of trees, the Dauphin and the King turn us all—we are like a swoop of birds, but various in our brightness, all choosing to change direction at the same moment—back toward the road.

Already the thighs of my green pants are drenched to a darker hue, and with one hand, I loosen the top clasp of my jacket. I am singing, no, yelling with happiness, and urging my horse faster for a moment, then easing off, responsibly, for my urging surprises him. I do not know who rides beside me, a blur of blue, and I do not care.

The horn sounds the signal that we are in pursuit of a stag, though I cannot see him. Alas, my bunch of riders slow, as though to prolong the chase. Those in the lead leave my group behind.

"Yonder rides your husband," the young Comte d'Artois points with his crop, and I see the Dauphin in his tricorn hat at the very lead, riding in a frenzy. My heart sounds the rhythm of romance, the rapid pitty-pat in imitation of hooves. Others have spoken of such excitation, but I have never before felt it. How easily the heart speeds after the manliness of a masterful rider.

But I would be master too! With a single whack, my good mount jumps ahead of Artois's and I gallop straight into the blinding dust to join my husband. My horse tosses his head and takes an adjustment on the bit, for he needs something more of freedom to navigate through these crowded, dusty shapes. Our brilliantly colored clothes are covered with dust of road and field, and I listen more intently to help me judge who is near and who approaches rapidly from behind. My horse listens too, and he is expert in all of this, and I know that the King has provided brilliantly for me in my mount, and I bless his care of my fate.

Far from my mother, that dark shape in a distant place, I am setting the pace for myself on this sunny road, and I dig my heels into the horse's flanks. His stride both lengthens and quickens, but we come close to trampling a limping dog, tail clamped between his legs, who thought he could cross before us. The horse is unhappy; I slow to win again his approval and trust, and I vow not to indulge myself in heedless speed again. Bending closer to the curve of his thick neck, I exalt that I wear no corset! Nor shall I—no matter what she sends from Austria!

It is fortunate that I ride at less than breakneck speed, for ahead the group has stopped. It is all men ahead, and some have dismounted. The first of my sex to arrive, I slow my horse to a trot and then a walk and guide him into the woods where the stag fled.

In a grove stand the King and the Dauphin. They have removed their hats, and so all the men's hats with their plumes hang in their hands. Ready with the knife, the hunt master lifts the head of the living stag by an antler to expose the throat. I look away, to scalloped tops of the leafy trees, where the green is interspersed with blue. Still, I hear the gurgle in the animal's throat. I do not look that way again but guide my horse back toward the group waiting in the road who did not bother to witness the climax. The cutting of an animal's throat is an obscene event.

I feel alone. I lean forward, and with the palm of my hand I pat and stroke the wet neck of my mount. He is noble, I tell him. The horse is indifferent to my caress. The pace of my heart is slowing, and I am glad and take satisfaction in this fact, and in everything.

Before we return to the château, ten more stags are taken.

As is his habit, tonight my husband will list them all in his journal, so as not to forget.

After such reckless excitement, all nature takes on definition—a stem of lolling blackberries growing beside the path, and the slender thorns beside the berries—they seem to embody a certain significant *puissance.* When I notice the hoof of my horse step close to a clump of violets with their heart-shaped leaves, the sweetness of their small purple petals have such surprising poignancy that tears start to my eyes. The violets seem to be lifting little faces toward me, and I am ridiculously glad that my mount did not tread upon them. Thus does the hunt heighten the senses and make the world more particular and real.

Already I lust after another day of hunting.

After the Hunt

Because there is no proper bath at Compiègne, my ladies bring tubs and porcelain bowls to bathe away the sweat and dust. I look with disgust at the limp rag of lace that I wore at my throat. Tossed on a dressing table, it resembles wilted lettuce, and I resolve to have a more enduring froth at my throat for future hunts, something more regal—a cascade of gold lace.

In one bathing bowl float several disks of orange to scent the water. I recall a crate of oranges boxed up from l'Orangerie at Versailles being lifted onto a wagon, no doubt for this purpose. Impulsively, I pluck a floating orange slice from the clean water, break its rind with my thumbnail, straighten it so that the fruit presents itself toward me in triangular tongues, and gnaw the juicelets to the quick. For my refreshment, immediately I am presented with a mound of grapes on a plate, but I ignore them and lean my nose over the white bowl with the floating wheels of orange.

"Please send for the perfumer for the hunt tomorrow," I say. "This aroma lacks complexity." But I cannot say what I want to smell. Something of lilac, perhaps, with the power of lily. Always I crave attar of rose, and yet none quite fulfills the need.

When I lift my face from the water, something in me feels older and more cynical than when I first mounted my horse today. Without reserve, I have given myself to excitement. I look at the ring on my little finger again.

After I looked at it while sitting in my saddle, when I glanced up, I saw that the King's eye had followed my gaze, and he too stared at my hands. Later, after hard riding, I recall the image of my ungloved hand rubbing the sweat-wet hair on my horse's thick chestnut neck. I wanted the horse to feel my bare hand. Now my ladies follow all my movements and my mood, even this moment of reverie. I take off my ring to bathe my hands among the disks of sliced orange. My hands are tired, and I spread and stretch my fingers in the water.

WHEN WE HAVE gathered together for the hunt supper, my fatigue makes me feel nervous. Drinking their glasses of wine, the others relax and shed their fatigue with the imbibing. Though I am tempted to join them, I remember my promise to my mother, and I know that in this she is right. I will never drink wine. *Draw your gaiety from your own heart,* she told me. *Be chaste in this matter and you will never regret the pure clarity of your mind.* Purple-skinned grapes sit in a tall silver compote before me, along with sugared peaches and candied oranges. I take a large grape and crunch through its simple skin with my back teeth. The pulp is good on my tongue, and I position the little seeds at the tip of my tongue and remove them with the perfect grace of a single forefinger, tucking the seeds into the palm of my hand till I choose the moment to discard them.

"Do you agree," the Dauphin asks me, triumphant in the chase, "the next-to-the-last stag was the most beautiful? He ran the most swiftly, threaded his way most gracefully."

"Lying on the ground," I say, "he did not deign to look at us."

"I noticed that as well. His gaze was on the sky."

"Or, perhaps, at the scalloped edge, where the treetops meet the sky."

The odor of a savory soup, one with parsley, greets my nostrils, but I do not want to bring anything hot into my mouth. I hated it when my ladies reapplied the circles of rouge to my still hot cheeks. The King asks me if I desire some token of our hunt, and I reply a necktie fashioned with lace of gold, one that will not wilt in heat.

"Our huntress deserves the gold," he answers enthusiastically. "You ride like Catherine de Medici."

"I think Your Majesty guides his horse with the hands of Apollo."

"But he had a chariot," the plump Comte de Provence puts in. "I wish I did."

The King asks me if I have been to the foot of the garden at Versailles and seen the fountain there of Apollo. When I say I have not, he offers to escort me on our return.

Quickly, the Dauphin reminds me that we are to have days of hunting before we quit Compiègne, and I smile encouragingly at him, for I do not want to leave either, till all of me is as tired as my hands. And I smile because I remember his promise as to what will happen between us, now that we are at Compiègne. The Dauphin quietly asks if there is any other part of my costume I would change.

"Not the pants," the King exclaims. "I adore her in pants, and how she rises from the saddle for the leaps."

Artois mischievously tells his older brother the Dauphin that I ride faster than he, though it is not true. "You will have to pant to catch her," Artois adds, and I recall that he has uttered this sentence before. But the Dauphin does not spare himself in the hunt—no one could urge his horse or himself with greater passion. When he draws to a stop, both he and the horse are gasping, and their eyes are wild in the same way. Now the Dauphin's eyes look down, heavy, sleepy, and hooded again. I wish he would not guzzle the hot soup, but he nods for another bowl of the creamy stuff on which float small islets of butter. I lay my spoon beside my soup plate, as though to give a signal.

Slender Artois also lays aside his spoon. He asks me if I prefer the lighter rigor of dancing to the wild rides on horseback.

"Today, I prefer the wildness of the hunt," I reply, "but when next we dance, you must ask the question again."

"Comtesse de Noailles plans a small dance in her rooms," the King says. "She attends to every detail and even consulted me on the guests—so much would she wish to please you."

Suddenly I am aware that part of my feeling of freedom is occasioned by the absence of Madame Etiquette. Beneath her insistence on forms is nothing but envy of my youth and energy.

"The King is so kind," I say, "as to wish all his family and subjects the greatest possible happiness at every possible moment."

"In that," the Dauphin adds, "he is like God, according to Leibniz—"

"One of his philosophers," Artois interrupts.

"But you read him as well," the Dauphin says to his bright little brother.

"However, I do not discuss him after the hunt."

"Please," I mediate, "Leibniz is an interesting name—German, I would guess."

"The princess would not leave all things German behind?" the King questions, but his eyes are kind and full of understanding.

"My mother wishes me to read books on devotion, as does the Abbé Vermond."

"Leibniz has his own thoughts," the Dauphin continues, but with some reluctance because of his brother's criticism of the topic. "Leibniz addresses the question 'How can a benevolent and all-powerful God allow evil to exist in the world?'"

Immediately, I think of the sudden death of my beloved papa, and the injustice of his taking, but I have never uttered that thought aloud, and I do not do so now. When the news of his death reached us, my mother looked at me, however, as though she could read my thoughts, and she ordered me to fall to my knees, handing me a cushion, and to pray for the soul of my father, which I did at once, with all the urgency of my being.

"What is the answer?" I ask timidly.

"Monsieur, you frighten your wife," the King cautions. Still his glance at his grandson is merely advisory, not unkind, not even a nuance of reprimand in his tone. Truly, I do love the King despite his moral weakness in concupiscence.

"Leibniz's answer is full of consolation," the Dauphin replies.

I recall the tenth stag, his neck presenting its curve for the knife, his eye rolled up to heaven.

"Your Majesty is so kind as to make my sensibility his care," I say, "but I am not afraid—of anything." Nervously, I laugh a little at myself.

The King chuckles. "Then your heart is still that of a child who has received perfect care."

"And are we not all God's children?" Provence asks. "It is a belief that none of us question. And yet we fear. We lack control in so many matters—"

"Such as the order of our birth," audacious Artois quips.

"I am my mother's tenth daughter," I say. "Yet here I sit, among you."

Oh, that was not wisely said before these boys whose turn at kingship is behind that of my husband and any progeny we may have! Around the edges of my ears, I seem to hear the crinkle of encroaching fire.

Papa-Roi rescues me. With the smile that shows him completely at ease in his own power and ordering of the world and in this moment most happy, he says, "Without doubt, God's wisdom rules the earth and all that comes to pass. Nothing could bless this moment more than the presence of our darling princess, the tenth daughter of our fortunate friend, the Empress."

"And that is Leibniz's very point," the Dauphin concludes. "This is the best of all possible worlds."

"Who can doubt it?" Provence speaks with his mouth full of venison, lifts his glass of wine by its slender crystal stem, and tilts outward to indicate the splendor and abundance that surround us.

"Voltaire thinks the idea absurd," Artois amends, with something of his own sneer.

"And where is Voltaire?" the King asks.

We all know that he is exiled to Switzerland for his attacks on piety and religion in general, so no one speaks.

"Voltaire . . . the *philosophes,*" the Dauphin muses. "Our tutors were chosen, my brothers, mainly to exclude those who sympathized with that crew."

I think of his hatred of his tutor Vauguyon which my husband has privately expressed to me. I eat another grape from the compote. I am eating very little tonight. I am almost too tired to eat. A sigh slips out.

"Are you thinking of your home?" the King asks. "Tell us, what image comes to mind?"

"I am thinking of the menagerie," I say. "My father kept many amusing animals for us."

"Monkeys?" the King asks, glancing around the crowded room, as though to be sure that all of his guests enjoy their conviviality.

I recall that Madame du Barry keeps a pet monkey. "I do not like monkeys," I say. "They are too mocking."

Artois laughs. "I heard that what's-her-name's monkey went on a rampage. He got in her cosmetics and powdered himself in a flurry and rouged his cheeks, just like his mistress." When Artois imitates the monkey, hunching his back and chattering his teeth, we all burst into laughter.

"What animals did you like, in the menagerie at Schönbrunn?" the King inquires of me.

"Clara, the rhinoceros, with her armor covered in red dust." I do not want to tell him of beloved Hilda, the hippopotamus, floating among the hyacinths, so peaceful and *vulnerable*. "And a leopard, with golden eyes lounging in the shade of a lilac bush."

"You must have a leopard skin," the King says, "to place under your saddle."

A HEAVY SILVER platter is brought forth, loaded with cakes in fanciful shapes, some like eggs, some like stars, or hearts. A whole group resembles the houses and shops of a small village, and all are covered in glittering sugar as though a great snowstorm had struck this darling hamlet. A golden platter is covered with pastries, their golden-brown crusts are shaped to make nests for jellies and cooked fruit, apricots and pears freckled with cinnamon, and some have a puddle of molten chocolate in their center. A large porcelain bowl decorated with Chinese bridges and blue willow trees holds an enormous pudding, and the aroma of cooked raisins and plums and cherries rushes through my nostrils to my stomach and makes it writhe with greed.

Nonetheless, I choose one of the snow-draped structures from the hamlet to nibble. The Dauphin has his plate covered with some of each of the wondrous sweets, and Provence has his plate covered, and then another layer, a second story, so to speak, of dessert built up on his plate. I have no doubt he will eat it all, but slender Artois, and I, and the handsome King have some sense in this matter of eating. I am sorry when the Dauphin asks for more.

Provence says, "I intend to live in the most *delicious* of all possible worlds."

When it is time to retire, the Dauphin accompanies me to our chamber door. He looks at the beautiful white bed, which is as bedecked with lace and satin-sided pillows as the little cake-houses of the village were with white icing and sparkling sugar, but he tells me he has indigestion, and, indeed, it is best that he sleep elsewhere, lest he disturb me in the night. He knows that he will be sick and need attending.

All my eagerness melts, but I speak with the utmost good cheer and genuine concern for his discomfort.

In bed alone, my legs are restless, as I anticipate the motion of the hunt tomorrow. My eagerness returns, and I think of squeezing the horse between my knees to make him jump at just the moment of my choosing.

Tomorrow our object will be the foxes, and we hunt another quarter of the forest.

Tomorrow night my husband will surely want to come to me—if the hunt is successful. Yes, it will be a sign. If the hunt goes well, surely he will want to bed his wife.

A Vow

The day has been a delirium of dust, speed, leaping, riding. I am triumphant not in the animals we kill but in the joy of the hunt, the excitement, the color of costumes, the sound of the horn, the hard thudding of horses' hooves, the independence of my own body, rising and settling, rising to fly, the good ache in all my limbs.

When we left the woods, I heard the quiet reclaiming the countryside. The trees seemed to be part of something almost holy, a vast *cathédrale*. But it was the quiet that called me back.

AT DINNER, we are loud and boisterous. The King always keeps his dignity, but the grandsons seem childish in their jubilance, especially the younger brothers. My Dauphin has moments of sullenness, which I have not seen in him for some time. Finally, he says to me, "I would hunt now, in the dark, if I could."

I understand: he is bored; it is only the chase he craves. The bounty of the table, the steaming meat pies, the piles of peeled fruits, and green stacks of haricots are poor substitutes for plunging into the forest astride a willing mount. Because he must wait for what he wants, he withdraws and sulks.

"The morning comes quickly," I say. "Refreshed, we will ride all the better."

"You love it too?"

"I do love the hunt, and all that pleases you gives me double pleasure, for I experience both your joy and my own."

His eyes look fondly into mine, with gratitude for my understanding, but they do not go so far as to promise any connubial joy for me. He needs, and he appreciates what he receives, but he is not strong enough to give.

The trays of candies arrive, nuts cooked in patties of brown sugar, a cake in the shape of a fox covered in raspberry fondant with a green grape eye. The Dauphin licks his lips. A lovely meringue shell holds a rich swirling whirlpool of chocolate pudding; a deep bowl with a scalloped golden edge cradles large mounds of beaten cream studded with strawberries and sprinkled with crystals of white sugar, and more and more; he eats it all.

At the door of our chamber, the Dauphin folds his arms over his stomach and bends forward in pain.

"I'm sorry," he gasps and runs doubled over away from me, as fast as he can, for a commode.

AM I TO GROW miserable at Compiègne? Soon will he not even accompany me to the door? I do not need to be a Bohemian Gypsy to predict the future. I know the answer is *yes.*

And what is my recourse?

I will remain patient. And I will visit the gardens of Versailles, and explore the bosquets, and revel in the basins of cavorting waters. I am his friend. Though the whole court laugh at him, from me, he will receive nothing but sympathy, mounds and mounds of sweet concern, as though each rejection were without history and engendered no impatience.

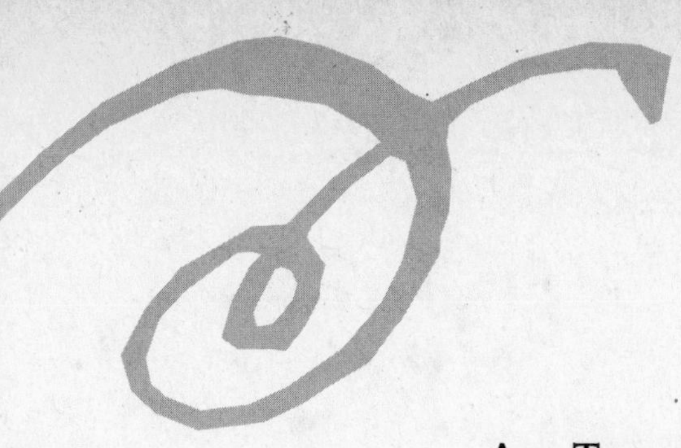

Act Two

The Princesse de Lamballe, Carnival 1771

I am so eager to reach the apartment of Madame de Noailles that I take the Dauphin's hand; we all but run through the rooms of the Château de Versailles, and we do run through the Hall of Mirrors. I watch us in the mirrors as we hasten out of one frame and past another, and another and another. It is the Versailles glide, smooth as ice-skating, but at a fine clip. Our attendants can hardly keep up. We shall have fun, we shall have fun! I remember how we rode lately to the hounds, leaping across ditches and over fences on horseback.

Before my husband and I reach the entrance to the apartment of Madame Etiquette, we can smell the aroma of roast pork and apples and cinnamon and game birds stuffed with sage, and something that must be a venison stew with much of celery and onions—all of the wonderful meaty smells and dishes that we shall have to forgo when Carnival is done and Lent has us in its fishy, forty-day grip. I know the Dauphin's appetite is keen, and everyone will attend the dance with a special eagerness to make merry. Over the winter months, without his beloved hunting, my husband has put on flesh.

It is time to walk more sedately. Slowly, slowly, we are becoming friends. When he comes to my bed, I chatter and amuse him with great success. Once after a fit of laughter, he suddenly fell asleep, with a mighty snore. My own laughter erupted, at him—but he did not awaken. Then I cried. Huge sobs—the bed shook with them.

As for me, tonight, the young Artois and I will dance till our slippers fall off, if I have my way, and I can feel the brightness already inhabiting my eyes. To dance, especially with the innocent and graceful Artois, is to forget that I am far from home and will never go there again to see the shining faces of my brothers and sisters. It is Carnival, my first celebration of Carnival, and I am fifteen. I have been here in France more than half of an entire year!

When the door opens, whom do I see but the beautiful Princesse de Lamballe. She is accompanied by her father-in-law, the Duc de Penthièvre, the richest man in France next to the King; his valet carries two simple pots of creamy clay holding living violets. With graceful gestures, the good Penthièvre indicates that one is for his hostess Madame de Noailles and the other is for his beautiful, widowed daughter-in-law.

To my amazement, the Princesse de Lamballe bursts into tears. Rapidly a seat is placed behind her, and half fainting, she sits upon it and weeps.

"Their sweetness is too great," she says, wiping her eyes.

To my second amazement, I find that tears have quickly come to my own eyes and are ready to spill. So appealing are the flowers that they appear to have been dug from the forest floor and brought by courier in all their freshness.

"She is overwhelmed by their naturalness," the duc says sympathetically of his daughter-in-law, and he gestures to have the potted violets removed.

I find that I am on my knees beside the princess, touching her hand, and looking into her eyes to console her.

"I too have been touched by the *poignancy* of their faces," I say, "when I rode to the hounds in the forest of Compiègne."

"Don't take them away," the sensitive princess sobs. "But, dearest Papa, may I make a present of my pot to the Dauphine, whose sensibility I share."

And suddenly, she smiles at me. The sun has come out from behind the cloud, and I am enchanted by the beauty of her wide-spaced blue eyes, and the steadiness of her gaze. She is neither afraid of me nor impressed by my position. It is myself whom she claims as a kindred spirit. And then I recall that she is of German origins, like myself. She continues to smile at me and clutches my hand in return, and I think of Charlotte, my sister, and how when we were girls at Schönbrunn, we would gaze into each other's eyes and hold the gaze, till the exact thought passed from one mind to the other, without a single word spoken.

So it is now, and my heart fills itself and sighs with happiness, for I have found a friend.

Oh, Mesdames are upon me in a moment. They would pry me away from her, but elegant Count Mercy steps forward and with his hands cups each of us under the elbow, the princess and myself. I rise with the pressure of his fatherly hand, as does the princess.

"Let me guide you to a more comfortable settee," Count Mercy says, "where you may speak of flowers and the friendship that I see blossoming between you."

The aunts dare not follow and intrude. Mercy has known my needs, and he stands close by now, an elegant sentinel, at his ease and in complete command as the guardian of our tête-à-tête.

The fair princess is twenty-one to my fifteen, but purity has kept her suitable for my confidence. She compares Count Mercy to her dear father-in-law in his thoughtfulness, and I tell her how I admired the family group of the Duc de Penthièvre as depicted in the painting *The Cup of Chocolate* in Madame Adelaide's apartment, and how I had wished that I might have entered that frame and become a part of that happy family picture.

I speak of how that first day, when I saw the little dog in the picture and thought of Mops, that I feared I might weep, and immediately, again, tears well up in her own eyes, in sympathy with my former longing.

"And do you love little dogs too?" I ask, smiling cheerfully.

"And kittens," she says, in a rapturous burst. A few tears brim over the edges of her eyes and course down her cheeks, but she bravely fights them off.

"And hippopotami," I exclaim.

She is caught off guard and says, "I do not know hippopotami. What are they?"

It turns out she has not heard of rhinoceroses or giraffes either, and I am glad, because for once I am not the most ignorant person in a conversation. With some fear (I am almost trembling), I ask her if she likes to read.

"Sometimes," she says, and she looks troubled, as though she fears her answer may not be adequate.

"I am the same," I say.

"There is one book that always touches me," she says, "and makes me feel that there are other sensitive people in the world."

When I ask her its title, she says her favorite book—she has read it many times—is a novel titled *Julie, ou la Nouvelle Héloïse.* She has forgotten its author's name.

"Jean-Jacques Rousseau," I say, "but I have not yet read the book."

"It is about nature, and friendship, and love," she says.

For a moment, I simply regard her. She is as elaborately and beautifully dressed as I am, at great expense. What is it I want to share with her? My mind scrambles to find some emblem of myself. I think of the little topiary trees in the garden here at Versailles and that night when I hid inside the folds of the curtain and looked out at them, so still in the moonlight. But not that! It is their *opposite* that I want.

"The forest is always murmuring," I say. "The great trees talk to one another with the rustling of their leaves."

"They put their heads together," she replies uncertainly, then smiles, "and share secrets, like sisters."

Already she loves me! I mind my husband's neglect a little less now.

All about us the drinking and dancing and eating of a party, late in the season of Carnival, goes on. At one point, I see Artois, beyond the princess's pink silk shoulder, looking at me as though he has been neglected. Recalling how many times he has rescued me by inviting me to dance, I rise to dance with him, after promising the princess I shall return.

When I seat myself beside my new friend again, we are presented with small private tables bearing plates of food, which my aunts have had assembled for us. None of my favorite things are on the plate, and I send it away. The princess also refuses food.

She whispers, "How can one eat when the heart is engaged?"

I tell her that we must walk the gardens together the next day or be carried in our litters, if the ground is damp.

"We shall compare our favorite fountains," she says.

"Let me guess," I say.

"I don't know if I could bear it, if you guessed wrong," she says.

"I will not guess wrong," I reply as confidently as though I were speaking to Maria Carolina, my Charlotte. "Your favorite fountain is Flora among the heaps of flowers."

"It is true," she says and sighs profoundly.

"Remind me, please," I say, "of your given names."

She begins, "Marie Thérèse—"

"My mother's name—" I interrupt.

"Is?"

"The Empress of Austria—" I hint.

"Oh. What is her name?"

I can scarcely believe the princess does not know the name of my mother, who has arranged my marriage and the Austrian Alliance, but I say all the more gently, "Maria Theresa . . . like your name."

"It is an omen," she says, "for I am older than you."

"And so you can easily guess which fountain I love best—after Flora."

"Tell me."

I see she has not studied mythology at all, and then I realize that perhaps the story of how Flora was taken from Ceres, her mother, to the Underworld by Hades, would be too heartrending for the princess. She has had a governess like my own darling Countess Brandeis, who guarded my sensibilities from shock, who ensured that I would have time to play, and who taught me very little.

"It is the fountain of Ceres, who was Flora's mother. Ceres made the wheat, and all the cereals and flowers ripen. The violets too," I add, "for which gift, I shall always honor your sweet and generous nature, from this night forward."

"I promise I will keep you in my heart," she says, and I feel that I have heard the truth. "Always," the princess adds. "To the death." She seems frightened.

To such sincere words I can frame no reply, but I reach out with my hand and squeeze hers.

"Now we must join the others and dance," I say, "or gossip will begin."

Blithely she rises, with airy lightness, but she turns back to smile at me, her face all softness, surrounded by soft, fair hair. As I dance—with everyone—sometimes I steal a glance at her, and I see that there is a touching melancholy about her face that makes her even more beautiful. I want to take care of her, but there is no need for that, since the good Duc de Penthièvre is devoted to her.

AS THE DAUPHIN and I walk through the state apartments back to our chambers, he softly touches my waist from time to time, and as we pass through the Mars state room, he dismisses our attendants. I glance up to see again the wolves who draw the chariot of Mars. My husband seems to want more intimacy, but I have been disappointed so many times by his slight overtures of interest that I do not let my mind evaluate what these gentle touches may mean tonight.

Instead, I think of the graceful charm of the Princesse de Lamballe, her small waist, her willingness to share confidences with me. I shall ask her about her husband, who, I already know, died of syphilis at age twenty-nine, consequent on his savage and insatiable appetite, and I shall tell her something of my own disappointments, of which, like everyone else at court, she must surely be already aware. Though they all know the problem lies with the Dauphin, they blame me anyway. They laugh at him.

The princess knows the fact of my situation; she cannot know the feelings within me, for they are shared only in careful and courteous language in letters to my mother. The disappointments of the princess and myself with the men to whom we have been bonded may concern quite different sorts of behaviors, on the husbands' parts, but the hurt hearts in the Princess and myself are surely kin.

Almost, tonight, I do not care whether my husband lies in bed with me, or what he does or does not do as we wait for sleep.

As we pass through the Venus drawing room, again I look up. When I see the gentle doves pulling the chariot of the goddess, I think of the soft face and hair of the princess whose name begins Marie Thérèse. Seated on the divan, she and I cooed together like doves.

When I look down, I see protruding from the hem of one of the curtains, the toe of an old and worn boot, one that I believe I noticed on the night of my wedding. Nothing happened in our bed that night, and I take the scuffed leather as an omen that nothing will happen tonight. *If I do not guard myself against expectations, I will go mad.* I must beat down my hope—I and only I can regulate my feelings. All sorts of people have access to the palace; one of them has left her boot behind. That is the only meaning of the scuffed toe protruding from under the curtain.

Tomorrow morning my husband will write *Rien* in his journal, if he bothers to keep a diary of married life. Certainly, our marriage is less exciting than hunting, though perhaps more important to the fate of Europe.

The curtain moves. My husband notices the movement; when he sees the boot, he pulls the brocade aside.

A female figure, about my own size, stands in a tattered skirt. She wears a cape, such as I have seen in drawings of the peasant Jeanne d'Arc, and its hood is up. Her face is turned from us, as though she has been gazing out the window at the moonlit garden.

For an instant I remember my nightmare of Mother Eve biting glass fruit, and I gasp.

"Don't be afraid," my husband says, but he is speaking to her and not to me.

Nor need he! I am not one to be afraid, no, not the daughter of the Empress of Austria.

The girl looks him full in the face. Her features denote only one emotion: wonder. Her delicate countenance is unlined, smooth; it shows no sign of hardship, though her body is too thin. There is a transparency to her skin. She raises one frail hand and presses her long thin fingers against her cheek. It is a gesture that seems to ask *Am I real? Her face somewhat resembles mine.*

She has but one short glance for me.

I realize the quickest of glances is all that is needed for me: she has seen me before. *Recognition* is in that single glance. Perhaps she sees me every day, so many people come and go through the palace, but her clothes are too poor for me not to have noticed such a figure. Her loose dress is the color of old moss draped in folds. She looks as poor as the fish market women. Perhaps she is one of their daughters. But no, her features are too soft to have issued from such stridency.

Too late, we realize that she is moving. She simply steps around us and walks toward the Mars room. Her heavy boots make soft, quick thuds as she hurries away, first into the Diana salon.

Because the doors of all the state rooms are in alignment, I expect to see her pass through the Diana room and into the Mars room, and perhaps she does, but my eyes slowly slide closed, then open, and she is gone. Perhaps she has used one of the hidden doors cut into the wallpaper, the secret doors that lead to the Land of Intrigue.

"We've lost her, haven't we?" the Dauphin asks. "Shall I look for her?"

"Perhaps we have other destinations this evening."

My voice is as quiet and neutral as her gray-green dress.

"Did you hear the story of the demented Comtesse de Guéméné this evening?" My husband's question guides our minds around some corner, and we seem back in the familiar world. "Lately, they say, she believes she converses with the dead."

"I would talk with my dear papa, if I could."

"And I with my older brother, the Dauphin who died as a child." My husband turns his head to look at me. Curiosity about my mood subsequent to this strange encounter is evident in his facial expression, though not in his words. "The comtesse communicates with the other world"—he cracks a thin smile—"through her dogs and their incessant yapping."

I laugh out loud.

"Come with me," my husband says and leads me to his bed.

WITH A STACK OF SOFT PILLOWS at our backs, we begin our nocturnal conversation. Every confidence we share is like a tongue of ribbon reaching out and connecting us. He tells me of the boy who died, the firstborn of his parents, who would have more rightly been the next king than he himself. He tells me the boy was brilliant and much beloved. For his brother's sake, Louis Auguste's own education was accelerated, as he was taken away from his governess in order to keep his brilliant brother company at his lessons. To whet their interest in history, the great philosopher-historian David Hume of Scotland was invited to visit. The older brother was frail, and their pious father, wanting his firstborn son never to be lonely, employed the second-born to serve that purpose.

The Dauphin speaks for a long time about his childhood, his brother's death, his parents' heartbreak at that loss and their disappointment in him.

"After the Dauphin's death, I was kept isolated with tutors, as princes usually are, and I developed no skills in conversing freely with other young scholars nor in quickly taking the measure of another person."

"What measure," I ask, "did you take of the young woman we saw tonight?" I rejoice in the informal coziness of our conversation. "We have spoken nothing of her."

His legs stir under the covers.

"Was she real?" he asks in a speculative tone. "If so, perhaps she was from the Gypsies. My brother Provence says they are encamped in tents outside the gates."

"Can two people share the same delusion?" I ask.

"Yes," he says. "A hundred can share the same delusion. A thousand, or tens of thousands."

He abandons the topic of our apparition. We talk until we fall asleep, though I only ask him questions to help him in his discourse. His face fills with brightness as he confides more and more of his childhood experiences with me. Perhaps another night, he will inquire further into my private history. Because sleep comes more slowly to me, I review the party hosted by the Comtesse de Noailles. By including the Princesse de Lamballe, Madame Etiquette has given me the gift of a special sister. With the Princesse de Lamballe, first one and then the other of us would tell one tidbit or another. The fabric of our conversation interlaced as naturally as warp and woof.

However, I did express my regret to my husband before he slept that the young Prince de Rohan has now become a cardinal, to the delight of both the Comtesse de Guéméné and the Comtesse de Noailles, who are his relatives. "He behaved most impudently to me in Strasbourg," I confided.

When morning comes, I wake before my husband. He sleeps with only a sheet pulled across his naked body. At the place between his legs stands a little tent of sheeting, held high by a single sturdy prod.

In the Garden: A Dragon

Weeks pass before I am able to spend more time in the company of my new friend. Her father-in-law has as many estates almost as does the King, and his household, like ours, travels frequently, at great expense, from one to another. She went southwest to Rambouillet, while the court traveled east to Meudon, which is said to possess the best air of all the estates. But finally, on a fine spring day, her family and mine meet again at Versailles.

Accompanied by our attendants, the Dauphin's charming little sister Elisabeth, the Princesse de Lamballe, and I are walking beside the dragon fountain, which for some reason has been turned off, though its large pool is filled with water. Exceedingly fond of her tall dogs, Elisabeth walks surrounded by her greyhounds, and she insists on wearing her winter cap of gray rabbit fur, though now it is well into spring.

"If it were not for the Dauphin's aversion to cats," I confide to the princess, "I would surround myself with them."

"I like it when they sit in my lap and purr," she replies. "But sometimes their toenails snag a thread and ruin the silk."

I wonder to myself if the Dauphin's dislike of cats is not rebellion, in a very small way, against the tastes of the King, who adores cats—particularly a pure white Persian, who is so spoiled and smug that my secret nickname for her is du Barry.

Glancing at my dear new friend, I wonder what the Princesse de Lamballe thinks of the du Barry and the King's immorality, but because my friend's husband was also a profligate, I do not raise the subject, which might be a painful one for her. How did she avoid the contagion he carried in his body? It took his life. With her pretty face and beautiful clothes, she seems the picture of health and content. Like myself, she enjoys the company of pets, but I do not think she likes to romp with the children of other people as much as I do.

One of the greyhounds trots so that his head travels just below my hand in case I should want to stroke his smooth, sleek head. He glances up at me—sympathetically, I believe. If I were with my sister Charlotte, I would be silly: I would cradle the dog's gray head in my hands, kiss him on his long nose, and say, "Now, turn into the perfect prince."

These animals are a relief—quiet and elegant in comparison to the spaniels of my aunts. Perfectly gentle, they are so strong that they seem to spring on their legs while they circle round and round their little mistress, Elisabeth.

The dragon is surrounded by large, gilded putti mounted on swans swimming in the waters of the basin. The fearless children aim their little bows and arrows at the monster. Reared erect, with spread claws, the dragon is fierce and scaly, his nipples pointed like weapons, his head thrown back and raised upward toward the sky. The children and the swans are far larger than life-size—perhaps they *could* slay the dragon, for all their innocence. Mythically large, they dwarf the adults standing at the edge of the basin.

Suddenly from out of the thrown-back head and open mouth of the gilded dragon, with a tremendous noise and gush, a mighty plume of water arises. The silent greyhounds erupt in barking. They crouch and growl while the water plume grows up and up to a truly towering height. All the greyhounds are barking, and some of them leap into the pool to join the swan-mounted putti in their attack. All the while we admire the dogs' fierce courage, we laugh at them for their foolishness. As they thrash in the water and crouch and spring and bark, Elisabeth shouts at them, "It's not real, it's not real!" but they believe the evidence of their own senses. The water spouting heavenward from the dragon statue means he is alive.

I laugh so hard that I begin to feel deep sobs starting in my chest, till with an awful gurgle in my throat, tears spurt from my eyes.

Quickly, the princess directs Elisabeth and her dogs and attendants to return to the château. Kind little heart, Elisabeth first kisses me on the cheek and whispers to me, her auntie, not to be afraid of the dragon. "He can't move." I try to seal shut my wailing mouth, and I give her a quick, reassuring nod, but as soon as she begins to climb back up the incline to the château, with the wet greyhounds frolicking around her, I sob again. Not one gray guardian dog has remained behind, but here is my friend, the princess, leading me to a stone bench.

She asks the source of my unhappiness, and when I cannot answer, she weeps with me a little. Still I cannot answer.

"Look how high the water spout has climbed," she says. "It seems to tickle the clouds."

But my eyes are shut in a hard firm line while I sob. The Princesse de Lamballe embraces me and tries to soothe me. Her cool fingertips and palm stroke the back of my neck, under my hair. Finally, I gasp out in a broken cadence, "I want to become a mother!"

Pulling back, the princess looks at me with startled horror, and then I realize she is glad to be spared the rites of married life and the pleasure of motherhood. As daughter-in-law to the wealthiest and most virtuous man of the kingdom, she is entirely content; she is like a large child.

"My whole being is afraid the Dauphin will never make love to me," I wail. "My whole body hopes to mother a child."

The princess sits before me in a lovely hat, bedecked with flowers; her wide-set eyes regard me as though she wishes to comfort me, but she is speechless. In her helpless distress, I believe she will begin to cry again.

I reach my hand toward her. "Every night," I tell her, "I thank God that he has sent me such a friend as you."

She smiles, and I make myself smile back at her. I straighten her pink bow that spreads its wide loops across her bosom. It is my duty to learn to command my feelings, or to hide them.

THIS NIGHT I SLEEP alone because the Dauphin has gone to Fontainebleau to hunt, and it being during the visit of the Générale, I did not want to share his bed. Nor do I ride with my husband, lest I risk the possibility on a galloping horse of a hemorrhage occasioned by too much exercise. Absentmindedly, I have arranged no entertainment for the evening.

As I lie in bed, the silence is terrible. Perhaps I should send for the princess to keep me company. Almost I decide to rise up and write letters to my mother or to my sister, but I do not reach out to anyone. In themselves, silence and boredom become terrifyingly interesting because they are *novel.* I want to *explore* the moment. I lie very still, staring for a while at the portrait of my mother, then at the one of my brother, Emperor Joseph. Their images are my guardians.

When I was at home, we were never bored—or afraid. We had amusements: we played cards, or games, or danced, or made music together. There were so many of us—I shudder to think that the Empress gave birth fourteen times—and the boys and girls played together like equals. Because our entertainments most often involved our talents—at the keyboard or with the bow, dancing or singing or acting—our ability determined who was dominant and most admired.

IN THE MORNING, after having coffee with my aunts in their apartment, as I walk with the King to Mass, I tell him that I must have more music in my life. I ask if my old teacher Christoph Gluck might be brought to court to give me lessons and to perform his operas.

"There is bitter controversy now about aesthetic questions in composing operas," Louis XV says, amused. "Should the music support the poetry, or the poetry provide a mere framework for vocal acrobatics? That is the question."

No. The question is whether I shall strangle on bitterness or shame. People say I am pretty and have great charm, but to my husband I am more hideous than a dragon. I want to throw back my head and spout up my misery. I want to be torn apart by dogs.

A Tempest

I have made my husband cry.

A double repentance is required: one with Abbé Vermond in the confessional box, another for political reasons.

Gossips soon will have told Count Mercy, who, I fear, will report the matter in an unadvantageous way to my mother, so I must tell him myself, and in the process learn more about the rumor that the sister of the wife of the Comte de Provence is destined to marry the Comte d'Artois; then we shall have much of Savoy come to Versailles.

As he enters my sitting room, Count Mercy asks why I have requested his presence in this private chamber and, of course, how delighted he is at any moment to serve my needs.

I look at his handsome countenance and pleasant bearing and know that he always makes an effort not to frighten me. I have been told that he keeps a mistress at great expense, but I forgive him because he serves my mother with undivided loyalty and is devoted also to me. In France such arrangements between men of power and common women are unexceptional and accepted, but that does not make me admit the Comtesse du Barry into my conversation, even if she sits in the same room with me. While Count Mercy sins, he is not corrupted by his sins, and besides, he suffers terribly from hemorrhoids and is thus punished.

Perhaps they hurt him at this moment, but because he is not only curious but also concerned about me, there is no trace of distraction in his face. His chin is an excellent feature, firm but well molded, with a certain delicacy. My own chin is something that has a bit too much of Hapsburg prominence, making me appear haughty to some, while friends speak of my dignity. Count Mercy always carries his head with utmost naturalness. It is when one meets his eyes that one encounters an intellect of remarkable cunning and dignity. And I believe I see there too a shrewd kindness reserved primarily for me—and perhaps his actress mistress.

I dismiss all attendants, motion to a chair, which the count draws closer as he sits.

"How can I serve?" he asks with avuncular goodwill.

"It would comfort me if you would listen to the story of the Dauphin's tears today." I seem so serene in my demeanor that I convince myself my royal bearing is unperturbed. "And I beg of you advice, if I have left undone any gesture needed to restore perfect tranquillity in the household. Have you heard already that I made the Dauphin weep?"

Truthfully, he says that he has heard of the incident—a mere sentence or two that did not criticize me in any way.

"You know the sad state of incompleteness, of course, in which the Dauphin and I live. I have given him every encouragement. My mother says always that I must express more caresses, and I do, but sometimes I feel it is conversation that draws us closer."

"It is true, and a disadvantage, that when Your Highness and His Highness were married, you scarcely knew each other. No one denies that, my dear princess."

"And to my mind, conversation, if it is to be effective, must sometimes convey truth—important truths."

With a slight smile, he nods and encourages me to continue.

"'There is only so much time in any day'—that is the way I began the conversation."

"An indisputable observation, my princess."

"And if we occupy the day and spend our energy in one way, then it cannot be spent in another."

"And you wished to convey that perhaps the Dauphin—"

"Would spend less time hunting."

In a confidential tone, the count remarks, with sad candor, "He has an intemperate passion for the sport, as does the present King, and the King before him."

"Yes, but I never thought a passion running through the generations would be instrumental in preventing the continuation of the family." I decide to describe my husband's habits in more detail. "The Dauphin hunts incessantly, and it leaves him no energy. After the hunt and eating, he collapses, night after night. Today, I asked him forthrightly, in front of Monsieur le Comte de Provence and Madame la Comtesse de Provence, if he was aware that his addiction to the hunt was destroying his health, and that furthermore it was destroying his appearance, making him look common and unkempt."

The count presents a mien of perfect neutrality, which means he is shocked by what I have had the unlucky impulse to communicate to the Dauphin.

Nonetheless, I continue my narrative. "I am sorry to say that my comment on his appearance hurt the Dauphin's feelings very much, and I know that I should not have begun as I did. But the comte is so overweight and Josephine of such a sallow complexion that it was clear to me that the Dauphin far outshines both of them, at any moment, and that he knew this fact and that he would not take offense because, in comparison to them, 'unkempt' was a minor flaw."

The count smooths the fabric on the thighs of his pants. He glances down and then up at me, as though asking permission to interject his own idea, and I signal with courteous silence that he may speak.

"Of course his Highness is hurt not by the specific content of your complaint against him but by the fact that he has been trained and counseled many times that even in his family, he is ascendant, and no one must seem to presume otherwise."

"I did presume," I admit.

When I remember the look of despair on the Dauphin's face that I who have always supported him in every situation should have suddenly failed, I feel as though I will weep.

I can offer only feeble defense of my indiscretion. "Sometimes the Dauphin has appreciated my concern for his welfare. You will remember, perhaps a month ago, at one of the parties of the Comtesse de Noailles when too many pastries were brought to him, I ordered the servants to remove them all, and I explained to his Highness that his digestion was delicate and that I could not bear to see him suffer from overeating. Then he was pleased and considered my behavior to be evidence of my tenderness for him."

"Is it really the same circumstance?" the count asks patiently, as he has so many times in trying to help me thread my way through a labyrinth of choices. Sometimes he speaks very earnestly and intently, sometimes with special pleasantness, as he does now, which makes me realize that he has probably been told the whole story already.

It is not the same circumstance, and I say so, noting that there is certainly a difference between a spontaneous act, prettily couched, and scolding.

"What happened next?" the count prompts.

"Before I could request that he change his hunting habits, he fled to his own apartment. But I followed him and continued discussing the disadvantages of a behavior, an indulgence, that not only drove me to despair but that was irresponsible in his duty to the King and to the citizens of France.

"The idea that he was robbing the people of a future king so humiliated the Dauphin that he burst into tears. He told me that I was right and begged my patience with him.

"Then I caressed him, and I wept with him and told him that I loved the French people second only to himself."

"And what was his response?"

"He asked with great feeling if it were true, then, that I did indeed love him, and I replied that I did, and even more I respected him, and that it broke my heart to think that I had been so wicked as to say things in front of his brother that should have been said in other ways and when we were alone. I called myself a goose, and then he kissed me tenderly."

Though I speak to the count only of what was said and done, I experience again how surprised I was by my husband's question—did I love him?

He was as vulnerable as a child. I had never imagined he worried about the question of my *feeling* about him, but that he simply accepted that it was our duty to be together. The frankness of this question from Louis Auguste struck through a hard shell that had grown (almost without my noticing it) around my own heart.

"So the reconciliation brought the two of you into greater intimacy."

"I believe it did, and certainly I feel most loving toward him," I confide in a burst of my own frankness, "for he has an excellent temper and rather than become angry with me, he shows me his sensitive nature and reproaches himself. I told him that a demon had taken control of my tongue."

The count smiles at me fondly and then asks if the Dauphin smiled at me.

"There is no one who has greater charm than you," the count says, "and I shall tell the Empress that I am pleased with the way you handled this small tempest. Perhaps flowers of greater affection will germinate between the two of you from this watering by tears."

I have not told the count that I excused myself with my husband by telling him that the so-called demon was sometimes a herald to the imminent arrival of the Générale Krottendorf.

"Ah, yes," the Dauphin said, "we will respect the visit of the Générale, and perhaps after that we will complete our reconciliation in a way that fulfills not only your expectations but those of France." He hugged me to him again and kissed my brow. Then he added gallantly, "And my own fond hopes as well."

Madame, My Very Dear Mother

The little tempest in the calm sea of my rapport with the Dauphin passed months ago. When we made up, tenderness was exchanged, but you will understand what I mean when I say that no real progress has occurred. I do tell you everything, and you must believe that I can justify myself on all the other points that concern you so much that you write to me about them repeatedly.

No, I cannot use the word *repeatedly*. I cross it out, I turn it into a black blob and rip the paper with the sharp point of my quill, but now I know that I must copy this letter again, for the Empress has scolded me about my handwriting and sloppiness as well as about matters of greater import. The corset—well, she has gotten her way about the corset, and the ones from Austria are more comfortable than those made here, and now that I am almost sixteen, it even pleases me to need to wear the appropriate womanly undergarments.

I am ungrateful not to appreciate her thoughtfulness more. Count Mercy has told me that my mother is profoundly worried about the impending partition of Poland by Austria, Prussia, and Russia. The French have no knowledge of what is about to happen because the young Prince de Rohan, whom I first met in Strasbourg and whom Louis XV has appointed as the French ambassador to Vienna, is too busy gambling and going to parties to even be aware of the international situation. My mother, so Count Mercy explains, is naturally worried about the effect this action against Poland will have on France and on the Franco-Austrian alliance sealed by my marriage. The Empress has been badgered into the agreement by my brother Joseph, who shares her office with her, as well as by the rulers of Prussia and Russia.

With her own hand, she has stricken the word *rightfully* from their joint decree of their intention to divide Poland into three occupied parts. Her anxiety about what she considers to be an unrighteous act has caused her great suffering, and that suffering is compounded by rumors she hears about my behavior—that I am flirtatious, that I spend too much time at cards and entertainments, that I neglect the Dauphin and have created a cool atmosphere with the King because I will not speak to that immoral woman he keeps in his presence—in his bed!

> *I feel desperate with sorrow that you believe what I must call LIES and gossip of a malicious sort instead of what Mercy and myself write you about the situation here. I am sure that the King himself does not want me to speak to du Barry. Mesdames Tantes have explained it to me: that he respects me for my stubbornness in this moral matter. That he himself hopes if I continue to snub that creature she will run away, and he will be restored to the bosom of his family, to his virtuous daughters.*

I see I have gone too far in my letter in revealing my dependence on my aunts for interpretation and advice. I will leave out those two sentences referring to them and say instead that my certainty about the appropriateness of my snubbing the Favorite rests on good and reliable advice from those who cherish my welfare.

> *I am sure that if the King wished me to change my behavior to the Favorite that he would have told me so, but he never even brings up the subject. Because I refuse to speak to her, the King has rewarded me with even greater friendliness.*

Part of the problem is that were I to speak to her once, then she and her circle would still not be satisfied. They would have me in their power and force me to make conversation with her as a matter of course, over and over. That would be intolerable for one who is the loving daughter of the paragon of Virtue, the Empress, my most dear mother.

The Empress's Reply

Because I am writing on the eve of your sixteenth birthday, I know that this letter will reach you days from now, but you will know anyway, today and tomorrow, that I am thinking of you, for you know my heart even as I know yours. I thank God every day, and I pray that He will keep you safe so that you can do good where you are and also make your family here happy insofar as you are able to celebrate the glory of God and promote the welfare of those who depend upon you.

I am glad that you write to me openly defending your behavior on the subject of the du Barry. Whenever you are candid and explain your sensitivity on an issue, you endear yourself to me. Nonetheless, I do not think your feelings are hurt so much by my remonstrances as you are experiencing impatience with my desire to guide and to help you. My feelings are hurt that you do not discuss your aunts in your letters to me when I am certain that they are at the bottom of your intransigence on the matter of being more courteous to the du Barry. They are the source of all your mistaken ideas.

I can assure you that the King's friendliness to you—and Mercy has made similar observations—is in spite of *your treatment of the Favorite and not because of it, as the aunts say.*

Do you count my love and my advice less than theirs? That is what really wounds my heart.

My heart bleeds when gossip is spread about you by the French ambassador, the dissolute Prince Louis de Rohan. He is not content to create gossip about his own outrageous extravagance and self-indulgence. He also creates gossip about you. For example, when you rushed to the friend of Artois, the handsome Dillon who fainted in public, and placed your hand over his heart, this simple gesture of compassion was interpreted by him as having a coquettish intent. Your chastity is your treasure. Even in appearance, you must take care....

What cheers me and fills me with joy is that your sister the Queen of Naples is pregnant, and, in addition, she was made fully a wife by the King of the Two Sicilies on the very first night after their marriage. Did you know that? Perhaps Charlotte is too modest to report her success with Naples. When the Générale visited so soon after the wedding, King Ferdinand expressed the greatest impatience.

As for the King of France, your grandfather, I implore you to speak to him often—writing notes to him, even if carefully phrased, is no substitute. He is readily available to you, living in the very same château, and he is genuinely fond of you. When you neglect him for other amusements, I picture you carelessly striding with unrealistic calm toward your own ruin, and I fear that you will have to suffer much pain before you can make up for all your mistakes. Understand that written language will not speak for you with the King; on the other hand, there is something so touching about you when you present yourself in your person with all your gracious manner that all hearts are moved.

The country suffers from crop failure, and also there is fear of smallpox.

Count Mercy Offers Advice on the Last Day of the Year, 31 December 1771

Having received a message from the Austrian ambassador that he would very much like to have a private conversation with me, I have invited him to the Dauphin's library. I would like to speak to him about many issues and to conspire with him about how Prince Louis de Rohan might be recalled from Vienna. His vices sicken the Empress. She does not want him in her presence, and certainly I feel nothing but hatred for this Frenchman who constructed an impure interpretation about my innocent hand seeking a pulse in the chest of poor Dillon.

Above my head, I can hear my husband pounding away, for he has had an anvil installed above to do his blacksmith work. When winter sets in and it is too rainy and cold for enjoyable hunting, he tells me that the smithy, with its cheerful glow of coals and the white-hot tongs, is quite the best place to be. He is fashioning a rose of iron for me.

Meanwhile, I embroider another rose, pink with splashes of darker rose and even moments of red. My eyes are delighted by the soft skeins of thread, and my fingers enjoy the slippery steel of the needle. I am creating the cover for a kneeler for my pious mother, as a remembrance of her birthday, and she will no doubt tell me that nothing could please her more. For my last birthday, she has sent me a small writing desk with the admonition that I am to think of her when I use the desk and that I am to write to her more often and to Papa-Roi less! But I know she is correct in this.

Count Mercy glides in with no pomp or fuss, but with the confident movement of a friend. He looks well today, but there is a bit of flush in his cheek. I tell him at once that my sister Charlotte is pregnant, and I see by the way he glances sideways before meeting my eyes that the news has reached me, via the Empress, before it has reached him. He speaks with sincere, quiet warmth.

"How very fortunate for her."

"Nothing could make me more happy, except to be able to convey to the world that I was in the same condition." I have spoken the perfect truth to the count. One cannot help but love any person whose character allows one's own to be proclaimed faithfully.

"Your generosity becomes you," he says, then continues, "although it pains me to discuss the Dauphin's strange behavior, I feel I must remind your Highness of *how* his recent promise to you for the proper and much desired consummation came to be broken. Do you remember it yourself?"

Quickly I recite the facts of a recent disappointment. "The Dauphin had promised that by a certain auspicious date, he would make me truly a wife. Although he has made such assurances in the past, nothing has occurred. This time, again, I believed him with all my heart, and while I was brimming with happiness, I confided my expectations to my aunts, who love me and always try to encourage the Dauphin to think well of himself and to have confidence in his prowess."

I see a predatory look in the enlightened eye of the count. He has the intelligence and swiftness of a falcon.

"Again, it pains me to bring up any injury," he comments, "but again I ask if you recall how Mesdames treated the confidence that you were so trusting as to bestow upon them?"

Some heavy tool is dropped on the floor above us. The entire chandelier sways above my head, and all the candles flicker. Outside, the winter day is the epitome of drab gray. I can understand why my husband has turned to his merry banging at the anvil.

"Most unfortunately my aunts said *to my husband's face* that they were happy to hear of his promise . . . to make me into a true Dauphine whom no one would want to send home for her failure." I have confessed the truth; he knows it already. I lower my eyes.

"Were they so unkind as actually to use such a phrase—'her failure'?"

Here I bite my lip because it is trembling. I do not like to admit, even to myself, that in some sense the aunts betrayed me. But I know my husband, the man working above me at the forge—that honest, lumbering, clumsy fellow—does not lie.

"I know that they did, for when the Dauphin came to me and told me what they said, he quoted them most exactly. He told me to imagine the surprise he felt to be so directly pressed on the matter of a private promise. I quizzed him on the point of the language with which they referred to me, and he swore they said exactly what I have quoted. Indeed, the words 'her failure' are branded into my heart as though by a hot iron."

Because I feel ashamed, my hand flies up and covers my eyes for a moment.

After a decorous pause during which I recover myself, Count Mercy continues. "And finally, dear princess, did their words inspire ardor and confidence in the Dauphin?"

"He told me, with some haughtiness, that now he could not be held to his promise because now the whole court knew of what had been his intention, and their curiosity and the thought of their whispering as the appointed day approached made him shrink with embarrassment."

"He canceled his promise. I believe that you are unwise to trust Mesdames Tantes for advice in any matter." Having spoken what is foremost on his mind and most certainly the reason for his visit, the count clears his throat. That small, discreet sound is his final comment on my latest humiliation. His hand rises to touch his lips, and then he lowers his hand, ready to pursue another subject.

"Just as the question of succession—of an heir—is of importance, quite naturally, to the King, so is another question, in a sense one could say again, *quite naturally* of importance to him. We cannot undo some of the damage the aunts have done, but we can put a halt to the damage they are doing every day when they speak ill of the King's Favorite and when they encourage you to flaunt your will against the King's wishes." Suddenly the count's voice changes. It becomes stern and threatening: "And to what do I allude? You are quick of wit, unlike the Princesse de Lamballe. You will not hide behind a timid and unimaginative mind but say directly, with German candor, what it is to which I refer, for your own sake."

"Why isn't it enough that you speak to the Favorite?" I ask petulantly. "You go to her chamber and you keep her company. Isn't that enough attention from one of us?"

The count merely rolls his eyes toward the ceiling. He has expected me to be more forthright.

I sigh and articulate what he waits to hear: "You refer to my refusal to speak with ceremonial politeness to that creature, the du Barry."

Suddenly the count rises lightly to his feet. He paces about to stimulate my attention and to add emphasis to his every word. I watch his elegant feet tread over the large plumes of feathers woven in the pattern of the carpet.

"It is my opinion, as well as that of the Empress, who has many informants about what goes on here at Versailles, and who, because of her vast experience in the ways of court life, has more wisdom than I could ever hope to attain, or in fact, than anyone could attain—except possibly Louis XV himself—that things are at a crisis, and you must speak." The count hesitates in his pacing as though to concentrate all his strategic ideas.

Then he continues. "When a group of ladies appear for the purpose of paying court to Your Royal Highness, Madame la Dauphine, it is your nature and habit to speak courteously to all those present. Tomorrow is the first day of the New Year, and we know that especially on this ceremonial occasion, the ladies will come to call. I know, in addition, that the Comtesse du Barry will be in that circle of ladies. When Your Royal Highness speaks to these ladies, she should also speak—once is enough, I assure you—to the Comtesse du Barry."

"Last year I just spoke generally—to the group she was in. Won't that suffice again?"

"Her Royal Highness might comment, for example, about the particular dress that the Favorite is wearing, or about a pretty fan she holds in her hand, or some other item might be the topic for a brief remark addressed in that moment, in the most natural possible manner but directly to the comtesse."

"My aunts will think I have lost my mind." Or my morals. But perhaps, in spite of my stubborn self-righteousness, the Empress and the ambassador know that morality *cannot* always override wisdom. I feel vanquished and ready to weep with vexation.

"Lost your mind?" The count's voice is low, kind, and understanding. "On the contrary, if they are present at the scene, they will know that you are no longer their toy, that you are a woman of judgment in your own right and need not obey their whims. I have observed many times, with great sorrow, that Madame la Dauphine is frequently used to express a hatred that *they* feel toward the comtesse or other parties but that they would not dare put forward."

Suddenly, the count places both hands on his hips—an awkward posture—and one that expresses his extreme exasperation with the situation.

"Not only have they intentionally alienated you from the very influential comtesse, they have also created a distance between you and the King over this issue. Let me be blunt as to why they wish to do this: they fear that you with your youth and beauty might take their places in the King's affections."

"They are his own daughters," I remonstrate.

"They lack charm."

The count throws himself back into his chair, as though he has been exhausted by the effort required to communicate with me.

He adds, "You may check the truth of my statement in this way: once you have shown courtesy to the du Barry, the very next time the King sees you, he will treat you with unprecedented consideration and tenderness to express his pleasure in your act. Then you will know that the Empress and I have given you excellent counsel. And please know also, in that moment, that we are most pleased with you, and delight in your triumph."

"My friend the count looks weary."

"There are other matters of state. What can you promise, in good conscience, on this issue that for all its triviality matters immensely?"

"I promise to perform as you have advised, tomorrow."

"Beware Madame Adelaide in particular. It is she who has the most boldness in interfering. Above all, do not tell her today what you intend to execute tomorrow. Remember that she ruined the Dauphin's excellent intention. Now I take my leave, with your gracious permission."

THUMP, THUMP, THUMP. My husband is pounding the metal. I feel that I myself have been upon the anvil, and my will has been beaten into a new shape. My nose and eyes begin to leak tears of chagrin. From my sleeve, I pull out a handkerchief and flick it open. The handkerchief is so bedecked with lace that the lawn square in its center is only half the size of the fleshy square comprising the palm of my hand. I place my nose in the lawn center and blow once. The capacity of the handkerchief is inadequate. Vexed, I ring for a servant to bring a handful of handkerchiefs so that I can attend to this dribbling.

New Year's Day, 1772

As I awaken, the terrible thought occurs to me that perhaps it is the King himself and not the Empress of Austria who has prevailed on the count to intervene in my behavior. My cheeks burn with shame, and I turn my face away from the light that streams into the room this cold New Year's Day. Have I really embarrassed the King and driven him to ask help of the Austrian ambassador? I will never know. But the possible logic of it all terrifies me. I pull the covers up to my forehead and find that my nightcap has fallen away. Yes, it was a restless night, full of concern about my promise and the imperative to keep it.

IT IS NOT AS THOUGH I have not tried to speak to the Comtesse du Barry before. In August, nearly half a year ago, Count Mercy made me promise to speak a few words to the Favorite. The idea frightened me—it was like going against myself—and I asked Mercy to be present for the occasion to give me courage. First he would locate Madame du Barry among the many game tables and go stand beside her—that was our plan. Then I would approach him, and it would seem almost by accident that I would drop a few words directly to the comtesse. Mercy made me promise not to tell Mesdames my aunts our plan, and I did promise, but some demon impulse toward truthfulness and full disclosure made me break my promise of secrecy.

When I saw that Mercy had located the Comtesse du Barry, I sent for him and told him I was almost too frightened to continue. He encouraged me, and again I promised that I would speak, but he told me I must hurry, for the card game was ending. Quickly I sent him back to her circle, but now all eyes were following him, for the aunts had told their friends of what was about to transpire. I could see that Mercy commenced a lively and friendly exchange with the du Barry, and I knew he would keep up the banter till I arrived.

I set out to cross the room; in fact I approached to within two steps of their table, when suddenly Madame Adelaide raised her voice and stopped me with her loud commands. She announced that it was late, we had dallied too long, that all of us must go. "The King is coming now to my sister Victoire's apartment," she said, "and we must meet him at once."

By invoking the name of the King, she made me turn and obey like a child.

Remembering this moment, I wonder if Mercy is correct. Perhaps it is time for me to relinquish my dependence upon my aunts.

IT IS THE FIRST DAY of the year, and I shall wear a new dress, one of a rosy warm hue, for, when I look out the window, I see that icicles hang from the nose of the nearest statue, and while the yew trees hold their greenness in tight little triangular shapes, the rest of the world appears flat and gray. Today I must make myself turn from my usual practices and obey the dictates of my promise to Mercy.

It is time for the ceremony of my *lever.* Every day, not just New Year's Day, is blighted by these boring and time-wasting rituals surrounding my arising and my retiring. Which is worse, the *lever* or the *coucher*? I mind it less at night because I am already tired then, thus the *coucher* does not occupy time that could be better spent. If the Dauphin and I ever do become King and Queen, perhaps we can abolish these tiresome ceremonies.

While I stand shivering and naked, the matter of who has the privilege of handing me which garment must be renegotiated when a lady of higher rank than those present enters the room. I see my chemise in the hands of Madame C, but then higher-ranking Madame B enters, and she is given my chemise; next, Madame A enters, and now my chemise, instead of being used to dress me while I stand exposed in the cold, is handed to Madame A.

"This is maddening," I mutter. "This is impossibly ridiculous."

Finally, I begin to be clothed, starting with the chemise.

The sun has gone behind a cloud, and the candles do little to brighten the gloom of January. I welcome the rouge for my cheeks, and I ask for another rose ribbon with tiny loops along its edge to be placed high in my coiffure. The picotee ribbon will draw the eye up and make me look taller, and at the same time complete the effect of warm rose already stated by my skirt.

TODAY I SPEAK to Madame du Barry. I have not decided what to say. (I and my ladies begin the long walk toward the reception room.) To comment on her dress or fan seems to me to sound a bit condescending. People will want to convince her afterward that I was snide or was not genuine in my courtesy.

Unexpectedly, as I traverse the state rooms and walk under their ceilings covered with paintings of classical gods and goddesses and their chariots, good cheer comes to visit me; an idea. The exercise of walking has refreshed me. Today *is* a *happy* occasion for the whole court to come to give greetings to the royal family as we, fellow travelers all, start a new year. Together, we journey through this frostbitten world. I pause in my progress to pull back a curtain.

In the garden, the water has been drained from all the basins for the winter, but it is wonderful to think that in a few months, spring warmth will come again. We must hope that we will all be here to greet the spring.

In May, I will make a pilgrimage to the fountain of Flora, with whom I identify my own self and all young maidens who must leave their mothers and dwell in the courts of men. I release the curtain. Not that my husband is anything of a Hades, for he persists in affection, is always kind to me, and I see often in the Dauphin an eagerness to please. Thinking of his admirable attributes adds to my happiness. If, in addition to his goodness, he is dull, then I must be bright enough for two.

As I walk through the rooms toward the reception, I remind myself of those who will be glad to see me just as I will welcome them. I resolve to be sensitive to their trials and tribulations. Although the Princesse de Lamballe did have intercourse with her husband, she could not remain the center of his attention or desire. But I believe the scars of that marriage are mostly healed now. Though our marriage remains incomplete, I have no doubt in the loyalty of Monsieur le Dauphin. I know that various courtiers, perhaps even his own brothers, have tried to interest him in a mistress, but the attempt has utterly failed. My friends have told me he replied without unseemly anger but in perfect control of his feelings. "I am charmed only by my wife," he said and left the matter at that. I do love him for making me feel safe, for his steadfast adoration. I am lucky in many ways.

Is it possible that someday I will become pregnant, that I will become a successful mother, that I will identify myself with Ceres, the mother? In the park, the fountains of Bacchus and of Saturn complement those of Flora and Ceres. I do not like the statue of Saturn, for he ate his children. Bacchus and his love of wine and debauchery frighten me.

Out the window, over the scruffy snow, I review the distant row of statuary. Mythology! Do not we ourselves create our myths of our own importance? Of all the marble statues mounted on pedestals, my favorite is Pan, who plays the flute. I love his hairy, goatish legs.

If I keep my promise to speak to the du Barry, I will allow myself more time practicing the harp, and I will not forget to play the spinet either. Madame Victoire is a fine harpist. No one can fault Mesdames for their love of music. It is true they have flaws. I feel in quite an imperial mood and lengthen my step.

My skirt rustles pleasantly, fabric against fabric, as I walk to join my family and the world.

THE KING GREETS ME with the flash of his dark eyes; from the first day when I met him in the woods of Compiègne, I have admired the luminous quality of his eyes. Memory makes history into mythology. Then he was the King of the World come to visit the woods. His eye is the eye of the dominant stag, crowned with a rack of antlers. This New Year's Day, he is the elk wandered into this realm of candles, crystal, and rustling silk. Nothing here speaks of the whisper of green leaves or the silence of the ferny forest floor. As I bend in a deep curtsy to the King, the room grows silent with admiration, for I do a curtsy as they have never before seen a curtsy. I curtsy with my heart. The King is happy to embrace me, in quite his usual manner.

Here is my husband, straight and tall, if fat and fattening, with a fond greeting on his lips for me. I know that he wishes to please me, in everything. This New Year's Day he wears the cloak of civilization with ease, but I have seen his eye when it was as wild as a horse's eye, waiting and wanting to be ridden, to be mastered because only then can the horse express what is within, his dream of speed, pursuit, power. And it is a pleasure to see my little sister Elisabeth, all sweetness, and still so fresh, and Clothilde, who has gained in self-confidence as well as in girth.

My aunts greet me with a pleasant kiss—they are aging, but they have endured and will endure—and they make way for others. There is delight for them in participating in this pleasant ceremony. For a brief moment I think of the New Year receptions at the Hofburg, and of my mother, who will be wearing black today as she does every day in honor of my father, and I envision too my brother the Emperor Joseph at her side, taking good care of her. Like the mother she always is, she will be telling everyone what to do. How rich I am in the love I have for my families.

And here come the Duchesse d'Aiguillon and the Maréchale de Mirepoix and with them the Comtesse du Barry.

I speak first to the duchesse, wishing her well, and then with a naturalness that is without awkwardness *because I do not feel awkward* and without pretense, *because I am still myself,* I say to the Comtesse du Barry, as I might to anyone, with pleasantness, "There are many people today at Versailles."

She has been acknowledged. Her beautiful face glows, and I see that she is indeed grateful to me, and in all honesty, I think better of myself than I did a moment ago. Immediately I speak to the maréchale. As the threesome turn away, one cannot help but admire the abundant hair and the lovely ample figure of the du Barry. Her beauty is the most important thing about her, and in itself it gives her grace, though the way she moves does nothing to enhance the impression she makes.

In place of my indignation—was it hatred—I feel toward her a blessed indifference, at least for this moment.

In the early days after I came to Versailles, it is true I was struck by her appearance, as I was by the beauty of the Princesse de Lamballe. When I asked who Madame du Barry was and learned that she was present in order to amuse the King, I was innocent of what the idea held. She is as beautiful as ever, but I have changed.

This day, understanding the ability of the world to press me till I do what I would not do, I have grown up. With what air I play my role—that is my only choice.

Now come others, and they will come and come, to pay their respects to all of us in the royal family, and I feel sunrise in my bosom, for these are my people, and the King depends on the support of the nobility and the clergy, and I am happy for his sake to spread goodwill and happiness all the day long.

It is a fickle First Day, for the sun comes and goes, and sometimes the estate looks drab and worthless and sometimes the vista is noble. When I stand in the Hall of Mirrors and look directly past the drained water parterres and down the Grand Avenue, and beyond to the frozen Grand Canal receding all the way to the horizon, I think with awe how all of this can and will go on forever.

With my acquiescence to the will of the world, I have grown up: now begins the second half of my life. I recall that first view of Versailles, when the coach stopped on a hill and I, a child, looked beyond the streets of the small town to the great engulfing arms of Versailles. Three sets of ever widening arms, emanating from the central bedroom of the King, Versailles held out to me. Now I have gone beyond that. I know the interior of the château; I look not at the three courtyards and the town but in the opposite direction, past the kingdom of the garden, past the grip of winter with splotches of snow and dripping icicles, beyond the leafless bosquets and the lifeless fountain statuary, beyond the basin of Apollo and the grandly frozen canal, a gigantic cross-shape of ice, to the vague horizon. Ah, I see a handful of villagers, small as ants, skating on the ice of the canal. They must feel that we inside the distant château are far too busy to glance out any window, though there are many, to notice them.

Throughout this day of greetings and good wishes, from time to time, I glance out at them, so tiny and black skating in the distance, and I remember my childhood, and how *immediate* seemed the full rosy cheek of my Charlotte, not an arm's length away, and the cocked leg of brother Ferdinand as he shoved himself off across the ice, and darling Madame Brandeis, looking after us all but especially after me. She was well bundled up in a mauve woolen coat, its seams trimmed with brown fur. Her strokes on the ice were small and careful.

After I have presided over our dinner, as I leave the table, I ask that Count Mercy come in to see me.

When we are together with Monsieur le Dauphin, I say to the count, "As you have perhaps heard, I did follow your advice." I smile at my counselor with perfect humor. "And I have in my husband, a witness to the truthfulness of my report."

The Dauphin also smiles at the count but says nothing.

Then the demon tweaks me and I add with a darkness that surprises me, "Though I have spoken to her once, I am resolved that that woman will never again hear my voice." I am shocked at my own petulance. I had thought I felt *indifference* as to Madame du Barry. I feel like a stubborn child determined to be destructive.

Neither the Dauphin nor the count acknowledges my addendum. My sentence sinks like a stone in deep water. My husband is unperturbed because he knows that no resolution has real efficacy at this court. My advisor is unconcerned because he believes he can always bring me round again to reason.

At this moment the King himself appears. He has come to thank me. All bow to him, but he comes straight to me. He kisses me simply, on each cheek, but with a tenderness I have never felt before. "All day," he says, "I have watched you or heard loving reports of you, for you are the angel of this house. When you smile and greet us, every heart is lifted, and you give us the courage to look to the future."

No one could behave with more kindness and courtesy than the King now bestows on me. The Empress and Count Mercy have been correct in interpreting the King's wish that I acknowledge his Favorite, and I have been in error. I am gratified by his increased attentions to me. It was my mother's parting wish that the French, from King to peasant, should regard my presence in just those terms so cordially employed by Papa-Roi.

I glance once again at Count Mercy, stylishly and perfectly dressed in blue and silver, his wig powdered to perfection, to acknowledge the wisdom of his counsel. There is no sign of gloating in his countenance. He is impeccable.

MADAME, MY DEAR DAUGHTER

I am not asking too much of you when I demand that you speak in a natural way four or five times a year to the Favorite. If you do so, you will feel more comfortable with the King, and you will want to talk with him and keep him company beyond a mere graceful greeting. You will feel more at ease because, having followed his wish and my own in speaking periodically to the Favorite, you will have no feeling of guilt (which always inhibits us in natural expressions) or fear of implicit reproach for neglectful or rude behavior.

My dear daughter, I advise you to recall all my love for you and keep this point in mind: don't ever say to others or to yourself that I am scolding you or that I am preaching to you. Instead, you must say, "Mama loves me. Mama is forever concerned for my welfare. Therefore I must take to heart what she tells me because I know it will console her for our separation if I follow her good advice."

My dear mama! How many times she has launched her ships, freighted with criticism, under the flag of love. Will I ever sail under my own insignia?

Madame, My Very Dear Mother

I am more faithful than ever to my dear harp, and many people say I am making good progress. I sing every week at a small concert given in the apartment of the Comtesse de Provence. I spend less time with the aunts and very much enjoy romping with my own young set. You would have laughed to see us trying to pack our trunks for a trip. Josephine of Savoy was behind a wall of baggage, trying to write a letter and consulting us about its contents, while I ran about like a dervish knocking things over as soon as they were packed, and while my brother Provence was singing, Artois was telling the same story ten times over, and the Dauphin was loudly reading a tragedy with mock solemnity.

On a more sober note, while the King is tranquil, the nobles have banded together to write an impertinent letter to him. On the bad advice of the du Barry, the King suspended the Parlement whose main function here is to make judicial decisions, and the King has proceeded to set up other courts, saying the old parlements were too slow and corrupt to serve the people. Of course the nobles care only for protecting their own interests and nothing for the welfare of the people who can scarcely buy the flour to bake their bread, but our faction believes that the King must not alienate the powerful Princes of the Blood. In some provinces rebellions have even arisen, and people begin to speak of Flour Wars.

Last Thursday, as part of Carnival, the young people, including the Dauphin—though people had thought he would be opposed to such an outing—went to the Opera Ball in Paris! All the women, but few of the men, wore masks, long dominoes that covered our faces, and everyone was cloaked in black. The well-illuminated room was immense. All classes of society mingled together and were equalized by the uniformity of our costumes and the masks. Everyone danced in unison to the rhythm of the music—a black sea of people. You cannot imagine how exciting it was.

For a while no one knew who we were, and I talked with many people as though I were just anyone and said, unguardedly, whatever I pleased, and danced with everyone, till in about half an hour, we were recognized. It was très amusant. *Then the Duc de Chartres and his friends, who were dancing just next door at the Palais-Royal, happened to come in and begged us to go to the Palais-Royal and greet the Duchesse de Chartres, but I felt I must beg off for my sake and that of M. le Dauphin, for we had obtained permission from the King to visit only the Opera Ball.*

We returned at seven in the morning, promptly attended Mass, and then went to bed for the day.

But now that I see the vast gaiety of Paris, I am determined to return as soon as possible. It is a city of some 600,000 people, much larger than Vienna, and really the capital of Europe, if you will pardon me for saying so. I am forever grateful to my dear mama for placing me in this position, when I who am the last of your daughters have been positioned as though I were the first. Again, we hear that the Comte d'Artois will marry either Mlle de Conde or the Princess of Savoy, the sister of the Comtesse de Provence. Mercy thinks that's rather too much of Savoy.

The King arranged for Monsieur le Dauphin and me to speak frankly about our physical beings to Lassone, the physician. The Dauphin spoke without embarrassment, and he was also examined by the physician and found to be well formed and of good parts. Lassone has reported to the King that the only problem is that we are awkward and ignorant, and for a few nights the Dauphin acted more forthrightly toward me. While eating no meat during Lent does not make me sick, it does disgust me, and the Dauphin has become ill with a fever and a sore throat. His illness made him less forward again, and progress is again delayed. There is a rumor that Monsieur le Dauphin is now truly my husband, but it is not true. The valets, who always gossip and report everything to everyone—even the king of Spain, through his spies here, knows what happens in our bed—have seen stains from certain emissions on the bed linens, but Monsieur le Dauphin has told me that at the crucial moment, entry is painful for him, and the fluids are deposited only at the threshold and not within. So there is no chance that I am pregnant, I believe.

Were I so lucky as to have a son, you may be sure that I would solicit the advice of my dear mama on every feature of his education.

Once the Dauphin and I are able to arrange for our official entry to Paris, you may be sure that our lives, especially mine, will become much happier. This time I saw nothing but the interior of the ballroom. It could have been anywhere—the place, I mean, but not the excitement, certainly not that! Paris herself awaits me! I will have my will in this. Versailles is a nunnery—for me—and I will be uncloistered. Fear not, it shall all be handled with utmost tact.

Entering Paris, 8 June 1773

The year 1773 has been marked by many small moments of private sadness; I am seventeen in November and still a virgin. I have lived in France for three years, and still the King has not given permission to the Dauphin for our official entry to Paris. Because the King is more unpopular with the people as every day passes, the Dauphin has confided, the King does not want to send us to Paris till we are older. Were it not impertinent, I would remind them both that to me the people have shown nothing but love. In Strasbourg, flowers were strewn in my path, and the fountains flowed with wine.

On this rainy spring day, I walk from window to window in the great long Hall of Mirrors and look out mournfully at the gardens. Their stiff elegance seems like a mockery of life. The trees, small and large, have been so closely clipped that their branches and leaves never stir in the breezes. Life? I am seventeen! Where is life to be found?

I feel locked in at Versailles. Visits to the other châteaux are but duplications of life here, though with different palaces and grounds. All of them are grand, in varying degrees, and all of them are isolated by a surrounding countryside of forest, fields, meadows. At Marly, I looked down at the lovely Seine river and thought of how, at no very great distance, it was flowing through Paris. I pictured graceful bridges, with people crossing freely back and forth in the most fashionable spring clothes.

The Danube, which I have not seen for three years—it too will be thawed now and flowing gracefully through Vienna. Here at Versailles, I watch the gray raindrops dimple the surfaces of the water parterres. The recumbent figure of Neptune, holding his trident, rules over the tiniest of ripples that move over the surface of the water in the slight breeze.

"Neptune has always been one of my favorite statues," a voice says behind me. It is the King.

I curtsy. "On a rainy day, the Hall of Mirrors is a lovely place for a stroll, Your Majesty."

"I like it best when you call me Papa-Roi," he replies. "Because of the rain, the hall is almost empty of the usual supplicants from Paris. And the court is enjoying afternoon gambling." With his hands clasped behind him, the King stands majestically beside me and regards the gray day.

"When it rained, the Empress always liked a small fire," I say, "even in summer. She said rain made her want to write letters to those she loved who were far away." His golden brocade sleeve stirs beside me, and he brings his hands together, over his stomach. With his fingertips, he twists a ruby ring on his other hand.

"Tell me, Toinette, if you were a mermaid and you were to ask Father Neptune for a wish, what would it be?"

When I turn to look at him, I see the King's eyes are luminous with knowing. He is fond of me. No matter how tardy the Dauphin is in responding to my charms, the King will never send me back to Austria.

"I would say, if I had permission, I would swim down the river Seine, I would come to a fair city, the fairest in your watery kingdom. May I and my husband visit Paris?"

"Granted," the King replies. "Now you must smile at me and dispel the gloom that should never visit the fairest brow I know."

ELEVEN-THIRTY in the morning of a brilliantly sunny day, the trumpets blast a fanfare, three cannon fire salutations—from the Invalides, the Hôtel de Ville, and the Bastille—and the Dauphin and I arrive at the gates of Paris. For the hour and a half that it has taken to drive by carriage from Versailles to Paris, we have seen nothing but the road and then the city streets lined with happy people, waving their hats and flags and tossing flowers at our windows as we pass. We have waved in return, and I am reminded of my entry into France, at the town of Strasbourg, but this arrival is twice as glorious, for I am with my husband.

Here is the governor of the city presenting its symbolic silver keys on a silk pillow, and the lieutenant of police, and the chief of the merchants of the city, and the market women, dressed in their best, presenting trays of fruits and flowers. After I take a bouquet of daisies and hand it to my lady-in-waiting, I cradle two pears in the palms of my hands, and the Dauphin holds aloft a long cucumber to be placed in the carriage, the rest to be distributed among our retinue.

The fishwives are full of glee at the Dauphin's cucumber. "Make us a child!" they shout. They cock their arms at the elbow, thrust their fists and sinewy arms up into the air and call "Give it to her; she's a pretty woman." Both the Dauphin and I laugh heartily, for they mean no harm.

"When yours is like this, Monseigneur," they shout, pumping their forearms, "you will give us a tribe of heirs."

Our carriage winds its way through the streets of the city, sometimes beside the Seine river, where hundreds, no thousands of people have gathered to see us pass and to smile and wave at us. The size of the city, the enthusiasm of the populace make our hearts swell with joy. Triumphal arches have been erected at intervals, but my heart leaps highest to see the twin towers of the Cathédrale de Notre-Dame rising from the midst of the Seine on the Île de la Cité. I saw an engraving of them when I was only a girl, in Vienna, and someone explained that they were left square, the intended spires never having been erected. Now, not tiny ink lines but the monumental edifice itself rises above the trees.

We pass over the Pont Neuf, that ancient bridge with the stone statue of good Henri IV, and into the throng of people massed in front of the high arched doors. I raise my eyes to the long outward-extended bodies of the high gargoyles mounted near the top of the *cathédrale*. When I speak lightly of demons, I think of nothing so sinister as these medieval realities, but now we are walking rapidly past the throngs of cheering people, and my ears are ringing with their glad greetings. A carpet has been spread for our feet, lest the paving stones bruise our heels.

Inside the enormous Notre-Dame de Paris, a solemn Mass begins. The aroma of the incense, the sight of the slow smoke rising and coiling ever higher, fills me with reverence. As the Mass is celebrated and we hear the solemn Latin words, I thank God in French and in German that he has made me acceptable to the people of my new country and for the joy all of us share in meeting on this day. Surely the little boy sopranos are not mortal children, but angels selected for the purity of their voices.

When we emerge past the carved saints that flank the door, the people are still there, and they call out their blessings. The Dauphin squeezes my elbow affectionately, extravagantly pleased with the acclaim and joyful goodwill expressed on every side. At one point, he whispers in my ear, "The future, the future! All this bodes well for our future."

Never has the sun shone with more cheerful radiance than on this June day! Both the Dauphin and I are dressed in gleaming white satin. We move like mirrors reflecting the light from our clothing onto the faces of the people. This is what it means to be loved and to love in return.

Slowly we progress by carriage to the palace of the Tuileries—where sometimes kings have dwelt—and therein to a lavish dinner. While the Dauphin eats with his usual good appetite, I can only savor a tidbit of meat here, and a few nuts there, some spoonfuls of soup. "How your eyes are glowing," the Dauphin whispers to me, and we agree to appear before the people yet again, on the terrace.

To my amazement, the greatest throng of people of all has had time to assemble in this one place while we dined. A mighty roar of love is lifted as soon as we appear—"*Mon Dieu*, how many of them there are!" I exclaim—and I cannot help but smile and wave, and then the second roar is even greater in their joy at our acknowledgment. Our civic hosts crowd about us, and the governor of Paris says that he hopes my husband will not take it amiss that two hundred thousand people are ecstatically in love with me.

"How could I blame them?" he replies with graceful aplomb. "They would be remiss if they did not fall in love with my wife."

To be yet closer to the people, we decide to go down from the terrace into the gardens of the Tuileries, and when we step forward, the people swarm past the barriers of the police toward us. "Let no one be harmed—no one," both the Dauphin and I say simultaneously to the chief of police who passes the order to his lieutenants.

For almost an hour we stand smiling and nodding, moving neither forward nor backward, but when we are both weary and take a single step back toward the stairs, and the police loudly but pleasantly shout that it is our will to depart, the crowd opens its ranks with utmost courtesy and alacrity. As we retreat inside the Tuileries, still we wave and smile, though my face is tired with smiling. My heart is brimful of a medley of feelings: love, happiness, triumph, and not at all the least of my emotions—gratitude to the innumerable citizens of Paris.

RIDING BACK to Versailles, neither the Dauphin nor I can speak. We are exhausted, but our spirits and memories are suffused with gratitude—we both speak of it, over and over—for the love the people have shown us. Their roars of love become the universe. Our attendants are amazed at the magnitude of our triumph and full of awe.

Along the route, many people have waited throughout the day and into the night, hoping to see our return, and occasionally we open the curtain at the window and smile and wave again, but we are too tired to continue our acknowledgments for more than a few minutes at a time. The Dauphin and I hold hands and nestle against each other.

AT THE CHÂTEAU, as soon as I alight from the carriage, Count Mercy tenderly congratulates me and tells me that every soul who saw me is under an enchantment. Messengers have brought the news ahead of our arrival.

Quite privately he whispers that the popularity shown us is in inverse proportion to the esteem held for the aging King, whose life of debauchery has appalled everyone.

"Your youth, beauty, and innocence promise a new age," he explains. Count Mercy has barely time to instruct me. "Here at the château, express your delight at your Parisian welcome with your usual gracious tact."

When we are brought to the King, I say with humility, "Sire, Your Majesty must be very greatly loved by the Parisians, for they have feted us well."

Madame, My Dear Mother

Mercy gave me your precious letter the day before yesterday, and yesterday a second letter so that I feel doubly connected to my dear mama.

Now I hope that my letter will serve, in its turn, as a conduit for joy flowing to you in Vienna. Last Tuesday, the people of Paris gave to me a fete that I shall never forget no matter how long I am to live. It was our official entry to the city, and every conceivable honor was heaped upon us. But it was not the honors bestowed by dignitaries that most moved me. What has touched me to the quick of my being is the love and eagerness bestowed on us by the poor people of France. Although they are burdened with taxes of a very heavy sort, they were in a transport of joy—merely to behold their future monarchs. Mercy tells me that everyone cried out about my beauty and charm and how they delight in our youth and innocence. In us, they see the rebirth of hope for the future of the country. I felt it most keenly and will work hard, as will the Dauphin, to alleviate the suffering of the people.

When we came out onto an open terrace, after dinner, and stayed there for a half hour, I cannot describe to even you, my dear mama, the intensity of delight and love which they manifested again and again. When I kissed my hand to them, or smiled, or waved my handkerchief to them, they went mad with joy. When we have so much and they so little, and yet they give us trust and love, I know that no experience can be more precious. I will never forget that they have given me this gift. I felt and do feel and will always feel profound gratitude. Were I to live a hundred years, I would not forget the outpouring of love given to us when we made our official entry to the city of Paris.

The King rejoices with us. Two days after our entry, the King freed 320 persons imprisoned for debt. The King made good on the debt which was owed to the wet nurses who had been paid to breast feed the children of the debtors. I am much moved that the King wants the helpless babes to be nourished in this way and for those who provide such nutrition to be honored.

I am glad to know that Mercy has told you he is pleased with the way I understand affairs of state. Really, it is my heart I count on for understanding, rather than my head, but Mercy has told me my first spontaneous response to persons and their words is something to trust, and not to be second-guessed. Even more than my intuitions, I trust the advice of Mercy, for I believe that it really is your advice that I follow when I follow his. I smiled to read your description that he thinks in a French way but as a good German. I believe that we have in his perspective the best of two worlds!

Now that we have made our official entry into Paris, the King says we may go as often as we like. Monsieur le Dauphin and I intend to see the shows at the Opera, the Comédie-Française, and the Comédie-Italienne every week, and we are to be greeted with just as much pomp and rejoicing as though it were the Monarch himself approaching, that is, with the welcoming roars of the cannon at the Invalides and the Bastille fortress. Now my life is much happier because the people of Paris have opened their hearts to me. If you had heard the mighty roar of the Bastille cannon, you would have exclaimed, "What punctuation!"

The Land of Fantasy: A Snowy Night, 30 January 1774

Snow has been falling all night, and the Dauphin, who loves me so much, like a protective brother, has wondered aloud several times if we should travel to Paris tonight for the Opera Ball. I tell my husband that in the snow, Paris will appear like a Land of Fantasy.

"You have been happier these last six months," he says to me.

"Since Paris . . . ," I begin. "Ecstasy. Perpetual ecstasy. I did not know life could be so amusing, so inexhaustibly entertaining." I am in a grand mood.

The Comte de Provence, who loves me (or anyone but himself) not at all but who can sometimes be amusing, insists that we must not hesitate to pile on our furs and climb aboard the sleigh waiting just beyond the stairs of the Marble Courtyard. He and his wife have come no closer together in the bedroom than have the Dauphin and I.

Comte d'Artois, who is always amusing and the best dancing partner to be had, has already announced that he and his wife prefer to sport at home tonight. Though Artois is full of little jibes about his marital pleasures, knowing that both his older brothers suffer from a painful disorder of the too-tight foreskin, I always forgive him. Perhaps one of his jibes will someday spur the Dauphin on to greater achievement, despite pain, but I doubt it. Perhaps I forgive brother Artois because his jibes are not directed at me.

Or perhaps it is because he is slim and lively and loves, as I do, the pretend world offered by theater.

My Partner in Pretend. Sometimes when the six of us play together, I pretend that he is my partner in life, instead of the stolid Dauphin. Had I been married to Artois, I would not find myself eighteen years old and still a virgin. But then I would not be Dauphine, a position I am learning to enjoy, since we can now visit Paris as often as we like. The fall season was jammed with theater, opera, dinners, balls, and receptions—a warm chocolate pudding embedded with darker chocolate morsels and iced with chocolate ganache!

After putting on my fur cloak, I cross to the window, so that I may look out at the snow in the courtyard before we ruin it. The sledges wait for us below, furnished with drivers and postilions, footmen, horses, but, without us, the scene seems empty and unreal. No, I witness an instance of simple *being*, caught in a still moment. It does not depend on us to have its reality. A footman leaning back against a sledge moves his shoulders forward, steps into new snow, and the scene is animated. It exists perfectly well—complete—without my presence.

Behind me sounds the ponderous voice of Comte Provence, and Artois is whistling the tune of a bawdy song. It is another way of bragging that he prefers his warm bed in Versailles to a cold trip to Paris in a sledge. *Artois, in Paris, you are interchangeable with other swains. If not you, some other young man will help me pass the time. I need the stimulation of the city. Paris itself will divert me from my imprisonment in a body that fails to allure its proper mate.*

The three brothers debate again whether the weather is too mean to permit our attendance at the Opera Ball. What is the speed of thought? Of intense imagining? It must be faster than anything that moves on earth, faster than a slate falling from a roof, or lightning. I wish that Artois were going with us. He is such fun to play with.

"Of course we're going," I say. "Anyway."

Full of merriment, I twirl from the window with so much vivacity that the heavy skins of my cloak fly out from my body.

"She looks so big, like a bear," Provence says. His own mountainous shape is shingled with animal pelts.

"I'd rather resemble a warthog," I reply and bare my side teeth as though they were tusks and run at him.

Taking careful stock, the Dauphin asks again if we have our dominoes, and all the garb suitable for a masked ball. He would be the shepherd to our frivolous flock. By taking responsibility for us, he fancies he prepares himself for assuming more serious royal duties. Why did my mother ever trade the lightness of pleasure for her somber desk and interminable work? But she would say that she always takes time for *proper* fun.

AS WE DESCEND the wide stairs, the cold of the night comes up to greet us. I feel it in my feet, and then my ankles, and then the calves of my legs, even though the fur cloak is long. At the foot of the stairs, my attendant ties on my separate hood with a silk cord under my chin. Now I look like two balls of fur stuck together, a big fur body, a smaller round furry head. I will need all this protection, for our sleigh is open to the night. From the footman's leather-gloved hand swings a small metal stove. Through the perforations of the metal, I see a red glow, for the heater is filled with hot bricks and glowing charcoal, to warm our feet.

It is ten o'clock, the perfect moment to embark on a starry drive. When I cuddle close in the narrow space to my husband, the lap robes of shaggy fur, lined with woven wool, are drawn up almost to our noses.

Hold on tight, Marie.

"What did you say?" he asks.

I have to laugh. "I didn't know I'd spoken aloud. I was giving myself advice, such as I was given when I was a child, about to descend a snow slope."

"But did they call you 'Marie'?"

"In Austria, I was called Antoine by those who loved me. Or as we say, Toinette. But, as a girl about to descend a snowy slope in the mountains, I seemed to hear advice: *Hold on tight, Marie.* It seemed to come from the mountains themselves, or from the future."

Suddenly another haunting phrase echoes from memory, but I do not articulate it aloud. *Now do you love me?* asked by little Mozart of my mother.

The driver takes his place high above us, and the postilion mounts behind. I recognize the postilion but cannot remember exactly where I saw him. When the sleigh suddenly draws us forward, it is as though my brain is hitched to the horses and is surprised that some external force transports its stillness into motion.

Between the blackness of the sky, glimmering with stars, and the whiteness of the snow-covered world, we slide toward Paris. Already I imagine the large room, the masks, the music, the jostling of bodies and the human heat, the vibrating sense of Opportunity and Surprise.

"And did you obey?"

"Obey?" *Hold on tight, Marie.* "Ah, you mean the voices of authority. Yes, I have always tried to obey. For example, did I not speak to the notorious du Barry?"

"Does it gall you still?"

"You like her no better than I. Does it gall you?"

"Always, we must be cautious. Then and now. Did you ever read Mr. Hume's *History of England*?"

"I began it—not only in obedience but because you wished it." I can feel my nose and cheeks growing pink with cold.

"And?"

"I found it quite interesting, but one has to remember that it was composed by a Protestant." I see a star overhead that I would like someone to pluck for me. That desire, as well as the snow, makes me think of my dear papa, for once I asked him to give me a star. Smiling, he said he could not, shaking his head from side to side. *Princes will give you diamonds*, he said and called me his beautiful daughter. But I replied that I'd rather have stars than diamonds, and he kissed me on the cheek.

"Maurepas, a former advisor who no longer lives at court, has sent word to the King that he foresees the weakening of England," my husband confides.

"Who is this Maurepas, who speaks of England?" I turn my head and glance at him to signal that he has my attention in a matter that has interested him.

"You don't know him, for Maurepas has been in exile for more than a dozen years."

Even in this bracing cold, as he looks ahead, the Dauphin's eyes remain hooded and sleepy. Because he rises early to do the manual work that he says "makes a man of me," I know he must really *be* sleepy, but voicing not one complaint, he enters into the spirit of fun.

"Still, this Maurepas advises the King?"

"He is a loyal subject; he would help his sovereign to see the future, if he could."

"And why was Maurepas sent into exile?" The Dauphin has sometimes complained to me of Louis XV's rather arbitrary use of power.

"Before Madame du Barry, the King's Favorite was Madame de Pompadour. Maurepas unwisely criticized her. For that he has been in exile these decades."

"I see," I reply soberly. My mother the Empress and Count Mercy should have told me of the fate of Maurepas. Perhaps they did not wish to frighten me. But it is said that Louis XV does not love the du Barry with the same intensity he felt for the Pompadour. Now, I fancy, he reserves a measure of his affection for me.

"We are so much stronger, with the Alliance between Austria and France, are we not?" I ask. "It's vain of me to feel pride, I know, but I do." It comforts me to know that my marriage has helped to strengthen France and assure peace, at least between our two countries.

"You and I are true friends," he says happily. "We can tell each other our true feelings. We do not betray our private confidences to others. You may not know how rare that is at the Court of Versailles."

I feel a moment of shame, remembering how I so unwisely told the aunts of my husband's plan to begin conjugal relations on a certain significant date, but I do not speak of this shame or remind him of my failure in the very area he praises. With gratitude, I think of how he is a kind and forgiving soul, a noble heart, and I wish to be more like him.

"And what event causes Maurepas to foresee the weakening of England?"

The Dauphin speaks but continues to look straight ahead. "Some say the American colonies are virtually in rebellion. Maurepas agrees."

"Would we support the rebellion of a people against their monarch?"

"If George III lost his English colonies, their empire would suffer. He would hesitate to engage in combat with France and Austria."

"Yes," I say, "because of our Alliance."

Still, I wonder if it is proper for us to hope for revolution, even if it occurs far from us, across the Atlantic.

THE DRIVERS, whose high backs rise above us, and the up-curve of the front of the sleigh have shielded us from the wind. Heat still toasts our feet. I listen to the merry music of the sleigh bells, and the steady swish of the runners over the snow.

"This is all so beautiful," I say. "Not just a means of transport to Paris, but a pleasure in itself."

"That's why I voted to come. I wished to be with you alone, in a beautiful place."

I turn to him again and kiss him on the cheek.

I hear the postilion jump off the runner behind us and run a few steps. I realize he must be doing it to stir the blood, that his feet are cold.

"Do you know the postilion by name?" I ask.

"He seems familiar to you?"

"Who is he?"

The Dauphin reaches under the cover to take my hand.

"Once there was a beautiful princess," he says, "who came to France to be married to something of a dolt—"

I stir and start to protest, but he says "Shhhh," and then reminds me, "We have promised to speak our hearts when we are alone with each other."

I am glad he cannot see me blush. He is in a rare mood, serene, here under the glittering eyes of heaven. Words flow from him as smoothly as our runners flow over the snow.

"Let's imagine, not a complete dolt but something of a dolt. Still, he had some sense of the goodness that might lie behind a pretty face. He liked to hunt, and fortunately for him, so did his bride, even though to do so meant disobeying the strictures of her most dear and beloved mother. But the mother lived in a faraway land. Still, people tattled on the princess—people like her mother's ambassador—"

"No," I said, "I don't believe Mercy tattles on me. Sometimes he brags about me, and I confess, in my own way I sometimes manipulate him to brag—"

"Well, someone who was in a position to tattle on her about her naughty riding to the hounds, someone—let's not say who—who had her complete confidence, and who had spies placed everywhere, but who meant well—certainly he means well . . . for the interests of Austria—did tattle repeatedly, but the princess bore up under her mother's continued disapproval because she so much wanted to please her husband—who also wants to please her. In short, she continued to ride across the country, after the hounds."

I know better: she rode to the hounds to please herself, for the exhilaration of it.

My husband continues his story in a low, confidential voice. "As sometimes happens during a royal hunt, crops are accidentally damaged. On this particular day, a stag who was being pursued ran into the vineyard of a peasant winegrower. The man tried to defend his vines, but the angry stag gored him. It happened that the Dauphine herself was nearby with her coach. Hearing the wailing of the man's wife, she stopped to investigate what had happened. When she saw the poor man's grievous injury, she took him into her own coach to convey him to a doctor, and, also, on the spot, she gave charity from her own purse to meet the immediate needs of the wife and quite a number of children—five or six—as well as to compensate for the loss of the crop. When it turned out that the peasant's wounds were mortal, the Dauphine took further steps of generosity. For all that, her husband blessed her, certainly because of the gifts, but more so for her brave sympathy and practical action in the face of the blood and pain of humble people.

"Although she acted entirely without self-interest, the people of France heard of the little Samaritan. Her deed was honored by pictorial engravings, by images woven into tapestries and paintings on fans. Often the images of the lovely, compassionate Dauphine bore the suitable title: 'An Example of Compassion.' And the people of France did not forget. When she made her official entry into Paris, they roared their approving welcome for the embodiment of goodness and beauty."

At first I cannot speak. Moved not so much by the story, precise in all its details, but by the loving manner in which it was told, I find no words.

I was never the most talented, the brightest, or the most beautiful of my mother's daughters, but I have tried to be good and to do my Christian duty, and I feel many old hurts healing in the wake of the idea that now I am loved.

Finally I say in a small voice, "But I asked you about the postilion."

Clearing his throat, for the Dauphin too is moved, he simply answers: "The postilion was the older son of the man whom the stag killed. When he felt his maturity, he came to the palace, asking if he might not serve us, in some humble capacity."

And so it is: a moral lesson—good deeds echo after us, long after we have forgotten their enactment.

I breathe in the frigid night air with appreciation of all the good things God has given us. My brain tingles with the thought of the goodness of God who dwells behind the stars. I have so much awe of the starry realm I am almost afraid of it. The night sky is remote, austere. The blue sky of day hangs lower, has always been my friend.

The Dauphin and I ride on. We feel entranced by darkness, the holy cold, and the pristine world. Soon, however, the sledge slows and then stops still in the midst of the great vacancy.

One of the drivers slides down from his high seat to approach the horses, and the young postilion joins him. Walking to the head of each horse, they remove a glove and place their bare hand over the muzzle of each. After each visitation, the horse tosses his head, shakes it, and then shudders his neck, with a sudden jangle of sleigh bells.

"Are they giving them sugar?" I ask. The earth seems covered with sparkling sugar.

"It is so cold that the horses' breath freezes in their nostrils," the Dauphin explains. "With the warmth of their hands, our men are freeing the horses' nostrils of frost, so they can breathe."

Suddenly I realize how desperately cold it is, and the idea ignites me with excitement. "What fun the ball will be tonight!" I exclaim.

To dance, to dance with all my heart seems a matter of survival.

WHEN WE ARRIVE IN PARIS, I notice that fewer people are about in the streets, and many of the men and women, of all classes, wear fur caps or some scrap of plain cloth wound around their necks, mouths, and noses.

Almost, I am sorry our intimate journey is finished. It is a night to make one fall in love. The ride from Versailles to Paris has had its own enchantment.

Suddenly I want to know more about the politics we spoke of earlier. I ask Louis Auguste, "And what of England and the colonies? Does their fate affect us?"

The Dauphin answers: "It need not."

Suddenly, I remember that he is nineteen years old, and I a year less. What can we possibly know about such matters?

The Dauphin continues: "But if England loses its colonies, then they have lost a resource and commerce is also diminished. Yes, they will be weaker."

The paving stones in the streets of Paris and the walkways are icy. People slip, fling out their arms, and come close to falling. Over it all sifts the jingle of harness bells.

Our sleigh arrives at the dome of l'Opéra and stops. Carefully, I dislodge myself from under the coverlets and, aided by a footman, leave the warm nest of the sleigh. I do not proceed immediately but pause to beckon the young postilion to approach.

"I remember your father well," I say. "He was a brave man, who, even as he was dying in my arms, spoke of his love of his family. I reassured him that they would never want."

The boy covers his face with his gloved hand and weeps.

AWASH IN MERRIMENT and mystery, never have the red velvet walls and curtains of l'Opéra looked more warm. We are stepping inside a great heart, thrumming with voices and music, pulsing with people embracing and greeting one another. Who is Who? Nobody knows!

Because the Dauphin has been taking dancing lessons, he bows to me more graciously than ever before, his black robe shrouding his body swings forward as he leans and bows deeply. I love the theater of it! We take our places at the foot of the minuet. Normally, of course, we would be expected to go to the head of the line, but here nobody knows! We look across the little space that separates us, and the rhythm of the music begins to infuse both our bodies. In spite of the fact that the domino covers most of his face, I know the Dauphin is as delighted as I am—I can tell just by his eyes. Suddenly he winks at me. Through the hole in his mask, I watch the lid of his eye come down.

Now it is time to reach up and touch the tips of our fingers, to turn, to promenade. We have joined the dance.

The night is full of dances, figures, rhythms, moods: gavotte, allemande, courante, a daring saraband. Suddenly, I am afraid to dance the saraband, a dance my mother, with medieval sensibility, considered lewd. The rhythm of it demands a thrust of the hip, with sudden passion, on the offbeat. In medieval times, the church considered it the dance of whores. But to me, its rhythm engages the body like no other rhythm. It makes the heart ache with loss and wanting. No, I would reveal my soul if I danced the saraband.

I heard the saraband first as a child of twelve, when they had put wires on my teeth to straighten them, after my mother and her counselors decided I was destined to marry the Dauphin. From a distant room in the Schönbrunn palace, I heard a saraband played on a low-throated stringed instrument. The ache in the music expressed the throbbing in my gums—urgent, almost desperate for release and relief. Later, I asked my teacher, my Gluck, what music that might have been. He told me it was by J. S. Bach, for the violoncello, from the Third Suite, performed by my brother Joseph. He added that my mother had also heard the piece and sent word that it was never to be played again, as she recognized the form to be a saraband, the forbidden expression. Was my mother so satiated by my father during his lifetime that she never felt the poignant throb of desire? As in so many instances, my imperial brother sacrificed his own pleasure to the will of our mother.

If I wrote her that during Carnival 1774, I had abstained from dancing a saraband, she would perhaps be pleased with me. That ghostly saraband I heard when I was twelve—the memory makes me want to ask now for a cello, and for lessons in how to play it.

I find that I have raised a finger to wipe under my eye. I am surprised to encounter the cloth of my domino. I had felt unmasked.

"And would you dance the next number with me, elegant lady?" a stranger asks. He wears no mask. Have I ever seen anyone so handsome?

"Elegant lady?" I ask. "We all look exactly alike! To make distinction is to indulge in dishonest flattery."

"Not at all, for with your carriage, when you simply walk from here to there—never mind dancing—all eyes follow the grace of your movement. Have your feet turned to wheels?"

"You would have to lift my skirt to know."

"I dare not, and more important, I would not, for my heart falls down before you, like the stag before Diana. Are you the huntress?"

"I will not tell my name. My mask is my name. The other ladies would feel betrayed, if all too soon, revelations of identity began to limit our freedom and allure."

"I swear on my kneeling heart that nothing could diminish your allure. Not even if you are a lady's maid in stolen garb."

The man is tall, with the elegance of Count Mercy, but young. Instead of shrewdness, his face is that of unprecedented romance. He is the embodiment of a gentleman, and though he speaks French almost to perfection, there is something slightly foreign in his pronunciation.

"A lady's maid? That I am not." I hear unexpected gravity in my tone, for I would not too thoroughly mislead a man of honor. For him, if he is as worldly as he seems, there may be honor, and *honor*, a whole cascade of levels, to suit the opportunity.

"No, that you are not, my lady. Would I be permitted to proffer you my name, without diminishing your pleasure in your freedom?"

"Your identity in no way could impinge on my pleasure."

The man restrains from repartee. He bows low. He could not be more formal, or more elegant, if we were at court. "I am Count Axel von Fersen."

By his tone, I hear he takes himself seriously. I do not think he would besmirch his name any more than I would. His bearing is that of all humility and simple fact.

"You are devoid of unbecoming pride, Count von Fersen." I make sure that there is no unbecoming haughtiness in my own tone. I speak as a simple milkmaid might speak to her master, whom she likes, though he is beyond her reach. "If you like, please follow me to the side, and we'll speak some more." He offers me his arm, and we progress to stand beside the velvet wall. As we approach a sconce of glittering crystal, I could swear the light glows more brightly. I position him to face the candles so that I can follow the nuances of his expressive face.

"And you have traveled here from Sweden," I hazard. I would not like to be mistaken, but it is only a brief and casual conversation, a pause between dances.

A gigue has begun, and I am glad not to be dancing, though I could have met the challenge. Now everyone dances with gusto, for they have caught their breaths while dancing the slow and measured saraband. The large room bobs with bodies, up and down and swirling round, like tops in a bowl of water.

"You are both correct and incorrect in your surmise." He laughs pleasantly.

"Which means," I say, taking up the challenge of his puzzle, "that your native country is Sweden, but you have traveled for—perhaps, two years?"

"Brilliant deduction!"

"You are too kind in pretending that I am clever when it is a commonplace that young men of your age make the grand tour to finish their educations."

"And you too are a foreigner in this most sophisticated assemblage?"

"Can you guess?"

"I hear a bit of Lorraine in your speech."

Suddenly I feel very serious. "Then you hear my father's influence, for he was from Lorraine."

Sensing my shift, he has the poise to hesitate. He does not tumble on, with immediate banter. With perfect courtesy, he waits for my direction.

"And have you yet been to court?"

"I meant to go early on New Year's Day."

On New Year's Day two years ago I made my formal, empty rapprochement with the du Barry. I remembered my own awakening on that day, shivering while I waited for the creaky gears of etiquette to bring me my chemise.

"You shiver. Perhaps you are remembering the recent bitter cold?" he went on. "It was so extremely frigid, with deep snow and ice hanging from the eaves, that I thought I should wait for a new fur cloak. But my tailor was behind. In truth"—he smiled in a most natural and friendly way—"I confess I wanted the cloak as much for the style as for the warmth. But you are correct in identifying me as Swedish, and hence my Norseman bones recognize momentous cold. I gladly give it the respect due. Wind and cold are no respecter of one's station in life. My departure for the château was delayed till nine in the morning."

"And may I ask whom you know?"

"Ah, a number of people. A few days later I was received by the Comtesse de Brionne."

"At her official *toilette*, I imagine. Being coiffed. And it was *amusant*?"

Yes. Amused to recall the scene, he chatters away, sometimes making gestures, in such a way as to make clear that he is quite at ease in such scenes. Without a hint of disrespect, he speaks of how she used a cunning little silver knife to scrape off excess powder. He described the varieties of rouge, six pots of different colors. "Very dark and imposing," he said. "One was almost black. And her daughter came in—like yourself, she hailed from Lorraine, but more directly, I think, than you have come."

Almost, I let slip that Mademoiselle de Lorraine is in fact my cousin, through my father, but I restrain myself just in time. I like my incognito too much to betray myself, if I can help it. Without revealing my own age, I discover that he too is eighteen, and two months older than myself. Lasting for several years, his travels allowed him to practice his Italian and German, in which he also converses fluently. I am delighted that on his travels he met my brother, the Archduke Leopold, and that without knowing of my relation to him, speaks of him fondly, though he adds the qualification that Leopold was said not to be so confident or so assertive as his older brother, Joseph.

"But that is only natural," I said, "for a younger brother. Of course, he himself is older brother to Ferdinand and Max."

For just a moment, I see him pause, attentive to my familiarity with the Hapsburg family.

"Are you yourself a younger or an older sister?" he asks.

"Ah, you mustn't try to guess my secrets," I tease. "But let me answer in a riddle: I am both."

"But mainly?"

"Mainly I am younger. And that goes quite far enough."

"Then let us dance the minuet."

And so we appear to dance, but my soul is flying. Has anyone ever danced as well as Axel von Fersen? Artois, almost. But he is at Versailles with his wife. The Swede and I dance until it is nearly three o'clock in the morning, at which time, I am definitely recognized.

At once, everyone presses around me, and the young Swede very politely gives ground. He looks at me with utmost admiration, but he is not in the least discomforted by the news that he has been speaking with the Dauphine, an archduchess of Austria. No, it is the human being whom he has engaged—what do title and position matter? I have rarely seen such self-possession, such ease with himself and others, not even in much older men than Count von Fersen.

"I depart in a month for England," he courteously informs me as he withdraws.

I nod, which is to say that he shall certainly receive invitations to a few *bals à la Dauphine* before his departure.

The number of people surrounding me becomes oppressive, so I withdraw to a box, where I am reunited with the Dauphin. In the little world of the box, we have hot chocolate in lovely cups lined with gold, and a pleasant chat with the Comte de Neville, whose china blue eyes and nimble conversation have always entertained the Dauphin as much as myself. The wig of the charming Comte de Neville becomes him so naturally that I sometimes wonder if it is not his own snowy white hair, powdered just a bit to keep down gossip. The Comte de Neville speaks of travel to Mexico in his future, to the silver cities in the interior mountains, and in particular to San Miguel d'Allende.

In duet, my husband and I exclaim with equal sincerity about how much we shall miss him.

For a moment I imagine cities made of silver, nestled in the mountains, every building gleaming and reflecting the light like a mirror. It is like a vision of heaven, only more exotic. But the comte explains the structures in Mexico are made of stone, stucco, and adobe—a sun-baked mud. They are called the silver cities because the Spanish discovered silver in the mountains around them. Rather mischievously, Comte de Neville says that in Mexico they enliven the hot chocolate with a pinch of pepper.

Long a student of geography, the Dauphin has been alert as our friend describes the location and history of the five silver cities tucked in the mountains of Mexico. It is clear they are not cities in the grand sense that we know—Vienna, Paris—but little nodules of nascent cities. Who knows what they may become?

"They have animals we have never seen," my husband remarks, and I know he is envisioning hunting in the jungles of the Americas.

The Comte de Neville remarks that the flora and fauna of Mexico have scarcely been described in print. He continues to tell us that the booksellers of Paris sell more books on natural history than on any other subject, even on piety. "But Racine and La Fontaine are still in great demand," he adds.

Although he is elderly, the Comte de Neville is capable and decisive, always in the know, always open to new horizons.

"Mexico," he says. "Perhaps not the final dream."

When the comte turns particularly to me and remarks how desperately the French opera needs to be enlivened by a pinch of pepper—or anything but more of Lully from the illustrious past—I recall how tremendously boring the opera entertainment had been at Versailles the night of my wedding.

And then I think of my old music teacher again, of the fact that I have missed him for a long time, and that the Empress has written that Monsieur Gluck is desirous of coming to Paris.

I note to the Comte de Neville that Count von Fersen is exiting the ball.

"Of course," the Comte de Neville says warmly as he looks into my eyes. "Having had a few moments of the company of the Dauphine, there is little point in prolonging his stay."

"He is a fine fellow," the Dauphin remarks. "I talked with him earlier."

"Do you think he knew my identity before I was recognized?" I ask.

"No," replies Comte de Neville, who is sensitive not just to the routines of etiquette but to genuine good manners. "Had he suspected your identity, he would have acknowledged that fact immediately. I know his father. The young count would not make a mockery of honesty."

"I have the same sense of him," I reply.

"His exit at this point is meant as an expression of his respect for the position and person of Madame la Dauphine," Comte de Neville adds.

The Dauphin smiles indulgently, his eyes half-closed by the hoods of his eyelids. He would rather be asleep, in a lonely bed dreaming of tongs and forges, than sitting in this red plush box with me. For myself, I am glad to have removed the hot black mask of incognito. I look into the mirrored wall at the back of the box. The mirror completes a half chandelier pressing against the glass, so that along with its reflection, a full circle of light and glittering crystal engages the viewer's eye. While it is not a perfect effect, I have always admired this particular illusion. Then I see my own face, flushed, in the glass beside the chandelier. I am amazed by how charming and alive I look. Who would guess that it is after three in the morning—I am too fresh!

Ah, I think, *if I cannot fall in love with the Dauphin, I can at least love myself.*

Then I ask myself, How can this be so? How have I attained in this last half year the power to love myself?

The answer comes in an echo of the roar of love and admiration I heard when we entered Paris. I can love myself, have confidence in myself (as the young Fersen, just my age, has confidence in himself), indulge myself because the people love me. The idea is intoxicating!

Winning and Sometimes Losing, Spring 1774

Of all our sacred Catholic dogma, the idea of indulgences has most successfully alluded me. When I asked the Abbé Vermond if I might not make amends in advance for indulging myself rather lavishly in gambling at cards, he replied that I did not understand the concept of indulgences, but, in answer to my question, no, sins of excess could not be excused before they were committed. His dear blue eyes looked troubled. His explanation was too boring to listen to.

What I know is that when I sit at cards and when I win, the happiest of giggles gurgles up from my soul. Everybody congratulates me extravagantly. Since the games are mostly luck, I believed at first such adulation was silly, but I have become used to it, and I love it when all faces turn to me with round eyes and open mouths, breathing, "Oh! You lucky dog!"

The first time I heard the expression, I gave a little yip-yap. Everyone was quite shocked; there followed a pregnant silence. Then all at once, to fill the void, almost everyone laughed uproariously. Madame Etiquette shot me a glance of complete disapproval. I bet all my winnings on the next hand.

When I lost and felt embarrassed, everyone looked away and pretended nothing had happened.

"YOU LOOK SO SWEET, peering over your fan of cards," someone says, and I flutter the playing cards flirtatiously. I have come to the gaming tables six nights in a row, and each has been more absorbing than the one before.

"Don't flash your cards at Madame Guéméné," someone cautions. "Our dear friend takes all the advantages she can."

"But I intend to take none at all," I announce saucily, feeling younger than my eighteen years. I think for a moment about how very boring it was to play cards with my aunts and how I had come to avoid their interminable games. "The betting makes it *so exciting*," I confide to Artois, who sits at my elbow.

"Do you think so," he replies. "Then let us conduct a scientific experiment."

"The Dauphin loves science," I reply. "I didn't know you were susceptible to its contagion." I speak so lightly that I feel no one could legitimately take offense, but I see the eyebrow of the Comtesse de Noailles arch itself.

"A different application of science," Artois answers. "This will be fun. Try betting more and more and see if your excitement rises with the amounts that you bet."

Everyone acclaims with pleasure Artois's bold and novel suggestion. I am happy to comply. After each wager, I report my level of excitement: "Moderate," I begin.

As we up the ante, I say, "Growing!"

Next I wager twice what anyone would expect.

"Ah!" they all exclaim.

"And again," I say, repeating my extravagance.

"How do you feel?" Artois asks with much interest.

"My head feels like a balloon!"

"Is it good?"

"So exciting!" I reply, and suddenly I have won the pot. I feel all the blood flow to my cheeks. I am burning hot, and I try to take deep breaths to calm myself. "Again!" I hear myself exclaim.

We play on and on, and I begin to hear the expression "She's lucky."

How they admire my luck! It pleases them to see someone so lucky, and they bet more wildly, remarking that perhaps my luck will come to them.

And it does. All of a sudden, I am left with nothing.

"You can always wager a bauble," Artois reminds me. His wife has pushed away from her table and stands with her hand on his shoulder. "Tired?" he asks her.

"It's two o'clock in the morning," she answers. "Could we say, 'To be continued'?"

Glancing at her face, I see not only fatigue but anxiety.

"Yes," I say quickly. "'To be continued.'"

But I retire with reluctance and cannot wait for the game to resume tomorrow. At the tables, I rarely had thought of the Dauphin. Full of the spirit of daring, I had forgotten my duty to make myself appear cheerful while I brimmed with my perpetual mortification.

To my surprise, I see that many of my friends are intoxicated. They need to hold to the backs of chairs or to more sober friends or spouses to make their way from the room. Someone stumbles. A lady's shoe slips off her foot and is left behind while she hobbles forward. For all the excitement of winning and losing, it never occurred to me to take so much as a sip of wine, for that is not one of my habits. My heart, however, is hammering against my ribs, and I know my face must be very pink.

Suddenly Artois clutches my elbow and holds me back.

"A game." he says, "Another game. One called Seek and Seek."

"How so?" I whisper back, a little embarrassed.

"Pretend we have an assignation. Arise at three in the morning. So will I. We will look for each other. If anyone finds us, we will say truthfully that we have met by accident."

"I'm uncertain," I reply, truthfully.

"My brother told me he is not coming to your bed tonight, that he thought it might be late when you retired. It's a game, pretty goose. And we are as innocent as children. We plan no meeting place. Use instinct, intuition!"

I think of the narrow corridors, sudden staircases, and private rooms hidden behind the linked state rooms. In those convoluted spaces, entered by secret doors, cut seamlessly in the wallpaper, people live secret lives. Sometimes, the Dauphin has entered my room by such a secret door.

With rising excitement, I whisper, "It would be mere chance if we met." Then I call to Madame de Noailles, "Would you be so kind as to lend me your cloak. I feel a chill."

The Land of Intrigue: An Adventure in the Château de Versailles

Thus, with no risk to my honor, I repudiate the disinterest of the Dauphin!

Although he is far from me in another part of the palace, at my own moment of arising, Artois is sitting up in bed; stealthily he lowers his legs to the floor, stands, pulls on a dressing gown, bends to house his feet in soft, flat slippers, and glides from the room. As do I.

His own soft curly hair floats about his face as he hurries along the corridor. This is not a time for wigs.

We have agreed not to assign for ourselves any specific meeting place. If we meet—and are discovered!—it will be a chance encounter on a restless night. I know only the location of his beginning point, and that is all he knows of me. The excitement lies in the aimlessness of our searching. This is no Hide and Seek; the game is Seek and Seek. We both surely feel it, in the same moment, the excitement!

The borrowed cloak of Madame de Noailles is a disguise. I draw its deep hood over my bowed head. I practice her awkward gait. Tremors of amusement shake my body. Incognito, I open the door close to the head of my bed that is cut into the wallpaper without a frame, a hidden door, and step into the vast and vague realm of the interior, itself a terra incognita. I decide to carry no candle but to depend on random light. Suppose rumors begin suggesting that Madame Etiquette was seen going to an assignation? What pleasant revenge for all the ways she has suppressed me.

Immediately, in the narrow corridor, I see two sleepy servants, sitting on a small bench, leaning into each other, dozing. At their feet, a lantern flickers dimly. My cloak brushes their knees, and the man stirs. I pass. If he looks up, he will just see the back of Madame de Noailles retreating. I add a dip to my limp. Almost I am tempted to say something, using her voice.

What rooms do I pass, for many of the state rooms have their private exits into the interior? Suppose I should stumble into the state room of the King? How can anyone ever memorize the angles and dodges of these hidden hallways? I hear someone coming—a familiar footstep? Here is a door, and I open it, step in, leaving only a crack. I push the hood back and stand here bareheaded, my hair a frowsy mess.

Through the narrow opening, I see a harlot pass, younger than myself. I hear her quicken her pace. And who is this behind? Could it be the Count Mercy? No, surely in that I am mistaken. He has his Favorite. He is too elegant and discreet to ply these corridors. In whose room do I stand? In the dim light of this large room, I see a naked man stretched on the bed, and beside him a woman with her back turned, her puffy night bonnet in place, like a swollen cheese.

When I leave their room, I again pull the hood well forward and hold my head down to conceal my face. I feel almost as an ordinary person might feel. How strange to live in a palace with so many people I do not know—nearly three hundred jumbled apartments exist behind the flat facades. Over five hundred rooms nestle under the roofs crowned with golden gilt. They do not all know Madame de Noailles. I could be anybody.

And who does Artois encounter as he moves through corridors on the other side of the palace, across the courtyard, on another level? I think he is almost running. He cares less than I if he is recognized.

Suddenly, he stops. Here comes a sleepy maid. Her mistress has rung for her. Having thrown on some clothes, she almost stumbles through the hall, rubbing her eyes. There is Artois, who pushes her against the wall. Recognizing him, she is amazed; her pretty mouth falls open, and he kisses her. But he does not hesitate to lift her skirt. He enters her.

Now she fancies she is loved by a prince. Her virtue sits lightly on her. Now she is awake and moves purposefully. She wonders what he will give her if they meet again.

Artois stops to think about where I might go. He imagines me, and he knows my heart is racing, though I do not run. He knows I do not know what will happen and that I am afraid. He feels like a fox, full of shrewdness.

It will be sheer luck if we stumble across each other. But I am lucky tonight. They said so at the gaming tables. But perhaps it would be bad luck? Artois knows I would never besmirch my virtue for him. No, not for anyone. He slows his pace for a while. He remembers how we have danced together, and my thrill when once my breasts—so plump and promising now—brushed against him. He knows I felt a vibration of desire, translated by the involuntary tightening of my hand in his. Quickening his pace, he steps around a stray chair left in the corridor, or a trunk.

Another young woman is coming toward me. I shrink against the wall and look down, my face curtained by the sides of the hood. Her drab, limp skirt passes across my averted gaze, but her boots—I have seen those boots before, worn by the peasant girl who somewhat resembled me. That night the Princesse de Lamballe gave me a pot of violets; that girl the Dauphin and I found in the drapery. This girl in the corridor was carrying something—I dared not look up—but with both hands she carried something, perhaps a bowl, in front of her. And the fresh odor of something earthy wafted by with her.

I hear a voice: *Your Majesty has had a pleasant evening.* It is the King himself, speaking of himself, to some confidante! To his *bonne amie,* the King has scarcely troubled to lower his voice. They are around a corner, approaching me. In his mind, it is not immorality that he practices, but what he calls his rights. His voice is full of ease and comfortableness.

I notice a wardrobe closet, abandoned in the hall. Opening its door, I step inside among the limply hanging skirts. Two pairs of footsteps, and the King is passing! Lest I sneeze, I scarcely breathe the musty air of the closet. My straying hand falls upon something hard and cold, a metal lever in the back of the closet. The back of the closet is a door, and my fingers wrap around its handle. I stand in no casual cabinet but the secret entrance to an apartment.

I open the door and step through.

I AM IN A VERY SMALL unfurnished room. I move to its center, and from this center, my spirit expands or dissipates. I could possess so small a space as this! I could fill it. The room has a low ceiling, and it is octagonal in shape. A small metal chandelier with no candles hangs over my head. A cunning little fireplace faced with glazed tiles stands against one wall, and a window is across from the fireplace.

When I go to the window, I see that this is one of those apartments that look out onto a small interior courtyard. The palace is riddled with interior courtyards, like moth holes in a woolen shawl. Only the birds who fly above us can count the number of these little vacancies among the rooms. The courtyards bring breath to the interior spaces and give those who inhabit them a square open to the sky, though the view across is but another wall with its own windows. Now, through this window, comes starshine to scantily illumine the room.

When my foot slides over some small cylinder lying on the floor, I stoop to pick it up. My fingertips encounter wax—a discarded candle. Though I have no way to light it, I hold it in my bare hand aloft, as though it could show me what I would see.

What else does this apartment offer? One room gives rise to another, and all of them are low-ceilinged, each small room having its own tiny hearth and unusual angles. Some are full of frightening darkness, but most have a window that faces the interior courtyard, or another open shaft. I am unsure whether the apartment wraps around a single courtyard or meanders across to another.

I love the tiny fireplaces the most, so different from the huge pretentious caves that warm the enormous state rooms. Of course it is right: small hearths, for small rooms. I have escaped the palace, and this is a house in the country where a woman orders her own household. *She opens a dusty drawer, puts away the candle that some careless child or husband has dropped on the floor.* At night, while they are sleeping, she has her privacy, can be herself. But the sparse furniture here is dusty, long out of use, the dregs of the palace. There is the shape of a chair covered by a white cloth. This place has been forgotten.

She remembers her husband, lying naked and unashamed upon his bed. She is proud of him, weary from a day of plowing. She thinks of the straight furrows of turned earth he has left in his wake; she is proud of how she has sewn a straight seam today and hemmed a sheet.

And where is Artois? He could never penetrate into this place. Here I am safe from his frivolity. How often my mother has said the French are a frivolous race. They do not know that to have proper fun, all etiquette must be suspended. To do that, one must live with people one trusts.

I do not trust Artois. To have fun in France, one uses cynicism, like a rudder on a boat, to steer the course. Or luck. Luck has brought me here. I sought excitement and found privacy.

I think I will come to these secret chambers again, if I can find my way back. I will describe this collection of small rooms to the Dauphin, who is my friend and who helps me get what I want. I have tried always to make him welcome, have never shunned him, but sometimes I am filled with irritation and impatience, for which dancing and laughing and teasing someone else are the only release. Now there is gambling too.

The Dauphin has his forge; he does carpentry and hauls paving stones and performs other heavy labor along with workmen. With such work—but it is really play, for there is no necessity for it—he exhausts himself. Why should I not have a place to play, or rest, some private rooms that none enter except by my invitation?

It is time to return to my lawful bed, but I take with me a new desire—for privacy and for an imaginative realm of my own designing. I shall occupy these rooms, and my guests will be people of talent—painters, composers, actors, singers. Here we will be snug in our delights.

What was it I saw in the starshine on a small, dull table near a window? There was just enough light to discern the color of the bowl—blue. And red was there too. I believe the bowl was full of apples.

The Chevalier Gluck

I am to have a new diversion. At last my old music master, *le bon Gluck*, will visit me at Versailles.

Until his arrival, Monsieur Leonard, my hairdresser, will dissipate the boredom. Curious, how my hairdresser has become one of the people I most look forward to seeing. Leonard has a certain insolence at times, but that makes him interesting, and he counterbalances his acid with the sweetness of flattery and fun. He has an interesting countenance: a long French nose, slightly crooked here and there, shiny, like a bony worm in the middle of his face. My Gluck will recognize in Monsieur Leonard a fellow artist.

Monsieur Leonard is creating something like a confection—or is it a towering nest for a bizarre bird—atop my head. I can scarcely reach the top of my coiffure! At his elbow, Leonard has an arsenal of aids: extra braids and curls, jars of stiffening agents, latticeworks to be concealed as scaffolding for the towering hair. Combing my natural hair straight up and stiffening it with pomade, he builds a steep cliff straight up from the forehead. High up in this hairy tree trunk, he will embed embellishments. His case overflows with fruits of all sorts, animals, especially monkeys, jeweled flowers, carriages, a herd of cows, a sailing ship larger than two hands with all its miniature masts, lines, and canvas sails. I have asked for something musical to plant in my coif today, in honor of the chevalier.

Wigless, his cheeks like bright apples, in blows Gluck! With Leonard holding up a large section of my stiffened hair (like a ridiculous rein for a horse), I rise to embrace my old friend, who has aged and whose body has grown stout and as round as his head.

"Madame la Dauphine," he exclaims in rapture.

He embraces me tenderly, kissing my cheeks over and over, as I do his. Then from inside his coat, he suddenly produces a little dog.

"What's this?" I ask, laughing as the dog begins to bark at me.

"Mops!" he exclaims. "Have you forgotten beloved Mops? Hush," he whispers, "they'll never know I've brought you the little Austrian fellow."

Alas, Mops does not recognize me, nor I him. There have been so many puppies between him and me and our childhood time together. But I lift him up in both hands, high over my head, and say, "His voice has changed from soprano to baritone." I place him on the floor, and one of my ladies, without needing direction, promptly produces a leash to lead him away. "But you, my chevalier, are exactly the same, only grown more dear."

"My little princess of the keyboard," he says fondly.

"Now let me sit down again, while Monsieur Leonard transforms me into something so otherworldly you will think we live on the distant moon."

"Monsieur, your talent is apparent," Gluck proclaims. He has dispensed with Leonard as adroitly as I dispensed with Mops. Now Gluck will focus all his attention on me, as though Leonard and his busy arms were no more than a hairdressing machine, a sort of spindle winding and stretching hair.

Gluck stretches himself luxuriously. "Ah, to breathe French air," he says. "The freedom of it!"

"I have never felt particularly free here," I remark in a low voice, even though I know that all my secrets are safe with my hairdresser. The Others have discreetly retreated to the corners of the room, or hover just outside, should I call them.

"My dear Antoine—"

"Toinette," I correct him.

"My dear Toinette, the Empress has whipped the Chastity Commission into a perfect frenzy. There is no privacy; she has a secret army, well paid, of emissaries and spies. Her knowledge of private matters has inspired terror in the court." Gluck's eyes glitter with delight. "Isn't that preposterous?"

"How do you account for my mother's strictness?"

Leonard gives a too-hard tug to my hair and meets my eyes in the mirror, as though to warn me not to betray *too* boldly my relish for all things that speak of home.

"Upbringing! *Her* mother, the mother of our Empress! Elisabeth Christina, your mother's mother's grief at not having a child until nine years after her marriage has thrown this long shadow known as the Chastity Commission."

(I shudder to think what would happen to me should my maternity be so delayed.)

"And then the mishandling and death of the infant Leopold and your grandmother's obsessive fear that something might occur at her court to displease the Deity. What did the French ambassador write of his stay in Vienna, during those days of your mother's growing up?"

"Pray tell me."

"The French ambassador said, 'I have led such an amazingly pious existence in Vienna that I have not had so much as a quarter of an hour of liberty.' He swore, 'I would never have come here if I had known what would be required of a foreign ambassador in piety and abstinence.'"

"But surely my mother has not been as severe as her mother?"

"*Au contraire*, I have heard Casanova grumble. Oh, there is plenty of money and plenty of luxury to be enjoyed at the court of Vienna. But the bigotry! The Empress has made any pleasure of the flesh extremely difficult."

I do not wish to seem to criticize my mother, not even to Gluck, but I cannot stop myself from saying, "Yet she demands that I wink at the behavior of... of..."

Here Leonard suddenly snaps open a little fan, which he places against my hair, as though testing its decorative appeal, but the fan is painted with ears, displaying numerous real earrings; as a discreet signal between us, the fan is to be deployed when my loyal hairdresser feels I should remember that Others are always listening. Just in time, I do *not* say "She demands that I wink at the behavior . . . of the King."

". . . of the du Barry," I say. Certainly I may speak ill of that woman in my own boudoir.

"Recently," Gluck continues, "the Empress wrote the Archduchess Maria Carolina that she has learned—from her spies—that her daughter the Queen of Naples says her prayers carelessly. Our Charlotte lacks proper veneration, proper attention to the meanings of the words. She must pray with deeper feeling. Oh, the Empress knows everything. The Empress warns Charlotte in just so many words that her whole day will be bad, after a careless beginning in her prayers."

I cannot help but shudder. At least so far the manner of my private praying has not been criticized.

Leonard folds up the fan. Conversationally, we are on safe ground again. As our own private joke, Leonard hitches a bronze bell at the apex of my hair to say we are all under the rule of the church.

"No bell," I say, shaking my head. The whole stretch of hair wobbles precariously.

"Sit still, please, my charming Madame la Dauphine."

Leonard squats to lower his head so it is beside my own; now he can see how my coiffure is progressing from my own point of view. The squat causes him to pass gas. The Chevalier Gluck laughs. The three of us laugh—comrades of like minds. With an impassive face, an attendant holds out a Meissen tray with two cups on it, one filled with chocolate, one with coffee, to the chevalier. The tea service is one of my favorites with a deep midnight blue band around the rims of the cups.

"Ah, coffee!" the chevalier exclaims. "And have you heard the 'Coffee Cantata' of J. S. Bach, dear Toinette?" When I reply that I have not, he continues to explain that when coffee first came to Europe, and the people in the German areas began to drink it for breakfast instead of beer, coffee was thought to be a morally corrupting substance—far too stimulating. "Bach's cantata told the story of a father so concerned about his daughter's new practice of drinking coffee that he promised she could marry the man of her choice, if she would only give up her dangerous coffee habit."

"And how does the story of the 'Coffee Cantata' end?"

"I believe the clever ingenue finds a way to have both coffee and the chosen husband. It's most amusing. You would love it, and I can rehearse the whole of it here—after an opera of my own composing is produced."

Leonard grabs his own tankard of coffee and swigs it down. Then he rolls his eyes about in his head and gestures wildly around my face with his hands, aping the behavior of a man gone mad on coffee.

We talk and talk. From the old days together in Austria, we review the triumph of the performance of *Il Parnasso Confusio,* for which Gluck composed the music, and also of how my brother Ferdinand and I danced in *Il Trionfo d'Amore* as shepherd and shepherdess, with little Max dancing Cupid, for the wedding of my eldest brother.

"And how fares my brother Joseph?" I ask, wondering if as emperor ruling with our mother, he is as tied to work as she is.

"He worries about you," Gluck answers and then rushes on to praise the performances years ago of the four Archduchesses Elisabeth, Amelia, Josepha, and my Charlotte. I must assure his success here.

Finally, it is long past the completion of my *toilette.* I inform the chevalier, as I will the entire court, that the Chevalier Gluck is to be admitted to my presence "at all times." I have not had such pleasure, such depth of pleasure, for a long time. One by one, with the pronouncing of their names, the images of my family and of our happy times together have risen before my eyes. My music master is much more than a diversion; he has given me a life-restoring whiff of home.

As a final touch to our meeting, Leonard takes from his bag of ornaments a hair clip shaped like a spinet and pins it high up—two feet from my forehead—in my towering coiffure. All those who look at me this day will know that today my friend Gluck, a composer and musician of great distinction, arrived at the Court of Versailles.

"Perhaps you recall?" I ask, unable to let Gluck leave me, "that Franz Xaver Wagenschon painted me at the spinet keyboard before I left home. I was practicing, and you were due to arrive for my lesson. I was wearing a blue dress, as I am today." I stand and slip out of the great dust jacket that always enswaddles anyone who is being powdered. "This dress too is trimmed in mink, like the one in the painting."

"I have admired the painting in the Red Room many times," Gluck replies seriously. "Each time, I have thought of how I miss you and of how glad I shall be, someday, to come to Paris and to make music for you and with you once again. Many times, your mother and I have stood before that portrait of you together and sighed deep sighs. The painting depicts the red curtain and red furniture in the room, as well as other paintings, rather dim, on the wall behind you."

"I hope I do not disappoint you today."

"You are as beautiful as ever. More so, for now you are a woman. Monsieur"—he suddenly addresses Leonard—"in that painting of which we speak, the archduchess, known to you as Madame la Dauphine, was depicted in her *natural* hair, fair and blond. A single, *simple* braid, with pearls twisted along it, crossed her head. But your tower is quite *à la mode*, and I am touched"—he drags himself heavily to his feet—"that the two of you have conspired together to crown this happy reunion with a barrette of a spinet."

He is taking his leave, though I can scarcely bear to let him go. I must return to a day full of formality but devoid of feeling.

"And in the painting," I say, "one can almost read the notes on the page of the music book. The notes are painted so as to resemble not exactly notes, but the impression that a score makes on the eye, when seen from a distance."

Like the family member he is, Gluck reaches out to pat my hand. First it is just a pat, and then he runs his fingertips over the tips of my fingers.

"Ah, I can feel the calluses. You have been practicing the harp."

"Yes."

"Good for you. Where there is a lack of other connections, of meaningful moments, in our lives, music can often fill the gap."

I feel as though I may weep, so thoroughly does my old master understand. Instead, I straighten myself and banish the tears. Serenity is a quality that earns respect—I know this truth well. My poor friend the Princesse de Lamballe has almost made herself ridiculous, crying on every occasion.

"My dear chevalier," I say. "My mother has written me of the Parisian resistance to your *Iphigénie.* Let me assure you that it shall be presented there, and lavishly. Paris will be at your feet." I beam at him and recall how our lessons used to end: with reassurances about my intention to practice; smiling, I pronounce the old words from childhood again: "I promise."

The Hall of Mirrors

In the faint starlight, all about me are the large, beautiful garlands of painted or woven flowers: in the wallpaper, in the hangings around my bed, on the screens, and in the upholstery of the chairs. My bedchamber is a pink bower. The scalloped edge of the canopy over my bed suggests the bed is a basket of flowers. Would I love it any more if this were a real garden displaying the beauty of nature instead of that of artifice? Only if it were at Schönbrunn in Austria.

Here at Versailles, sleep does not come. Slipping on a dressing gown, I arise and walk about restlessly. I consult the portraits of my mother and my brother Joseph positioned above the mirrors. What do the Empress and the Emperor of Austria think is more beautiful—art or nature? My mother looks mildly amused. She says there is no need to choose. I do not consult the portrait of the Dauphin, my husband. It is his absence, the total absence of ardor in his constitution that galls my soul.

Something soft and furry winds itself around my ankle; I hear purring. It is a black and white kitten, one of the new favorites of the King. Chaconne, the King has named him, a dance form similar to a saraband. I pick up kitty Chaconne and cuddle him to my breasts. Together we walk from my chamber into the Peace room, which forms the southwest corner of the château, and then into the Hall of Mirrors, which faces west. I see the slipper of the new moon riding low on the horizon. I turn to see if it is reflected in the mirror opposite the window.

But what I see there is an image of Louis XV, looking at me. Quickly, I check to see if the reality of the reflection is in fact standing close to the window, also looking over the gardens at the moon.

"Your Majesty," I say, with a deep curtsy, still holding the soft kitten against my bosom.

"Ah, it is the cat's wet nurse," he says playfully. "How is my daughter?" Already his more decorous tone has shifted keys. "How is the always charming Dauphine?"

"I was unable to sleep."

"The attentions of my kitten awoke you?"

"It was the beauty of my room, with its new spring hangings, the floral ones. It was too exciting to sleep there. No doubt I'll soon become accustomed to the spring decor."

"Excited by beauty?" He slowly walks toward me. "From the beginning, I recognized the Dauphine as a rare and spontaneous creature."

"I hope, also, that I exhibit patience."

"Yes," he replies. "That, and more. But your patience with my grandson does not go unnoticed or unappreciated by me." Because he looks in the mirror to see our dual reflection, I too turn to see us.

"We are informal this evening," I say sweetly.

"Lit only by the shine of the sky," he replies. "Usually the room blazes with thousands of candles, doesn't it? The chandeliers are in their glory, the torchères illumine the faces of the dignitaries. What did you think when you first saw the Hall of Mirrors?"

"On the morning you first escorted me to Mass, we passed through this great hall quickly. I was too much in awe of Your Majesty to regard it carefully."

"But our progress through the state rooms went more slowly. We admired the ceiling paintings, the gods in their chariots—Mercury pulled by two little French cocks. Rather far-fetched, I always thought. Allegorically appropriate, I suppose. Those paintings in the mythic state rooms are easier to see, not so high above us as these."

"What do these paintings depict, Your Majesty?"

Indeed, they are high above us, a great swirl of rich, dark colors of overwhelming complexity.

"They are all of Louis XIV, my great-grandfather." He sighs. "The history of my immediate predecessor."

"I have always loved the large medallion painting of Your Majesty on the wall of the Peace room."

"Yes, I was nineteen, about your age. The female figure there is Europe, whom I offer the olive twig of peace. The nursing mother represents Abundance—the Prosperity promised by Peace."

No sooner has he uttered the words than I can hear the age in his voice. Even his face, in this dim light, looks more worn. His usually luminous eye is dull.

"This Hall of Mirrors," I quickly go on, "embodies the majesty and glory of France, in the old days and in the present."

"It was designed to do so. To humble all who entered here."

When I first saw this grand hall, with its seventeen windows on one wall and the seventeen light-reflecting mirrors on the other, with its cavernous length lighted by seventeen crystal chandeliers, I could not believe there were only seventeen.

"The Hall of Mirrors has the sweep of eternity," I say. "The windows, mirrors, and chandeliers seem innumerable as the stars at night."

In a startling moment, I recall our great hall at Schönbrunn—we thought it so stately—with two chandeliers made of wood. The architecture and decor of Austria suddenly seem rustic to me. Massive in comparison to the grace of France. But I will not confide these thoughts to Louis XV; I will not belittle the glory of my mother and brother.

The King chuckles. "When my daughters were young—if you can imagine that now, of Adelaide, Victoire, and Sophie—I had goats, cows, even an ass walk across this space to provide *mes enfants* with the freshest milk."

"Your Majesty was a most dear Papa," I exclaim affectionately.

"The moon has just slipped beyond the horizon."

"I should return to my chamber."

"Give me the little cat, then," he replies tenderly, "for company."

As I turn to go, he speaks again. "Tonight is a night of poetry, but I would speak to you, just for a moment, of politics."

I am surprised. The King never speaks to me of policies and politics.

"Gladly will I listen," I reply, "for I understand so little of these matters."

"You are your mother's daughter. You could learn, if you needed to." He glances into the mirror at himself. "During my lifetime, people have begun to speak differently than they did during the time of my great-grandfather. We have achieved the peace; your marriage is a part of its future. We have built up the navy and are building it up more, but at a cost five times greater than we have been accustomed to spending on the navy. All of our expenses—the beauty you enjoy about you—have expanded. I turned to the Parlements, hoping that they would see the necessity for increasing taxes. But they rebelled against austerity like bad children. They put all their energy into trying to limit the absolute power of the monarchy. There is a bold minister who speaks openly about reining in the power of the monarchy—Malesherbes."

In uttering that name, the King's voice sinks to a mutter, followed by a pause.

"Is he a traitor?" I ask, alarmed.

"No, Malesherbes is not a revolutionary. But he speaks out against what he perceives as 'despotism' and 'tyranny.' He would limit us. People used to say proudly that they served the King. Now they do not use the word *King* so often. What they say is that they are glad to serve the *state*. They wish to reinterpret history by claiming of my own coronation that I took an oath to the nation. I reply and have insisted my oath was to God."

Again, he pauses. I know that the Empress also considers her role to be her duty to God and her power to be bestowed by divine right, which is passed through our blood, down the generations. Suddenly I fear that the King will chastise me as I stand in this great hall in my dressing gown—I have failed to produce an heir, but it is not my fault. I have been willing, sweet, and amusing—the charm-of-three attributes needed to please one's husband, according to the Empress. I have tried to attract the Dauphin to my bed, but the Empress's charm-of-three has not delivered him to me.

The King continues. "In March of 1766, when you were still a young girl, I spoke without compromise to the Parlement of Paris." He seems now to gather that moment to himself. He stands tall and takes a huge breath, then speaks loudly into the empty Hall of Mirrors, his words reverberating throughout the space.

"In my person alone resides the sovereign power! From me alone does this Parlement and all the Parlements derive both their existence and their authority. Such authority can be exercised only in my name. It can never be turned against me." The great hall echoes and reechoes. "All legislative power belongs ultimately to me. The entire public order issues from me because I am its supreme guardian, anointed by God. My people and my person are one and the same. The nation has no body apart from the body of the monarch!"

The kitten Chaconne leaps from his arms and runs silently away from the thunder of his voice.

Very meekly, I say, "It is just the way that the Holy Church represents the body of Christ. Would I be right, Your Majesty, in thinking the ideas are parallel?"

Quietly, he replies, "I gave that speech to the Paris Parlement. And, yes. The Roman Catholic Church, holy and apostolic, is the body of our Lord and Savior. Some would presume to make the interests of the nation into a separate body from that of the monarch, but the two are necessarily united. The good of the nation is united with my own good, and the good can rest only in the hands of the monarch. In my hands. Malesherbes, the *philosophes*, the encyclopedists, Voltaire, Rousseau to the contrary."

Their names echo through the great hall, bouncing from the hard glass of mirrors and windows. Silently, we both stand and wait—I do not know for what reasons. Till the echo dies and peace descends?

We stand like shadows until I inquire respectfully, "Should I bid Your Majesty good night?"

"Do you have an entertainment for tomorrow night?" His voice is conversational.

"Gluck's opera opens in Paris."

He slightly bows his head to me. A painting forms in my mind: the two of us standing a little apart, facing each other in the dark Hall of Mirrors—an old man and a young woman. From the edges of crystal pendants and baubles, only glints of mild light illumine the dusky chamber. Outside the window is the sleeping world. I would name the painting *Politics Triumphs over Poetry.*

"Good night, Madame la Dauphine. May God keep you."

"Everyone would be most honored, should Your Majesty the King choose to be entertained by Gluck's *Iphigénie.*"

"No. . . . No," he says, his lips barely parting to admit the words. "I choose . . . not to attend."

Iphigénie en Aulide, 19 April 1774

Unlike the Italian operas of Piccinni, in Gluck's operas the lifelike human *emotions* as manifested in the events are of the most importance. To Piccinni, the story is but the framework for presenting vocal acrobatics. In the old style, the human story ceases altogether, while musical technique is displayed. One loses the sense of dramatic tension and continuity in order to focus merely on the voice box of the singer or the high jeté achieved by the legs of the dancer. Gluck is persuaded that it is for the sake of the poetry, the strong and subtle feelings conveyed by the words of the narrative, that the music of the opera should exist. The music should support but not supplant the story.

As we are seated, we are giddy with gaiety, and I project an air of confidence as we chat among ourselves. Twinkling with jewels, the Dauphin looks splendid. I see the Piccinni devotées ready to hiss and boo my Gluck, but not their leader, Madame du Barry, though she may be behind a grille. It was reported to me that she spied on a rehearsal of *Iphigénie* in just this manner.

As I look out over the gathering audience, I think how difficult it is for an audience to accept innovation. They have come with certain expectations based on prior experience; they are too lazy to make the effort to revise their views and to enter into the spirit of new ideas. Gluck's music has already been compared to the yowling of ten thousand cats and dogs.

But the good Rousseau, renowned as a music critic as well as being the author of the fabulously popular novel *Julie, ou la Nouvelle Héloïse,* took it upon himself to attend a rehearsal, and Rousseau found Gluck's music to be expressive of genuine emotion—indeed, he thought Gluck's music to be humanly powerful and sensitive. I cannot understand the King's hatred of Rousseau.

It lies to me to be expressive of my approval at the earliest possible moment of the performance. Wishing to please me, surely the audience will follow my lead. I take a moment to catch the eyes of my friends, of the Dauphin's brothers and their wives, and also the Duchesse de Chartres and the Duchesse de Bourbon. The eye of the Princesse de Lamballe is already damp with sympathy, and she smiles encouragingly at me. *Yes, much is at stake,* the expression on her face conveys. *I feel both your joy and your fear on this occasion.* My eyes moisten with gratitude.

Of all of us, the Princesse de Lamballe is the most lovely. Though her throat is brilliant with the diamonds her father-in-law has given her, she herself has forgotten them. She is merely herself, no matter how richly dressed. The blond sheen of her hair, visible through the light powder, complements the pastel hues of her dress. She is a young woman who has what she wants: the admiration of all for her virtue and beauty.

If the Comtesse du Barry were here, her languid, sensual appeal would not be able to compete with the perfect poise of the Princesse de Lamballe. Suddenly, the princess blows me an affectionate kiss off the tips of her fingers. Immediately there is a sigh from the hall, and I am reminded again how closely we are watched. Where I look, the audience looks. What I choose to see, so do they. A number of those whom I know, seeing the princess's gesture of respectful affection, also blow kisses toward me, off their fingertips.

I smile and nod at all, and they squirm with delight, the planes of their dresses reflecting the light in small flashes of various colors throughout the hall. The hum of conversation, the odor of perfume fill the room. Members of the orchestra tweak their instruments into tune—the fifths of the strings, the breathy run of a flute.

I wonder what my dear Gluck is feeling now. He is a thorough professional. I do not believe that he doubts himself or his genius in any way, and yet, even the most seasoned professional experiences, at times, what we all call butterflies.

In a flash of diamonds, Madame du Barry takes her seat, quite at the last moment. Partly because she is despised and blamed for the excesses of the court and for the miserable financial condition of France, the King's popularity is so low that he dare not appear in Paris. Last night in the unlit Hall of Mirrors, the King pretended to choose not to come, but the King would be hissed if he appeared here. How is it possible to fall so low in the esteem of people who have a natural propensity to love their monarchs? The du Barry still has her supporters, enough so that she does not hesitate to be in public. Perhaps she comes at the last minute as a precaution.

My Gluck walks onto the stage. We begin! From the opening measures, the music of the overture has both sparkle and pathos; it forecasts the rapturous melodies and rhythms that we shall enjoy for the next five hours. People are still settling their clothing and looking about to see who else is present and what they are wearing. If they would but listen, the music would delight them. To my fury, though my face reveals nothing, I note that Madame du Barry makes a point of yawning several times during the overture. She scarcely uses even the edge of her fan to cover her gaping mouth. People have admired the evenness of her teeth. She fidgets with the diamonds at her throat. With a bit of satisfaction, I remember my crushing reply when she tried to bribe my friendship by offering to have the King give me diamonds of outrageous expense. "I have quite enough diamonds," I replied.

But now comes the opening recitative of King Agamemnon, passionately addressing the goddess Diana, who wears a moon on her head and appears in a shimmer of light. Like a true father, Agamemnon begs the goddess to relent in her demand that he sacrifice his own daughter, the beloved Iphigénie, so that the wind may rise and the ships may sail to meet the enemy. The king's heart is wrenched by what he refers to as "the most dreadful of all sacrifices," and immediately I am seized by the agony of his position.

How can this goddess, the "shining author of moonlight," not be moved by the plea of a parent? Who has not felt wrenched between the love of family and the love of country? My hands spring into applause. The people follow me! The entire hall resounds to the sound of our approval and pleasure in the marriage of Racine's words and Gluck's music.

Racine, as much as Gluck, deserves this appreciation. But I understand immediately the success of Gluck's innovation: *yes*, the music magnifies and intensifies the poetry of the language, without overwhelming it. This music has not been created to serve the egotism of the performers while they display mere technique and virtuosic ornamentation.

As the performance progresses, whenever I applaud, or whenever I show that I am moved, the audience allows itself to feel the same emotions and expresses them with vigor. Even the du Barry understands that she must join in, or risk being whispered about as an enemy.

Tomorrow I shall ask Leonard to place in my hair an embellishment shaped like a moon, and perhaps some black ribbons, for this story must end tragically.

During intermission, I try in vain to train my opera glasses on the expression of Rousseau, who has been seated in the stalls below. I would like to see if his face is animated with pleasure, but his head is bowed, and he is writing copious notes on a pad of paper. No one dares approach him or interrupt his writing, so I cannot deduce his disposition. To Gluck, during intermission, I send a footman to express our total triumph. As they come to congratulate me, my friends are jubilant.

After intermission, the tragedy builds. All of my attention is absorbed by the drama, though I know how it must end. Only once the face of the du Barry catches my notice. She is speaking to her little black page, Zamore. Her features are fond, maternal. Like myself, she lives without tasting the sweetness of motherhood.

AT THE END OF THE OPERA, the ovation is tumultuous. A friend brings a statement from the connoisseur Rousseau. The great music critic congratulates me for having introduced so successfully a work of originality that heralds a new approach to the concept of what opera can be. I glow with his words. My Gluck will be appreciated!

As Dauphine, I can enrich lives.

The Maid of Versailles

Stiff from over five hours at the Opera—our triumph—we are exercising our legs, though it is just after midnight, with an impromptu promenade through the state rooms of the château. (The Dauphin announced that he was ready for sleep and has already retired.) I feel too flush with victory to consider sleeping. My party is composed of ten of our friends as we turn the northwest corner of the château, into the War room, the antechamber on this end to the great Hall of Mirrors.

An apparition appears to us all. I am astonished by her presence.

"It is the Maid of Orléans," I exclaim, for once again her head and shoulders are covered by a tan hood and cape, such as I have seen depicted in paintings of Jeanne d'Arc.

Quickly I look at her feet to see if I recognize the rather mannish boots that I have seen at least twice before—first on the night of my wedding, secondly, when the Dauphin and I together found her behind the curtain.

"Don't frighten her," the Princesse de Lamballe remarks. "I know her. She sews for my gifted couturière, Rose Bertin."

"She made the shroud for my baby," the Duchesse de Chartres says.

We are all stunned by this information.

"I am sorry that such a sad reminder of your loss should occur tonight," I say to the duchesse. After the success of Gluck's opera, in the midst of my friends, I am not pleased to be accosted by this intruder. She seems an emissary of darkness.

"The beauty of the little garment was my only consolation," the duchesse replies. With that she leans forward and embraces the little seamstress. "Let me thank you, Marie Jeanne, for your stitchery. For your design."

"You know my name," the maid replies in a soft, alto voice.

Did not Madame Etiquette tell me, long ago, that the du Barry was named *Marie Jeanne*?

"Yes," the Duchesse de Chartres continues, "for I inquired of Mademoiselle Bertin. I asked her to give you my gratitude—and a painted fan as well."

Despite my initial annoyance, suddenly I am much moved to learn that the work of this unknown person, a peasant perhaps, could have helped the duchesse so much in a moment of grief.

I ask the girl, "And do you call this midnight upon myself or some other member of my company?"

"I have the gift to console," the strange girl confesses.

"Then you are an emissary from heaven," I reply. A fear like quicksilver runs through my veins. "Who among us is in need of consolation?"

"Where is the Dauphin?"

"He has retired." I feel a new wave of petulance. Who is she to inquire of the whereabouts of the Dauphin?

"Then I offer *you* my condolences."

"But no one has died," I reply. "Pray, Marie Jeanne," I murmur, "I share both of your names as part of my own extended name, though I am called Toinette." Suddenly it seems ludicrous to me—this telling of my familiar name to a stranger, a seamstress. "Would you tell us, Marie Jeanne, something more of your mission?" I speak as softly and as coaxingly as I can to her, and I reach out my fingertips to touch the back of her hand. "My friends are distressed."

"Valet!" the Comte de Provence orders in a harsh tone. "Conduct this interloper to the gate."

Though I know she should, indeed, be escorted out, I raise my hand to delay her removal, in the hope that she will speak first.

"The end of an era approaches," she says simply and turns. She is willing to make her exit.

One of the little guard spaniels, yapping furiously, runs toward her ankle. I fear he is going to bite, but suddenly the valet kneels and intercepts the little brown and white animal. Then the valet turns his body, and as he holds the dog against his chest, he looks directly up into my eyes, like a supplicant. I recognize him: he served the château as a postilion, and it was his father who was gored by a stag.

"Yes, gracious Madame la Dauphine," he says. "You do recognize me. And she is my sister, who lives in Paris now to work."

Aghast, I ask, "And is the stipend I send your family not enough to allow your sister to remain at home with your mother?"

"You have provided with utmost generosity. We are grateful beyond anything you can imagine." The young man's eyes are a deep, liquid brown. He is very comely, more so than his sister. "My sister wants independence, to provide for herself in a way that uses her extraordinary talent with the needle and her ideas of fashion."

"You both may go now," I say. It is on the tip of my tongue to tell them to go "in peace," as a priest might, but I restrain myself. "Perhaps it is best," I say to Marie Jeanne in a sweet but serious tone, "that you do not come here again." I have not spoken harshly.

She lowers her eyelids, and the expression of her face changes, as though she is sad for me. She pushes the hood off, exposing the back of her head, and follows her brother, who places the spaniel back on the floor. The dog trots along behind them, as though he were now their pet. Her hair is cropped short, to the nape of her neck, as is the hair of Jeanne d'Arc, who dressed as a boy to come to aid the French in throwing off the yoke of foreign tyranny.

I wish that Marie Jeanne had continued to appear only to myself, or to myself and the Dauphin. She could have been something like a secret self to me—a companion.

WHEN I ENTER my chamber, I am surprised and pleased to find my husband there. Disturbed by my entry, the Dauphin suddenly sits up in our bed. "Iphigénie is offered as a sacrifice to please the goddess," he announces.

Then he falls back into the pillow and continues to sleep.

Catastrophe

While going on a hunting expedition, the King has been taken ill. Because he felt uncharacteristically weak, he actually rode to the hunt in his carriage. Though he is now in his sixty-fourth year, he is of an unusually sturdy constitution. Perhaps in a perverse way, Louis XV's life of debauchery has contributed to his physical vigor. This illness comes as a surprise. Of course everyone takes any illness of the King seriously, and the frivolous entertainments have been suspended in Paris.

Because of the King's illness, it is imperative that Gluck's production be terminated now after only a few days. Quite naturally, he is in despair, but I cannot intervene in any way.

After the King has been taken back in his carriage to the Grand Trianon, his private palace beyond the fountain of Apollo at the foot of the garden, he has continued to feel nauseated. While his ailment might have been caused by unfortunate eating—though the King has mostly retained his figure by *not* overeating—he also has a high fever. In the night at Trianon, Madame du Barry is summoned to ply cold cloths to his forehead, for he suffers from a terrific headache. Now he is no better, but I have not been informed if she is still in attendance.

Declaring "Versailles is the place to be sick," his doctor has mandated his removal from the Grand Trianon to the château, a careful trip of only ten minutes. When I enter the sick chamber, crowded with doctors, I kneel by his bed and say, "Papa-Roi, all my prayers are for your recovery."

Ever gallant, he replies, with closed eyes, "The mere sight of you gives me strength and a reason to live. I thank you for your sweet prayers." To keep the light dim and comfortable, very few candles burn. Like a clock set to chime mechanically, his words to me are automatic. Though he enunciates from rote, his compliment has its usual charm of sincerity offered with affection, even though he is very weak. The dark blood under his skin makes me wonder if he shall not soon be bled.

Behind me, I hear someone murmur that the du Barry has been invited to care for him by night, though she is not among the present assemblage. Quickly I must give my place to one of the doctors, who wishes once again to take the King's pulse.

Surrounding the bed are six physicians, five surgeons, three apothecaries. They are accompanied by sixteen attendants skilled in the art of nursing. Opinions are whispered back and forth as to the diagnosis, but no idea wins consensus.

The King himself appears helpless and bewildered. He knows that he who has ruled over the whole of France is now at the mercy of the expertise of these medical people. When he asks for water in a begging tone, I am the first to understand what he wishes, and I am honored to take the cup to his parched lips. He does not know who has helped him. I would attend him longer, in these simple ways, if it were allowed, but my aunts, his three daughters, have arrived, and I know that their claim is greater than mine.

I look from their grim faces to the window curtains, where a narrow slit tells me it is yet bright daylight outside. Feeling that the crack of light may hurt the King, I myself back up to it and quietly struggle to close the gap. A servant sees that the drapery is too heavy for me to move and comes with a long brass extender to push the rings along the high rod.

The King groans a long and piteous moan, and his daughters, in spite of themselves, echo his suffering. The chorus of woe is extremely unsettling. Is this what it comes to? I ask. Life? When he moans a second time, they have mastered their voices and make no sound except the kind of cluckings that mothers make to soothe sick children.

IN THE EVENING, the Dauphin and I sit waiting for news in the hall outside the large anteroom. Over and over the beads of the rosary slip through my fingers. The Dauphin's face is set in a kind of anxious seriousness that lends a certain nobility to his features. We watch the Comtesse de Noailles quickly cross that great anteroom, packed with courtiers, which separates the King's bedroom from the Dauphin and myself. The black space of night is visible through the oval-shaped window, the Oeil-de-Boeuf, and it seems as though a dark eye is looking down on the assembled mortals. Now Madame de Noailles slowly comes to speak to us. Even *her* sternly controlled face bespeaks sorrow instead of protocol. The closer she approaches, the more small, frightened, and childlike I seem to become.

"They have bled His Majesty twice," she says, "but still no one knows the nature of the illness. I am commissioned to bring you to him to say good night."

As we walk near the King's bedroom, a terrible stench greets us. *He is rotting*, I think, and a wave of nausea, followed by a measure of panic, sweeps through me. What can be done? I remember my mother, and her great calm when faced with difficult or distressing scenes. Though I am walking through foul air, I lift my head and do not forget that I can yet move with grace.

Entering the room, I see that they have prepared a comfortable camp bed at the foot of the royal bed, and the King lies there, resting in the smaller but more accessible bed, his eyes closed. My shoes crunch spices that have been scattered on the floor to mask the horrible odor. The room has a degree of darkness I had not anticipated, and it is difficult to tell how many people are standing in the shadows.

I do not try to approach too closely but say in a clear voice, "May you sleep well this night, Papa-Roi, and awake restored."

"Amen," the Dauphin adds, and I hear his voice soaked with grief, not hope.

Suddenly someone ignites a torch and brings its blaze close to the King's face. There we all see the red spots and pustules that speak smallpox. The King is asleep. As the room gasps, he makes no movement of recognition.

"We will stay to nurse him," the voice of Madame Adelaide sounds in determined tones, full of pity for her father.

"I have been inoculated," I say, "when I was a child. Let me stay with him, Mesdames, for you run a great risk."

"I will be here always." It is the voice of Madame du Barry, in the dark. Even now there is something languid in her voice, something too layered with honey.

Someone says to the Dauphin that he and his brothers must leave the sickroom and not return.

"But the King has always said that he had smallpox as a youth," the Dauphin remarks.

"He was mistaken," a physician says. "You must leave at once."

It takes little courage for me to say again that I will gladly stay.

After the smallpox took so many of the family, the Empress bravely and wisely insisted that I and the others be inoculated. We could have died of the inoculation, but she weighed the advantages and the risks and bravely made the correct decision. Again I say, "I can nurse the King, whom I love so dearly, more safely than you, my aunts."

At my elbow, I feel a hand—one determined to guide—the hand of Count Mercy, who tells me I must be a companion for my husband at this time. Remembering how many times the Empress has written me that she now speaks to me through Mercy, I acquiesce.

IN THE DAUPHIN'S apartment, we are quickly joined by the brothers of Louis Auguste and their wives. We six young people sit in silence. I am glad we are all together. We depart to our own chambers only to sleep.

NO ONE TELLS the King of the diagnosis. Day by day he grows steadily more ill. At some point, they *must* tell him, for he must make confession.

When we are visited in our quarantine, I make the argument, on behalf of the King's soul, for telling him of the gravity of his illness. Again and again I am told that there is yet time.

THIS IS THE NIGHT of 3 May, and the King has been ill since 27 April. The Parisians were right to close the amusements. Still, my mind cannot embrace the fact that with the King's departure from this life (sure to occur, if not with this illness, then in the future), the role of the Dauphin (and of myself) will change forever. No, I cannot imagine us without Papa-Roi present to make all the decisions while we play. Our ignorance is immense.

I walk to the window and look across the small interior courtyard to another window where a candle burns. Beautiful light, full of hope! As long as it burns, I know the King lives. The signal is prearranged: should he die, someone will snuff out the candle.

My soul feels bleak.

These interior courtyards are barren places where nothing green or pretty is visible. These open squares let in only air, light, odors, temperature; they are forgotten spaces, though apparently necessary. Nothing elevates them in the slightest above mere functionality. I find myself irritated with the minds of the architects responsible for this neglect. Hovering above the shaft, a snatch of night sky is visible. The night I learned the pleasures of gambling—now a favorite pastime—I entered a little apartment in the interior and coveted it.

Across the way, a single star burns steadily—perhaps the candle, like the star, will continue to glow and never be snuffed out.

FONDLY, I RECALL how my mother called in new tutors for me, corrected my teeth, improved my French, discussed the role of religion in her life, talked to me of the needs and urges of the male body, and in a hundred other ways tried to prepare me for marriage and life at the court of Versailles. Now who will prepare me? Us? In whom can we have confidence, and why have they let us live as though our roles would never change?

For a moment, someone stands beside me. An emissary from the sickroom, because her clothes emanate the terrible decay of that room.

"The King knows," Madame Campan, whose duty it is to read aloud to me at my request, murmurs. "He knows he is dying."

"How does he know?" I ask in the same quiet tone, but everything inside me quakes with fear. Then must I too know the truth?

"He has looked at the flesh of his own hand and arm, brought it close to his eyes, and said without hesitation, 'It is smallpox.'"

I hear the Dauphin burst into tears. He has feared his grandfather, but his sympathy for any human who must face his or her mortality is boundless.

Looking across the way at the lighted candle, I can only say, "The candle still burns."

I think of the very long road that runs from Versailles to Vienna. Probably the Empress has moved to Schönbrunn now because spring is well on its way. As always, of course, I can rely on my mother. But she loves Austria more than she loves France—or me.

Not her love, but the gift of love by the people of France has come to me without stint. It is they who make me secure in my sense of worth. Through Count Mercy I will learn what is best for France and for the Alliance, and Louis Auguste, when he becomes King, will listen to me.

"Now my grandfather must be led to repent," my husband says to someone. "For the du Barry, for all of them."

Will we become King and Queen before we are truly husband and wife? The fact that I cannot assert my will over even that small rectangle of the marriage bed fills me with a frantic sadness. I have failed, but it is *not* my failure. My mother criticizes me for my frivolity, but so long as this . . . reticence . . . of my husband continues . . . I have a right to divert myself in whatever ways I can, so long as my virtue is never compromised. The bedside readings by gentle Madame Campan have not sufficed for a long time in soothing my restlessness.

4 **May**, deep night again. In these long days, we play no cards; we make no music. Sometimes the six of us speak of other deaths, in other lands. I do not tell them about the death of my father, how, as though he had had a

premonition, he stopped the coach, descended, hugged my little body one last time. Here, they are not my true family, and my love for my father is too precious to show them.

I have sent for little Elisabeth and Clothilde to stay with us. They are both afraid, and Elisabeth leans close against my body, as close as the wide panniers of my skirt allow. She has a need for my bodily warmth to reassure her. I have asked that their favorite dogs and cats come with them, and their small hands seem to draw comfort in the act of stroking fur or watching the dogs and cats go about their oblivious play.

Here is an account of the King: he has told the du Barry that she must allow the Duc d'Aiguillon to take her to the château at Ruel. I wonder if hope has been with her till this moment. Now, even if he should survive this devastation, if he sends her away and repents, he will not recall her. No doubt she knows the story of the Duchesse de Châteauroux, who, thirty years ago, was sent away during an illness from which no one expected Louis XV to recover. When he did recover, he could not have her back, for fear of offending God.

They say he spoke to the du Barry with dignity, telling her that he must send her away, that he would not have kept her beside him in the sickroom had he known the nature of his illness, that he would always have "tender feelings of friendship" for her.

But she is finished.

I am too sad for the King—his waste of life, his enslavement to passion—to feel much triumph over this wanton woman. How I admired her golden beauty and voluptuous figure when I first came here with my little flat chest and naive ways. She is still beautiful. I cannot deny I am glad that her carriage is now departing—I can hear the rattle—from these gates for the last time. I am relieved of an irritation, of a burden. Involuntarily, I breathe more deeply and lift my head.

The days of the du Barry, here, have come to an end.

It is not my victory, but God's and Nature's triumph.

In the window across the interior court, the candle still burns.

More news: at the permanent departure of that creature, whom he tried in vain to call back, a large tear from each eye rolled down his swollen face.

They say his voice never rose above a whisper like dry leaves rustling, but the urgency in his voice, the urgency and regret when he called for her! She was gone.

Is this gladness or sorrow that I feel?

THEY SAY HIS FACE is covered by scabs, and the fever never abates. I wish that one more time, I could take cooling water to his encrusted lips.

The Abbé Mandoux, my own kind confessor, has wanted to serve the King, but he must wait till he is summoned. The Duc de Fronsac actually lay hold of the priest's shoulders, turned him around, and commanded him to return to his church, Saint-Louis de Versailles. In years gone by, Louis XV laid the cornerstone for that structure. When I think of its cool stone interior and of the mighty organ, it does seem to me a sanctuary, a house of an enclosed God. I wish that He, like his priest, would come out of His home and try to make His presence known here.

At once, I am ashamed of my impious thought.

But the King is in despair. He needs succor.

7 MAY—it is scarcely daylight but Madame Adelaide is close to my bed.

"The viaticum ceremony," she says to me. Her voice jars in my ears like the clap of a bell. "The King is ready."

"Has the Abbé Mandoux been summoned?"

"At two-thirty this morning."

I hear the drums sounding outside the walls of the château and sit up in bed. My ladies are standing behind Adelaide, ready to dress me.

"The bodyguards and the Swiss Guard are lining up now in the courtyard," Adelaide says firmly.

WHEN I SEE my husband, I note that his eyes are red and his face is swollen with his weeping. I embrace him to comfort him, and I touch the shoulders of his little sisters to reassure them that they are not alone and forgotten. Behind the canopy of the Holy Sacrament, all the Princes and Princesses of the Blood line up in ceremonial parade because the host is to be taken to the King. Carrying lit candles, we walk from the chapel toward the sickroom, between a double row of the Swiss Guard. In his beautiful and holy vestments, the Grand Almoner, a tower of swaying clothes, leads us through the galleries of the château, till we reach the bottom of the marble stairs. Here the Dauphin kneels and prays. With all my heart, I pity my husband and his youth. He must not go nearer to his grandfather.

I wonder if the King's thoughts turn at all to the yoke settling upon his grandson, kneeling on the hard marble. When asked, once, what he thought might be the future of France, the King muttered, "After us, the deluge."

The confession of the King is extended, and it is only after a long wait that the Grand Almoner reappears to make public the repentance of the King, who has humbly agreed to his humiliation.

"The King instructs me to convey to you that he asks pardon for his offenses and for the scandalous life that he has lived before the people."

THE MINUTES, and hours, and days drag on. They say he is turning black, that his body decomposes, and yet he lives. I believe it is 9 May today, and we have been told, once again, that the condition of the King is worsening. They say his swollen head resembles that of a Moor. The sight of his gaping mouth terrifies all those who see him, and the stench in the room is unbearable.

Yet we bear what we must—that is what the Empress used to say to me.

10 MAY. I glance wearily at this endless afternoon. It is but three o'clock, and I have just requested that the curtain be set aside for a quarter of an hour. Though the sun is shining brightly, I hear strange thunder in the distance.

It is a sound composed of many small sounds, each very much like the other. I remember the roar of love rising for me from the voices of thousands of throats—at Strasbourg when I first came to this country, and again, when the Dauphin and I, all dressed in gleaming white, entered Paris. The sound grows—not human voices, but something rumbling and building like thunder. The sound is bearing down upon us!

Suddenly I am on my feet, and the Dauphin beside me.

"It is the sound of people running!" I exclaim.

Together we fall to our knees.

The terrible noise of feet, running, running, grows louder and louder.

The door to our little chamber bursts open, and the Comtesse de Noailles runs forward to greet us—to congratulate us in our new identities.

Together the words tumble from our mouths as we kneel. "Dear God, guide us and help us. We are too young to reign!"

The room is aswirl with men and women who want to congratulate us. Because of the brightness of the day, we did not notice that the candle had been snuffed out. The guards draw their swords and declaim in unison, "The King is dead, long live the King!"

The sunlight plays all silvery on their blades, held aloft.

Act Three

THE FIRST GIFT OF THE NEW KING TO HIS WIFE

They tell me that the body of Louis XV has been wrapped, disinfected with spices and alcohol, and bundled off to be sealed in his tomb. The carriage has traveled at breakneck speed, as though he were going on a hunt, and the peasants who have seen the coach rattling past have cheered the passage of his corpse.

It is a terrible image, one fit for the pen of the caricaturists. One that fills me with horror. I do not know how the King, who was once admired and loved, could have fallen so far in the estimate of the French people, who are so naturally disposed to love their sovereigns. It is the people, not the nobles, whose spiritual lives include the monarchy as appointed and blessed by God. But the people jeer their passing king.

I think it must be a reaction to the long anxiety during his illness. They express their inappropriate relief that his suffering is over, and that the monarchy is renewed and born again with my husband and myself.

Our own carriage has been at the ready for days. Just as rapidly as the old King must be taken to the tomb of his ancestors at Saint-Denis, so must we be conveyed to healthy environs, to the château at Choisy.

The six of us stir from time to time as our coach hurries away from the pestilence. It is as though we have been asleep during the illness of the King. Now it is time to awake and to be young again.

"Does Her Majesty think of the benign Hilda, the hippopotamus, or the armored Clara, the rhinoceros?" the young Comte d'Artois asks.

"Why do you ask?" I say, startled.

"Because I see a slight curl at the corner of the pretty mouth of Her Majesty."

Although he takes care to address me in the third person, with proper titles, his tone is as boyish and free as ever. He is only seventeen. I am very glad for his youth, and his gay countenance is an antidote to the image of the old King's mask of black suffering.

"You are right," I tell him. "I was thinking how lucky we are to be young and together in this carriage. And when I think of youth, I think of the patron saints of my childhood, St. Hilda and St. Clara." Wickedly, I cross myself.

The whole carriage, even the somber new King, bursts into laughter.

Soon we are punching one another with the points of our elbows, and giggles erupt from us at the slightest witticism. We are free.

AT THE CHÂTEAU de Choisy, the King and I take a private walk in the gardens. We are full of the good that we hope to do for our people. As we walk among the fragrant rosebushes, we speak of the need for advisors, and the King mentions that his late father, the Dauphin who never became king, had a great respect for the Comte de Maurepas, now long in exile for writing scurrilous verses about Madame de Pompadour. The King worries a perfect pink rose from a bush and gives it to me. Unused to picking roses, his thick fingers struggle a moment with the wiry stem.

Of course I pronounce no criticism of the King, but I say, "Maurepas has paid a high price: many years of exile."

When I bury my nose in the petals of the flower, the aroma of perfect sweetness refreshes me and replaces the stale and pestilential air of the galleries of Versailles. On our wedding day, Louis Auguste sent me a single pink rose by little Elisabeth.

"The people have faith that I will never betray my moral duties," the King says proudly. "There will be no scandals of mistresses and Favorites. I will not repeat the mistakes that tarnished the reign of Louis XV."

I reply, "We will keep the confidence they bestowed on us in Paris." Unused to interfering directly, I hesitate before speaking.

"Would it be appropriate," I ask, "to recall Prince Louis de Rohan from his position as ambassador to Vienna? His immoral behavior has long fretted my mother. Because of his gossip about me, I count him a personal enemy. My mother would regard his being recalled as a mark of your consideration for both her and her innocent daughter."

"Nothing will be easier to do," my husband gallantly replies.

Breathing in the aroma of the rose, my own confidence bestirs itself—that perhaps now the King will more strongly feel a man's urges, that he will know me in the biblical sense, and that we shall produce an heir. The people need to have a sense of *next.*

I admire the blue cornflowers as we pass and wonder if it was their abundance and satisfying color that caused Louis XV to select this color for the livery here at Choisy, where one visited only by invitation.

Suddenly, the King stoops and picks a handful of cornflowers, to which he adds white Queen Anne's lace, and yellow-eyed daisies, and lavender clover, one of which he snatches right out from under a bumblebee. Then he takes the pink rose from my hand, adds it to the group, and returns it to me.

"To you who love flowers so much," he says, "I will give a whole bouquet."

Because he is flushed with the pleasure of his gallant gesture, I lean forward, stand on tiptoe, and kiss his cheek. "Your Majesty is my delight," I reply. "With all my heart, I thank you."

"Do you like the little house, the Petit Trianon?" he asks.

Small and square, made of stone, with large windows on every side, the smaller of the two structures referred to as Trianon sits not far from the large one, both being situated at the foot of the immense formal gardens of the Château de Versailles.

"Nothing could be more exquisite in its proportions than the Petit Trianon," I reply, recalling that the late King had it built for Madame de Pompadour, who despite her poor morals had exquisite taste.

"The du Barry was rarely there," the King adds. "As my first act as king, I intend to give it to you. Really give it to you, in your own name."

I am astonished. Not even queens hold property in their own names.

"I shall have a new key made for it, with your name on it. The Petit Trianon is the bouquet I will give you, as your own private retreat, to do with exactly as you please, a haven from the etiquette of the court."

I cannot speak. I am completely surprised, and enrapt with delight I kiss him again, seeking his lips.

"And may I have my own livery there?"

"You may do exactly as you please."

I had hoped that one day I might have a private apartment within the Château de Versailles. He has given me much more—a private house, almost in the country, and the land around it—the Petit Trianon.

Maria Theresa to Marie Antoinette

Everything I hear about you heartens and pleases me. It is difficult to find the words to express how very pleased I am. The entire world is right in being ecstatic over the change in France. Now they will have a young king, only twenty, and a queen who is only nineteen, and both of you are known for your human kindness, your generosity, not to mention prudence and even wisdom.

Religion and decent living will be your watchword, for they are essential to attract God's blessing and for the guidance of the behavior of your people. My heart soars above me on the wings of joy. I pray God to keep you well for the sake of your people, for the entire world, really, and especially for your family, and for your old mama to whom you have given both joy and hope.

The gift to you of Trianon, which I hear is a most lovely and comfortable place for relaxation and close enough to the château at Versailles to walk there in less than half an hour, is an amazing token of the King's esteem for you.

Most of all, I am proud of you and the King for refusing the tax called don gratuit, *even though it is your right to tax the people upon accession to the throne. Instead, you take pity on their impoverished state in refusing the so-called Queen's Belt, and I congratulate you on your witty statement of denial: "Belts are no longer worn." When one can marry wit to kindness, the people remember, and the countryside buzzes with your own words.*

Let us hope that when the late King's private strongbox is opened that millions will be found there.

I must express too my admiration for the aunts in staying with their father and risking smallpox; however, I advise that you take the King away from them, if they have come to Choisy.

Think of me not just as your mother, who loves you, but as an intimate friend. If you are too busy to answer this letter immediately, be assured that I understand and that I know you must attend to your duties. If the King wants to write me more often, urge him to be completely informal.

Remember what I wrote in my last letter to you: try to be the King's trusted friend; both his happiness and your own depend on that friendship.

The Château de Marly, June 1774

Most of the family of the King and his brothers, and the Comtesse d'Artois are rather ill. Following the King's lead, they have all decided to be inoculated against the smallpox. And so I walk beautiful Marly almost alone, with only my attendants trailing along. Rousseau thought it good to be alone at times and that perhaps our natures bloomed most purely at such times.

It is hard to say even to myself what my nature is. I know that I am overjoyed in my soul that my dear mama is pleased with me. I can only be happy when she is pleased with me, and for the first time, I think this is a fault in my character. I should have the ability to be happy in myself, to be pleased with who I am. Not the Queen but who *I* am.

I am glad that I had nothing to do with the King's decision to be inoculated in this hot season. While everything at Marly is verdant, we humans wilt in the heat, and I think it makes the body less resistant to serious illness. For three days, I have been truly worried about the King because of his high fever, but when the eruptions on his skin began, then the fever went down.

He will not be disfigured in any way, but he did have large pustules on his nose. It would have been comical had he felt less weak and sick, but he himself laughed at himself when looking in the glass. I am fortunate in his sense of humor. Also his wrists and chest showed eruptions, but the doctors lanced them at the base, and, thank God, I can write my mother that he is doing much better.

I am sorry to have to tell her that the late King's strongbox was a disappointment. It held only fifty thousand francs—not enough to be any boost to the treasury worthy of note. They say that the extreme heat will hurt the grain harvests throughout the country, for those plants lack the deep roots of the trees, which are capable of reaching far down in the earth for water. Now that we are the monarchs, I almost feel responsible for the weather. I worry that the people hold us accountable for all features of their well-being.

From the hillside at Marly, I look down at the beautiful Seine winding its way toward Paris. The vista is incomparable. If I were to construct my own landscape, an artificial one, it would certainly include water. Not like the Grand Canal or the Swiss Lake at Versailles with their straight and regimented sides, but something with soft shores that bend in here and there, something sinuous like the shape of the Seine.

Here at Marly, my thoughts turn often to the Petit Trianon. After the death of Louis XV, we have wandered some six months—to be sure that Versailles is well aired from the pestilence—but soon I will return and claim that beautiful, natural place for myself and the friends I love most. Part of my promise to myself as Queen is to reward those who have been good to me, who have been pleasant company, and sympathized with my trials. I can do as I please now, and I shall have my friend the Princesse de Lamballe as the superintendent of my household, instead of the Comtesse de Noailles.

When I return to his bedroom, I present my convalescing husband with diverse flowers of the field, like those he gave me at Choisy. He smells them, and we ask for a vase, but while we wait, he falls asleep again.

I sit beside him and prepare to write a letter to my mama. I suppose had he died of the inoculation, I would be able to return to Vienna, but I am very glad he did not die. With the old King gone and Comtesse du Barry sent to a convent—it was the King who decided she should go there, not I—I feel larger, more free. This beautiful place, Fontainebleau, Compiègne, and all the others, are ours. It is not the châteaux but the beautiful trees and meadows and the sky above them that I love most. When I was a child in Austria, I did not properly appreciate nature, except for the mountains. Now it all seems beautiful to me, and I wish that I could embrace it.

"To whom do you write?" he suddenly asks me.

"To my mother, to tell her you are better."

"She has been very affectionate to me, and I am grateful."

I ask if he would like to append some such words to my letter, in his own hand.

Willingly, he sits up, propped with pillows, and takes the lap desk in hand. There is still a very large white pimple on the end of his nose, and I can see he has been scratching his wrists. He writes:

As my wife says, I am completely over the inoculation, my dear Mama, and I actually suffered very little. I would ask for your permission to kiss you if my face were cleaner.

TO FURTHER ENTERTAIN the King, I send for my Inoculation Pouf. Rather like a hat, this incredible concoction is to be worn high above my head, some thirty-six inches or so above my forehead. "Headpieces have grown so tall," I tell the King, "that ladies must now kneel in their carriages to accommodate their new heights."

His eyes glint with merriment. "And how does this pouf represent inoculation?"

"Here is an olive tree, and this is a snake wrapped around the trunk."

"A garden of Eden?" he asks.

"But here the snake does not triumph. This is a club made of blossoms, and it will vanquish the snake. Science in the shape of the club conquers evil pestilence."

"And will you really wear such an outrage on your majestic head?"

"With pride and dignity."

The King looks skeptical. I kiss the end of my finger and plant the kiss on his nose, next to the white wart. "It is the style," I say in a tone that cannot be challenged.

The Dressmaker

There have been bread riots throughout the kingdom, including Paris—against which the King has sent troops to restore order. If Monsieur Turgot, the minister of finance, had his way, the coronation would not occur at the ancient site of Rheims, but in Paris. He says it will be less expensive there and also that the economy of Paris will flourish if people pour into the city for the event. The King thinks Rheims will add dignity and history to his ascension, and Rheims is farther away than Paris from troubled areas. It shocks me that the people riot just as we come to power, even in Paris which has shown such love for us.

I HAVE A NEW DRESSMAKER—Rose Bertin! She unpacks her trunks of dresses and hats as though she were unloading the costumes for the most sumptuous of plays. She will fashion my dress for the coronation, and I shall be simply encrusted in jewels.

When she comes to my apartment today, I ask Rose Bertin if she has in her employ the little seamstress named Marie Jeanne.

"Marie Jeanne de France?" she asks, her voice a river of energy.

"Yes."

"She stole from me."

At that moment, Rose Bertin throws open the lid of her trunk, and I behold such an array of baubles and feathers as I have scarcely seen before. Whose fingers would not itch to take up a pin shaped like an emerald bird or a unicorn all aglitter in diamonds, or a peacock feather with its velvety blue-green eye?

"What did she steal?" Surely the seamstress had no need to steal.

"A crust of bread."

I am taken aback. "Real bread?" I ask.

"Such as only the rats would relish."

"I am amazed. I know her family to be well fed." I wonder if my contribution for their care has gone astray. I stammer, "They want for nothing."

"She said it was for her neighbor."

From the tray of her trunk, Rose lifts a pouf. To be worn atop a tower of hair, the pouf is a miniature stage, featuring the tomb of Eurydice, and beside it stands a miniature figure of Orpheus holding in one hand a flute with a shaft punctuated by tiny diamond keys and a lyre outlined in pearls in his other hand. I offer to swap my Inoculation Pouf, now out of style, for it, but she says firmly that we must start afresh.

"None of Monsieur Turgot's ideas of thrift for us," she says stoutly.

I have had only the tiniest impulse to economize, but my objection is a mere pebble easily tossed aside by the rushing torrent of her words. Rose is a genius of inventive design, and who am I to stand in her way? I adore her.

"It is such a shame," Rose suddenly says, "that your dress for the coronation shall arrive crumpled."

"Crumpled?" I am horrified. "I arranged that it be carried on its own stretcher all the way to Rheims."

"But at what cost?" Rose asks.

"Twelve louis," I reply.

"The Dame d'Atours, the Duchesse de Cosse, has refused to sanction the cost."

"It is unthinkable that my dress be packed in the ordinary way," I reply. I am aghast that an underling would refuse an expenditure, but I can see by the expression in her eyes that Rose has a solution to the problem.

"Exactly," she replies. "I myself will arrange for its transport."

"Folded into a trunk?" I feel anxious.

Rose snorts, "On a stretcher, made especially to accommodate its dimensions."

"May I ask the expenditure?"

"Of course it is much more for a private citizen than for a representative of the royal family." Her eye is positively twinkling.

"How much?"

"Ah, forty or fifty louis will be my charge," Rose replies.

"Let it be done, and say nothing more to me about it. Not folded," I remind her. "On the special stretcher. Well guarded."

Hunger and Riots

Like Catherine de Médicis, in 1547, for the crowning of Henri II, I am to be a mere spectator of my husband's coronation. The French scarcely know what role a queen should play; the last three kings, Louis XV, Louis XIV, and even Louis XIII, were too young to have been married at the time of their coronations. Well, I have been compared to Catherine de Médicis before in my ability to sit a horse at a gallop.

If Count Mercy had his way, I would be crowned Queen as Louis Auguste is crowned King, but I do not think he will have his way in this, and I don't care, one way or the other. Crowned or not, I am myself, and it is the love of the people that buoys me up and lends radiance to my presence.

On 5 June 1775, the King and I leave Versailles for Compiègne, where we rest for two days. Our progress to this, the King's favorite retreat, has been along roads lined with spectators; in every village and hamlet, the bells sing out in celebration. We are grateful that there is no trace of discontent or rioting. Only at one spot, when our coach swings around a bend in the road, we see a lone man standing there. Sunburnt and gaunt, he faces us—his mouth wide open. With a single finger he points into the little cave of his empty mouth.

"Hunger," the King interprets quietly, just to me.

Then the King comfortingly squeezes my hand, which suddenly feels very white and plump.

AT COMPIÈGNE, the King comes to my bed to talk. He speaks of the importance of the ceremony, for it is the meeting of church and state. He speaks of the divine right to rule, and how with the anointing of his body with the holy oil, before the noble assemblage, he prays that strength and wisdom will come to him.

I remind him of the strength he has already displayed in standing up to the people, even when they marched to Versailles, protesting the price and the quality of the bread they were offered.

"When some of the bread was examined, it appeared to be green and black with mold," he says, "but it was found to be a fraud. The bread was painted."

I am shocked by this piece of information, and I tell him that my mother wrote to me praising his conduct and suspecting that conspiracy was at the base of the uprisings.

"Some of those arrested, who claimed they were starving and penniless, were found to have sacks of gold on their persons," he continues. His eyes look wounded and troubled. An honest man himself, he does not know how to understand deceit.

I tell the King that I hope the flour riots have not been widespread.

Sitting beside me, without his wig, he runs his fingers through his natural hair, as though he would like to pull it out. I have never seen him so worried and distraught, and I remind him that Turgot, as well as my mother, has had nothing but words of praise for his conduct during La Guerre des Farines.

Swiftly, he summarizes the disturbances of the Flour Wars. "Of course the winter beginning 1775 was the coldest on record—"

I think of my sleigh rides with my brothers-in-law, how we were bedecked in furs, how the golden bells jingled on the harnesses of the horses, my enormous fur headdresses, and the giddy laughter, while all the time, the King worried about the people.

"By spring, there was almost no grain left for the making of bread. The harvest of 1774 had been a total disaster, and then the extreme cold. . . . In the early spring, in March, disturbances occurred at Meaux, Lagny, Montlhéry, and Pont-sur-Seine. By the next month, even more desperate demonstrations occurred at Dijon."

I am shocked by the number of places involved—one, two, three, four, five—I count their names on my fingers.

The King continues, "In the last days of April, the unrest reached Beaumont-sur-Oise, and then Méru and Beauvais. Pontoise is a major supplier of grain to Paris, and the eruptions were there on the twenty-ninth of April, and by May Day, in Saint-Germain and Saint-Denis."

It is a list of sobering length. Eleven locations of discontent.

I shudder at the thought of rioters at Saint-Denis where the smallpox-ravaged body of Louis XV and of so many royal ancestors lie entombed.

"It was only 2 May—remember, I was about to go hunting—when they arrived at the gates of Versailles."

"And you organized the Swiss Guard, and the crowd was dispersed." I smile at him encouragingly, sit more upright, and press my back into a stack of feather pillows. *Twelve.*

"What worries me most is that the police in Paris did nothing to quell the riots."

Twelve, did I count twelve? "But the coronation will not be in Paris," I remind him. "We go to Rheims, as is prudent not only in terms of safety but also according to tradition, and what everyone expects."

"Perhaps having the coronation, as Turgot suggested, in Paris would have led to a prosperity there that would have settled the nerves of the people."

I lean forward and touch his elbow. "The winter is past. Already gardens are beginning to promise a good yield." I know little of agriculture, but it does no good for the King to show the people a tense or worried face. Of this I am sure. I add, "And the lieutenant de police has been dismissed and replaced in Paris."

"It is orchestration of unrest that I fear." He stares into the room, focusing on nothing. He continues, "After Versailles, Paris was pillaged two days later." He slowly shakes his head in disbelief at the enormity of the outrage. "Four or five hundred people, armed with sticks, broke into the bakers' shops all over Paris from three in the morning till three in the afternoon."

"But you acted exactly as a king should act. You stood firm."

"I am twenty years old." He pivots his body to look me squarely in the eye. "I rely on my ministers while I try to grasp the root of the problem. Let me recite to you what Veri wrote to Turgot: 'Keep your master firm, for the happiness of his life. A King who yields to a mob will find no rest except in his tomb. Even if it has been a mistake to set up free trade for corn, the sedition perpetrated in the name of famine must be resisted. Only after a show of force can the King do the right thing toward helping the people—from his own position of power.'"

"I think that is well said," I reply. "We have come to Compiègne to rest." Certainly, the King is in no mood for even a bit of cuddling. It would be wise for him to return to his own bed and let me refresh myself in sleep as well.

"Yes, but if we insist on limiting the privileges of the nobles, from what base do we draw our strength?"

"The nobles are happy. You have reinstituted the old Parlements, as they wished. You have restored their power. You have undone the work of your grandfather and of the du Barry."

"The du Barry," he says, rising. "How small a problem she was, after all."

"My mother has criticized me for sending her away."

"But my grandfather sent her from his deathbed and from the château, and it was my decision that she should live in a convent for a while—my decision, not yours. The trick is how to keep the nobles happy while responding to the needs of the people. The du Barry's stay in the convent is short; she will return to luxury—to her lovely château at Louveciennes—if not power. Neither you nor I intend to abuse our powers."

"I have thought already of what I wish to say to those who have crossed us in the past."

"What is that, my dove?"

"I shall say, 'The Queen does not remember the quarrels of the Dauphine.'"

Hearing my remark, the King strides to my bed, bends down, and kisses me on the forehead. He squares his shoulders, replaces his wig, and walks out confidently, as though he is, indeed, ready to rule. He intends to be a monarch governed by a sense of goodness and justice.

In the morning, the King will leave early, but I will linger and rest until eight in the evening to be escorted by my brothers-in-law.

Entering Rheims

Because night is falling, the road to Rheims is lit by torchlight. My bosom is bedecked with jewels, as gleaming and sparkling in the mellow light as though illumined by an enchantment. Once in my bed in the coronation city, I dream all night of a path of smooth jewels softly glowing in moonlight as it winds its way through a shaggy forest.

In the morning, I awake in the most gracious of moods. Because the King has not yet arrived, it falls to me to greet everyone, and it is a pleasure to do so. Never has my tongue found it more easy to compliment those who come to pay their respects, to remember in what activities they have lately engaged and what family matters are causes of happiness for them. Nor do I ever remark on anything that might cause a shadow to cross their faces. They are beautiful in their happiness.

Not at all fatigued, though the weather is quite warm and the clothing very heavy, in the early afternoon I take a seat on a balcony near the cathedral to wait for the King's arrival. These streets are arched with garlands. Statuary has been brought here to add a regal air, and tapestries are displayed along the way.

From far away, I hear shouts and know he has arrived at the edge of Rheims.

The cheering becomes ever louder till here is his coach, drawn by eight white horses with tall white plumes. Fanfares and kettledrums combine with the pealing bell of the cathedral to make the most joyful and royal noise imaginable.

The King looks round for me. When he sees me on my perch, he rises to acknowledge me, and the crowd is wild with joy.

I SLEEP THIS NIGHT with the image of the beautiful carriage and the white horses, stepping with such high elegance, crossing and recrossing my mind, and the thumping sound of the cathedral bell which is the same as my heart.

Before the Throne of God

Morning, and I am in my seat to watch the procession enter the cathedral, which has been so fitted with boxes for guests, rich hangings, and Corinthian columns that it scarcely resembles the austere Gothic structure of engravings. Instead, it is as modern as the Opéra and just as fashionably elegant.

I see the Duc de Croÿ, a wonderful witness to pageantry, and remember how he came to me at my wedding and spoke to me of the view from the roof of Versailles. The Princesse de Lamballe tells me that he came here at four in the morning to take the seat with the best perspective, right on the end of his bench. I see the King's elderly minister Maurepas; how glad he must be to be released from that long exile over verses about Madame de Pompadour! Now he is in the thick of things, with a fine seat for viewing the coronation of a youthful new king. Maurepas's cheeks are dry and papery, like the wings of a dried moth.

I see robes of such magnificence as neither I nor any of this great throng of people filling the cathedral have ever seen before. The mantles of the presiding officials are cloth of gleaming gold in the morning sunlight, and their linings of ermine are exposed from time to time. Last, the King himself takes a position under the canopy erected at the very center of the cross formed by the nave and the transept of the cathedral. From behind a screen behind the altar, the King's own musicians begin to sing the *Veni Creator*, and as they sing, the procession bearing the holy oil solemnly moves forward.

The holy oil was brought here from the Abbey of Saint-Rémy by the prior riding a white horse. All those throughout the countryside took note when his sacred journey intersected their ordinary day. I myself wish that I had seen him ride by, for I know it would have touched me no less than it touched the quick of the common person who knew that in this small way, he or she, in that moment of the passing white horse, partook of history.

Now I hear the voice of my husband taking the oath before God to preserve His Church and to protect the people. His voice is clear without being loud. It is firm and it rings with the goodness of his dedication. Wrapped in a silver surcoat, he seems the embodiment of a ray of light. Is light more silvery or gold?

"I promise these things in the name of Jesus Christ to my Christian people subject to me."

The Bishop of Laon and Beauvais (was not that one of the places where the people, uncontrolled, rioted for bread?) asks if the people accept the King. Those congregated here, including myself, offer our consent with our total silence.

Now the King speaks in Latin, which I do not understand but know that he sounds as serious, as wise, and as dedicated to God as any priest. In the way that he stresses each word, it is as though I can hear him say *Je m'engage à cela de bon coeur,* "I promise this with a true heart," for he is the most sincere of men.

After Louis approaches the altar, he takes off his silver mantle and reveals his scarlet camisole. The color red sings of the flesh, the naked flesh, for so comes he, before the throne of God, and this garment is made cunningly with openings, so that, indeed, his very flesh will be anointed by the administration of the holy oil. Next, his feet are shod with silk shoes worked with fleur-de-lis. But it is the sword of Charlemagne, of Charlemagne! named Joyeuse, taken by the archbishop from the altar, and the girding and ungirding of my husband with that noble, ancient blade that most stirs me.

"Take this sword given to you with the blessing of God, by which, in the strength of the Holy Spirit, you may be able to resist and repel all the enemies of the Holy Church and defend the kingdom committed to you."

So it is that we are undressed and dressed to signify our transformations.

Now, through the openings in his garment, my husband's body is anointed, with a small golden bodkin dipped in holy oil—first at his chest, then between his shoulders, and then in the crook of each arm. With this oil upon his flesh, the distant Almighty conveys upon my husband the divine right of his inheritance—to be one of the kings of France. Throughout this anointing, the choir sings: "Zadok the Priest and Nathan the Prophet anointed Solomon King in Jerusalem. And all the people rejoiced and said, 'May the King live forever.'"

Next, the King is clothed in ways that remind everyone of the union of church and state, in a deacon's blue dalmatic, and over that is placed the coronation robe, also blue and embroidered in fleur-de-lis, with a lining of ermine. He extends his hand and receives a ring and a scepter.

The moment to receive the crown itself, the crown of Charlemagne, has arrived. After the twelve peers of France came to stand beside the King, the archbishop raises the crown over his head.

"God of Eternity, leader of all virtues and victor over all enemies, bless this thy servant who inclines his head to Thee."

The crown rests on the head of he who will be known through all time: Louis XVI.

Following those solemn and culminating words, the King climbs the steps to the throne, which has been erected high above the choir screen, and each of the twelve peers climbs after him to bow and to kiss him.

Then! The church doors are thrown open, the people throng in, thousands of birds are released, the trumpets blare, everyone cries and applauds—applauds, which has never before happened in this noble ritual—I am acknowledged—and my tears flow so copiously that I must use my handkerchief, and everyone weeps the harder for the joy that has come to us, that God has sent a new king.

Marie Antoinette to Her Mother, Empress of Austria

My dear Mama,

The coronation was completely perfect. Everyone, whether noble or common, seemed pleased and delighted during every moment and with every detail. At the moment of the crowning itself, the people could not contain themselves but broke into demonstrations of adoration, and those accolades caused every heart to swell with tenderness. I tried to control my emotion, but I was as unable to do so as everyone else, and the tears of joy rolled down my cheeks, and when the people saw that I was crying, they cried all the more, joyously, and all of us vibrated in sympathy with one another.

Throughout the journey I have also tried at every moment to be responsive to the people, to show them that what they feel, I feel, and what I feel is in harmony with their own desires for the welfare of all of us, throughout the country. It is amazing and wonderful that the people believe in us as they do because the rebellions occurred very recently and the high price of bread, most unfortunately, continues to oppress their daily existence. The French people have a remarkable trait of volatility in that they can go from one extreme to another, from wicked rebellion against order to loving and loyal devotion to us.

For myself, having seen their participation in the spirit of the coronation, in spite of their own hardships and distress, I know that we are more obliged than ever to repay their love by working as hard as we can for their welfare and happiness. This truth fills the mind and heart of the King as much as it does my own. I know that throughout my whole life—even if I should live to be very old, my dear Mama—I will never forget my obligations to the people or the wondrous love expressed the day of the coronation.

An Heir to the Throne of France, August 1775

The English queen, Elizabeth, we know with awe as the Virgin Queen, but she was never married.

When Madame Campan wakes me by shaking me gently by the shoulder, I feel that I am passing from nightmare into nightmare.

"The baby is coming." Like a small, warm flame Henriette's voice licks my ear.

Opening my eyes to the darkness, I know that the Comtesse d'Artois has begun her *accouchement*. It is she, and not I, who will present the first child of the next generation to the court, the public, the world.

"Here are your clothes," Henriette whispers.

At least I do not have to be dressed in ritual manner, one petticoat ceremoniously waiting on another. Henriette skillfully helps me to put on my things. She straightens my hair. She holds a lighted candle close to the glass, and my own image appears there. Quickly, I smile at myself. It is a wonderful thing for a child to be born into the family. And just as quickly first my eyes and then my whole face become sad. I will rejoice, as best I can.

Here is a cup of chocolate to give me strength.

Half asleep, I take Henriette's hand for the few steps that bring us to the door of my room. Warm and steady, her hand in mine gives me strength. Soon I have joined the dozens of others whose rank entitles them to witness the birth as we hurry through room after room together in the same direction. Like a magnet, the event pulls us toward the room of the *accouchement*. Our faces are all mingled with excitement and anxiety that things may not go well for either the mother or the new child. When the Princesse de Chartres joins us, I note that her face is starkly white, but she has tried to disguise this fact by hastily applying two circles of rouge to her white cheeks. I see the beads of her rosary trailing from her fingertips. Her own baby was stillborn, and she nearly died.

WHEN WE ENTER the room, the comtesse is lying propped up on her pillows, her forehead weeping the sweat of her labor. For a moment, I think of the death of the old King, and of his agony. But here the pain is mingled with a wild determination, and the comtesse moans and calls out that she is progressing, progressing. Her cap is askew, and no one would consider it less than sacrilege to straighten or correct anything about her bearing.

The Comte d'Artois stands proudly beside her head. He does not look at her or bend to tend her in any way but stares straight ahead, like a proud, well-dressed statue. The lace cascading from his throat is starched and pristine, as though he were participating in a ceremony of satins and gold instead of one of flesh and fluids.

I take a position near the foot of the bed. No one shields me from the moment when the linens will be removed from her draped knees and that private door of her body will open to issue forth the child, who if he is male, will be third in line for the throne.

The comtesse's excitement is communicated to all the ladies present, who stand about in a rainbow of colors, like so many good fairies. While those who have already had children show faces of patience and confidence, those of us who have not had children struggle to retain a calm mien. We are afraid for her; we cringe at her pain; we would like to shriek when she does, but the most we can allow ourselves is to wring our hands or to hold and clinch the hands of one another.

The men are remarkably calm. They do not look directly at the bed, and certainly not at that curtain of sheeting rising over and down from the high bent knees of the Comtesse d'Artois. It is soothing to hear the men's deep voices occasionally making some brief, appropriate remark to one another. Sometimes they catch the eye of one of their wives and smile in a friendly way. *This is the fate of women,* their glances acknowledge. *For this we honor you and are dependent on you.*

The comtesse has now begun to pant, and the interval between her moans or shrieks grows shorter. The sheeting has been removed, and a doctor stands nearby with each half of a forcep, like large, open-bowled spoons, in each hand. The sun has come up, and the curtains are drawn back to illumine the portal for the child's arrival. Fluids issue forth from time to time, and occasionally clean towels, white and absorbent, are positioned under the naked buttocks of the comtesse.

Her sister, Josephine, takes her hand on one side, and suddenly the Comte d'Artois gracefully kneels beside her on the other side.

Looking into his wife's tearstained and distorted face, he says elegantly, "The moment approaches. Take courage."

All the ladies begin a chorus of brief encouragements, and suddenly, with a gush, the wet head of the child issues forth from between her legs. My whole body gasps with the agony of it, and my being convulses with her pleasure. Aided by the hands of the doctor, the sleek little body comes sliding out, and we see, and all exclaim, "A boy, a boy!"

"My God, I am happy!" the comtesse screams.

ONCE THE CHILD is cleaned and wrapped—the room atwitter as everyone congratulates everyone else to the degree appropriate by their kinship—and handed to his mother, it is my duty and pleasure to congratulate the mother. Her face is beautiful in her motherhood. The Comtesse de Noailles keeps a strict eye on the etiquette of it all.

I kiss my sister-in-law tenderly and tell her how this birth blesses all of us present and how I shall be the most devoted of aunts and how the whole kingdom is made happy. Even as I say so, one can hear the cheering outside, for hundreds of people hurried from Paris at the news that the labor had begun.

Now it is my place to withdraw, but first I kiss my sister's cheek again with all the tenderness in my heart. I only wish that she might have been my true sister, or that I might have been present when Charlotte gave birth to her firstborn.

SCARCELY HAVE I BEGUN to progress toward my own room, when I note the way is lined with the fishwives of Paris. Yes, I remind myself, it is the custom for these women to be allowed in the proximity of royal births. But their faces are not friendly. They are angry that their Queen has not produced the heir. They speak roughly and loudly to me: "Where is your babe?" "Why have you not given us an heir?" "You spend your nights dancing." "You have neglected your business as a wife." "We are mothers! Why not you?" "Hurry, run to your husband." "Do it tonight!" "Can't you spread your legs?" they say. "Behold the virgin," another remarks scornfully. One of them adds a word of urgent courtesy: "Please," she says, "get busy."

All the time, I keep my legs from moving faster. All the time my countenance must remain serene. I simply pretend that they are not present, or if one manages to catch my eye, I nod in acknowledgment. I allow myself not the slightest sign of discomfort or impatience.

Occasionally, I say to no one, "Let us rejoice," or I smile prettily and remark, "It is a day to be truly happy."

Only when I spy the door of my own chamber do I allow myself to hurry my steps.

As I slip through the doorway, a tall harridan with a lumpy nose makes the last demand, "When will you give us a Dauphin?"

Inside, I lean against the closed door, panting, terrified. Suppose any tender child were actually to fall into the hands of such coarse creatures as those women?

Madame Campan takes me in her arms. I am sure she heard their mean voices and saw how they formed a gauntlet through which I had to pass.

"Darling," Henriette says to me, and with that word of sympathy, my tears begin to flow.

It is all right. I am safe in the arms of a friend.

"They did not mean to frighten you," she soothes. "They are only the market women, come from Paris. It is their custom."

I do not describe to her their rude gestures. How they formed circles with the fingers of one hand, and entered that space with the lewd finger of another, how they cocked their arms and pumped them up and down, how they patted their own bellies, or pointed to the place between their legs and said, "Let him in, let him in!"

I say to Henriette, "They are disgusting. They frightened me." My chest is heaving as I try to repress my sobs. "What barbarous customs they have at Versailles," I gasp.

"They meant no harm. They are only eager for a dauphin to love, for an emblem of the future."

"The King and I represent the future, in our persons."

"So you do," she said. "But they long for a straight line of descent. For the sake of their children's children. A dauphin signifies peaceful transitions in the future."

I quiet myself. "Yes," I reply. I make myself look calmly into Henriette's kind eyes. "Your words comfort me. What they wish is nothing less than what I myself have longed for these many years. They are honest women."

"Now," Henriette says, "let me have some warm milk brought to you, with a sprinkling of cinnamon. We'll sit here by the window and look out. The crowd is all on the other side of the building. Come here and look out at the fountain of Latona."

Obediently, I follow the suggestions of my friend.

"What is the story of Latona?" I ask. I watch the clear waters of the fountain, which is mounded up in a series of ever smaller circular levels, with water tumbling down from the highest level to the next. The August sun plays on the cascading water.

"You've noticed that the people in the fountain are turning into frogs and lizards?" Henriette says, so that my gaze will remain on this living work of art. Some of the heads of the people are those of lizards, hands have transformed into the webbed hands of frogs.

"Yes. And there are many turtles."

"When the people ridiculed Latona and her children—Diana and

Apollo—she asked that the gods punish the rude peasants. So Venus transformed them into those grotesque creatures."

I think that Latona's story would make an interesting opera—an opportunity for costumes—frog masks with bulging eyes, foot coverings that resemble flippers. I have always loved the idea of metamorphosis. Several of the paintings at the Trianon shall represent the ancients of mythology as they transform into trees or myrtle bushes. "And why were the peasants ridiculing Latona?" I ask Henriette.

"Because she was one of the mistresses of Zeus; Hera, out of jealousy, arranged that Latona and her children be hounded from one village to another."

Suppose, with a wish, I could have transformed the market women who hounded me into nothing more than a chorus of crickets! Suddenly I smile. I recall that great theatrical moment when the base of a woman's body opened, and a new human being came forth. I promise myself that someday—yes—I will be such a portal. To be fair to Latona in her illicit amour I say that a woman could hardly resist the caresses of the king of the gods, but then I remember the du Barry, whom I hated for her immoral, seductive ways. For the first time, I wonder if my condemnation was not more political than moral, or perhaps it was personal—a sort of envy that Papa-Roi loved her more than he loved me and that her position allowed them to do together exactly as they pleased.

I am no longer a child who lost her father at age ten. As someone whose ears listen to the passing comments at court and add them up to an unexpected sum, I now know that my own beloved father, like Louis XV, often responded to a new and pretty face. Yet my remembrance that we were a loving and loyal family in Vienna remains strangely intact.

"Here's your milk," Henriette says as she hands me a goblet with a glass stem composed of two strands of glass twisted about each other. "Now sit in this most beautiful and comfortable chair." It is a sunny, yellow fabric with medallions of pink roses centered on the seat and the back. "Here's a bench for your feet. Tell me how you're feeling. A little better?"

I think how good milk is, especially with a dusting of cinnamon or nutmeg, and wonder why anyone would ever prefer wine.

Should I ever have a babe, I would nurse the child myself, as I am told Rousseau advocates. Surely there is a bond between mother and child. Yes, there must be a *natural* bond that a woman feels for a child, and one that is mutual, especially when the child is young—a bond like no other. At least, it would be so for me.

Fontainebleau: A New Friend, Comtesse de Polignac

Perhaps late summer is simply the time to be bored. Everything stays the same, even though we travel to Fontainebleau, and the draperies and colors are different. The days are endless. And now it is time for another ball. Another endless night.

The Princesse de Lamballe does not know how to dwell in the realms of fun; she is too serene. She offers no challenges but quietly fits in as well with the worldly circle of Madame de Guéméné as with the loyal servitude of Madame Campan. She has no variety of affect: she is the same whether she is riding at breakneck speed or sitting with a fire screen between her and the hearth fire as she embroiders. I love to ride, I love my needlework—but I am not the same person when I perform one or the other. We Hapsburgs have something of the chameleon in us. I am tired of her steadfast angelic sensitivity, her blond innocence. She *wants* nothing.

And with a wish—there! In the midst of the ball—I see someone new. Her face is as perfect in its beauty as that of the Princesse de Lamballe, but this unknown lady is dark brunette. She is not buxom but possessed of a delicate figure. There is a modesty and grace in the way she stands. Quickly, I approach her, smile so as not to frighten her, and ask why I have not already made her acquaintance.

"I lack the means," she replied in a simple sincere but musical voice, "to appear often on grand occasions."

Oh, I need not have feared intimidating this frank soul!

"Let us promenade together," I reply and slip my arm around her narrow waist. As we walk, I ignore all others to whisper to her. "Never has anyone answered any question of mine with such unpretentious honesty." And then I giggle, a cascade as tinkling as any uninhibited falling of water.

She laughs in reply. "I could think of nothing else to say, once having said the truth."

She has entered my mood exactly. Strolling beside her as I am, I cannot see her face, but I can feel the smile in her body, the release of tension till her emotion matches mine. She is the Comtesse de Polignac.

"It is my immediate and spontaneous wish," I tell her, "that you attend court regularly, and you must come and stay in an apartment I shall appoint at Versailles."

Then I guide her through doors till we step outside the crowded ballroom into the summer heat. Immediately my mood shifts to languid. The very air is sensual. Our bodies wilt and relax, as I still hold her about the waist. I kiss her cheek in friendship, and she takes this kiss as the frank offering that it is.

My own frankness causes her to speak of her situation. She wishes me to call her by her given name, Yolande; and I reciprocate immediately: Toinette. Without apology or embarrassment, she acknowledges that her husband, the Comte de Polignac, is the most obliging of husbands in allowing her to have her own amusements, and that she enjoys a liaison with the Comte de Vaudreuil, known for the amusing circle of artists and musicians he often entertains. "One is never bored with that graceful man," she says.

Ah, like the du Barry, my new friend lacks the virtue of . . . the virtue of what?

The virtue of virtue.

I laugh out loud, having amused myself.

I have changed: I have no impulse to chastise her, let alone send her into exile. Instead, I ask about the artists they befriend, and I confide that I am never content with my portraits, not since the one made when I was still a little girl, just arrived at Versailles, and wore the costume of an equestrienne. "My mother, the Empress, still treasures that portrait," I add, "but of course now, I am much changed."

Arm in arm with this slender creature, I suddenly swell with pride in my own voluptuous figure.

Suddenly I say exactly what has come into my head. "I am chaste and ever will be—for that is the only wise and politic course for me—"

"At least till you have produced an heir," Yolande de Polignac interjects mildly.

"But I wish to be filled with evanescence, with *fizz*."

We both cover our mouths with our hands and giggle. She looks almost as though she is merrily vomiting.

"Flirtation," she says, supplying the very word that could certainly enliven my dreary existence.

"I can easily draw the line of propriety between myself and any *gallant*, for I am the Queen, the power is all mine."

TONIGHT I GO to sleep quite happy, after talking with my new friend till well after midnight. I go to sleep thinking of her and picturing her as though I were a painter. Her nose is particularly charming, small and shapely, but her eyes are large, and her dark hair softly frames her face. Her chin is particularly beautiful, just the right length and shape, softly rounded. I would paint her with parted lips so that her perfect pearly teeth would show. Above all, her expression is one of relaxed sweetness; her mien is calm, utterly natural, and lacking in egotism—Yolande de Polignac.

Amusements

His amusements are not mine. He has the smithy; he has his hunting. No, I will not play the role of Vulcan. Were I to play the role of Venus and stand beside him in diaphanous gowns, he would be displeased.

So I amuse myself. What else can I do? It suits me to clothe myself in fun, even if at its edges there is nothing but the black lace of desperation.

I have the theater, I have my balls, I can gamble and dance the night away.

An Englishwoman, Georgina, the Duchess of Devonshire, joins us in gambling. Though not a queen, she is the English version of myself. Married to a cold husband, she delights in fashion. But it is her charm and grace that make her shine. Like myself, she loves Yolande de Polignac, whom she calls "Little Po." Like myself, she loses large sums of money and covers her wild distress with hysterical gaiety.

We three adore each other.

Sometimes we gamble all night. There's no need to lie alone in bed, waiting. What is the fruit of rejection, of loneliness? Only slow tears seeping from the corners of my eyes. How utterly silent they are. I only notice them when they draw across my temples into my hair.

But the King has given me my Trianon! My own little house, a key with my name on it. He flouts the convention that women can have nothing significant, no property, of their own. For that I am grateful to my impotent husband. And I remind myself that I must be of good cheer.

Sometimes now he grows hard. He makes a halfhearted attempt to enter. I have hope. The endless parties are nothing more than a visible enactment of my gaiety. He needs—the world needs—to know that I am happy, that no foot is more light or definite than mine, that no smile is more ready or dazzling.

Now there is Trianon to decorate, and around my little pleasure house all the gardens to rebuild in the new Chinese-English style, which replaces regimented greenery with the riotous abundance of blossoms. He has been good to me. With good humor, endlessly, he opens his purse to me.

OCCASIONALLY, I still hunt with my husband. This bright day, as I sit in the moving coach, I look at the houses of the peasants, and I wonder what it is in their lives that most brings them joy. Perhaps it is the sunshine, which also brings me joy. Glancing out the window, I see a blond boy—four or five years old—standing in the doorway. His face is dirty. We'll hunt nearby. His cottage is thatched, and a clump of violets blooms on his roof. Suddenly the coach swerves. The boy no longer stands in the doorway.

Under the hoofs! I hear someone cry, and I scream for the coach to stop.

Bursting through the coach door, I fly from the vehicle to run back to him, crumpled in the sandy road, and I lift him in my arms, shaking him gently to revive him. Suddenly his eyelids raise, and I look into the bluest eyes I have ever seen.

"He is mine! I will have him!"

I am amazed to hear myself shrieking. The child clings to me as much in fear as in desire. Naturally, he is crying. But he is unhurt. Not a single hoofprint has nicked or bruised his arms or legs or his broad fair forehead, not in the least. I know that he has run into the road because he heard my heart calling for him.

A woman emerges from the roadside cottage. She says she is his grandmother, and his mother is dead. Yes, now he will be mine. The grandmother says five others are inside, like him.

She is told I am the Queen and that I would like to take him. Yes, that was my urgent whisper—*make it happen: he will be mine.*

In dulcet tones, as though I were calm, I promise that she and all the others will be cared for, forever, if she will give him to me. (My need for him is desperate. I have no child of my own. Why else was he sent under the hooves and wheels and then sheltered by the invisible hand of God?) Yes, I am hysterical. My hands are shaking as they do when I shake the dice, for high stakes. Here, indeed, are high stakes. A child. A boy.

She has no objection if I take Jacques with me to Versailles. Now. Forever.

The horses' heads turn back for Versailles. I send a messenger to the King. All the way back, I hold Jacques in my lap. Passive with wonder, he merely clings to me.

ONCE HOME, he is washed and dressed in white, the color of innocence. I tell him that the Dauphin and I wore all white when first we went to Paris. Jacques is to share the food from my plate. Now. Just as Mops used to do, when I was a girl in Vienna, and no one was looking.

Let the market women see what I have now! Jacques! There is no more beautiful child, dressed in white, of fair skin, hair like ripe hay, eyes as blue as the cornflowers growing out of the dust.

Yes, I will see to his education. Yes, he is to be brought to me as often as is possible.

But one day I do not see Jacques at the table, and I do not send for him. They bring him less often. Jacques will always be a part of our household. I will always speak to him with kindness.

But Jacques has not redeemed my life.

Jacques is not really mine.

The Queen's Bed

At first the dream is pleasant: I am young, only four or five, and I am visiting the cottage of my wet nurse and her son, Joseph Weber, who is just my age, and who suckled, as I did, at the bountiful breast of his mother. The Empress has made sure that I know something of the peasant life, that I be a part of their joys and sorrows, that I know the furniture and the food and the fabrics that contain their lives.

In the dream, I am made welcome as I step inside the cottage of my dear nurse, but no great fuss is made of my presence. I often come here to play with Joseph Weber.

Then I remember how he cried a few days before I left Vienna to come to France to be married. But in the dream, his face, red with grief, becomes flushed with anger.

Then he holds out his hand to me, and for a moment he is Artois, my brother, whose newborn child is third in line for the throne. Artois, the young father, is asking me to dance, but no—I am a child who has come to play in a humble Austrian home, and all the adults with their watchful, critical eyes have gone. Little Joseph Weber holds out his hand to assist me. I step up easily, light as an airborne milkweed seed, onto his parents' feather bed. Our bare feet sink up to the ankles in the soft down, and then we hold hands and begin to jump in unison.

Higher and higher we jump, breathless and panting, our heads so close to the low ceiling I begin to fear injury. Our jumping then becomes ragged in its rhythm, and when my face is low, his is high, just under the square beams of the ceiling, and his face has been transformed into that of an angry peasant woman. Not his mother's face with the smooth round cheeks, but a French face, the face of hardship and of the scheming marketplace.

Now the figure above me becomes one of a bat or harpy, and she cocks her muscular arm to knock me flat on my back. Her beak and talons tear at my body. She massages my bare breasts—*oh yes, they are large and attractive,* she says, *and what man who is a man would not want the abundance of your body?*—her fingertips hard as horn explore my secret places, and I awake with a little yelp, such as a puppy might make when her toe is accidentally trod upon.

It is my own hand and my own fingers on my breast and in my body. Slowly I withdraw them from these forbidden places. Lying curled on my side in my own ornate bed, I place the palms of my hands together, press my cheek into the pillow, and pray.

Indecent Verses

While I am walking in the lower garden, not too far from Trianon, where work is progressing on the new garden and on the grotto of the Belvedere, I decide to walk into the Bosquet of Enceladus, which depicts a man in agony.

Today I visit agony, for my amusement.

Enceladus has tried to scale Olympus, and he has been cast down. He lies, all smooth and golden on an island, and he is half-buried in rocks, the textures of which are as rough as art can make. The fountain is a study in contrasts—the smooth, gleaming metal of his body and the rough rocks that represent the wrath of nature.

The King is with me, and at my elbow, he says, "It is a lesson in the vice of pride. We must control our ambition, and that of others."

"You mean the nobles, who feel entitled to receive every privilege and obliged to return nothing."

"Yes. We must not be greedy."

Does the King mean to criticize me? Does he suggest my expenditures seem unbounded?

"I need pretty things," I reply, "as you can imagine."

"But your wardrobe allowance is a hundred and fifty thousand livres."

"And my debt with Rose Bertin is five hundred thousand livres."

At this moment, I am tempted to say that in the old days the du Barry ran up a bill with Rose Bertin of 100,000 livres a year *just* for ribbons and lace, when suddenly we both see a pamphlet that has been stuck among the green leaves of a topiary trimmed to resemble a large green vase. The King plucks the pamphlet—a poem—from the bush.

Its title is "Les Nouvelles de la Cour." The drawing depicts a sad Queen. Between every stanza, the words repeat the question "Can the King do it? Can't the King do it?"

His face is scarlet with shame. My eyes fill with tears and mirror his shame, but we continue to read what has been written about the novelties of the court. The most pure and innocent Princesse de Lamballe is maligned: the verses suggest that with her little fingers she has done the work of the King. My mother, the Empress of Austria, is blasphemed as one who does not care who fathers the successor to the throne, as long as the deed of impregnation is finally done. I cannot look at my husband.

The King rips the pamphlet to shreds and throws the pieces into the basin of water that surrounds Enceladus. In his gleaming misery, we both see the mirror of our own. Who dares to throw us down and trample on our dignity?

Suddenly the King says, "I will pay your debts for you, Toinette. You and your Rose will construe whatever fashion pleases your fancy."

"My mother hopes my brother, the Emperor, will travel here. She thinks he has advice for us, that he will help us."

"Yes, of course he must come." The King smiles at me. He is glad to think of something other than obscene *libelles.* There is a graciousness in my husband's forehead when he releases tensions. Smiling, he tries to make my moment a happy one.

"When Joseph comes, I want the entertainments to be lavish beyond anything he has ever had mounted in Austria." My gaze roams over the clenched body of the statue, follows the spout of water rising into the air from the Titan's tortured mouth into the beautiful blue of the sky. "During his visit, my brother must never be bored."

Madame, My Most Dear Mother

My joy is not complete, but progress has been made. The King is less lazy. One night he knocked at the door—so to speak. The next, he opened it a crack. I praised him to the skies, with the most endearing phrases. He wept for joy, and I wept with him.

Last night, he has been two-thirds of a husband to me. He says that he does not think the dreaded operation on his member, which we have only just begun to talk about, will be necessary, and I heartily agree, as I do with all his judgments concerning the marital bed, for I believe that all my restraint will pay off in the future. I know he wants to be fully man and fully king. I sympathize, and I myself do not know entirely what is best to do, but my little Polignac tells me that I can think of our state as consummated, or almost consummated if not complete.

Unfortunately, the King confides that his body is experiencing a drought, and the fluids are not emitted even when he is asleep. I continue to hope and to pray, and I am sure my dear Mama joins me in this.

Madame, My Very Dear Daughter

I write from Vienna, on the second day of the New Year, 1777. *This year you will be twenty-two. You have been in France and married some seven years. In a month, the Emperor will arrive at Versailles. How I wish that I could join my son in his visit to our beloved Queen of France.*

I know that you will speak to him with the trust and love he deserves to receive. Loving friendship between the houses of the sovereigns of Europe is the only *means by which we can ensure the happiness of our States, our families, and the peace of Europe.*

Speak to your brother about your connubial state with frankness. I know *he will be discreet and will be capable of giving good advice. Seeking his help is of the utmost importance to you.*

Dawn

My friend the Comte de Neville has recommended I become acquainted with Marmontel's *Histoire des Incas,* so that I might have some idea of the customs of the New World. There, life is actually conducted much as Rousseau has described it should be, in his philosophy. People behave in a simple, natural way. They are in tune with nature; they worship nature, which I do not find at all incompatible with the love of God, who created all that is. Those people have their own version of Genesis, of how God made light and set the great ball of light we call the sun into the heavens.

Like the Incas, the Princesse de Lamballe and I, chaperoned by the Comtesse de Noailles, other friends, and our bodyguards, will venture forth to a remote area of the estate where no building is to be seen. Made comfortable with cushions and cloths to spread on the ground, with natural snacks of fruit and cheese, berries, nuts, and milk, we will behold the dawn.

The Princesse de Lamballe is happy that I have chosen her, and not the Duchesse de Polignac, to accompany me. I am not sure my Yolande would like this sort of excursion. Almost I wish I could go entirely by myself. When I hunt, sometimes I cause my mount to run so fast that for a few brief moments I am alone among the mighty trees of the forest. Often I would have liked to sit alone on the grass, very quietly, and be still, just to think, and to tell myself about the shades of green to be seen in the leaves and grasses and moss, and what birds I see fly by. Sometimes I considered sitting directly on the grass itself—though I have never done so—without benefit of cushion, or I consider the possibility of sitting on a clean, smooth rock, with my feet washed by an icy stream, though actually I do not like cold water. I would do it for only a moment, if I did it, and then wrap my feet in a warm towel.

This night, when we shall greet the dawn, we start out at three in the morning without ever having gone to bed. This way I avoid the tedious ritual of my official *lever*, of being clothed in glacial ceremony. Because I want to experience the darkness, we set forth while the sky is still inky. Louis has granted permission for this excursion on the basis that his sleep will not be truncated in any way. It is the princess who takes my hand, and I think for a moment what a good friend she is, one who never says no to my ideas about how we shall amuse ourselves, though she has no suggestions herself.

"Thank you, dear friend," I say, "for agreeing to sit outside with me and wait for the sun."

"I think we already know all there is to know about sitting *inside,*" she responds cheerfully.

"As is my duty as well as my pleasure," the Comtesse de Noailles adds, "I must make sure everyone sits at a proper distance from Your Majesty, even in the wilderness, with myself beside you, ready to serve in whatever way you wish."

"I would like the sky to be pink at dawn," I say to her. "Would you arrange that?" I am teasing her, of course. She always overestimates and overstates her abilities. Sunrise has its own protocol, and the Comtesse de Noailles has no power in its realm.

If the sunrise party is a great success, I shall have Leonard weave ribbons of the proper hues into my tresses and create a sunrise in my hair. *Aurora*, the word comes to me, a beautiful word. Suddenly my feet are racing over the grass, and my slippers are wet with dew.

On a whim I order the servants to douse the torches, and now we move in true darkness. For a moment I am blinded by blackness. I hear the rustle of the grass and the call of an owl, a sound I have not heard once all the years I have lived in France. My feet would like to hesitate, but I do not allow them to be cowardly. I feel a pebble under the sole of my slipper, and a wiry briar pulls at my skirt, but I do not pause. Holding the hand of my friend, we sail like twin ships over undulations in the land, places where a small slope rises up or drops down. Because Nature is not always symmetrical, the terrain delightfully surprises us. Rapid walking in the dark is an adventure for the feet. I raise my hand for silence, so that all may hear the sound of our slippered feet moving through grass. We become mysterious as a flock of ghosts. At the crest of a long grassy slope, I stop.

"Here we pitch our tents," I exclaim.

The cloths and cushions—sleek satins in shades of pink, gray, and silver—are spread. I inquire which direction is east. Like the Incas on that distant continent, we settle ourselves and face east to wait for the appearance of the sun.

"And what happened," Provence poses the question, "when Apollo allowed an inexperienced driver to hold the reins of the chariot that brings the sun?"

I am not altogether pleased that he refers us to Greek classicism, when I am in the mood for Incas and Rousseau.

Artois interprets the import of his brother's question. "He is speaking in political riddles, my dears. He refers to our illustrious ancestor, Louis XIV, the Sun King." When no one comments, Artois adds, "And those who have held the reins of state after him."

Together, they are questioning the fitness of my husband, their brother, to rule, and I know it well, but I decline the riposte. Louis does not need my defense against his aspiring brothers. I've seen my own brothers playfully banter and jostle for position, like young ponies.

Just now a golden plank of pale sunlight appears at the bottom of the sky. I will allow nothing to mar the glory of the moment. With perfect composure, I reply, "When Apollo allowed an inexperienced driver to ferry the sun across the sky, he lost control of the steeds of state; the sun collided with the earth and a great fire followed. The earth was scorched and burnt."

Frankness settles the question.

Now the sky shows bands of rose and lavender, and the entire east begins to pinken. The radiance and majesty of it all! No one speaks, but I hear even the guardian of etiquette, Madame de Noailles, sigh in wistful appreciation of the quiet spectacle in the sky. A single stray cloud floats past, and its puffy edges are outlined in gleaming gold and silver.

"How wondrous it is!" I exclaim. "How truly beautiful!" I cannot stop myself from repeating those words over and over, while everyone else sits in reverent silence, their familiar faces flushed rosy in the light of God.

I take the princess's hand again, squeeze till I feel the bones within her soft flesh, and whisper, "At the last moment of my life, I shall remember this dawn."

THE DAYS THAT PASS after our witnessing of the rising of the sun have a new tranquillity about them. Less than a week has passed, and I am inspecting my gardens near Trianon when the King appears. He is in full court regalia, and I am surprised at what a discordant note this finery strikes beside the simple loveliness of flowers. The King asks me to walk with him to the Belvedere. As we walk along he thumps the satin leg of his breeches with a rolled-up pamphlet of some sort. I tell him of some of the flowers to be planted: narcissus, hyacinth, myrtle, laurel, and how the surrounding gardens will remind my guests of some of the paintings from mythology inside the Trianon of mortals being transformed into certain flowers. The King murmurs a bit to show that he is listening, but he is abstracted and troubled.

We stop at the edge of the water to look across its bright surface toward the grotto.

"People say those groups of statuary are the most beautiful ones at Versailles," the King says. He points at the figures of Titans bathing the horses of Apollo, after their day's work of pulling the chariot of the sun across the sky. "It's carved from a single block of Carrara marble," he remarks. Another statue depicts Apollo's repose among the sea nymphs of Neptune.

"I suppose," my husband continues, "that in some part of Greece, one can actually see the sun both rise from the waters in the east and sink into the sea on the west. I would like to see the wonder of that someday."

I recall my own lovely moment of watching the sun rise, but I say nothing. Suddenly I realize the King is trembling with anger.

"Look at this," he says, and he unrolls the pamphlet held in his fist.

Its title is "Le Lever d'Aurore." Something has been published about my watching the rising of the dawn. Suddenly I am cold with fear.

"It was a beautiful moment," I say.

"I am sure it was. Without the slightest impropriety."

"The Comtesse de Noailles was at my side every moment. It could not have been more decorous. Our brothers joked a bit. But the beauty of the dawn was an inspiring event, as Rousseau—"

"We are looking now at statuary," the King interrupted, "of transcendent beauty, of utmost purity and power—the noble horses, the lovely maidens. Yet how easy it would be for some rude villain to besmirch them with handfuls of mud." He fills his lungs with a huge breath, and I know he would breathe fire, if he could. "I promise that whoever wrote this pamphlet shall find that a cell in the Bastille awaits him. He has the effrontery to address you, yourself."

"What does he say I have done?"

"He describes a drunken orgy that lasted till the sun rose."

"I was surrounded with witnesses, my family, the court, bodyguards! How could anyone imagine any such thing even to be possible?"

"He claims that you escaped surveillance by crawling away into the bushes."

"I intend to greet this libel with complete indifference," I announce, and then I burst into tears.

The King gently positions my head on his royal chest. I feel I have placed my cheek against the flank of a volcano.

Finally, I lift my head and say with composure, "We will not speak of such calumny at Trianon. Because of the generosity of Your Majesty, this idyllic spot is mine to be transformed into paradise. I wish Trianon and its gardens to be the place where nothing can ever vex me or trouble my tranquillity. Look how brightly the sun shines! Here the flowers will always bloom, and these small trees will grow tall as cathedral spires and just as magnificent, for the future queens of France to enjoy." For a moment I think of the lovely pearls that Anne of Austria bequeathed to the queens of France, and I think with pride that my gift will bring with it just as much pleasure, or more.

"It will be your refuge," the King assures. "No one will come here except by your invitation." The Petit Trianon is just enough removed from the Château de Versailles to give it a good measure of privacy.

"And I will have a small theater built nearby, may I not? And when I and my family tire of the beauties of nature, we will go onstage, and pretend with one another, and inhabit a world of artifice."

THIS FANTASY of my own *petit théâtre* to be newly constructed within a very easy walk of a thoroughly renovated Petit Trianon buoys up my spirits when we return to court. Then one of my ladies confides to me that Prince Louis de Rohan has taken care to spread both near and far the news of the libelous pamphlet "Le Lever d'Aurore." Recalled to France, that noxious Rohan weed may prove more troublesome to me than he was in Vienna. I thoroughly hate him, though I cross myself and ask forgiveness for the sentiment. But that he would help to besmirch my sunrise party. It was not only an innocent but a genuinely spiritual event in my life!

A Visit by the Queen's Brother, Joseph II, Emperor of Austria

My brother comes incognito, known only as "Count Falkenstein." They say he travels in gray with none of his medals on his chest, and he rides in an open carriage, without fanfare or entourage. They say he intends to sleep in a humble inn on the skin of a wolf.

Because Count Mercy is in bed with hemorrhoids, I meet my brother almost alone and without the interference of protocol. When his carriage arrives, he is guided straight to me, up a private stair. Alone with my brother, I am taken into his strong arms and held close for the longest of embraces, which seems only a moment but surely partakes of the completeness of eternity. For a long time, we are silent in our embrace, for no words are adequate to express the profundity of our mutual emotion. Near the end of our moment, I begin to sense how lonely he is for embraces, since the loss for the second time of a wife.

Finally he steps back, still holding my hand, savoring my presence from top to toe, and tells me I am so pretty that were I not his sister, he would surely want to marry me.

We talk for two hours, and the Emperor is utterly responsive to all my lively chatter. He smiles and laughs with complete sympathy and wonderful familiarity. There is no ceremony between us. When I tell him my anxieties and struggles, his face becomes the mirror of my distress.

When I take my brother, the Emperor of Austria, to meet my husband, the King of France, for love of me, they embrace each other with perfect cordiality. I cannot help weeping with joy, for this is the fulfillment of my mother's dream and the reason for which I was sent here.

To my amazement, my husband speaks in a direct, confident way to my brother, as he would to a true friend. All shyness aside, my husband enjoys himself with my brother. Our days are spent in gay conviviality, and the Emperor meets my aunts and my friends as well.

BEFORE OUR VERY PRIVATE dinner at the Petit Trianon, Joseph delights in and admires each of the six rooms of Trianon, and he remarks on how the decorations complement the views in all directions from the large windows, and how the house, with all its elegance, is really a celebration of all that is beautiful in nature. His favorite room is the large reception room, and he exclaims with joy on seeing my harp there, standing at the ready, and a pianoforte. Lifting my hand to feel my fingertips, he says fondly, "I can feel your calluses, which means that you have kept up your practice."

"Our Gluck made a similar observation. My music always transports me to Vienna," I continue, "and the happy times we had there when we practiced all the arts as children." Of course my brother was already a man when I was a child, but I can see that my words evoke happy scenes in his memory of when he was younger.

While we stand on the rosy carpet woven with plumy golden arabesques, I feel almost that it is a magic carpet. Perhaps it will rise and take us to tour the world, if we can but engage the charm! My brother asks me to explain the metamorphosis in each of the paintings above the doors, so I point and speak of Narcissus changing into a flower that now bears his name, and Adonis changing into an Anemone, and Clytia becoming a sunflower, and then Hyacinthus.

When we retire to the dining room, he admires the four paintings of the seasons, especially the scenes of fishing and of the wheat harvest, and the painting over the door of Flora.

"Often I identify with her," I remark.

"Because of your love of flowers," he replies. His smile is so like sunshine, that I wish I, too, could turn into a flower and bask and grow under the influence of his radiance. In the presence of my beloved brother, I feel taken care of and understood.

"I, like Flora, was taken from my mother's world into another, stranger realm."

"But the King is far from being Hades," my brother answers with a smile. What honest eyes he has!

"Indeed," I reply, and then say frankly, "Certainly, as you know, he does not ravish me."

"In this case, restraint is far from kindness. I am here to help you both on that score."

He has written to me that when he travels he always eats the cuisine of the place—that this habit helps him to better understand the constitution of the people among whom he moves. Now he relishes the hearty French stews, replete with six meats simmered in mushrooms and truffles, the roasted ducks, the fatted goose pâté, but I am too excited to do any more than sip a thin consommé of chicken stock and carrots. As he eats, we speak of our family, especially our dear mother, for whom he has sacrificed so much.

When I take him for a garden walk after dining, he lectures me.

He dislikes my rouge and tells me I could easily look just like a Fury if I put the color under my eyes and nose, as well as on my cheeks. With the rather roughened tip of his finger, he traces the space between my mouth and nose to show me just where I could add more rouge. He stops to thrust his nose against a rose, then tells me that my friends are unsuitable, that they are frivolous and know nothing. He tells me I must treat the King with more tenderness and warmth, that in his presence I appear to be not merely indifferent but cold, bored, and even repelled. He snaps off the head of an orange marigold beside the garden path and presents it to me. My brother loathes my gambling and the expense of my jewelry and gowns. Trailing my hand behind my back, I secretly drop the marigold into the pebbles. Throughout the Emperor's scolding, I adore him and bask in his familial affection.

I agree with him at almost every turn and promise to reform on all counts. I turn the conversation to the menagerie at home, and he speaks fondly of the visit of Clara, the rhinoceros, but he has no memory of Hilda the hippopotamus and tells me sternly that I must have imagined her. He speaks with admiration of the elephants we keep at Versailles, male and female, and suggests they be brought together in marriage.

He promises again to have a frank talk with my husband.

OVER THE COURSE of his visit, my brother informs me that the King is not without ideas, that he is an honest man, but weak and indecisive. He tells me that my intentions and instincts are good, that he is most pleased to find me to be both a decent and virtuous person, but I must trust my own heart—he sounds a bit like Rousseau—and not be a slave to the habits and conventions of others based on their own selfishness. All of this he writes down so that I may read his words over and over, after he is gone back to Austria, and I readily promise to do so, and really I do think that I can do more to make the King happy, and I feel more warmth toward him.

My brother chastens me because he loves me and cares about the welfare of France.

Only when Joseph criticizes my Yolande do I refuse to acquiesce. Standing beside my chair, he says she lacks substance and is of easy virtue. When I speak of her adorable children, Armand and Aglaië, he waves their existence aside and criticizes me for expenditures that have gone toward the comfort of her family. He does not know that I paid all of my favorite friend's debts—some 400,000 livres—or provided her daughter's dowry of 800,000 livres, but he has heard of many other expenditures, the commission for her son-in-law plus an income, a pension for her father, the appointment of Yolande's permissive husband as postmaster-general, which everyone knows to be one of the most lucrative appointments in France. As my brother walks to the window, he rages that the Polignac family is costing

France a million livres a year, and he quotes Count Mercy that my largesse to my friends is almost unparalleled: "Never before, in so brief a period of time, has royal favor ever brought such enormous financial benefits to a single family!"

Far from arousing shame, the idea causes me to smile a bit, that I have used so much power for the happiness of my friend. My brother catches the upturn of the corners of my mouth and rages on. "You may call your favorite friend an angel, but those downcast, modest eyelids conceal her shrewdness. Not Madame de Maintenon, not even the Pompadour have been such a drain on the royal treasury!" This idea is delivered as we stand in the Hall of Mirrors at Versailles, and for a moment, he is distracted with the grand and sweeping view out the window. I believe that he is admiring the sheer size of the Grand Canal and the little boats that sit so picturesquely on its waters.

"And the morals of this court!" he goes on, pointing out that when a certain duc was so careless as to come home at the wrong time and find his wife in bed with another, he apologized profusely to his wife for his inopportune arrival.

"Your friends are as bad as any. Especially the salon of Madame de Guéméné, which is nothing but a dive—"

Here I interrupt and remind him of the perfect virtue of the Princesse de Lamballe, the mistress of my household and a very close friend indeed. Now I have played a trump card, for no one ever impugns her. My brother quickly dismisses her as a "pedigreed fool," and the truth is I cannot defend her mind. But she really has no *need* to make decisions of any moment about what she does or where she goes. One setting is as good as another to her. Even I feel superior to her in that regard.

What makes the criticisms of the Emperor tolerable is that I know without doubt that he speaks only out of love, that he wishes me to do my duty. And I appreciate that he has behaved like a good family member to my husband, who has told me that my brother has been comfortable, honest, and helpful in all their conversations.

My brother tells me that our mother the Empress warned him, before he left Austria, that he might find me so pretty and charming, so capable of conversing with lively wit and endearing manners, that he would find himself captivated by my flattery, and that, he admits, *is* exactly what has happened. "How often," he says, "I have found myself surprised not only by your quick wit but also by the depth of your insights. To me, my sister is the most charming of all the women in the world."

Letter of Joseph II, Emperor of Austria, to His Brother Leopold Concerning the Conjugal Relations of the King and Queen of France

In the marriage bed, the King has normal erections; he introduces his organ, stays inside without moving for about two minutes, then withdraws without ejaculating, believing that he has protected HIS HEALTH by avoiding orgasmic ejaculation. Still strongly erect, he bids the Queen good night. Yet the idiot confesses to me that he sometimes has night emissions in his sleep, but while inside and in the process of attempting to produce an heir—NEVER. He is happy with this style. He tells me frankly that he only performs at all out of a sense of duty and that he does not like the act. Oh, if I could only have been in their bedroom, I would have taken care of him! I would have ordered him whipped until he discharged his sperm like an infuriated donkey.

Unfortunately, I also have it from him that our sister is as ignorant and innocent as a child lying in bed beside her immature brother. Between the two of them, they are complete incompetents. Fumblers!

The Aftermath of the Visit

Because my brother has gone home to Austria ("home"—have I really allowed myself to even think that word about any country other than France?), I read over the notes he has left me:

> *Are you not bored or absentminded when he touches or talks to you? If so, is it not inconsiderate of you to expect a man who has no experience with carnal pleasures to be able to feel intimacy, to be aroused, and to bring his love to a successful climax? You must focus your attention on creating a physical link between you, for that is the strongest link you can forge to happiness in your life. You must never allow yourself to feel discouraged, and you must always give him hope that he will be the sire of children. Never give up. Never despair. Your only power is your charm and friendship.*

He has reminded me that our mother wants me to improve my mind, to spend two hours a day with serious books. My most serious flaw, my brother says, is not my gambling or my love of entertainment or of parties, but the fact that I do not love to read. Reading, he claims, would broaden my experience of the world. The ideas to be found in serious books would deepen my thinking about every choice I make. I do not see how reading would draw my husband to feel more passion within our marriage.

On the table beside my chair is one of the novels the Emperor has condemned for its licentiousness. But those novels that describe the pleasure of love do *help me* to long for better success in the marriage bed, to display more warmth and charm toward my husband.

All my life my mother and my older brothers and sisters, except Maria Carolina, have confused me with their directives! They tell me to follow my heart, but when I start down that path, they insist that I turn my feet in another direction!

I hear myself sigh. I pick up the novel on the round table; my hand is hungry for the feel of its soft leather binding, for the theater it builds in my mind. Though I miss my brother and wish he were still here, despite confusion and a certain impatience, I will try to follow his advice. I lay the bright red book on the table. I will try to create a real life of love instead of experiencing it vicariously through the pages of a novel. It is necessary for me to change, and I will try again to do so.

The Emperor left me with very serious words:

> *I tremble not only for your happiness, but for your safety. I have seen enough in this country to know that the finances and welfare of the state are in a desperate condition. Your marriage and the lack of an heir is also a desperate matter. In the long run, perhaps much sooner than anyone apprehends, it will be impossible for France to continue as it has. The revolution will be cruel, and I am sorry to say that it will be of your own making.*

A Bath, 18 August 1777

Sometimes the water in the bath is of such a compatible temperature that it is bliss to submerge my body in the fragrant liquid. I wonder if, before the Fall, the waters of Eden were just as these, and that of all Eve's pleasures, walking among the open flowers and fondling the rounded fruits of the garden, perhaps Eve preferred bathing. My attendants always test the water, so that it is neither very much too hot or very much too cool, but they cannot regulate the water to a temperature that is consistently perfect because they do not take into account the temperature of my skin. This morning the water feels like warmed silk.

Lifting up the hem of my gauze bathing dress, I point my toes down as my foot enters my bath. The water-smoothness creeps over my arch and encloses my ankle like the finest stocking and then up my leg almost to the knee. Then the other foot follows, and I stand in a medium that is slightly warmer than myself. My calves feel gladly surrounded. The temperature is so close to the heat of my own body that the flesh does not in the slightest flinch back. The warmth of summer air gives way to the more congenial warmth of water. As I lower myself entirely into this universe of comfort, the aroma of attar of rose with tincture of orange is released. When I am seated in my bath, I cannot resist raking my fingers forward in the water to further liberate the fragrance.

I submerge the globular sea sponge until its cells and fissures are filled with warmth, and then my attendant squeezes water from the sponge over my back, and next she rubs my shoulders and spine with a circular stroke that stimulates the circulation and makes me want yet another pass of the warm wet sponge, and another. My flesh develops an appetite for the motion of the sponge, and then I take it from my attendant and stroke my bare neck and then my breasts, myself.

With a hand cloth of silk, my attendant follows the trail of the sponge to smooth away any roughness. By scooting my buttocks forward in the tub, I submerge myself up to my neck. The thin fabric of my bathing dress floats around me like a gossamer lily pad. Now my knees break the water before me and rise up like round-top twin mountains. My breasts are buoyed up, and my entire body wants to float. Feeling like a fish at play—or a mermaid—I twirl myself in the warmth so that my breasts hang down into the water and twirl around again. My bathing dress twists around my body. If only I had a lovely emerald green tail to splash!—though I make quite a nice splash in my rotation.

I see my attendants are smiling at my play, but their smiles are ones of understanding. They too would like to cavort in water of perfect temperature, smoothness, and scent.

"Some moonlit night," I say, "we should join the statues bathing the horses of Apollo. We could stand in the waterfall and imagine—"

"The King is passing," my attendant suddenly whispers. "He is walking back and forth, just outside the door." For just a moment, I imagine she refers to the old King, Louis XV, whose luminous eye always took on a new luster when he beheld unexpected feminine beauty, even when I was fifteen and quite flat.

"Let him come in," I reply.

Skillfully, she opens the door as he passes, and with the same gesture my attendants slip silently away.

The King stands in the open door and looks at me; my hair pinned atop my head hangs half-loosened in wet ringlets. Placing my hands on the sides of the tub, I suddenly rise, my muslin gown quite transparent and clinging to my body. The water rushes off me, as though I am a living fountain.

"Would you be so kind as to help me," I say, and I hold out my hand.

Gallantly, my husband holds out his hand to steady me as I step over the high edge of the bath. The water from my gown and body streams onto the floor.

"Who was the consort of Neptune?" he asks. "You resembled her, lounging against the high back of the tub as though it were a watery throne."

"Toinette, my Lord," I answer and slowly lower my eyes to half-mast, as I have seen the du Barry do a hundred times. "A towel, please, Your Majesty?"

"First, let me help you with your wet garb," he answers.

Tenderly he pushes the loose wet sleeve over my shoulder, on one side and then the other. I raise my shoulders from the slumping bodice so that my bare breasts emerge. Slowly, I sit down on the edge of the tub behind me, the wet muslin falling over my lap. The King kneels, with no regard for the puddles on the floor, and takes my pink nipple into his mouth. Here is real bliss, beyond the lapping warmth of water. My bosom heaves, my head tilts back, and I know that I am panting.

Finally I say—I can hardly speak—"My other breast is dying of jealousy."

Glancing up, he smiles happily, and encloses the tender pinkness of my other nipple.

Soon he rises, and holding his hand, I too rise. With a gentle hand, my husband shoves the sodden gown down my thighs to wreath my feet. When I step on the fabric, I feel water squish between my toes. Wearing nothing more than the blue ribbon tying up my hair, I follow him as he hands me a towel and leads me to our bed.

My Dear Mother

Every fiber of my being thrills with happiness. Complete *happiness. It has been more than a week ago that my marriage was completely consummated. I do not think I am pregnant yet but now I have hope based on the fact that I may be.*

To Honor the King, the Opening of the New Gardens at Trianon

I am giving a night fete, and I am sending word to everyone to collect objects to be sold. For this fete, we will contrive a fair throughout the grounds surrounding my little pleasure house! Yes, a fair such as country people might hold at the end of summer when the harvest is starting to come in. But we will have shops wherein we sell not butter and eggs and cheese, but precious objects—bracelets and feathers of exotic birds, ribbons and jeweled buckles, vases and brooches. Everyone must sell something that she knows others have much admired, and the proceeds will be given for charitable needs. Yes, a country fair! But with all the elegance and finery of the court on display. The ladies of the court themselves shall tend the shops, and I shall dress as the proprietress of a café.

My friends can serve such pastries that the King always relishes, and for once I shall allow him to buy and feast on all the dainties that he wishes. Perhaps I shall even charge him for a kiss, which I believe he will now bestow with hearty goodwill and not a touch of embarrassment!

By planning this open-air fair, a late summer night's fete, we will let the people know that we wish them to share in our joy, that we do not selfishly contain our happiness in cloistered chambers hung with velvet but that we bring it outdoors, under the night sky illumined with torches, for all to enjoy. We make the night into day.

I myself, dressed like a peasant girl, will pour from my pitcher into the flagons of all my friends the bounty of the earth—spiced cider will be the wholesome brew, stirred with sticks of rarest cinnamon, and at the top of each whorled stick I shall have affixed a pearl of some size and value, as a memento of when the King and Queen rejoiced in their marriage, and the Queen thanked the King for his great gift to her not only of the small palace of Trianon but also for the gardens, recast, as they bloomed with abandon and profusion.

And music! Yes, the French Guard shall supply its musicians, who will twiddle and toot and blow and bow, and drum and tee-dum till ears overflow—and nostrils are full of fragrance of flowers, and eyes fill till they blear with beauty as offered by nature and artifice, and hearts burgeon with happiness.

The King's seed is within me. Soon I may be pregnant.

Madame, My Dear Daughter

The gazettes and other sources tell me that your mania for gambling is worse than ever, and worst of all you stay up very late, when the King likes to go to bed early. Your brother has said all that needs to be said on the subject of gambling, and I say no more. You are losing money that the King and you could put to much better use, and you should forbid gambling at court. Everyone knows you are losing vast sums and that your finances are exhausted, and that you spend all your time whispering into the greedy ear of the Comtesse de Polignac, who encourages you in all your dissipations and causes you to ignore everyone else at court. You must not isolate yourself from the nobility. Your brother is greatly worried about the state of France, and the day may come when you will need all the loyalty of the nobility and the loyalties that they command on their own estates to surround you and protect you.

Your brother is even more savage *about the future of France.*

The news of your completion in your marriage has filled me with joy, but I am very sorry to learn that the King does not like to sleep with you throughout the night—not of course just for the matter of having children, but because sleeping in the same bed promotes unity and trust, which is also of spiritual importance. Write to me every month about your period. I fear that often my young Queen forgets to account for this most important matter. I do not forbid you at this point to ride horses as long as you are not astride, but do not get overheated. The jolts of a carriage can be worse than riding.

I do indeed gently kiss my dear little woman whom I love, and whose essential goodness I never doubt.

Madame, My Most Dear Mother

Though it is well into October now and we have been at Fontainebleau for eight days, I often feel overheated and take many baths to cool myself. The King has had a bad cold since we arrived, but his health does not keep him from hunting every day. I do understand the importance of our spending the entire night together, but it takes time to change his habits. I am quite willing to sacrifice my entertainments in order to keep him company. I know better now about how to spend my time which is filled with reading and needlework.

I truly love my embroidery, as it puts me in a kind of trance. I am not transported into another world as I am at the theater or even when I read an engaging book, but I enter a deep, still place within myself as I create flowers in thread. I feel calm and happy, which is a good balance for the thrill of the gaming table, though I gamble much less now and only in my own apartment; instead, I often play billiards.

More important, I have started drawing again, and knowing how you have always treasured the artwork of Marie Christine, I hope that I may one day draw a scene worthy of sending to you. Even here at Fontainebleau, I am visited by two music masters, one in voice and one in harp, and my harp teacher tells me that I can sight-read music for the harp in a way worthy of a professional musician. I like to play music that is expressive of my mood, and, indeed, it amazes me how perfectly music embodies even the most intimate feelings of longing or of happiness.

These are my dissipations—my diversions—and the French term dissipation *properly cannot be construed in a moral sense, as the English construe it, should you have read in pamphlets about* dissipations *at court in which I would never dream of engaging. These pamphlets are not even the half-truths of gossip. They are vile fabrications.*

I hardly ever ride anymore because people think it stops one from having children, but I am sure that it does not hurt. Nonetheless, I am now cautious about anything that can be misconstrued as insensitivity on my part to the future happiness of this country. I cannot tell you how much it hurts me that enemies have tried to destroy the love that the French people showered on me so abundantly when I first came to France. I do not jar myself with riding during my period—not even in a well-sprung carriage.

Happily, my brother Ferdinand writes that he is well and that Joseph has kept him current on matters here and has given him an excellent report of me.

My Dear Daughter

Vienna, 5 November 1777

Your letter of last month delighted me because it was full of important details. Be assured that I am never bored by the smallest detail because I care so much for your good health and good reputation. I am especially happy to hear about your music, your needlework, and above all your reading. Gambling is a terrible pleasure because it causes other bad behavior, and you cannot win, ultimately, at Pharaon, though the game bewitches you to continue to play and increases your desire to win, but honest players never win in the long run. If you add up the sums that you wager and lose, or that anyone does, you will find the mathematical truth of the matter.

You are losing much of your popularity too, especially abroad, because people believe that you indulge yourself in reckless gambling while the country suffers for basic needs. I know that when you are at the gaming table you think of nothing else but winning, and you allow yourself to become overly excited and egged on by the almost bodily thrill that occurs when you either win or lose because gambling cultivates both immoderate joy and desperate desire and mingles and confuses these sensations. Away from the table, your mind is occupied about other matters, and so it is my duty, as one who dearly loves you, to ask you to rein in this habit, and if you do not do so, your mother will have to ask the King himself to save you from this great danger.

It gladdens my heart that you ask for the painting of you dancing onstage with your brothers when you were a little innocent girl here, and I will send it to you to hang at the Petit Trianon, but first you must send me a portrait of yourself as you now appear, for which I have been waiting some eight years. As a mother, I long to see your face again.

I am sorry that gossip says you do not maintain even the appearance of friendship with the Princesse de Lamballe but bestow all your favor on the Comtesse de Polignac, and that you even treat the Princesse de Lamballe in a way such that people can easily see—and that you want them to see—you are annoyed and bored by the company of someone known for her virtue.

You must realize that the Polignac aligns herself with the Duc de Chartres and the Orléans family—who would like to be the rulers of France themselves. The princess is of Choiseul's party, which is made up of people who favor the Alliance between our countries.

My Very Dear Mother

I was beginning to have diarrhea, along with a cold, so I danced very little at the December balls, which are just beginning. I went to the ball but did not dance, which I'm sure my very dear Mother will be glad to hear.

With horror, I reread what I have written to the Empress. I am ashamed. Never before have I allowed such a tone of impertinence and irony in my letters to her, no matter how I chafed under her criticism or control. I do not give this nasty little note to the courier.

The Générale Is Tardy! April 1778

Who can I tell?

The Princesse de Lamballe would keep my secret; the Comtesse de Polignac would not. And somehow those two facts make it impossible to confide in either.

In the old days, I would have run to the chambers of my aunts; I would have sat among the three of them while they petted and flattered me as though I were their prettiest lapdog; I would have sipped a cup of hot chocolate, and over its gilded rim, my lips would have formed the words, with no fanfare: "I believe I may be pregnant." Then their happy trio of exclamations! Their discreet questions bursting at the seams with eager excitement to know all there was to be known. But I am no longer their pet. When I am not with them, I never think of them.

This morning Rose Bertin, down on her knees, was measuring me around my hips. Suddenly she stopped, leaned closer to examine just which line marked the end of her measure. Then, with her thumb, she ran around the inside of the measuring tape to be sure it had not folded over or deviated in its path as it encircled my form. No, the tape made its usual smooth circuit. Just once she glanced up into my eyes. Was that a *sad* question I saw in her gaze? I said nothing.

"Perhaps the mere breadth of a line bigger this week," Rose said quietly.

I said nothing, but I felt my posture grow more erect, and I lifted my chin. No doubt I looked a haughty queen—as those who do not know me have accused me of appearing to be—but I knew I lifted my head and stretched tall my body to better fit into my destiny. I am a Hapsburg fulfilling the role prepared for me as the mother of the Children of France. Perhaps.

I must not tell my own mother till I am sure. *Have you seen the Générale Krottendorf?* I might ask her, whimsically. *She has not made her usual visit to Versailles this month.* How the heart of the Empress would gallop at that question! But I will not cause her pulse to race for nothing. Too many times, I have expressed hope and had it come to naught.

No more riding, she would say to me now. *No, indeed*, I would reply.

But I have the urge to walk the grounds, to parade myself past the long line of statues and to encircle the fountains. I will take Elisabeth with me, my little sister whose devoted sweetness is as great as that of the Princesse de Lamballe, but who has much more sense, despite her youth. The formal paths of Le Nôtre's old gardens are magnificent at least for their vast size, for what they lack in intimacy and unbounded joy. With Elisabeth, I am with family. Who better, at this moment, to walk beside me? Perhaps I carry the beginnings of a child within me who will someday behold these same rows of severely pruned trees and the careful edges that form the parterres which are as well-defined as scroll-figured carpets.

Elisabeth knows her role in this world the way a foot knows a well-constructed shoe. The steps of her quadrille are always the proper ones to fulfill the duties of her royal birth. She has found the trick of filling her shoes with her own true self, and she is content to do so. Now she is quiet because she knows that my thoughts are busy. She does not chatter but waits for when it is my pleasure to engage her in conversation. Glancing about, she gladly entertains herself with the distant view or with a nearby flower.

Like my little sister Elisabeth, the Comtesse de Polignac also embodies her own natural self, but she is direct—unassuming?—rather than sweet. Blessed with good nature, my friend has almost black hair, and when she is close, I am always aware of the darkness of her hair, and how the light touches it so that sometimes it gleams purple as aubergine or iridescent like a raven's wing.

Like that bird, my Yolande has an attraction to shiny objects—and to her own advantage, yet she is so casual about it all—the incomes, the positions for her family—that I never think of her as in any way domineering. Unlike my mother, she never gives me a moment's stress when she makes it known that this or that appointment would please her. Still there is much transfer from my purse to that of the family de Polignac. But Yolande accepts my faults, and that is what puts me so much at ease with her, along with her warmth, and so it is only right that I accept her also as she is, and her needs. Proudly, I do lift my head—that I am Queen, and my greatest pleasure is to serve my friends.

I smile at Elisabeth and give her the pleasure of choosing the direction for our stroll. I step carefully on the little pea gravel underfoot, lest my foot should slide and I should fall. Protectively, I find that I have placed a fond hand on my belly just below my waist. Yes, I will shelter the little being who lives there, the fruit of my womb, the King's first child, for whose sake my body has become a house.

Elisabeth has seen my gesture, perhaps. In any case, she slips her slender arm around my waist and draws me close. She is still immature, and I can feel the difference in our bodies, how mine is softer and more womanly, as is Yolande's, who has already become a mother. I wish my mother could see me in my maturity. Yes, there will be a new portrait. The Empress so far away, in another country whose particulars of gardens and statues are now rather dim in memory compared with these marble figures on their pedestals—we pass the flute player, my favorite, with his furry loins and stony curls. In Vienna, probably at the labyrinthine Hofburg (for the weather is not yet warm enough to move out to fair Schönbrunn), the Empress sits in her widow's weeds. Dressed all in black, quite stout now, she works at her desk, quickly reading with her beady eyes the papers of the state. Absorbed in business, she does not think of me. It is she instead of Yolande who resembles a large black bird, clasping a wintry twig with yellow feet.

Here it is spring, and I have a bud within me. I am sure of it.

Elisabeth is often my walking companion now, for mild exercise is good for her in her youth as for me with my expectations. As we stroll, I ask her if she noted when the dancing stopped at my *bal à la Reine*, how the elegant men raised their fists in the air and shouted with joy, just as though an announcement of war did not mean mud and hardship, sweat, terrible fatigue, danger, blood, and suffering. "And how the ladies fluttered their fans in approving excitement?" I add.

"I shuddered," the gentle soul replies, "when I heard of alliance with the Americans."

"When the Comte de Provence made the announcement, straight from the King's Council, did you notice how his square face was filled to its corners with smug satisfaction?"

(While I was gently dancing, swaying my secret within the cradle of my body, in another room, my husband had been choosing death and war.)

"The King explained to me long ago that the weakening of the English is the object in allying ourselves with their colonies." (Perhaps it is because I may carry the future within me that I wish for an earth safe for all who dwell thereon.) "I have never found glory in humiliating others—English or not," I mention to the princess.

She does not reply but points to a flock of song sparrows rising in a single dusty cloud from the pea gravel.

"Perhaps with the exception of the du Barry," I amend, honestly.

In a comforting squeeze, Princesse Elisabeth tightens her arm around my waist. "Do you recall," she chirps in her sweet voice, "when you told the offending chevalier, 'The Queen does not remember the quarrels of the Dauphine?' It was then that I knew you would make the best of queens."

"I promised myself to rise above my revengeful impulses."

Our legs move in tandem as we walk, the princess and I, over the expansive grounds of Versailles. Our skirts bob forward at the same moment, orbs of pale blue and pale green, for within the silk our legs stretch forward at the same moment. Now I really do triumph over the du Barry. If I am pregnant, my power over King and kingdom increases.

Days pass. Slowly, one by one. The Générale has lost her way. Yes, I know my brother Joseph has invaded Bavaria without even consulting my mother. Yes, I know that she begs me to intervene in matters of state, to entreat my husband to support the Austrian aggression. But Louis XVI is not one to be persuaded by his wife; nor can the mother of a future king of France advocate any step that might endanger our kingdom years from now.

Elisabeth Vigée-Lebrun

In my bath, glancing down, I move the wet muslin aside to see if my nipples are more pink. I smile. Yes, they are more pink, for I have an eye that can remember an exact shade of any color. After asking for a glass, I consider my reflected face: my cheeks have taken on, quite naturally, something of the same pink as my nipples. The frame of the looking glass inscribes my countenance with a well-wrought wreath of silver flowers, repoussé. How well art improves nature! The oval embrace of a frame focuses my eye, the eye of any viewer, to look for other ovals—the rounding of the chin, the curve of the cheek—and brings all into harmony. Perhaps it is time to have my portrait painted, time to meet the young woman artist who is just my age, recommended so often to me by the Comte de Vaudreuil, the special friend of my Yolande.

Perhaps in years to come, I will look at this new portrait and think: *At that time you yet contained your secret. But see the hope in your eye, the color in your cheek? Then your body knew, though your mind did not, that you carried a new life within, a precious secret.*

When I see Madame Lebrun, I see a sprite with dark hair, loose curls about her shoulders, much like those of Yolande. This girl does not enter my apartment with the easy confidence of Yolande. This is a person who makes her way not by her birth but by her talent. She is unsure of her welcome. Seeing that she holds her curtsy, waiting for a word, I speak quickly, with much lightness.

"I feel we are friends already, Madame Lebrun, for I see we both love nature. We are of an age, and you are the friend of very dear friends, who speak both fondly and admiringly of you and of your gift for painting."

She rises gracefully, blushes, gives a quick downward glance, then raises her eyes again, this time with a gaze that is inquiring, one that looks through the appraising lenses of an artist.

"How do I look?" I ask her gaily.

"As any queen would die to look." Her voice has more confidence in it than I would expect. "As any woman would hope to appear—full of life and goodness."

"I think you cannot paint such abstract qualities." I smile at her.

"Indeed, if you will forgive my saying so, I believe I can." When she smiles back at me, I see small dints of dimples at the corners of her very pretty mouth. Her eyes rove my face and body in such a way that it is a pleasure to be so regarded, for she takes pleasure in seeing me. She is not afraid; only a little nervous.

"Can you guess my favorite colors?" I ask, seating myself. Now I look up at her, as she yet stands, and each of us has a different angle from which to regard the other. Because I am sitting now, a warm light floods my countenance, a reflection from the rosy silk that covers my lap.

"I believe that Your Majesty might have some inclination herself for brush and canvas?"

"All of my sisters, and I, were given lessons in all the arts. I do enjoy drawing and painting, but my best grace lies not in my hand but in my feet."

"The grace of Your Majesty's carriage as well as the beauty of your dancing is known throughout France."

I stand again, gesture, and turn my head, as though I were addressing an unseen audience. "I have two ways of walking," I explain. "One is to express my happiness when I am within the circle of my friends and family;

the other is used to express dignity, among the courtiers or foreign visitors, but it is devoid of haughtiness. At least I intend it to have nothing of stiffness about it. Shall I show you?"

"I should not aspire to witness such a demonstration."

Quite modestly, she lowers her eyes, and when she does, I feel deprived. I would much prefer to regard their warm, clear depth.

"I think we are opposites," I say cheerfully. "My hair is fair, my eyes a grayish blue. Your lovely hair is chestnut, your eyes a deeper brown." She raises her eyes to me again. "You make your way by your talent alone, while I was born to a life at court. I think us equally fortunate."

"Your Majesty makes too much of me."

With that phrase, I suddenly recall my last moments on Austrian soil, the last moments with my ladies, colorful as butterflies, while we stood on an island in the midst of the Rhine, the sound of its powerful waters rushing around the walls. As they fluttered around me in a whirl of love, I modestly said to them *You make too much of me*. I recall the tapestries on the walls there, depictions of feasts and celebrations, woven red apples cradled in a blue bowl. Later someone told me the tapestries were the pride of Strasbourg, lent just to honor me, and that they depicted the marriage of Medea, from ancient Grecian times.

"Do you know the story of Medea?" I suddenly ask the painter.

"I do, for someday I aspire to paint the subjects of mythology, or those of history."

"I was just recalling something of my own history. Your phrase 'you make too much of me' is striking in its grace. And it is one I once used, when I was little more than a child whose greatest desire was to please, to be loved. I was leaving Austria to come to Versailles, to be married."

I am struck by my frankness in naming Austria to this child. Not a child, but a young woman my own age, but because she is more slender, less made up with rouge and powdered hair, she seems younger than I.

"Usually," I confide in her, "I do not mention my native country by name. The French do not like to recall my origins."

"Your Majesty must say what she pleases to me." She speaks with charming seriousness. "As an artist, I hope that I may rise above the common prejudices, that I see with my own eyes and hear with my own ears, tuned just so, to suit myself." She pauses, meets my gaze in the most warm and confiding way. "And in saying *that*, I too am being more frank than I would usually dare to be. But I believe an artist had best be international in tastes. Otherwise, she misses too much that may nourish her spirit."

I hold out my hand to her. "Then we are comrades," I say. "And you must walk beside me as I demonstrate locomotion *à la Reine.*"

Together we promenade about the room, and I point out the portraits of my mother to her and of my brother Joseph II. When she asks if she might view the full-length portrait of Louis XIV, I escort her through the grand rooms till we reach its position in the Apollo drawing room.

I remember how it was when Papa-Roi escorted me through these chambers and pointed out the mythological paintings of Mars, Diana, and Venus on the ceilings, but now I am in charge. I recall how dominated even Louis XV felt, nearly a decade past, by the representations of Louis XIV. I mention to her that I have always much admired the Bernini marble bust of Louis XIV as a young man, but she is more interested in the full-length painting of him, displaying his elegant leg, a preference quite understandable, since she herself works in oils.

In a whisper, I comment that Louis XIV's face now looks to me—he was over sixty—rather hard and cruel. I feel almost as though my sister Charlotte were with me—so free, indeed so unguarded, is our exchange of ideas and tastes. Charlotte, being three years older than I, always took *me* by the hand and led me hither and yon, but now I am the superior one, and perhaps I am pregnant. I giggle at my thoughts of dominance and bliss.

She glances at me first with a question in her brown eyes—she had not anticipated such a frivolous attitude—then with relish. Suddenly I flush, embarrassed, for the hand I hold is not that of a child, but one of an accomplished artist, for all her youth and beauty. Everyone says so, and the courtiers even attend her parties, held in cramped, bourgeois quarters. She displays no signs of pride; and why should she? Her gifts, like mine, came with her at her birth. Still, she has worked hard cultivating her talent and her graces. Truly, she has *earned* the admiration of all who know her. Yes, Elisabeth Vigée-Lebrun shall paint my portrait.

The Bavarian Question

It does seem to me that Bavaria, left with no heir, due to the untimely death of the elector of Bavaria, should more naturally become part of Austria than an appendage of Prussia and Frederick II. If only my husband shared my brother's suspicion of the bellicose King of Prussia, but Louis and Joseph are truly at odds on this matter. I could both please and impress the Empress if I could persuade my husband to consider as an aspect of the Bavarian question the importance of the Alliance between Austria and France, of which our marriage is the sacred seal. In the past my heart has always been in Austria, but perhaps the interests of France are growing now within my body.

As often happens in moments of confusion, Count Mercy appears and is admitted at the door of my apartment just as I am about to open a letter from my mother. His attendants must have seen her courier descending the stairs.

He bows to me, and again I admire his bearing, as I always do. Though I practice the feminine version of the bow, it is from him and not my dancing master that I have learned to convey so much in a gesture. His bow tells me that he is my friend, that he is wise, and that he will help me to understand the tangled skeins of loyalties.

"The Queen's brow is clouded," he remarks, with kindness in every syllable.

"I have a letter from Vienna—"

"I saw the courier in the courtyard."

"Will you read it to me?"

I hand the letter to my trusted friend to interpret for me.

He reads, "'Mercy's illness comes at a very bad time when I need him to be active'" (he does not glance up but keeps his eyes steadfastly on my mother's handwriting), "'just as I need your own feelings of loyalty to me, to the House of Hapsburg, and to your native country of Austria. You must take to heart and you must tell the King that the King of Prussia is unscrupulous, and if an alliance with France should be formed with Prussia, we will be in great danger. Prussia fears only you—'"

"Let me read for myself," I interject. My heart swells with pride that my mother acknowledges our importance. I read on to myself, silently: *The alliance between France and Austria is the only natural one, and though I cannot here go into all the details, you must turn to Count Mercy as soon as he is able to see you. He will make clear to you not only the usefulness of the alliance to both our countries but also its goodness. I oppose any change in our Alliance, which would kill me—*

On apprehending those words, I exclaim aloud, and I can feel all the blood draining from my face.

"The Queen has turned very pale," Mercy says.

"Read what she has written." I give the page to my counselor.

". . .'Any change in our Alliance, which would kill me.'" His elegant fingers tremble as he holds the page. The Count hesitates and looks directly at me, his face full of concern. Thoughtfully, he says, "The Empress has underlined those last words."

Because I feel dizzy, as though I might slide off my chair, I grasp the edge of the little table in front of me. Though my vision seems to spin the elegant chairs around the walls of the room, I see my choice. Very deliberately I address the count. "At your approach, I anticipated consultation with you to aid me in my confusion. After this moment, I myself *know* what path to pursue with the King. From you, I will need only the particulars for a reasoned argument. The spirit and direction that my remarks must take is abundantly clear to me. I will use all my power and influence with the King to assure the Alliance with Austria."

"Even in her obvious distress, no one speaks more clearly from the heart than does my Queen," the count replies. His own clear eyes flash their approval of my words. He looks down at my mother's page again and summarizes her words in a quiet tone. His hand and voice are steady. "She says that many of her people are sick and that she kisses 'my dear daughter.' She says that soon she hopes she will be able to add the phrase 'my dear little mama' to the phrase when she sends her love to you, her most dear daughter. In closing, she says that everyone she knows is praying for you and that you may be pregnant. 'I am always all yours.'"

My heart brims with love of my mother, and with guilt that I have not yet told her of my hopes. Even while she worries about the politics of Europe, nothing causes her to forget my situation. She says nothing of my sisters and brothers: *I am always all yours.* Those are her final words.

Now I will focus all my attention on Count Mercy as he explains to me what will be the best arguments to protect the King from the seductions of Prussia. I invite my friend to sit down. With a simple gesture, he parts the skirts of his coat, seats himself, rests his tapered hands on his thighs, and begins my instruction.

"My Queen's eyes are beautiful, even when they are clouded," he says gallantly. "Soon the skies of Her Majesty's eyes will be their usual clear and charming blue again."

Never have I listened so carefully. *Not only . . . but also,* he explains, and *moreover* and *however. Perfidy, insinuation, calamity.*

Madame, My Very Dear Mother

Count Mercy can tell you that I grew pale at your words and that I am resolved that no concern in areas where I myself have influence will in any way weaken the health and heart of my beloved mother. It is painful to recall your suffering over the partition of Poland, and now this Bavarian business! I am well aware in this delicate situation that your worst nightmare is that the kingdoms of your children should war with one another, and I will use my own preeminence to assure that none of our countries become combatants.

Frederick II has created clouds of confusion for the King, but I have spoken with Mercy so that I can learn enough to dispel any such obscuring clouds created for the King. The King of Prussia is full of perfidious and persistent insinuations; he has already sent five couriers to our court in less than half a month. Count Mercy has explained the politics so well that I can see for myself what has confused the King, and those little clouds that others have created will soon vanish so that no change is made in our Alliance, which is based not only on the closeness of our affection but also on its usefulness to the general good of Europe. Moreover, I believe that no one can be more dedicated to our purpose than I am.

Talk has begun here that when the current Grand Almoner dies the young Cardinal de Rohan will inherit his position. Nothing could be more abhorrent to me, but he has powerful relatives among both the Noailles and Guéméné families. I am urging the King to resist their pressures. That brother Ferdinand's health is improving is news of great importance to my own happiness.

The Return of Count Axel von Fersen, of Sweden

When the King dutifully approaches my bed to perform his conjugal duties, I surprise him—it has all been orchestrated—by holding out a warm cup of chocolate to him, over the bedcovers.

"Let us sit propped up together," I say and smile at him. I am wearing a blue ribbon in my hair, and I have combed the soft blond curls over my shoulders in the natural manner as the painter Elisabeth Vigée-Lebrun wears her hair. I feel like a shepherdess looking at her swain. "Let's exchange gossip and news for a few minutes." Then I add quite honestly, "I wish to share a confidence."

"The Queen looks exceedingly pretty, and more important, very happy," he says.

He himself is relaxed, for now he knows that he can perform the deed, and his self-confidence is much increased. Unfortunately, he has also become more firm and active in his political decisions, but tonight I will say nothing of Prussia and Austria.

Tonight I speak to him as a member of his family and as one who will, in the dead of winter, bring new life to the family bosom. In my imagination, the little being within—for I feel sure of his nascent existence—will become a valentine for all the world to see, held up lovingly, between us, in the arms of both his parents.

The King sits beside me in the bed, and once he is propped up and comfortably rests his back into the plump pillows, I hand him his cup, a beautiful green one of Sèvres porcelain decorated with a wide golden rim and lozenge portraits of deep pink roses. Then I reach for my own cup, as deep and satisfying a green as the forest itself.

"To Compiègne," I say, lifting my cup in a toast.

"To Compiègne, always rich with game," he says and tactfully waits to hear my explanation. I can see the questions rising in his expression, and also his love for me as a friend and not just as she who must produce an heir.

"For I am quite certain," I say, "that the lateness of that monthly visitor whom my mother calls the Générale is a signal of our success."

"You are often early—" he begins.

"But never late," I finish.

Suddenly, with a blur of liquid chocolate, he tosses his cup and saucer into the air—they do not break, for I listen to their muffled thud on the carpet—and he embraces me with both arms. He has spilled the hot liquid all down the front of my white nightgown in a long brown stain. I lay the cup and saucer aside, on each side of me, and pull the King closer to my bosom.

AS THE SUMMER progresses, I often entreat the King to oppose Prussia—I even speak in very strong terms to his ministers Maurepas and Vergennes—but the King listens to them and not to me. To his credit, he never says a harsh word to me, and in fact he is quite sympathetic when I tell him of my fears for my mother's heart. Nonetheless, he will not budge on the issue. I know now that the invasion was something my brother did, behind our mother's back, and she considers it to have been most unwise. I hate it that it is another woman, the Russian Empress Catherine, who has humbled Austria by threatening to take the side of Prussia. But my mother is more wise than proud—she will not sacrifice her people to vanity—and she has agreed to give up some portions of Bavaria, keeping only Silesia.

Somehow the people know that I have advocated the cause of Austria, and I am unpleasantly referred to as *l'Austrichienne*, the Austrian, though I know that as my pregnancy progresses, I become more and more French. The appellation darkens my joy, for it hints of treason.

Lewd pamphleteers have the audacity to suggest that it is not the King who fathered the child I carry; they propose a ridiculous list of others. The King and I only laugh at them: we know the truth. What hurts me most is that the King's younger brother, the Comte d'Artois, is named first on the lists of putative fathers, and Yolande has whispered to me that my husband's other brother, the Comte de Provence, may well have paid the pamphleteers to do so. With a successful delivery, the Comte de Provence will no longer be next in line for the throne.

But I am introducing a wonderful new style of dresses—I and Rose Bertin.

Sometimes down on her knees, sometimes up high on a little stepladder, she drapes me in light silk fabrics in the colors I love most: pastel blue, a pale yellow soft as sunshine, turquoise that teases the eye between blue and green.

When she measures me around the hips, Rose pretends she cannot reach around me. Instead she marches around me with the tape, remarking like a character in a comic play, "What a distance, what a journey, I now must make!" Behind me, she begins to pant and puff theatrically. Seeing I am amused and pleased, she stamps her feet in place to prolong the charade. At last she comes wheezing around in front, closes the tape, and exclaims, "Four inches, you are already four inches *fatter.*"

I burst into laughter, for never in my life has anyone ever applied even the shadow of the word *fat* to my person.

"I am remembering Racine's play," I say, "and how the Jewish priestess wore flowing garments of surprising attractiveness. I have no intention of lacing myself and this child into any sort of corset."

"As I recall, you have never had any love of corsets." Rose's good round face is wreathed by her smile and twinkling eyes. I love her because she is as jolly and frank as a peasant with me.

"My mother used to scold me about corsets," I say. Soberly, I recall how my mother's recent correspondence has been full of much more serious matters, and that for all of my efforts I really was not effective in helping her. A cloud of anxiety about her health passes through my mind.

"These gauzy garments," Rose says, "might be named for one of the tribes of Israel and called Levites."

By the end of summer, I know that I will be grateful to have clothing loose enough to allow the breezes to enter and fan my body.

ONCE I AM ASLEEP, I sleep and sleep and drink in yet more sleep, as though it were a flagon of nectar, but sometimes I have difficulty falling asleep. My appetite is excellent, and I have never felt happier. I was happy when my marriage was fully consummated, but that was only act one of this masque: I think that only maternity itself can eclipse the joy of pregnancy.

Just once have I felt the slightest discomfort. When I wrote my mother that I vomited a little, she replied she was glad even to hear of my nausea, for it is a common feature of a normal pregnancy. I confessed to my mother that because I had longed and hoped and waited so long, praying that I might have a child, sometimes I feared my present condition, here in the height of summer, might only be a dream. "Yet," I wrote, "the dream does continue. . . ."

NEVER HAVE I FELT more alive or more satisfied with the life I live. The King and I speak together most congenially of our plans for the care and education of our child. Having strolled all the way down the Grand Avenue from the château, we sit on a bench outdoors—the fresh air being so good for my health, despite its summer warmth—and admire the basin of Apollo. As Apollo's horses pull the chariot bearing the sun out of the water, their powerful shoulders and forelegs rise above the surface of the basin. The breeze brings drifts of spray to cool our faces with the fine mist.

"Perhaps I shall nurse the child myself, at least some," I say. I long to feel the little babe's mouth at my breast.

The King is not aghast. He treats all my ideas about our coming child with utmost tenderness.

"Nor shall he be tightly swaddled," I say. "He shall have the freedom to toddle about, and his nursery shall be on the ground floor, for greater ease of access to the outside world."

The King agrees by taking my hand in his and very gently squeezing my fingers. Rapt with happiness, he now looks the very figure of both King and husband.

An imp makes me say, "I believe you too are putting on weight as the weeks pass."

The King blushes, and he has no rejoinder. I regret having given him discomfort.

"It is but natural," I add hastily, "as we grow older."

The image of his grandfather, Louis XV, comes to mind, conjured up by yet another imp, and I recall how even when he was old, that king was called the most handsome man in Europe—a title my Louis will never possess. For a moment I feel ashamed of my own superficiality.

"You are such a good king," I say. "All the people say so."

Again the King blushes, but this time with pleasure. Again he finds no words with which to reply.

Finally he says, "Rousseau," quite enigmatically.

I smile at him encouragingly.

"You have caught the ideas of Rousseau—from the very air, it would seem. I do not think any of the queens of France, for two hundred years, have considered sparing their children the oppression of protocol and custom. The royal children of France have simply been turned over to others. I was."

"I see virtue in motherhood," I reply. I feel proud that the inclinations of my heart are congruent with the thinking of the revered philosopher Rousseau. "Even when our children are babes, I myself will inhabit the role of mother."

I tell him that I want my darling Yolande at some point in the future to become the governess to the children of France, that I have seen her with her own adorable children, and there is no one whom I can trust so fully with the welfare of my son or daughter. The King agrees so readily that his very acquiescence makes me remember for a moment, in contrast, the grave face of my brother Joseph, when he criticized my Yolande as superficial and manipulative, but we do not always agree with Joseph. It was Joseph's decision to annex Bavaria that cost many common soldiers their lives and weakened the heart of our mother.

"Perhaps we should return to the château," I remark, "and prepare to receive guests."

I am only a little bored. During the good humor of my pregnancy, I have found court more entertaining than usual. As we slowly ascend the slope toward the château, I hear the waters of the fountain of Apollo grow more and more dim, like distant rain.

"The populace of Paris was overjoyed," the King says enthusiastically, "when they heard of your pregnancy."

The slope is steep, it is very hot, and contrariness causes me to picture not joy but the hard fierceness of the faces of the women who taunted me after the birth of Artois's first child. They seemed almost dangerous—but that was years ago.

My mother used to remind me that contrariness showed a failure in obedience, the cardinal virtue in a princess. Suddenly I feel tired, and I stop in our progress up the slope and look back at the figure of Apollo. Heavily gilded, he gleams golden in the August sun.

Though I am tempted to exclaim *What a magnificent figure of a man!* I restrain myself. Perhaps the King would feel that he was being adversely compared with the god. Sweat trickles down his brow from under the edge of his wig.

"My mother wrote that she is sure the happiness expressed by the citizens of Paris could not equal the ecstasy throughout Vienna when the news arrived of my pregnancy." My tone is petulant.

AT COURT, THE AUGUST heat is oppressive to many. The women fan rapidly, with the serious intent of stirring up a breeze. The men shift their position from foot to foot; sometimes they hold open their heavily embroidered waistcoats to admit air. But I breathe deeply the perfume of my handkerchief—lavender refreshed with mint—and feel quite comfortable and happy. The lemonade in my goblet refreshes me even more. Heat is like cold: one must give her body to it and then one is relaxed and comfortable.

I know the courtiers would love to toss their powdered wigs, en masse, into the air to cool their pates. I smile at the comic image and feel even more delighted with the world.

For all their discomfort, their elegant rainbow clothing makes them beautiful to behold, and besides, I stand close to an open window where puffs of cooling air enter from time to time.

Yolande de Polignac stands on one side of me, and the Princesse de Lamballe on the other. Today I have no trouble speaking to them both in tones that are smooth as pearls. Though her dark ringlets are damp against her neck, Yolande accepts the summer heat as a natural state and makes no complaint. The Princesse de Lamballe has a heart (and mind), I think, that moves more slowly than most and never overheats her; the skin on her neck and chest is like porcelain and would feel cool, if touched. They are both as gay as I am, and like the three Graces, we are gradually making all hearts glad.

No, it is the mere fact of my pregnancy that pleases them all. I glance down at my belly with enormous satisfaction, for it is more beautiful than a large bouquet of the most pleasing flowers.

The crowd before us moves this way and that like a giant organism, like a flight of bright birds, or like daisies bent together by a unifying breeze. At the corner of my eye, I note a posture and movement that is so elegant that I think for a moment it must be Count Mercy, but the figure is too tall.

And too young.

And even too handsome.

The man is hauntingly but not immediately familiar, like a figure from the past or from a foreign land, a memory or a traveler too good to be true.

"Ah, it's an old acquaintance!" I exclaim, catching his pale blue Swedish eye.

I nod, and the crowd parts to allow his approach.

He bows, yes, with all the elegance in the world, plus the grace of youth, and begins to speak, but I speak with him, so we say his name in duet. "Count Axel von Fersen."

We laugh, and I say simply, "It has been too long a time since I saw you," but I know my eyes are dancing. He is the lad, grown into a man, that I saw in the dead of winter when I was eighteen at the Opera Ball in Paris. We are exactly the same age, I recall.

"Four and a half years, Your Majesty," he replies and inclines his head respectfully, but he is not solemn or awed by me—no more than he was at the ball. His bearing is perfectly simple, that of one human being speaking to another whom he respects in the most natural way.

"The new happiness of Your Majesty lights not only her face but the entire room."

I nod to acknowledge his compliment; he has noticed my pregnancy, the most important thing about me.

Naughtily, I confide in a playful hiss, "When I see the bright disk of the full moon, I stick out my tongue at Diana and all the flat, virginal goddesses who have known nothing of the round fullness of maternity."

He throws back his handsome head and laughs. I think of Triton blowing his horn. Not that his laughter is overly loud, but that it seems to come from another realm. There are rubies in his laughter.

"And where have you been these years?" I inquire.

He takes neither too much time nor too little, he neither overly ornaments his sentences with rhetorical embellishments nor speaks too bluntly. But he tells me in a style that exactly pleases that he went to England intending to marry, but his intended would not leave her native country for a foreign home. "In a phrase, she wouldn't have me," he replies with sudden informality.

"You seem happy and well."

"I shall seek a military life, attaching myself to serve in foreign countries, as my father did."

"Even in these days, your father's good service to Louis XV is spoken of with admiration and appreciation," I reply. "And so I assume you have your father's blessing."

I hear Yolande say sotto voce, "He looks like the hero of a novel."

Beyond her the Duchesse de Chartres replies, "But not a French novel."

"My father is the wisest of friends to me," the Swede continues, ignoring the twitter of my ladies, "and as I journey, many letters pass between us." So confident is the young count in his independence that he makes not the slightest excuse for his obedience to his father. I see strength in this foreigner's face, and kindness. One never sees such nobility in a French face, be he fictive or actual.

I lower my voice just a bit and wish that we were speaking privately. "So it is with my mother and myself." To my surprise, a tenderness for my mother that I have not wanted to admit even to myself sweeps over me. Certainly, I have loved her, but some new element in my own feelings is surprisingly available to me.

Fersen replies, "You showed great courage in making a new home far from the land of your birth."

"But I understand well—now—though I did not at fourteen, how your lady might have hesitated to do so, especially since her journey would have been over water."

"I believe Your Majesty herself crossed the Rhine?" A slight smile lurks around the corners of his mouth.

"The Rhine is a mere ditch compared with the Channel," I remark. As soon as the words have crossed the air to his ear, I feel ashamed to have described that imposing river in demeaning terms. I remember how the sound of the rushing waters of the Rhine filled my ears with fear, or was it my own inexperienced blood seeking a place to hide, when I stood naked on that neutral island between two rival countries?

"All the waters of Austria have their beauty." He speaks sympathetically to me, his sentence anything but a corrective. "And Your Majesty is a daughter of the Danube."

"My mother has always said as much." I add diplomatically, "It has been a very long time since I have thus thought of myself," but in my addition is a truth about myself that I've not intended to reveal. His eyes are those of a traveler who brings back in their depths something of every place he has seen. "You fetch me my youth with your words."

"You think, then, of words as so many little baskets, bearing tidings of times past and things yet to come." Surely he did not address me thus, as "you"? No, he would have continued to say "Your Majesty," with perfect correctness. Wishing for familial intimacy, my ears have twisted the words of Count Axel von Fersen.

MY NIGHTS ARE a luxury of utter relaxation, for once my pregnancy became an established fact, I suggested that safety required us to refrain from connubial relations, and the King acquiesced with the perfect tenderness that will someday make him a beloved father to our child. This August night, I call for Madame Campan to sit beside my pillow and read to me of fairies and enchantments, of Puck and Oberon, and dances in the moonlight.

She reads until I drift away from the realities of my bed, the woven coverlet and droning voice, to journey toward a moon made of rosy quartz. I arrive in a Venetian gondola shaped like a smile, with a single sail, such as those we are privileged to board here to float on the Grand Canal of Versailles. The rudder of my gondola is steered by no Italian, but by a nobleman of the North. To light the way, through the midnight blue, he holds a candle in one fist. Like a whisper moving forward, we rise up from the waters into the sky, the prow of our green boat parting the haze of clouds.

Full of peace and drowsy rest, I press my cheek into the soft down of a pillow; a frail circlet of stars crowns my brow, and I name myself the Queen of Clouds.

Giving Birth, 19 December 1778

I tell my friends the Swede must be invited to every fete, and he is. As I grow rounder and ever more serene, so does our friendship grow, that of Axel von Fersen and myself. With him, I have no impulse to flirt, as I may have done with other courtiers. Whether he speaks or whether he remains silent, his presence is unfailingly both virile and gracious. He is exactly himself, and for that every man in France should envy him. Every woman adores him, and I mark his courtesy to all with great approval. I write nothing of him to my mother, and I suppose Count Mercy does not mention him either. Since she makes no summary judgment or directive to me concerning this friend, the Empress must be ignorant of his existence.

Mercy tells me everyone is jealous of the favor I show Count von Fersen, but I say they would be jealous of anyone standing in the light of my favor. "Better a foreigner," I reply. "He asks nothing of me. It is only my regard that he receives."

Mercy tells me that all the courtiers believe Fersen "has captured the heart of a Queen," and Mercy cautions me *they* (meaning the Polignac circle, and now I can admit they *are* a circle) have *plotted* that he do so because if it were a Frenchman who became the Queen's Favorite, he might "win all the favors of appointments and incomes for himself or his relatives."

For their part, Madame de Polignac and her lover Vaudreuil encourage me to give full expression to my appreciation of the handsome count, to give him the pleasures of the flesh. It makes me laugh for people to imagine that anyone could manipulate Axel von Fersen, for his respect for his father has brought him wisdom beyond his age. He and I understand each other completely: our joy is of the spirit.

Look at me: I am enormous!

IN HIS PRESENCE, my heart is light. With the most perfect serenity, I watch the fall season progress. The dark comes earlier every day. The leaves of the trees at Versailles are half dropped, and I see the black skeletal branches emerge from the thinning foliage. The sunsets grow rich with a heavy red and roiling gold.

Sometimes the little being inside me kicks his tiny foot, and I tickle the place where he is making room and yet more room for his growth. The King glows with his happiness for me, and once in the presence of the count, I placed the King's hand against my side to feel the movement. Without the slightest embarrassment the good King exclaimed, "Ah, Fersen, what a thing it is to be an almost-father!" Nor was Fersen the slightest discomforted. We are all three most natural with one another. Royalty aside, we are simply three friends. They both love me, and we are in perfect balance.

Fersen once remarked to us that in the nature of geometry, the triangle is the most stable of forms. We three were admiring a pediment of that shape; his comment was no sly remark on ourselves. At least he had no awareness of it being so. But just as he knows the private, unworded recesses of my mind, so can I discern the shadow of his thoughts, of which he is unaware.

Once I saw Elisabeth, the King's sister, looking at Fersen as though she too was about to join the ranks of ladies who come close to swooning at his glance. Her eyes quite glazed over when she saw him in his Swedish military uniform, looking like an actor in a play, a spectacle of glorious manhood, but authentic and comfortable.

"Elisabeth," I said gently, for she could not help herself.

Her lips parted and she looked as though she were awakening from a daze. "His boots are so beautiful," she murmured. Then her truthful eyes fully met mine. "I am so glad your Highness has such a noble friend," she said. "We could follow him to the end of the world."

"It is good there are such men," I replied. "The King likes and trusts him entirely."

Meager words! The real essence of this moment is that in its private folds I saw the sincerity of my sister-by-marriage. She does not want what is mine. Always, there has been a bond between us, from the day I arrived for my wedding, and she—a perfect, natural child for all her royalty—flitted about me. She was the little messenger for the Dauphin's pink rose. And now she fills her role to perfection: she is my true friend. Almost, she wants nothing for herself. In her proximity to the King and myself, it is her will and ardent desire to enhance—in every way—our position. I know no way to repay her generosity.

I FEEL THE LABOR pains begin soon after the clock strikes twelve. There is no need for haste or alarm. Soon enough I will be surrounded by dozens, perhaps hundreds of people, but this moment is mine. Who is this little person who knocks at the door of the world? And what a strange portal is the female human body. So it is beginning: pain where there was no pain. A tightening and a squeezing, and the pain passes. While I wait, I know that I am smiling.

I think of my mother, and the joy that will be hers. To her, I and my arrival had been no mystery. There were so many brothers and sisters before me. *Yet another*, she probably thought. *And what shall we do with her?*

But for me it is the beginning. I am doing what I was born to do, but more gloriously than even my mother had dared to hope. I shall bear the next king of France, God willing. This new being is made of the royal blood of hundreds and hundreds of years. Old Louis XV must be smiling in his tomb. How pleased he was to join my six-hundred-year-old house of Hapsburg to the Bourbon line.

But the coming child—my body compresses him again, I pray he feels no pain—is but a child. He knows nothing of these proud thoughts. But I think he senses his world is changing. Birth and Death—I think it must be like this when we die: that we but exchange one world and its close limits for a more expansive kingdom. Here in the dark inhabiting my bedroom, I think of the light of eternity. My mother would have me pray at this moment for France and the happiness of Europe, as well as our own, and I am glad to do so. The beads of my rosary slide with their angles and smoothnesses through the tips of my fingers; that they are connected one to another connects me to the intangible beyond.

The clock strikes one, for half-past midnight. How forlorn that gong sounds.

Yet I love this darkness, that I am alone. I want to remember this black peace. I can see the curtains at the windows. I suppose soon I will get up and pace about. The King will come, and I will feel his love for me and I for him that together we have made the reality of this little life. I wish Maria Carolina were with me. One after another, her children have come easily. She would tell me what to expect, and how best to help the progression. When I close my eyes now, I can feel her lips kissing my forehead. Such love. The pain attacks again. If she could, Charlotte would labor for me. How often she took my hand, when we were little together, to lead me forward to some new play. To the menagerie! To see Clara, the rhinoceros, plated like a knight of old, but dusty.

Here comes another pain.

The clock bongs. I give myself another half hour of solitude. Then I'll ring the bell, and its silver sound will announce the impending event. Probably never in my life will I be again so alone as I am in this moment. I am not afraid. Blessed solitude. Sweet secret! Is it possible that what is now within will be soon without, and separate from myself? But my arms will comfort him and hold him close against my flesh, this outer wall of the room of his unborn life. *Remember*, I'll say, *only hours ago you were inside.* My hands smooth and soothe my big belly as it goes rigid again with pain.

I test time by counting to sixty, and yes, those moments are gone, and another minute is here to be counted out. Such is life! Such is life: the passing of moments, none more or less real than another, for all their difference in import. The moment it takes to move my eyes from left to right is as real as a moment of love or fear. I read my way across the room, starting from the tall door frame on the left, spelling out draperies and cabinets, chairs and paintings till I arrive at the other wall and view the high door on the right. So we spend our moments, which have their own will and will spend themselves whether we are aware of their passing or not. Suppose we could give away time, like a sparkling bracelet. The lapis bracelet I received when I arrived for my wedding comes to me, a broad band, with diamonds, and the clasp I have liked to wear next to my pulse. My cipher *MA*, with the letters intertwined, two mountains, with three peaks among them. *Hold on tight, Marie Antoinette*—it is the voice I heard at home when we rode our sleds through the snow, the voice of the Empress, giving good advice. I wish it would snow this December night, for the world needs to be new and pure as white linen, as white as swansdown for my baby.

I am glad it is December, the month of Christ's birth, when Mary herself had her firstborn son and wrapped him in swaddling clothes. *Hail Mary, Full of Grace, Blessed art thou among women.* And blessed am I. *Mary, Mother of God, Mary, my special patron saint, and that of all my sisters and of our mother before us, may the fruit of my womb be blessed, for the sake of the people, for France, which I shall love better than ever I have before.*

One. The clock chimes once again for half past one in the morning, 19 December 1778, and I ring the call bell for those who will attend me. Only a few moments pass, and here they come. First is the Princesse de Lamballe, as superintendent of the household, her pale face a lozenge of love, who dispatches the news to all the royal family at Versailles and beyond, by pages, to Saint-Cloud, and on to Paris with the news. Men scurry out, then ride away from the palace into the cold, full of my news. I hold out my hand to be assisted from this stately bed, leaving the print of my warmth behind me. Before I return to this bed, I will have given birth. I arise to begin my pacing, which will hasten the process and prevent my blood from pooling.

IT IS EIGHT in the morning, and the pains come too close together, and my body is too weary for any more walking. I look at the little white bed that has been prepared for the actual delivery of my child. Were it my tomb, I would lie in it now, for respite. Daylight appears in a vertical slit where the draperies meet.

It is the face of my husband and King that most comforts me now. They called Louis XIV the sun king, but it is my husband's big round face, beaming at me, that most resembles the sun. His gentle, hooded eyes sparkle encouragement to me. All the others, I ignore. The room is stifling with the press of people—there must be two hundred crowded about me—many faces I know, all those of the court who must have the honor of being present, but beyond them crowd the curious people who have walked out from Paris, and others who happened to be in the palace. I see the little seamstress among them, but her name is gone from my weary mind. I think "Rose," but that is the name of her mistress, not her own name—Rose Bertin who has made me beautiful in softly draping garments during my pregnancy, with soft feathers for my hair. *Mon Dieu! The pain!* And two strangers are perched on top of high cabinets to get a fine view of me lying here, trying to open my body. *Mon Dieu! The pain!* They are like the gargoyles leaning out on Notre Dame. *Mon Dieu! Mon Dieu! I count eleven bongs of the clock, mon Dieu!* If it strikes noon, and I have not delivered, I will die. I am resigned to it.

And yet I think of the Empress, my mother, who delivered fifteen times, as though it were no more difficult than a hard sneeze. The throng is breathing up all the air and leaving none for me.

I wave my hands toward the windows, sealed against the winter cold, but no one understands I am stifling for lack of breath, that I beg the windows be reeled open. *Use force, use force!* I command, but they think I refer to the babe within me, and awful hands enter me, searching. I will not scream. Never let them make you cry out, the Empress told me. Never for any pain or injury that is personal to yourself. One shrieks for the state, only for the kingdom.

One! The clock is at half past eleven. It is Yolande de Polignac who tells us all: *Now, now the baby crowns.* And with all my heart I love her for her tidings. I open my eyes, just a slit, to see her face once more before I die. Her countenance is calm and happy. She sees nothing awry. Her gaze meets mine. "Very soon," she says in a low voice like the purr of a cat. I believe her.

I push, then relax; the child is born. The room falls silent. I fear he is dead: that is the meaning of their silence. There is no applause, no exclamations of joy. The heat of the room engulfs me. I sink into the fires of hell.

HOLD ON TIGHT. Yes, the sled sped along, down and faster. Faster. The frosty wind hits my face, streams into my nostrils. Bits of ice sting my cheeks as I rush down, and faster, colder, down.

But I am not in Austria. They have opened the windows. The air in the room is fresh, and it is French. It pours over me like a spray of snow.

The King presents our child to me and tells me we have a daughter, healthy, robust. "Keep her warm," he says to me.

Ah, they greeted her with silence because she was not a dauphin.

"Little Marie Thérèse," I say to her, holding out my arms to this bundle, my child. Never have I heard such gentleness in my own voice. "All France wished you to be a boy, but never mind." I look at her small head, a tiny version of myself, fair of skin with sweet light hair. "To me, no child could be more dear." I touch her petal-soft cheek with the back of my finger. "Now you are mine." Having come out of me into the world, someone to touch and see and smell, I know she is more mine than when she was closeted within. "The court, the people would have owned a boy, but you," I tell her again, "dearest little girl, you are mine." She is asleep and swaddled; I check the wrapping cloths, and they are not too tight. I hold her close to myself. My breath touches her face. "I will take care of you, and we shall share our lives and comfort each other."

I tell them I am quite revived: they must close the windows tightly, lest the winter air chill my daughter.

"She is so newly born," the King says wonderingly, and I look at him. His countenance expresses all that I knew it would. He continues, "I could not be more pleased with her, or with you."

My husband's kindness causes me to weep. I know the courtiers think I am disappointed to have birthed a daughter, but that is not it at all. My travail is finished, and a new chapter of my life begins. I have had a child. I can have another.

"My little daughter will suckle at my own breast," I tell my husband.

He nods, and I know that he will support me in all that I ask.

Farewell to Count von Fersen

Three months old, my daughter is only in the next chamber; should she whimper, and should she continue to whimper, then I will leave all these lords and ladies, to give my little tyrant the breast she most prefers.

People remark on how lovely I looked last night at the Opera Ball. Of course the King was too busy to attend, but I walked with Count von Fersen, and if I did not look radiant it would indeed be a great shame, for I felt myself to be nothing but aglow. Always attentive to my moods and thoughts, always approving of me, and always himself, he and I both felt a perfect happiness, for we are kindred spirits. As I walk about and speak to friends today, in my mind I stroll again with him, my dearest secret friend. In the glamour of candlelight, reflected prismatically, with all the jewels appropriate to attendance at the opera glinting around us like fairy lights, we did glow from within.

And yet this daylight scene is lovely too, with flowers—tulips and narcissus, pussy willow, and forsythia bending in a yellow arc—blossoms and fronds beautifully arranged in vases wherever one looks. Flowers look best in daylight, and I love the lighter dresses of daytime that complement the flower petals quite as much as the princely robes of night. The day speaks of the freedom of nature, the night of the glory of jewels and regalia.

A whisper reaches my ears that one of the ladies has said she is grateful she is not in love with the Swedish count—how helpless one is before him, she says, be she lady or queen.

Yolande de Polignac asks if we are to have music this afternoon, and I reply, "I am waiting only on my Gluck—and Axel von Fersen." I can confide in her almost as well as I can in him, but the nature of my confidences changes, depending on whose ear is inclined toward me. With Yolande, I am my most wicked self—imperious, a bit greedy for what is not yet mine, full of criticism for others, and making light of their vanity and pitiable judgment. While I will not flaunt my power, my pride is that I can give her anything she wants.

As I muse, in the midst of many, my fingers travel up and down, over the gray fuzzy nodes of pussy willow, and I recall how recently in the dead of winter, my fingers visited the hard beads of my rosary as I prayed for deliverance.

With the count (as with my child), I am my best self, I feel my deeper urges, experience delight through all the levels of my psyche at the beauty of a buckle or of a song. The fingers of the musician at the keyboard have never seemed more nimble or true, as when I listen with the count at my side. The hues of the flowers in their vases, the floral forms and postures, never please me more than when he is near. Ah yes, flowers like people have a distinct carriage of their heads and lifting of their leaves. When Fersen stands beside me, elegant, amiable, intelligent, and kind, I have no impulse to criticize or complain of anything or anyone; with every breath I want to enjoy, enjoy. Secure in my happiness, I know that he will never ask anything of me.

And here is my friend Axel von Fersen, of Sweden, come again as he has come countless times to my entertainments. I simply smile and nod; the crowd parts—they disappear from view, they melt away as his figure commands all my sight. He fills the frame of my seeing as surely as if he were a painting commanding all my focus.

Far from fixed in the eternity of art, he moves toward me, through the golden light of the afternoon, among the March blossoms, past the vases whose very forms break the heart with their grace, his face fairer than any lily. The colors in the carpet before his feet are more vibrant than they ever were before.

I am not the least afraid—though today he is more compelling than ever before in his appearance, but I think just so every time I have the pleasure of looking at him. Because he approves of me, his perfection improves any inadequacy I may have ever felt about myself. I meet him on equal terms, with equal joy. All is perfectly proper; no one can claim that they themselves have been greeted by me with any less joy. I please them all, assembled here today, the princes, the ducs and comtes, my ladies, and it is effortless.

"And tell us all the news, for our number and our happiness are complete," I say to him so all can hear, "now that you are among us."

He clicks his heels together softly, brings his hand to the knot of lace at his throat, slightly bows, and speaks, "All of my news is good, for the desire of my father has come to fruition. I have many kind friends to thank. The King of Sweden has spoken to the Comte de Rochambeau, and my dreams of military service will be given opportunity."

"You have received an assignment," I say with a smile, but I can feel a cloud pass over my brow. I actually touch my forehead as though to wave it away. Yolande is at my side. She whispers in my ear, as is her privilege, but I cannot hear what she says, though her very lips tickle the porches of my ear.

He is wearing a coat of bright claret, a color I have always favored, and while I drink no wine, I am always pleased when others drink claret so I can admire its color in the lifted crystal, when the sun passes through the liquid.

Again he bows his head. "If it please Your Majesty, I have been appointed the aide-de-camp of the Comte de Rochambeau."

There is a buzz in the room, or have bees entered my brow, mistaking it for a hive.

The Comte de Rochambeau is the commander in chief, and he embarks for the American colonies forthwith. My heart panics. *Express panic as pleasure caused by the presence of all assembled, for their eyes are upon you*—thus, my dramatics master instructed me, before I floated onto the stage from the wings, so long ago, when I was a daughter of the Danube.

Yolande whispers in my ear, "The Americans have done nothing but cause trouble since they came into existence."

"You must bid my little daughter farewell," I say to Axel von Fersen, "and take your leave of her before you sail. Perhaps she will then be old enough to form a phrase with her own lips." I feel confused. I fear the room will begin to spin, though my eyes are fixed on nothing but his eyes. The Princesse de Lamballe is suddenly at my other side.

"Ah, look," she says with great spontaneity, "it is the Chevalier Gluck, come to entertain us with exquisite music."

I shift my gaze only enough to see that my old friend has arrived. My Gluck seems to pant, as though he has come in haste; his hair is badly powdered, and much of its natural color shows through. His short stocky figure is always most welcome, but my eyes pass from him back to the elegant count. Modestly, he waits till I address him again, but I cannot.

Yolande asks him, "And what time, in the morning, do you sail? We are so sorry to think that this must be farewell for a while."

Could she have said *in the morning*?

"I apologize to Her Majesty and to all my friends that I have come late to our gathering only to announce that I leave early in the morning. But Chevalier Gluck is here, and let us not delay further the moment for music."

He looks at me in such a way that tells me he understands my sorrow, that he must go, as it is duty, that we must go forward with our gaiety, which is also our duty.

"I claim my privilege to go first," I say, "for after Gluck has played for us, no mere amateur will dare to sit at the harpsichord."

"Because the performance of the amateur springs from love," the count says to me, and smiles with exquisite grace, "such music always moves me most."

Slowly I sit myself on the hard little bench. When I was a child in Vienna, Gluck told me the bench needs to be hard so that our backs are never seduced to slump. I spread my skirt about me, a lavender one today, which evermore I shall associate with death. At each elbow is a round puff of the pale purple. "Yes, an amateur is one who plays for love," I say quietly. "And I hope there will be some charm in my effort, for all of you who are so kind as to listen."

I place the tips of my fingers on the smooth, flat keys. How cool they are in their repose, waiting to speak at my touch! "Listen with your hearts then, for I play with mine, and forgive my fingers should they stumble." Indeed, I feel uncertain, but I lift my eyes to him and begin.

I sing an aria from *Dido.* My fingers ply the keys well enough, but my voice betrays my feeling and trembles. To steady myself—*to perform, perform*—I imagine the dramatic reality, the world of Dido, and not my own distress. I sing her words, "Ah, what a happy thought led me to admit you to this court," but the word for *court* is slurred and sounds almost like *coeur*—heart. Yes, I have admitted him into my heart; it matters not whether he attends my court.

Though I look only at him, his eyes are modestly turned downward. For my sake, no action of his ever betrays the bond between us. All is done in such a way as to efface himself, to belie the fact of the special position that he holds in my regard. No egotism mars his natural compassion; he asks for nothing. My eyes fill with tears. And if they see my tears—I do not care!

When I rise from the keyboard, I indicate to my old music master that now he is to entertain us, and he does, playing Rameau's "The Mysterious Barricades." Alas, the barricades that hem me in are anything but mysterious. Rameau's music boils with energy, played in the brightest of the major keys. I fade into the group, and soon Fersen, without displacing anyone, is standing beside me. I hear him breathe deeply: it is the opposite of a sigh.

"I hope you will write letters to your friends in France when you are in America?"

"Nothing would please me more. For those who are true friends, however, distance—I know Your Majesty agrees—cannot separate their spirits."

He glides away. I circulate among my guests. "Is it not wonderful news?" I say brightly. "And I understand Lafayette is going, as well."

At the moment of farewell, I hold out my hand to the noble count. He bends and kisses it, glances up just once, his soul in his lifted eyes; then he raises his head and chest, squares his shoulders, smiles, softly clicks his heels, turns, and leaves the room. My eyes follow his back—straight without stiffness, all ease, all grace—and he rounds a corner and is gone. I listen for the sound of his feet on the marble stairs, but I hear no hint of his passage. The back of my hand hums with the whisper left there by the feather of his kiss.

LATER IN THE EVENING Yolande comes to me and tells me I do not look well.

"I have a bit of fever," I say truthfully. I will not give her any news of my heart.

When she asks to see the backs of my hands, I give her the one that Fersen did not kiss.

"Those red spots on your fair cheeks suggest measles," she replies, her voice full of concern. "Several people not at the musicale are reported to have the disease."

"Was it not a delightful afternoon?" I feel hot and listless.

"I overheard a most interesting exchange between the Duchess of Fitz-James and our count."

"Do tell," I urge and feel brighter, interested.

"She said, 'What is this, Monsieur? You are deserting your conquest for the sake of American liberty?' And he replied, with perfect composure, 'If I had made a conquest, do not imagine I would desert her. Because I am going away quite free of connection, I am leaving—so much the worse for me—with no other person feeling any special regret.'"

"He displays not a hint of pride," I reply, well satisfied with my friend's discretion.

"And yet, I think," she replied with a toss of her dark head, "that he would certainly be able to give bliss to any lady who wished to bestow favor and true trust upon him."

I smile at my friend with perfect equanimity, but I do not find her remark amusing.

"Indeed, I have heard testimonials of just such happy ladies," she adds, examining her nails, adjusting a diamond bracelet I have lately given her because I saw her admiration for mine with the lapis clasp and my cipher.

I glide away and look out the window. Had she been able to do so,

Yolande would have goaded me to seal with the count, ere he left. It needs no seal: my confidence in his devotion cannot be shaken by gossip. "When summer comes again," I say, watching the gardeners transporting carts of roses toward their planting beds, "perhaps we shall take nocturnal walks again, among the bosquets and fountains, as we did when I was pregnant, with fragrant music wafting on the breeze."

"Madame Vigée-Lebrun, the painter, tells me there is no music more gay than Mozart's. Vaudreuil finds all her opinions about aesthetic matters to be worthy of attention."

"I'm told Mozart came and went during my pregnancy, declining the offer of a position of some sort."

"Many say that he exceeds Gluck as a composer."

"He is just my age. I heard him play, as a child. The Empress gave him—Wolfgang—a splendid suit that my brother Max had outgrown."

Memory presents the scamper of small feet across the large room at Schönbrunn, his running toward my mother, his confident occupancy of her lap. Yes, I would love to cuddle a little boy, my own cherub-child with plump cheeks and stubby wings in my lap.

How life has changed for me, how I have grown, since I envied Mozart as he kissed the Empress!

"I suppose he has grown up, now, as we all have. Really, I do not feel well," I tell my friend. "I must send for the doctor."

COVERED WITH THE MOST hideous red spots imaginable, I have removed myself to Trianon and have dwelt there—night and day now—for three nights.

When I first look at myself in the glass, I weep at the sight of me. I open my mouth to inspect my tongue, to see if even it has become spotted, but before I can see, I burst into laughter. What would Axel von Fersen think now of my beauty!

I send for the four most amusing of my male friends and tell them they shall be my nurses, and their duty is to make me laugh throughout this siege of spots. Baron de Besenval, though a colonel in the Swiss Guard, tells the most delicious stories, complete with witty dialogue. Does the King care? Not at all—whatever pleases me, pleases him. My only regret is that he and our daughter must stay their distances till I am free from contagiousness.

Count Esterhazy, my favorite of the four, for he loves me most, tells me that the whole court and half Paris is laughing, and what if the King should come down with measles—would he have four ladies to nurse and amuse him? Toward such barbs I present the tough skin of a rhinoceros. I could not have survived the onslaught of obscene pamphlets continually circulated about me had I not learned to ignore all but what I myself know to be the truth. The King hires spies to try to find the origin of such horrid printing, but I know he cannot stem the tide, for all his fury and indignation.

TONIGHT, THE KING stands under my window—deemed a safe distance by the doctors—and speaks with me and tells me how much he misses me and how our little one is faring. Thriving, he says, though now she has only her wet nurse's milk. *My God! How I long to nurse her!* In her letters, my mother reminds me endlessly that I thrived on nothing but the milk of Joseph Weber's mother. Milk is milk, she claims. My breasts are aching hard with unused milk. She fears that nursing makes another conception for me less likely, but I doubt the science of such a belief.

It is God's will to make me fertile or not, in his own time, just as He warms the earth and makes her fertile when He would have her so. Nor do I look superstitiously to the stars for guidance; the things of this earth and the goodness of trees and flowers and grasses where I myself can walk bring joy to my spirit. The gardens of this earth speak to me of paradise and give me hope. Why should I send my imagination questing for answers about the ways of the universe?

"I plan to have a hamlet built close by, such as peasants and humble folk inhabit," I tell the King. Dressed in dulcet tones, my words drop down to him, waiting below among the new-planted rosebushes. *My breasts feel as though they will burst.*

"What do you envision?" he asks.

"There will be a mill where wheat is ground into flour, and a millpond where folk can fish, and I will have cottage gardens and rustic cottages."

"How do you see the cottages? Small?"

"Quite small. And appearing to be old—painted with cracks in their plaster and with thatched roofs so that they will blend with nature. The cottages to be constructed of beams and plaster, with casement windows, and houses for doves. With spiral wooden staircases to open balconies, with clematis twining up their pillars. I have seen such a village at Chantilly, looking as though it has spent such time with nature, though human work has weathered, mellowed, and blended the village with the trees."

"The stars are winking at us."

"I do not look up, when I can look down into the face of my dear and generous husband."

Swayed by my tenderness, he shifts his weight from foot to foot. "Perhaps you'll need a lighthouse in your hamlet," the King whimsically remarks, "lest anyone be lost at sea?"

"At sea?"

"I imagine your pond expansive enough to suggest a miniature sea."

For that good thought, I throw down a bouquet of spring lilacs to my husband and bid him bury his nose therein.

Almost I look forward to the time when he shall plow me again. Suddenly a gurgle of laughter falls from my lips. When yet I lived at home and I was sent a portrait of the Dauphin at his plow—was that what was meant? That he would someday plow my body, be my husbandman who brings forth abundance from the fields he tills?

"I shall dress as a shepherdess," I say. I am glad that the dusky night masks my spotted face.

"And I as a shepherd."

I blow him a kiss.

"Surely I strive always to be a good shepherd to my people," he says, and I hear the goodness in his voice. "They bear such heavy burdens. If only the nobles would join me in bidding the farmers and laborers to rely on us, for succor. But the nobles are outraged at the thought of paying equitable taxes."

I feel his distress for the people, but I cannot think of any advice to offer. For myself, I wish to live more simply—not only because it suits me but also for the sake of the people. My *Hameau* will celebrate life as the peasants live it. I twist the diamond bracelet around my wrist. "Nevermore," I say, "give me gifts of diamonds. I will not have such jewels when they could buy a ship for our navy or bread for the hungry."

And yet I know the hamlet will be very expensive to construct. Earth will have to be moved, and a stream diverted. Still this embellishment of the land does not seem sinful in the way the embellishment of my wrist or my throat with diamonds would be. Its reality will embody and celebrate the ideal of simplicity. I wish that the Princes of the Blood had the noble heart of my husband, but it is only their titles that bray their nobility. I wish that he could be surrounded by men like Axel von Fersen.

"The burdens press heavily on the shoulders of the peasants," the King adds sadly, "when I would give them peace and prosperity."

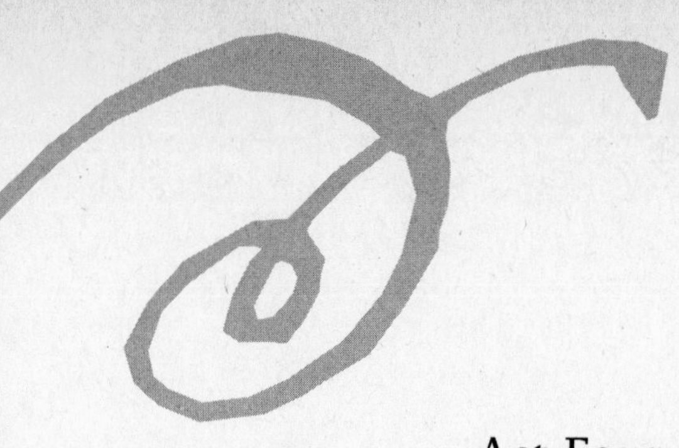

Act Four

The Death of the Empress of Austria

On 11 October 1780, I write to my most dear Mother.

I have been more than a bit worried during the last three weeks because my daughter has had pain and fever, at the eruption of several new teeth. You will be proud that even though she experienced considerable pain and suffering, she showed always sweetness and patience. I am touched to the quick by her courage. Because of my dear mother and my dear daughter, who bears her name, I feel inspired to the marrow of my bones to always take courage, no matter what life may bring to me.

I am at Trianon while the King has gone to Compiègne to hunt, which he enjoys so much. Here these gardens which I love are, as they say, being put to bed as the winter season approaches. With the loss of flowers and foliage, I am glad that the windows give views of the small but most charming structures in every direction. Architecture and statuary know no limits of the seasons in their ability to inspire pleasure.

Now I sit at my small secrétaire, *positioned so that I face out the window, and I see the beautiful circular Temple of Love, built on a small island and linked to the shore by darling bridges over the moat. A mat of autumnal golden leaves floats slowly in the water, which reflects a white cloud or two. Within the colonnade of the domed temple is the marble statue of a slender, youthful Cupid fashioning his bow from the club of Hercules.*

I have always loved that passage of Scripture in which pruning hooks are made from spears and out of the implements of aggression come the tools that represent love, harvest, and abundance. How I wish all wars might end, and the brave men who fight for liberty might return safely to those who love them, and I pray for them all, as I am sure my dear mother the Empress does also. Always, when I look out at beauty such as still waters, golden leaves, and azure skies, and all but worship it, I think of my most dear mother, the Empress of my affection.

Perhaps you have heard of the painter Elisabeth Vigée-Lebrun, who, like our beloved Gluck, has risen in the world entirely by her own artistic talent and her bright and natural sociability. She is my favorite painter, but I have modified my manner of dress since she last painted me. Now I prefer muslin to satin or silk. I think that perhaps Madame Lebrun has not only the aesthetic resources but also the amiability to produce a new portrait of me that would please my dear mother, the Empress, so that when you view my likeness, you will feel the essence of my presence. You used to scold me for the elaborate artificiality of my dress and hair, but now you will find that fashions in France have modulated. I am still much in fashion, but now I influence dress and decor. The new styles are much more comfortable and economical as well.

It gives me much pleasure to look through the windows at the combinations of nature and art wherein my Trianon and I are nestled. I like to imagine that my dear Mother, free from the worries of state, sits beside me.

May I beg permission to borrow Cupid's wings, then to fly over all the distance between us, thence to kiss my dear Mama most lovingly, with all my soul?

ON 3 NOVEMBER 1780, the Empress takes time to think of me and to write to me.

Because it was your birthday, I spent yesterday more in France than in Austria. I pictured you being greeted by your friends and sitting down to enjoy a delightful dinner or an amusing entertainment. Memory allowed me to revisit, as well, so many shared happy times, now gone forever. Still, memory is a great consolation to the old, as is the thought of new young life, such as that of your so very sweet little girl. And because you assure me that your relation with the King is good, I think of the future and of what will surely be the consequences of that good marital relation. To think that you will soon produce an heir to the throne of France, one that unites the blood of Bourbon and Hapsburg houses, as you were sent to France to accomplish for the peace of the world, is the greatest consolation I can imagine. At my age I need assistance with my work and consolation for my spirit because one after the other those of my own generation are inevitably lost to me, and I am quite overcome.

Because I have a good deal of pain from rheumatism in the arm and hand that hold the pen, I myself am writing to you with less control. Though the letters I am forming may be shaky in appearance, and I feel that now I must end, take note not of their form but only of their message, which unwaveringly assures you of all my love.

Thus ends our correspondence.

So I read again my last letter from my mother, the Empress of Austria, dated 3 November 1780.

I can scarcely see her crooked letters through the blur of tears, but this page I hold in my hand is my last link to her. It was the side of her own right hand that rested on this page as she wrote, pausing to have the strength to continue, regripping the quill with her fingertips from time to time. Would that I could cover her hand with my kisses and wet it with my tears so that she would know my love. When the news came, I thought that my face would explode with sorrow.

It is now December. My mother died 29 November 1780.

I take a deep breath, trying to empower myself to step forward through my life. I cannot imagine the future in which no letters from her will come.

These ten years I have been in France, she has been my guide, the prop to my soul. She has taught me to pray, and I will not forget her lessons.

TO MY BROTHER, Joseph II, 10 December 1780:

Though I struggle with every breath not to drench this page, I am crushed by the misfortune of our loss, and I cannot stop crying. Oh, my brother, my last link to my Austrian homeland, my friend! Our mother who watched over us is gone. Take care to watch over yourself—For me, I cannot see to write. You will surely not forget we are friends, allies, as she wished us ever to be.

I implore you: Love me. Kiss me.

Out the window, I see the broad terraces, an empty world blanketed in December snow, and where is a coverlet for my heart?

A Friend

Here is my friend, my Yolande, come to stand quietly beside me. She waits. I look up at her and know she sees the red misery in my face from crying. She smiles at me encouragingly. Yes, she has in her hands a little tray bearing the potion that often calms me when my spirits soar too high or plunge too deep.

Gratefully, I take the chalice of orange-flower water; she empties a fresh spoonful of sugar into the liquid and swirls it round.

Through the glass, I feel warmth, for she has had my orange water potion heated to counteract the chill of the weather.

Yolande asks if I would like the curtain loosened from its loop so as to shield me from the bleak view of the frozen courtyard, but I shake my head. "No, dear friend," I say, and again she smiles at me, and her eyes glow with love. "I must see things as they really are."

She is looking very well, already quite slender after the birth of her new son. I inquire of his health.

"It has been nine years since the births of Aglaië and Armand," I remark. "But I see you have not forgotten how to mother."

"Nor shall I ever. Here, let me put my shawl around your shoulders."

It is a gorgeous piece woven of wool and gleaming silk, the rich reds and golds of last fall intermingle—a fantasia representing her soul. I gave her this token of my affection.

Impulsively, I reach up and take her hand. While I drink the orange-flavored warmth she, ever patient, joins me in gazing out the window.

"It will soon be spring," she murmurs.

"Nothing perturbs you," I reply. "Not the coldest blasts of calumny."

"And why should it, when the Queen has chosen me as her friend and confidante?"

Always, she is direct in her speech and goes to the heart of every attitude.

"And did it not infuriate you, when last fall, certain pamphlets claimed that I, the Queen, was the *father* of your child?" I give her a wan smile.

"The King himself visited me and the babe in my private home in Paris. Why should I fear gossip when the King so marks me with his favor? No one else has received such a mark of distinction."

"The King appreciates how you give yourself to me."

"In truth, it is the two of you who make my life so complete."

I release her hand, for I hear her baby boy crying just beyond the door. I know she must want to go to him and take him from the arms of his nurse. "Go," I whisper, and I feel a small, real smile curve the corners of my mouth. With her halo of dark curls, her face is lovely to regard.

No sooner do I give her this gentle command than my husband brings us some white chocolate candies from molds shaped like sheep. They are coated with sugar crystals.

"I have a box for you as well," he says to Yolande, "but I believe you prefer the jellied fruits to the chocolate bonbons."

"Your Majesty remembers everything," she replies.

"You have come to us when we very much needed comforting, my dear countess," he says and warmly takes her hand in his for a moment. Her baby whimpers again.

Yolande turns from us. Perhaps God will give me a son this time. I listen to the crying of the boy baby in the room beyond and memorize the sounds of his tiny male voice.

People at court say that Yolande's lover, the Comte de Vaudreuil, is the father of her child. Protected, she cares nothing for such gossip. Certainly she feels no shame but inhabits her life as she lives it, her head held high. She has charmed even the King, who does not much like women, myself excepted. Because he is devoted to me and to our duty as King and Queen, I have no fear that the King would take her or any other woman as a mistress.

I resolve that I will prevail upon my husband to give my friend a new title by summer: Duchesse de Polignac.

Perhaps I live a lucky life, fortunate in my husband and in my friends. At twenty-five, I am still young. If I am no longer a daughter to any living woman, then I must pour myself into being a mother. And should I bear a son, I fulfill not only my mother's ardent desire but also the hopes of my husband and of France.

I DREAM I AM at Schönbrunn, tucked in among the skirts of my sister and the ladies of our court, and I am watching the little Mozart—*Wunderkind*—from across the room. As he performs his marvels at the keyboard, he sometimes swings his heels, which dangle high above the carpet. His notes swirl and swoop like the arabesques beneath his dangling feet. When the keys are draped, still he touches each one with perfect accuracy.

Then comes the moment of daring. After the harpsichord notes have fallen like an amazing silver shower from his small fingers, the little Mozart slides from the bench and runs as though winged across the room to throw himself into my mother's imperial lap. I have become Mozart and I kiss her big on her naked cheek and demand, "Now do you love me?"

She kisses him—Mozart again—as though he might have been her own dear child.

Letter from Axel von Fersen

My dear Friend,

Having just received the dreadful news of the death of your most dear mother, I hasten to write that my deepest sympathy is entwined with your sorrow at every moment. I know your nature and how its sweetness and sensitivity also make it vulnerable to the most profound feelings of loss. Let me express the idea that I hope will be consoling to you that even as you ache for your loss you are honoring her.

I know perhaps better than anyone that you have the ability to continue an intimacy based on spiritual affinity; thus, your spirit and hers can never be truly separated. Death is not an insurmountable barrier, no more than are our earthly constraints of place and time.

I know this letter will be some weeks in reaching you across the waters of the broad Atlantic, yet as you hold it in your hand, now, in this moment, you are aware that my spirit is with you. What matter time and place?

So it is with your beloved mother. Look for her in your heart. You will find her there.

I can write to you now that my men and I are in good spirits. We have been forced to stay here in Rhode Island during the previous summer and winter while a heavily armed British warship patrols the harbor.

I have tried to imagine sometimes how the officers on the deck of the British ship are thinking. Surely, they must think they own the world. They take it for granted they have the right to hang any man who is not where he should be, and they have surely destroyed letters from my dear sister Sofie, whose health is always of great interest to me.

Our soldiers have been pinned down this long winter. I am sure you can imagine their restlessness and despair—so far away from their loved ones and from the nightlife of Paris. I have had to choose my words carefully in talking with the other officers. Otherwise, we get involved in pointless arguments.

Tomorrow, we set off for Philipsburg and then New York. There are hundreds of men in my force and Lafayette surely has a thousand more. Together with Washington's army we will surely prevail.

In October, I met George Washington outside of Hartford. He is the most famous of men—a hero in our times. His beautiful face is mild and polite showing his moral character. He is cool, speaking few words and yet he is good-natured and kind. There is a sadness in his eyes that intrigues me. His men walk in the snow, many of them without shoes. If they must, they leave a crimson trail of footprints, yet they march on. All about me is the spirit of courage.

You, too, most dear of women, possess such courage. You are not alone, nor will you ever be.

Faithfully, your servant

LETTER TO AXEL VON FERSEN

My bravest friend,

It is exactly as you said. My eyes devour your words; my fingers hold your pages tenderly between their tips, and your spirit is with me. Inside myself, I always hold you dear, but with this tangible connection, I feel I exist inside the aura of your compassion. Light fills my soul when you remind me that you are with me and will be always.

I would have you feel my presence, despite the paradox of my absence, just as strongly. Sometimes I fear that you feel alone—that my spirit is not robust enough to be a real presence in your life. Yet, I do not want you to think of me too much! I want you to be free to meet whatever dangers lie in America with your full attention.

The loss of my mother sits like a stone in the base of my throat. At this point, it is a smooth stone, a weight, an impediment to happiness, but my swallowed tears have worn it smooth. In the first month, I felt the stab of the sharp edges and rough cruelty of her death.

To you, in whom I can safely confide everything, I can speak the truth of how I loved my mother and how I treasured every sign of her affection for me. At the same time, I was sometimes afraid of her. I feared not her person but her displeasure. With her death, I feel that she has forgiven me my shortcomings, that from her heavenly position she understands my human frailty and weakness.

It is particularly in relationship to my gambling mania that I feel forgiven. (What a luxury it is not to feel the need to conceal from you anything about myself!) I wasted vast sums of money at the tables. I cannot excuse myself. Never! But from this perspective in time, I do feel that I lived in desperation then. I felt like a toad. No wonder my husband shunned my bed. My fear of losing money, my desire to win astonishing riches were like an intoxicant. Worse, I'm sure, than any wine or spirits. At the tables, I entered a trance, as some are said to do when they communicate with the dead. There I escaped from my own body, my lack of charm, my bad chin, my too large lower lip, my uneven shoulders. You have seen them all, yet you never see my imperfections. You do not wish to change me.

But my mother always hoped for my improvement.

Sometimes I am filled with the anguish that I may have disappointed her. Then I think of you and bask in the glow of your affection.

I am grateful to God for allowing our bond to exist. That your friendship with my husband is as steadfast as that for myself makes my happiness complete.

I pray for your safety. I wish I could envision you more exactly in that raw country across the water. As my mother used to write to me, I delight in knowing all the details of your daily life. I think that you must find their General Washington an admirable leader? Though he lacks noble blood, I am sure he would be at home in the Hall of Mirrors here at Versailles, just as Monsieur Franklin was.

Sometimes I look at our nobility and think what a worthless lot they are! Have you ever felt so? Once the King said so, when he discovered us playing forbidden games at the gambling tables. He never scolds. I am ashamed to say how many times he paid my debts.

Our debt to you for your allegiance to France—yes—but for your personal friendship and devotion can never be paid. Yet you can be sure that it is met in kind.

I reread this letter and see that I have not accounted for my escape from the bouts of hysteria that could be dissipated only by immersing myself in gambling. Becoming a mother has given me fulfillment. Being known by the dearest of friends is like having an angel who guards my happiness.

A new happiness is that I am pregnant again. Of course we hope that this child will be the longed-for heir to the throne, but in any case I await with impatience the moment when I lie down to begin my labor. Almost, I want the pain of it. I relish the thought of being filled—brim-full—with my pregnancy.

At no moment do I forget you! The thought of you—just the thought—makes all my moments joyful.

Red Stockings

The so-called Nords arrive today, but they are really the heirs, traveling incognito, to the throne of the Tsarina Catherine of Russia. It is one thing to act the part of the Queen of France among mere nobility, another when royalty are to visit. As I watch their splendid coach approach the Marble Courtyard, I drink a large glass of water to try to steady my nerves. At least my Rose Bertin has been so kind as to tell me the "Duchesse de Nord" has ordered the most fashionable clothes possible in which to appear so that she will not be nervous about her clothes during her visit to Versailles.

Suddenly my stage fright melts away, and I feel every fiber of my body vibrate with confidence and graciousness. This is Versailles, built to daunt visitors from any part of the world.

IT IS THREE O'CLOCK in the morning and still they have not left, but the supper was exquisite, and in the Peace room I arranged for a performance of Gluck's beautiful music from *Iphigénie en Aulide.* Many more fetes are to follow, and of course each must be more magnificent than the one before.

HEAVENS! The tsarevitch has confided the most inappropriate information about his mother to me. My face must have blushed scarlet. Certainly the Hapsburgs never stoop to revealing such private secrets. And then the tsarina has had the effrontery to mention the name of Madame du Barry. I simply reply that she has been provided for with a lavish home at Louveciennes.

"And when did she move there?" the Duchesse de Nord inquires.

"I believe it was about two years after the death of Louis XV," I reply. "I do not keep track of her life."

"But your brother visited her, did he not? Joseph II reported she was happy."

To that stunning piece of information I make no reply. Can they not detect that silence signals detour! New conversation, please.

Instead, the tsarevitch adds, "I understand the Duc de Brissac has made her happy and that his sickly wife takes no notice."

"De Brissac is said to be of a sweet disposition, as well as handsome and tall," the tsarina gushes.

I wish that I could pinch her lips closed. "For the final night of your visit," I announce, "we will have a grand masked ball in the Hall of Mirrors."

I COULD NOT be more pleased with my costume for the ball. In a dress of shiny silver gauze, my head topped with enormous white ostrich plumes, fastened by diamond pins, I represent Gabrielle d'Estrées, the mistress of Henri IV. My pregnant state is not overly noticeable, as the outline of my figure is diffused in the misty gauze.

With our reflections in the mirror and the reflections of the thousands of blazing candles, the Hall is enchanting with its glow and sparkle. In a way it seems a simple thing—that the Russians should come to call from St. Petersburg, that so much distance could be traversed, and all of us, for all our glittering finery, are after all mere people. How could I have forgotten such a fact a few days ago when I watched their coach arrive and wondered if I could adequately play my part? Still, I will be glad for their departure.

Just as the customary fireworks begin to ignite the sky, another color catches my eye: red. The red of stockings! And who would wear red stockings to this occasion? And who would dare to come without an invitation? The Cardinal Louis de Rohan! Would that he lived in Strasbourg or even Vienna!

Immediately, I demand to know who admitted him. How contemptuously pitiful that when he found himself not welcome at the ball for the Nords, he should so much desire to be present that he would stoop to bribery!

The answer is that he bribed a porter. His deceased uncle, the old cardinal I met in Strasbourg, would turn crimson with shame.

ONCE THE PORTER was identified, I had him dismissed from service, but dear Madame Campan has had him reinstated. She did it so simply. One evening after the departure of the Russians, Madame Campan was reading me to sleep with a fairy tale about a serving boy who offended a queen. Her dismissal of him caused his family to suffer terribly from hunger. I shed a tear or two, and my dear Reader asked if we could not allow our porter to resume his duties after all.

I am glad that I said yes. A slight, wise smile hovers at the corners of Madame Campan's mouth. Everything about her balances: the two corners of her mouth, her smoothly curved cheeks, her mild eyes, the poufs of powdered hair on each side of her face, the simple sheer white scarf that encircles her shoulders and is tied in a knot between her bosoms, her inclination to balance justice and mercy. She offers no excuses for the intrusive cardinal and his telltale red stockings but just for the porter who accepted the cardinal's bribe.

The Hope of France, 22 October 1781

I awake to gentle rumblings in my belly. These subterranean grippings are certainly recognizable to me: a child wishes to be born. But I do not attend to the process immediately; instead I drift back to sleep. (Perhaps I am remembering how long the process of giving birth took with my first child; just now, I do not wish to rush headlong into this protracted event.)

I dream of the latest visit of my brother, the Emperor Joseph II, a short visit. At that time, I was seven months pregnant. My brother was as kind to me as ever, indeed in my dream he is so proud that he struts as though he himself were the father.

Then the dream turns dark, and he is replaced by my friend Yolande de Polignac. "Never mind," she says, "I am the true father." I gnash my teeth with anguish, for I imagine these words emerging from her mouth in a little balloon, as in the crude drawings of the obscene pamphleteers.

Then a birth pain rocks me, and I wake up. I puzzle for a moment as to what has yoked my brother and my friend in this distasteful way. And I remember. The dream is my revenge: she has been critical of him. No wonder, perhaps. Even at his first visit, in the midst of my joy at our reunion, my brother had scant good to say of my new friend's character or of her circle. He only wished to guide me because he loves me; however, I find that I do not tolerate her criticism of him very well. I feel the cooling of my love for her because of it.

The thought terrifies me, and I vow to make some appropriate gesture that will bring her back close to me again. I banish the impulse to plan: I have work ahead of me, and I wish to be of clear and pure mind while I do it.

Another cramp seizes my abdomen. Still it is not severe. How strange to be in no hurry—none at all. I ask for my bath.

As I luxuriate in the warm water, I think that I resemble a great turtle, with its humped shell on backward. I think lazily of how I float in the tub, and the babe floats in me.

"Shall I cancel the hunt?" I hear the King say at the door.

I rake my spread fingers through the bathwater. I envision the King riding through the forest in pursuit of a wild-eyed stag, its antlers lifted high.

"Yes," I say, and realize I have meant to say no, but that none of it makes any difference. Yes, I am in the soft grip of my body now, and what the rest of the world does or doesn't do is of little concern. Soon, nature will squeeze me hard. I hold out my hand to be helped over the edge of my tub, for it would not do to take a fall now.

I allow myself to be dried, my big belly buffed a bit with towels. It is a rich moment. I feel like a pomegranate and wish that my skin could take on its hue, a blend of orange and red and rose, a streak of gold, some drops of black, the little crown on its top fit in shape if not in size to sit atop the head of a royal babe, a boy who would be king. I am a pomegranate mother.

Yes, I think, it has come about, it is coming about—all these events—as my mother promised before I left my country. I see her now, a dark wedge at her desk; she rises: *You will copulate, you become pregnant, nine months later you give birth, you will give France an heir. They will say I have sent them an angel.*

Suddenly I shake my head to clear it of these dreamy thoughts.

"This time," my husband says, "only a few will be present. The Princesse de Lamballe, the Comte d'Artois, Mesdames Tantes . . ." He goes on to name only a few more, and I think of his goodness to break with the traditions of over a hundred years, to give me a modicum of privacy.

"No." I smile at him. "Not like before, this time."

Again, I approach the little white birthing bed and lie down, unafraid, curious as to how this birth will resemble and not resemble the earlier one.

"There will be plenty of fresh air," my husband says, "and no fainting for lack of breath."

He himself pushes the window out, and I note the smells of dusty autumn leaves, nothing of the frigid winter breath of December almost three years ago.

The pains are strangely close together, and much less terrifying because they are familiar. I hear the long bonging of a clock, and though I do not count the strokes, I am familiar enough now with this sequence, in a musical way, to know that the noon hour must have been struck. "Twelve?" I say, and my husband looks at his watch and nods.

THE BIRTH COMES. And it is greeted with silence. Ah, I know what this silence means. The child is a girl, but I hold my counsel, smiling to myself.

She will be the friend of Marie Thérèse. I picture them holding hands, running through the rooms of Versailles, as Charlotte and I did, when I was the happy little sister, at Schönbrunn. I see again the lovely painted lattice walls of our playroom, with ivy twining through the interstices and painted birds here and there: blue, red, yellow. I think there is a little gap in consciousness, though I do not faint. A painted hibiscus flower trumpets orangey red; all in a cluster, the golden pollen points in its center thrust beyond the petals, awaiting the legs of bees. I am aware that the King and the babe have left the room. I wish for my mother. I see the mild, kind eyes of the Princesse de Lamballe, wide spaced and wet with emotion, but I cannot interpret what they say. *Let my new daughter live*, I pray.

The King enters, and I look at him with the new baby, small and well swaddled, a beautiful child. A sweet and tiny face.

"You see I am behaving very well," I murmur to the King. "I have asked no questions."

"Madame, you have fulfilled our hopes and those of France; you are the mother of a Dauphin."

My heart brims full and overflows. Leaning forward, I kiss the cheek of my mother. Promises and hopes *fulfilled*! I cannot speak, for joy. I feel her cheek against my lips.

The King fills the silence. "At precisely a quarter past one—for I looked at my watch—you were delivered successfully of a boy."

Joyful Noise

The labor done—oh, the fun and triumph of it all! Two weeks have passed since my little Louis Joseph came into this world, and the world is inflamed with joy—the King has told me all about it.

Some of the celebration I witnessed myself. Because she is the royal governess, the Princess de Guéméné received the baby, held him close against her, and sat in a chair, which was paraded through the château en route to her apartments. I could hear the shouts of joy and exclamations of admiration as they marched, even while I lay in my bed. The King witnessed it and told me that the crowd adoring our son was enormous, and many wept in their happiness for France. In one household, that of the Marquis de Bombelles, we heard that the giddy man literally ran through his house, shouting to everyone, "A Dauphin? A Dauphin! Can it be true? Is it possible? Oh what are they saying and doing at Versailles?"

The King himself was so moved that he wept throughout the christening ceremony, conducted the day after the child's birth, and Madame Campan tells me that he deploys his sentences so that he can utter the phrase "my son the Dauphin" as much as he can.

The wet nurse is actually named Madame Poitrine, which means Mrs. Breast—it delights me so!—and anyone can see she is the very embodiment of robust country health. The tsarina of Russia has bestowed a rattle upon our son fashioned from coral and a multitude of diamonds. All these details are told and retold in every village and on the streets of Paris, where strangers suddenly embrace one another. At great expense, the King has caused the city to be illumined with torches burning at the crossroads, and all the fountains are filled with wine.

How I wish I could have risen from my bed to see the tradesmen who came out from Paris, in a long procession of decorated wagons or floats ending at the Marble Courtyard. The guild of chimney sweeps carried a wonderful chimney from which sprang a tiny boy representing the Dauphin, and the locksmiths—how Louis loved to tell it, he himself being a crafter of locks—created a lock with a little Dauphin inside! I was told too that the league of wet nurses carried a woman in a sedan chair exhibited in the very act of nursing a child. Ah, Rousseau! Today you are vindicated!

TODAY THE MARKET women have insisted on coming all the way to my bed. Dressed in black silk—their finest—they recite verses in praise of the event. One of their number—she has a splendid, firm voice, almost like a man—has the speech written on the back of her fan. She can read, and she consults her prompt from time to time, first peering down into the fan, then rolling her eyes upward and fluttering the fan like a coquette. What a droll sight!

Then the fishwives recite couplets that they themselves have composed—some on the spot! The King and I laugh and we call for encores, and the entertainment is merrily repeated till we can whoop no more.

We have a bountiful feast served to all their company.

I LIKE TO THINK over it all and to tell myself again and again the details of the celebrations. But nothing compares to gazing at my little son as he lies in my arms. He has a more delicate face than his sister, and his eyes already seem thoughtful with a strange light in them. I am glad for him to have all the butterfat that Mrs. Poitrine's ample breasts afford. Unlike my daughter, he is the heir to the throne. He is a treasure, not to be nursed by a mere mother!

AH, AND THERE is more cheering and noise, about war, for we have heard that the Americans, aided by the French, have triumphed at Yorktown, and the British General Cornwallis has surrendered. They say that Lafayette will soon be home, and Count von Fersen and all the other gallant young soldiers. To think they have been gone three years.

How difficult it must be for mothers to watch their sons go off to war! I hope that my dear baby boy will never have to lead his country into battle.

As my husband and I look down into his crib, I ask, "Why is it that we rejoice in the happy conclusion of this American revolution? I know that this war has weakened England, but they have rebelled against their lawful king."

"George III and his Parliament taxed the colonies without regard for their prosperity. Because the king did not act as a good father to his American children, they felt it necessary to rebel."

"But was it truly right to do so?"

The King sighs and strokes the small cheek of our little son. "We must try to be good monarchs to our people so that they are content and loving."

I feel that he has not answered my question in a direct way, but I do not wish to press the point. While Fersen and Lafayette have returned, unharmed, surely many people suffered and died in this war across the sea.

"With the fruit of your womb comes the happiness of France," my husband says, reaching out his hand to me.

"You speak from the abundance of your heart," I say, "and your words are beautiful. I am happy."

He does not utter a syllable but leans his whole body forward to cover my lips with his. Shyly, his tongue enters. Never have I received a richer gift.

"Perhaps as a token of my appreciation of the birth of a Dauphin," the King says quietly, "you would allow me to have furnished for you some small chamber within the Palace of Versailles. A quiet and intimate place such as you like so well, but near at hand, so that you need not go all the way to the foot of the gardens to your Petit Trianon. Would you like such a private apartment?"

All in a flash, I remember the unused apartments I discovered deep within the maze of the palace, when I played the game of Seek and Seek with Artois. I think sadly how we are not such good friends now, of how he and his brother the Comte de Provence succumbed to jealousy once the King and I began to have children. With the birth of the Dauphin their own hopes for themselves or their children ever becoming king have surely dwindled to nothing.

"Yes," I reply slowly. "I can think of just such an intimate space. Its rooms have low ceilings and many little nooks and strange angles. The fireplaces are small and cunning. A daybed could be built there where I could rest in the afternoon."

"The Méridienne," the King says, naming my retreat for afternoon naps. "There will be many symbols of the Dauphin there."

I think of the pastoral style of my Petit Trianon and determine that the style of this chamber will be quite different. Something in the newer style, called "antique," that reflects the Roman culture, with Greek sphinxes and perfume censers as gilded carvings against the walls, the wainscotting and carved ornamentation all gold on white. Upholstery to be in a seeded light blue damask for the draperies around my little bed, and its coverlet, and the chairs nearby. Yes, gold and white and blue.

I am quite overcome by the King's desire to surround me with comforts and beauty of the types I find most refreshing.

ONLY THE FACT that the Cardinal Louis de Rohan, now established as Grand Almoner, will hold in his hands our precious son at his christening upsets me. When the event occurs, I know that my heart will rebel against that hypocritical prince of the church. Yet people tell me that he would do anything to win my favor and admission to my circle of intimate friends. These ideas make me shudder. He must appear, it would seem, like an evil fairy from time to time in my life.

Simplicity

I wish to dress myself more simply. Here at Trianon, I do not lead a public life but a private one, and it is ridiculous to apply big circles of bright rouge on my cheeks, to tread my garden paths impeded by skirts with wide panniers. Sometimes a rosebush leans a bit into the path and snags my stiff and cumbersome garment as I pass. It is nature's reprimand. Muslin would be better—and much less of it! Thirty-six yards to clothe a single person? Absurd.

Leonard has cut my hair short and feathery to help it thicken after the ravages of pregnancy. My whole head feels lighter and more airy. When I stroll in the autumnal garden, I simply wear a broad-brimmed hat instead of a towering coif topped further in an ungainly mound of velvet and ostrich feathers.

From whence come these new ideas about fashion and decor? From the air. From the spirit of change. Ideas and feelings more invisible even than clouds can float into every brain to whisper: *we must cast off old customs;* they are too confining and inadequate to our present temperament and needs.

My son, behind me, carried in the arms of his nurse as I stroll, makes sweet babble. Perhaps it is his presence that causes me to want a new world for his fresh and lovely being.

Behind my son, another nurse holds the hand of my daughter, who insists on walking on her own two feet, though it makes our progress slow and almost tedious. I sigh. I feel grateful that there are so many lovely grasses and birds to observe. I lean over and pluck two blue asters, bits of star-shaped sky come to grow beside my path.

Louis Joseph sleeps, his face wrinkled against the sunlight. I turn back and hold the flowers on either side of my daughter's pink cheeks. Yes, the flowers' color matches her eyes, blue as English asters in autumn. She reaches for the flowers, and I give them to her. I kiss her diminutive knuckles and return to the head of the procession to continue my musings and our walk. A blue jay flies across my way, screaming his raucous cry.

I think if God looked down at me, He would see a shepherdess, taking a simple stroll, in a remote corner of France, with her babies and their nurses, among the last flowers of the fall, and He would approve. He likes simplicity, for He is the God of nature, and it is His first creation. "Consider the lilies of the field, they toil not, neither do they spin. Yet Solomon in all his glory was not arrayed as one of these." (Louis Joseph lets out a feeble cry, as though he were hungry, but I know that cannot be so.) Here at Trianon and in the decoration of new rooms in other châteaux, I will strive for simplicity.

If they knew of it, the pamphleteers would describe this quiet half hour with my children as an opportunity for debauchery, with an assortment of lovers—male and female—hidden behind every pear tree, underneath each pile of autumn leaves.

The Return of Fersen from America, 15 July 1783

My soldier returns! When he walks into the room, the courtiers stand aside to clear an aisle for his approach. They part like the waters of the Red Sea, for the passage of Moses. Completely at his ease, the count walks briskly, as though returning from an absence of three days instead of three years. One of the heroes of Yorktown, he is unscathed, intact, only his skin seems more weathered. His eyes are almost the same, but they have changed because they have read my letters while he was away. Even from a distance, his eyes look into mine with the love of a true friend, and with the kindness and understanding that envelop love as the husk encloses the corn. Everything about his deportment is perfectly appropriate: he returns to the Queen of the country for which he fought; in no way does he claim more. His modesty resides in his elegance.

Now is the time: he places his hand on his heart and inclines his head, lowering his eyes. At that moment, I rise from my chair and curtsy.

The room gasps at the favor I show him, but it is fitting: he is a hero who has served the interests of France in the wilderness of America, one who has fought a triumphant war against the English. When he raises his head, he sees me standing, and he blushes.

I hold out both hands to him. Ah, to join my hands with his! It is he himself! For this brief ceremonial moment he takes my hands in his. Our flesh is of matching warmth, and that fact is our secret and ours alone, for the courtiers know only what they see. Our hearts kindle and meet in one warmth, but our eyes betray nothing of our feelings. We would like to squeeze our hands together in rapture, but we do not. We touch. We release. My hands are glowing.

"Nothing could ever bring me greater pleasure," I say, "than to welcome you to a court that I hope you will regard as home."

"I most sincerely thank Her Majesty for the honor she bestows on me. May God grant that I am permitted to serve the causes of Her Majesty all the days of my life."

He calls me *Majesty* with perfect propriety but his eyes say to mine: "More than queen, Lovely Woman, I lay my heart and life at your feet."

"I see you come decorated. And what is this new medal?"

"The new medal is the order of Cincinnatus."

"And who or what is Cincinnatus?" I ask. I know the answer, for his letters have told me of his honor, but I wish the lords and ladies assembled to know of his glory.

Very slightly, he tucks down his chin to signal his reluctance to speak of his own valor.

"Cincinnatus was a tribal chieftain among the American Indians who lived in the Ohio River Valley." I see a cloud of melancholy pass over his countenance, but it does nothing to mar his attractions; indeed, it adds a degree of maturity and depth to his mien. "He was named for a Roman statesman of antiquity."

I invite everyone to extend individual greetings to our Swedish count, and soon they swirl about him in tides of color and glittering jewels, and their faces too are bright with gladness. Because he is a foreigner, their greetings are more genuine and less calculated than if he were one of them.

The Princesse de Lamballe stands beside me and remarks, "If he has changed at all, it is only for the better."

The Duchesse de Polignac says, "Your Majesty is pregnant again, and again the count comes to court—a conjunction of lucky stars. The Queen is always in her greatest glory when she is pregnant—her skin is radiant; her eyes sparkle."

"My dears," I reply. "I am unspeakably happy."

For all the frankness of my admission, standing between my two dearest friends at court, I try not to sound too jubilant. Yolande's lover, the Comte de Vaudreuil, is off with the King's younger brother to play at fighting in Spain. I miss the comte too, for he is the most talented of our amateur actors, but he is a dandy, his gambling debts and expenditures are enormous, and in short, he entirely lacks not only the noble bearing but also the noble character of Axel von Fersen.

To our surprise and delight, the King suddenly appears to extend his own welcome to our hero of the American Revolution. He kisses Fersen on both cheeks and then pats his shoulder and beams upon him. Like two brothers, the men are glad to see each other, and again I admire the balance in the count's decorum—he is perfectly respectful, with no shred of familiarity, but at the same time, his manner is one of companionable ease. Because he is secure in his own character, he is not made artificial by the presence of royalty.

When I join them, the King compliments me on my glowing appearance. Only our closest circle know that I am pregnant, but of course I have hinted in my letters to so close a friend as the count of my happy state. Placing his arm around me to draw me close to him, the King continues his happy conversation with the count, and all of us seem like a family reunited.

ANOTHER DAY, at Trianon as we stroll a little apart from the others, I am able to ask the count how his plans toward marriage have progressed, for I know it has been his father's fond hope that Axel will marry an English heiress.

The garden is in its high summer bloom, and never have we had such an abundance of roses. Their perfume makes the air itself intoxicating. I am dressed in the simple white muslin I love so well, and the count has expressed his admiration of my straw hat, with a pink ribbon hanging off the brim in back. He says what a fortunate hat it is to be allowed to grace the head of the fairest woman and queen in the world.

He answers my question with the frankness and honesty I so appreciate in him: "I am very glad that Miss Leyell of England is married now. Of course she will not be mentioned to me again, by my father. It is my ardent desire that he will propose no other possible marriage to me. My own mind is quite settled—I do not wish to marry. For me, such conjugal ties would be against nature at this point. I cannot belong to the only person to whom I want to belong, the one who really loves me, and so I do not want to belong to anyone."

Because we are almost alone and the path curves around a very large specimen of *Rosa rugosa*, he is able to pause and to face me as he pronounces that last sentence. Should the wind carry his words to some waiting ear, still there would be no incrimination in what he has said—a confidence to a close friend, who listens to him with sympathy. With utmost sympathy, my eyes linger, feast, on his.

"I live in your eyes," I cannot stop myself from whispering.

He resumes our walk. "And so we understand each other," he says.

I glance up at him and see the beautiful muscles of his cheek flex and set themselves. His manliness causes my knees to melt and tremble. We continue to walk.

"We understand," I say.

There is a scurrying behind us, and it is the Comte de Vaudreuil, returned now from his pretense of warriorhood, pursuing Yolande, whose face is as pink as a raspberry from running.

"Don't let him catch me," she cries to Fersen as she slips past us.

Always gallant, the count turns to face the on-charging Vaudreuil and holds out both arms. "I command you in the name of an unnamed lady"—Fersen laughs—"to halt in this headlong pursuit."

Vaudreuil stops, with perfect good nature. "I was pretending to be Almaviva. Beaumarchais has a new play. Quite revolutionary, really."

"Revolution? I've seen enough of that," Fersen replies.

Because it is the hot part of the summer day, Vaudreuil's face is running with sweat. He yanks off his powdered wig and beats it against his thigh. Really, he is quite disreputable in appearance. "Someday we must get rid of these abominations," he says carelessly. "Did your George Washington review his troops wearing a powdered wig?" The little cloud of powder he has created blows away over the tops of the purple clover.

In the distance, Yolande calls, "I am first in the swing. Come push me, all you swains!"

"Some time ago, I conceived of having a hamlet, a village to play in, back here, beyond the gardens of Trianon. The swing is a harbinger of the rustic fun to come."

"If I were an artist," Fersen replies as we view the lovely Yolande waiting for us, sitting in the swing, "certainly I would want to paint her."

It is a lovely picture. The long ropes of the swing are fastened high above in an enormous chestnut tree; its leaves are green-black and are of amazing density and profusion.

"Boucher already has painted a lady swinging so gaily that her slipper has flown off into the air. We will have a world of gay abandon, back here, when my peasant play-village is complete."

THIS IS THE BEST, most carefree summer of my life. Occasionally, I am visited in the early morning with vomiting, but by the time the count makes his daily visit, I am quite well and eager to enjoy myself in his dear company. I do not like to stay up too late because the fatigue of my condition visits me by ten in the evening, but earlier than that, we stroll in the dusk while musicians play. If I become warm, we stroll—I and my ladies, sometimes with the count, occasionally with the King—close to a fountain, and its cooling misty spray refreshes me.

One evening as I walk with the count, my hand through his arm, lest I turn my ankle, accompanied by Elisabeth, the King's sister, as well as by many others, I remark, "Now since I am become a mother, twice over, and soon, I trust, to be a third time, it is Ceres with whom I identify myself."

The Duchesse de Polignac says fervently, "Pray that no child of yours, then, is snatched off to the Underworld."

I am startled by her comment and wonder if she has noticed some change in the Dauphin's health. Hers is not a welcome comment on a summer night.

"My children always prosper in the summer," I say. "They do not need to be watched so closely."

Axel von Fersen asks me if I am aware of the Botticelli painting titled *Primavera.* I say that I am not. He mentions that he saw it in his travels with his tutor before he first came to France. In one part of the painting is a lovely blond Flora, he explains, in a diaphanous white gown printed with many colored flowers. "The remarkable thing is that she is quite pregnant. In her rotundity, she is even more beautiful than the central figure."

I call to my painter friend, Madame Vigée-Lebrun, who is with us this evening, asking if she knows of this work. She replies that she has seen engravings of it, but not the painting itself. "Did you see also the painting of Venus rising from the sea?" she asks Axel.

He replies that he did. "Born of the foam of the sea," he says, and I know without his telling me that her figure is lovely and nude, for we are all born naked. I recall that scene of my own girlhood nakedness when I was born anew as a French *citoyenne*, but I do not speak of it. It was too long ago.

The King arrives in a sedan chair and calls to us with informal good nature. He has grown quite portly, and the evening is too hot for him to walk any distance without endangering his health. Ever considerate of my needs, he has had a second chair brought for me, for the path from the park back to the château is all uphill.

Gladly, I accept the transport.

As I return to the lighted palace, past the various fountains, I particularly admire the fountain of Latona. It was long ago that the market women reduced me to distress after the birth of Artois's child, and Madame Campan pointed out the window at the fountain of Latona among the amphibians. Like her, I have two children, but I live in utter safety while she was forced to wander from village to village. I am grateful my husband is a more loyal spouse than Jupiter.

It is good to see him comfortably transported, not far from me, but each in our separate chairs, moving toward the beautifully illuminated palace. As is my custom when pregnant, I encourage no conjugal acts, and the King acquiesces willingly, glad to have no royal duty to perform, glad to provide with his abstinence greater safety for the unborn child.

My two children are not of the gods and goddesses, but they are beloved human children. I have a twinge of guilt that my attention to Axel von Fersen has caused me somewhat to neglect my little ones, not in any observable way, but just a wee bit, within the walls of my heart. Steadily, the King and I float uphill toward the château.

Sometimes, framed by the windows of the Hall of Mirrors, I can see the twinkling lights of the chandeliers, or their reflections in the mirrors. Sometimes I hear a few harp notes on the air and suppose that my Aunt Victoire is practicing her instrument. The open sedan chair allows us to enjoy the slight summer breezes. I feel almost that I am rising magically toward the beautiful château and my rest. In his chair, the King is dozing and emitting soft snores. The ground glides past as the men carry my chair, and I listen to their feet moving on the grass or the gravel.

These nights, these days—what blessings they are. We are all happy because a regiment has been bought for Count von Fersen, with the help of his father and the recommendation of his king, Gustavus III. Axel is most happy of all; indeed, he said that his entire happiness depended on his acquiring the regiment. The expenditure was 100,000 livres.

Montauciel

My only regret has been that summer turns into September, until a less expected regret occurs: that same King of Sweden who contributed toward Fersen's regimental appointment has reversed himself; Gustavus now wishes the count to join his entourage as he travels. Instead of commanding a regiment of his own, Fersen is to be the captain of the bodyguard for Gustavus. Utterly devoted to the monarchy, his obedience is instant. I only note the clenching of his well-chiseled jaw, which sometimes betrays that he labors to master his natural inclinations for the sake of duty.

The day before his departure on September 20, we are to view an unprecedented spectacle: the Montgolfier brothers have requested of my husband and received his permission to launch a hot-air balloon from the broad courtyard that stands between the palace and the town of Versailles. Exhibiting an amazing degree of anticipation and curiosity, thousands of spectators, conveyed here by their own feet, by carriages, by sedan chairs, pack the courtyard.

Journalists have speculated that if the ascent is successful, it will open a new era of possibility and not only in modes of travel. Many things that have never been accomplished before will be brought to pass. From the publication *Correspondance Secret*, the King reads a most humorous pronouncement to all those in our viewing party: "The invention of Monsieur de Montgolfier has given such a shock to the French that it has restored vigor to the aged, imagination to the peasants, and constancy to our women!"

We are separated from the crowd by our own, slightly elevated viewing area, but there is a press of people here in the vast courtyard. If the balloon were to fall on the mob, a panic could ensue, with many lives lost. But all is orderly, despite the degree of eager excitement in the air, and the sun is shining brightly.

A few clouds drift lazily over the high ornate ridge of the chapel; it is indeed hard to believe that anything invented by man might float up to such a height as the chapel roof. Perhaps the balloon will float over the ground at only the height of a man's shoulder over the ground, rather like a carriage but without wheels or horses.

It is a strangely exciting day, though my heart sinks when I remember that soon Axel von Fersen will leave—tomorrow! At least we are assured that Gustavus plans no transoceanic adventures but will confine his journey to Europe. "Are humans to make the ascent?" I anxiously ask the King. What a horrible omen if people were to fall from the sky the very day before Count von Fersen's departure.

"No," the King replies. "The balloon will raise a basket wherein will be housed a sheep, a duck, and a rooster."

"At least the duck has the gift of his own strong wings," I respond, "should the experiment fail."

"I think that the door of the wicker kennel will be closed," the King answers. "Perhaps the animals have been trained to lift the latch of the gate, should there be need of an emergency disembarkment."

"But what of the sheep?" I ask. "Once out of the cage, he would surely fall to his death." My whole body cringes at the thought of the helpless woolly animal named Montauciel plunging to the hard earth below, be it courtyard pavement or the hills of the countryside.

"Let us have confidence in these scientists," Fersen advises.

The King chuckles, "So as not to frighten the ladies."

Fersen smiles in return. "Just as Bottom promised in Shakespeare's play not to roar too loudly when he played the part of the lion—so as not to frighten the ladies."

"You read him in English?" the King asks, but he already knows that Fersen is fluent in English and has also read in English his own beloved Hume.

I can see young Elisabeth glancing at Fersen with utmost admiration. Lean and martial in appearance, he resembles a sculpted rock fashioned into a man. The King has grown soft and portly from many hours of sitting at council tables and at his desk, or reading, in spite of the hard riding of the hunt. The gossips compare him to a hog, a description that hurts me, for his sake. I would remind people that he is a moral and well-read man, one who considers the good of the people and not just the comfort of the nobility.

"I do not want the Dauphin to witness a disaster," the King continues. Lovingly, he picks up our two-year-old son in his own arms. "Let's inspect the balloon," he proposes. To Fersen he adds in a low voice that so many undifferentiated people have not packed the courtyards of Versailles since the flour riots, soon after he became king. But this is a happy crowd, on holiday.

Some sixty feet long, the balloon lies in an immense azure puddle on the ground. His eyes large with the wonder of the expanse of fabric, the Dauphin points his little finger at what he correctly identifies as his father's insignia painted in yellow on the limp side of the great balloon. Attendants lift up its huge mouth, and we look into the blue cavern. Soon it shall be pulled up, like a tent, by a hook-and-pulley system attached at the tops of two great wooden masts. A fire will be built beneath its opening so that the close-woven fabric will catch and retain the heated air until the balloon is inflated. When the great bubble is sufficiently filled, its gondola loaded with the animals and the tethers severed, we shall see if it will float upward, or run along the ground, or perhaps utterly collapse.

From our platform we watch the lighting of the fire, open our picnic baskets, and serve lemonade to our group. We share our picnic with two young Englishmen, William Pitt and William Wilberforce, who are members of the House of Commons in England, drawn here by their admiration for French culture and their desire to become proficient in our language.

Some hours pass before, at one o'clock in the afternoon, a startling drumroll is heard, and the great axes, made shiny for the occasion, are raised in readiness. The poor sheep, named Mont-au-ciel ("Climb-to-the-sky," Fersen explains to the Englishmen), bleats pitifully. She does not like the proximity of the duck. Even more, she fears the sharp beak of the rooster, who crows loudly, as though to demonstrate his self-importance in this great experiment, and then pecks at the sheep's eyes. Standing beside the fire under the balloon is Étienne Montgolfier, dressed very simply, all in black, the soul of modesty in his matter-of-fact demeanor. Thunderous applause for the creator of the balloon joins the drum as it rolls on and on. Then Montgolfier raises his hand. The crowd silences; the drumroll suddenly stops. There is an astonished quiet, the axes fall, the tethers are severed, and ever so slowly, the great balloon begins majestically to rise.

The crowd lets out a terrifying shriek of joy as the balloon continues, in stately manner, to ascend. On one side the duck thrusts his head through the bars of his cage, and on the other side appears the bright comb and wattles of the rooster. The sheep's mouth is open, but I can no longer hear her distressed bleats. More quickly, now, the balloon rises, the crowd urging it on as though it were a racehorse. For as far as I can see out into the throng, tears of joy are flowing down the cheeks of the common people. The balloon rises to the level of the second floor of the surrounding buildings, and on up to the third level. Now it is even with the mansard roofs.

Will it actually rise above the chapel roof, crowned in gleaming gold? To do so almost seems sacrilege. But, yes, the balloon glides higher than the House of God. The crowd groans with fear, for suppose it should be divinely struck down in its vaulted pride, as well as all those assembled below who cheer this conquest of the air, heretofore the realm of angels and of birds? Though it is floating away from us, the balloon climbs not so high as the clouds—I could not bear it if it went so high as that.

Even should God allow such a man-made miracle, my heart would burst for fear of what human beings have become capable of achieving.

Now many of the crowd rush out of the courtyards in an attempt to follow the balloon as it drifts majestically away. It is like a large blue mushroom, proudly bearing the golden fleur-de-lis of the monarchy. The dangling circular kennel is dwarfed by the girth of the balloon and seems dragged after it, an afterthought. The balloon tilts a bit, as a sail would, because of the prevailing breeze.

Suddenly a rent appears high in the canopy of the balloon, and a quantity of the hot gray smoke is emitted. The balloon wobbles, and the crowd shrieks in fear, but it continues its journey out toward the countryside.

Consulting his watch, the King notes that the balloon has been aloft some three minutes.

"The possible uses for such a machine challenge the imagination," Fersen says.

For the first time, his countenance looks fierce to me. As though he senses my thought, he quickly looks at me, and smiles. "Does Your Majesty think it a pretty spectacle?"

"I am afraid and happy all at once," I answer truthfully.

"Look at the faces of the people," the King says.

We see their wonder. They feel as though perhaps they too were lifted a little off the ground, when the balloon rose up. They seem to walk on tiptoe.

The King suggests that all the royal party return to the palace, for music and celebration.

THROUGHOUT THE HALL of Mirrors, on this eve of Fersen's departure, we dance to mannered minuets, gavottes, and allemands. Our skirts swish and tilt over the floor in something of the manner of a herd of hot-air balloons. In one corner stands the dark column of Montgolfier, and all the brightly skirted ladies crowd around him, some with coifs to suggest balloons.

The ladies flutter their fans, decorated in anticipation of this gathering with pictures of balloons among the clouds. A few fans sport the figure of Montgolfier in the dark clothing of a chimney sweep standing next to a fire. Aloof, the man of science pays little attention to the coquetry of our ladies.

Because of my pregnancy—though I have gained little girth—I am careful not to dance too much. As I rest in a chair beside the King, all about us the courtiers speculate on the possibilities of human balloon travel—

that it could be used for smuggling, that it might engender war in the skies with blood raining down on all those below. Someone expresses concern that the ascent of the balloon will undermine religion, because the Assumption of the Virgin into heaven may cease to appear miraculous.

Some wag suggests that, with the aid of hot-air balloons, lovers might be able to come down chimneys, then ascend back into their waiting balloons with the daughters of the house, clad only in their nightgowns. Glancing at the count, I cover my hand with my fan and giggle.

We learn that the balloon traveled for eight minutes before it landed in the woods a few miles beyond the château. The basket having opened, Montauciel the sheep was found nibbling greenery, as though she had not been the first sheep in history to fly. The cock and the duck huddled in a feathery trans-species embrace in a corner of their gondola.

BEFORE HE TAKES his formal leave, the count chooses the single moment when we are alone to offer me reassurance. He looks at me, bends toward my ear, and says calmly but with intensity, "Of course it is impossible that we can ever be parted."

Fearing that someone at the ball has learned the art of lip reading, I merely nod.

A Bitter Birthday, 1783

It is my birthday. I have lost the unborn child on my birthday. Soon after Fersen left, the King and I admitted to each other that our beloved little Dauphin Louis Joseph is not robust, and this new child was very much wanted. I confessed one of my nightmares to the King, that I hear the Dauphin cry in the night, his little body afire with fever.

And now a miscarriage. A child who will never cry.

It is a bitter thing.

For my birthday, the King has given me a prayer book, a precious illuminated volume titled *Les Très Riches Heures du Duc de Berry.* Indeed, the pictures, very wonderful copies of the medieval original, are enchanting. Some of the colors are like stained glass. Other scenes possess all the charm of real life, one of harvests and of peasants living in France in the fifteenth century, so long ago. Idly, I turn the pages. Rich hours? The title of the book seems ironic, on a day when I have lost an unborn child. These hours are leaden.

The poor King! Sitting beside me, he cries as though his heart would break! He covers his large face with his large hand, and weeps.

I AM ALMOST TOO WEAK to think. Too weak to look at my gift or to offer comfort to my husband. How many baskets full of cloths soaked with my blood did they carry away? One after another, with a clean cloth folded on top, so that I would not have to see the evidence of disaster. But I saw the blood through the weave of the basket, once, and I saw a drop fall down and be absorbed by the carpet.

Because Fersen was here, during the summer months of this pregnancy, I thought God had sent me a good omen, for Fersen has always come during my pregnancies.

How Count von Fersen pleased me with his presence. Every moment was a treasure. Everyone said his gaze has grown more icy, since his time in the American War, that now he rarely smiles. His reserve tempts the ladies, for each wishes that she might have the power to restore his spirits to animation.

But I notice no such lack of animation in his spirit or his features. For me, he always smiles.

I ache with the misery of this loss.

When Fersen first appeared at court, in July, I said to him again, "Ah, an old acquaintance," which is how I greeted him before, after a long absence. *I close my eyes; yes, better to remember the hours, days, afternoons that were years ago.* He recognized the phrase, smiled, softly clicked his heels together, and all was between us exactly as it had been before, magnified, because now we knew our affection had outlasted time and distance.

He told me what a joy it was to be once more in my Private Society.

Almost, now, I want to smile. His presence now would cheer me.

BALLOONMANIA

After several weeks in bed recovering from the miscarriage, I feel well enough to dine with my friends. Yolande has promised an amusing time. She does not usually employ the word *amusing*, so I am full of curiosity.

It is a pleasant dinner, but I cannot say that I have been amused. Nonetheless my appetite has been good, and I have eaten beef, because the doctors say it strengthens the blood.

"For dessert," she says, her face exceedingly merry, "we shall have fruit tarts and fruit itself."

A very large dish is brought in, capped with a silver hood. At a nod from Yolande, the cover is removed by a servant, and there I see the tarts and fruit—but, behold! The fruit begins to rise! To my amazement—yes, vast amusement!—apples, oranges, a pineapple, limes, pears, a bunch of grapes, are steadily floating upward in the air!

"Balloons," she shrieks, "filled with methane gas."

"They are lighter than ordinary air," the King explains, his eyes twinkling, "so they rise."

IT HAS NOT been long since the fruit-shaped balloons rose up from the table, past the decanters of sherry and port, up to the level of the putti near the ceiling, that the King comes to my private chambers within the château to read me an article describing the first human ascent by balloon: a young physician of the last name of Rozier, age twenty-six, along with an army officer have been the first human beings to be carried aloft by a globe of hot air. While the King reads, I work at my needlepoint. The King explains that methane is too susceptible to explosion to be trusted in such a venture at the present time. Large balloons bearing people are best filled with hot air.

The King goes on to read aloud Pilâtre de Rozier's life. To provide interaction with the public for scientists excluded by the Royal Academy, he created an open Musée des Sciences containing books and scientific equipment, in Paris. Not only men but women might be given admission to the museum—but only if they were recommended by three male members. Rozier has written a book titled *Electricity and Loving.*

"What is this electricity?" I ask.

"It was discovered by the American statesman Benjamin Franklin. It is the force in lightning that lights the sky and has the power to kill people and to knock the bark from trees."

"How is it related to *loving*?"

The King lays down his lorgnette. "I can't imagine," he replies.

Both of us look at one another, dumbfounded. Then we laugh.

It is the first time we have laughed together since the miscarriage.

ON THE FIRST of December, very formally at dinner, the King announces, "What months these are!"

We all wait to hear what he will say next. He lifts a glass of Bordeaux to propose a toast. All of us rise—we happen to be dining with his two brothers, the Comte de Provence and the Comte d'Artois, and their wives, planning festivities for the Christmas season—though we do not yet know what solemn occasion has just occurred.

"Congratulations to Messieurs Charles and Robert. From the Tuileries gardens in Paris, they have soared aloft for a full ninety minutes, come back safely to earth, and been greeted as they stepped from their basket by the Duc d'Orléans."

We all shout hooray, as though we were the triumphant aeronauts, but I can see that the King wishes with all his being that it had been he who had had the honor of greeting the heroes.

I notice my husband's eye falls with interest on another item in his paper, below the fold.

"Is there more to the story?" I ask.

"No, no," he replies. "Only here it says that in one's own kitchen one can make a miniature balloon from the bladder membrane of an ox."

All the rest of us burst into laughter.

The King looks a bit sheepish. "It says to use fish glue," he adds.

A Double Portrait, Spring 1784

In a rapture of excitement, though I try not to show it, I watch my friend paint my children. We are all outside at Trianon, and they sit on a large stone step. As I watch her transport their actual beauty to the world of the canvas, I am radiant with pleasure. Such an art she has, Elisabeth Vigée-Lebrun!

Not long ago, the Dauphin lay so ill with a consuming fever that he could not pass water, and his body bloated. The physicians explained that such an ordeal strengthens a child against future maladies and surely he would recover. Yes, I said, it is unthinkable that he will not recover. And he did, but when I look at him now, dressed in pale blue satin beside his sister, I want to say to her, "Hold him to you more closely."

Her arm is around his little shoulders; his sweet hand touches her forearm. In the painting they appear to tend some little gray birds, though actually the birds are products of taxidermy. When my friend paints them, she imagines them back into life; she paints the one in the Dauphin's hand with an open beak.

His fingers enclose the feathery bird, a meadowlark, so gently, as though he would not for all the world squeeze the life out of it. In the hand resting on her lap, Marie Thérèse holds the nest, with a number of other occupants.

The Dauphin's eyes look right out at us, but they are wistful, and I can easily see the traces of illness in his expression. My friend paints it just so—his large, tired eyes—for she knows my anguish and how I treasure him for his delicacy.

She is no less accurate in capturing my daughter's expression: her smile that curves slightly down, the tight little pressure that is often between her lips. Her taffeta dress is the technical masterpiece of the painting: peach and blue stripes, smooth here but slightly crumpled there, reflecting the light in a hundred different ways. A wisp of scarf softens the neckline, while a pink flower—is it an apple blossom?—is pinned to one side. My daughter's gaze is partly on her brother, partly on the twiggy nest; her gaze seems partly unfocused, or focused on inward thoughts. Sometimes I feel just like that—softly absent. The pointed toe of a white satin slipper peeps out from under the hem of her skirt.

I love the softness of Madame Vigée-Lebrun's touch, the vibrancy of her colors, even when they are pastel. I wish there had been such a painter in Vienna to capture the enchantment of my own childhood.

My children hold a nest, but they themselves are little birds with open beaks, needing the careful care of those who would hold them tenderly.

The court calls the time I lavish on my children *frivolity.* They criticize me for wishing to take care of my own children, for they feel I neglect my duties as Queen, which is to say, spending time at court with them. But what do they want of me? Only favors and gossip. They are behind the times in not appreciating the appeal of children, and when they are old, they will regret that they preferred to hold stiff playing cards in their hands instead of the trusting fingers of their children and that they studied the faces of jacks and spades instead of the sweet eyes and lips of innocence.

When my friend painted me in my muslin dress, the courtiers demanded that the picture be removed from the Salon. They said it was unseemly to portray the Queen in her chemise, her undergarment, yet less of my bosom is exposed than if I wore a court dress. Moreover, this same Salon accepted Adélaide Labille-Guiard's portrait of Madame Mitoire breast feeding her babe, a subject never depicted in modern painting. When they scorned the simple appeal of my straw hat, I knew all their criticism of my portrait was actually an attack on me. They call me Madame Déficite. I think they wanted to criticize the very rose that I held in my hand, but it is my favorite painting of myself, and the one that is truest to my spirit. And such simple clothes are less expensive.

Now my friend proposes to paint me again in the same attitude, only this time dressed in blue satin.

I am glad the Dauphin is wearing blue satin for his portrait, for I could not bear it if they criticized my son. I would want to run away to another country, and then they would have no king and no future! I would want to lock us behind gates that they could never enter, and there we would have an uninterrupted idyll, my dear family, my true friends, and I.

The Season of the *Hameau*

Count von Fersen writes to me that my letters are all about the building of the hamlet of late, and that I mention the theater less and less frequently. This observation surprises me—certainly it is not a criticism. It is an observation about a change that is perhaps made so slowly that I hardly detect it.

I fear such changes. Sometimes I wonder if the Dauphin is not slowly losing ground, and because the change is gradual, I fail to take proper note of it. The doctors are so determined not to upset me that I sometimes wonder about the veracity of their explanations. When I mention my fear to the King, he only looks at me sadly, his eyelids at half-mast. He grunts in a troubled, sympathetic way. He offers no opinion. When I press him, he says we must rely on the doctors.

It is true that thoughts and plans for the *Hameau* delight me. We have a model of how it will all be built. When I look down on the model, I feel rather like a goddess viewing the earth from Olympus, only this is a very French earth, with tiny model French cows and French sheep beautifully placed in the pasture of the miniature working farm, to be located at the edge of the village and to supply the wholesome things we shall eat there, our cheese and butter.

But certainly I have loved the theater well. Last spring I was playing the roles of Babet and Pierrette, both of them simple, loving country girls. In contrast, this spring I talk endlessly with Hubert Robert and Richard Mique about our designs for the *Hameau*. I shall have over one thousand white porcelain flowerpots, decorated in blue with my own monogram, modeled on that lovely superimposition of the letters *M* and *A* on the clasp of the bracelet I received at the time of my marriage. These rustic pots will be placed on the wooden staircase that spirals up to the balcony and on the balcony itself, lined up like so many little soldiers. And the darling pots will also adorn the winding stair up the Marlborough lighthouse tower, overlooking the pond. I think the pots will be filled with red geraniums, but the air of the *Hameau* will be redolent from spring through summer with the aroma of lilac, roses, jasmine, and myrtle. And I will have nightingales to sing during the evening hours! Wild ones, but so well fed with the nicest seeds that they will never want to fly away.

My white lawn dresses, tied with a simple sash, topped with a straw hat, can be worn whether I am in the artificed world of the *Hameau* or receiving guests in the château itself. Passing from one world to another—is not that the provenance of spirits?

I've already spoken to the artisans at Sèvres about my milk buckets, made of porcelain to resemble rough wood. Every detail will be artistically perfect, and I've already named the cows Blanchette and Brunette.

And so, does my attention wander from the theater? I think I am taking the world of imagination off the stage and into the real world. The sets are no longer flat paper cutouts to be slid out of the wings into the glow of the theatrical lamps, but real places, where one can go in and out.

NOW WHILE THE *Hameau* is half finished, it seems especially to hang between two worlds. The model village was like a seed, but there is the life-size reality, half completed. I myself have often felt half created, hanging between my past and my future.

I step through the frame for a doorway and inhale the aroma of newly cut lumber. Just as easily, I pass out again between the studs of an uncompleted wall, an improvised and temporary door. In future days, this passage will be as impenetrable as the walls of a prison. I look out at the flat stone where my children sat to be painted. Now the stone is blank, but I fancy I call to them and they rise, then step forward out of the flat world of canvas to join me among the rustic cottages.

We admire the heavy thick thatch at the edge of a completed roof. A meadowlark visits to tug at a reed for her nest, but the thatch is too tightly compacted, and she flies away with nothing. I rejoice in being outdoors under the puffy clouds. The builders sit over there beneath a chestnut, eating lunch.

I will walk back to the château, change my dress, prepare to be painted myself, to be placed on a flat canvas. In this moment, I fill my lungs with sweet country air. All laziness, I recall my out-of-doors play as a child.

Portrait of a Queen in Blue Satin, Holding a Pink Rose

Having heard that the bloom of youth begins to fade after one turns twenty-eight, I have determined to have myself painted again, and this time I look forward to the sitting, for Elisabeth Vigée-Lebrun shall be the portraitist. My request is that she present herself to me in my private apartment, in the interior of the château, where all the rooms are small and cozy. Long ago, the King gave me these small rooms, and I have claimed them as my own intimate nest, exquisitely decorated. When I cannot escape to Trianon—just as my husband planned—they provide me with privacy. While I have been painted in my state apartment with my harp, by Gautier-Dagoty, in 1777, surrounded by my friends, by a singer and a reader, I do not like the expression he gave to my face—more like that of a doll than a living person. Here I will be myself, with a true friend.

Madame Vigée-Lebrun sets up her easel with an expert flick of its tripod legs, and takes out a new wooden palette on which to mix her colors. While she prepares the other implements of her art—brushes, rags, turpentine—she glances quickly at me, as though she is taking impressions and looking for just the right angle. I stroll about a bit restlessly, for it is wise to dissipate excess energy before attempting to remain immobile, for the sake of the artist.

As though she reads my thoughts, Madame Vigée-Lebrun tells me that she will not require that I stand perfectly still. Then she asks if I have forgotten to wear my pearls. Touching my throat, I find, indeed, she is correct, and I send for them. When I was painted *en chemise* I wore no necklace or bracelets. Perhaps it was the omission of jewelry that made me appear naked or half-dressed to the objecting public.

It is rather delicious to surrender oneself to an artist; I really cannot account for the pleasure to be derived simply from being regarded by an aesthetic eye, especially when that person is a friend. I find that I lift my bosom and that my flesh seems to glow, as though a magic candle moved beneath the skin. It seems satisfying in the same way that it satisfies to allow dark chocolate to melt in one's mouth. In fact, there is a melting of the will. Now one is not in charge; now one is malleable and about to be re-created. The mind seems to empty itself of cares.

"I wonder," I say to my friend, "if Adam and Eve enjoyed it, when God created them?"

She looks at me quizzically. Then asks, "Do you enjoy being painted?"

"Not usually," I reply. "But today I feel all *melted* at the prospect. A languor comes upon my body."

I am standing beside a large bouquet of pink roses, for we have agreed that I shall be painted again among the flowers I love so well. Suddenly my friend plucks one of them from the group and deftly winds a white silk ribbon around its green stem, as though to protect my fingers from its thorns. Leaving a dangling tail of ribbon, she hands me the wrapped flower. A number of attached rose leaves and two large buds are part of the arrangement, along with the spent sepals of three or four other blooms that have now vanished.

"Would Your Majesty please to hold the loose ribbon in your other hand, so that the two hands are brought rather close together."

I do so, just as I did in the earlier painting, such that the ribbon passes between my thumb and forefinger, and I enjoy feeling its silkiness between my fingers. Keeping her vigilant eyes on me, she mimics the posture she wishes me to assume, and I see instantly how the position of my arm crossing my body makes a graceful curve under the neckline and, parallel to it, of my dress.

"And you want the pearl necklace to echo the curve of the cheek," I say, as an attendant fastens the double strand around my neck.

"You have a lovely Grecian neck," my friend says.

I wonder that she wants no adornment for my earlobes, but I say nothing. Who am I to question the decisions of the artist?

My dress is a medium blue satin, with a double ruffle all around the neckline, and a blue-and-silver-striped bow directly in front. The sleeves come to my elbows and terminate in a flounce of gathered lace.

For a moment I turn the rose so that I can look into its center, which is a deep rose, while the outer petals, a perfect overlapping cup of petals, are a paler pink. The darker center lends depth to the rose's perfect face as I look into it.

"But you must let the rose face the viewer," she says, "a smaller version of yourself looking out at us, to inspire benign admiration."

As she speaks, I feel the soft round weight of my curls against my neck and resting on the tops of my shoulders. For this portrait, I am powdered with a silvery powder that complements the silver sheen of the blue satin as it bends around my upper arm.

She sketches and tries out dabs of color, an interplay of blue, white, flesh tones, and pink.

"The background will be quite dark—a large tree with a massive trunk, at an angle something like that of your arm, but in the background."

"What is the most lovely place you know?" I ask her.

Now she pauses, holding the brush dipped in bright blue up in the air. I have not meant to interrupt the flow of her work, but she knows exactly how long she can hesitate before inspiration dissipates.

"Marly-le-Roi," she replies. "I saw it as a girl and remember it perfectly. On each side of the palace were six summerhouses connected with walks covered by jasmine and honeysuckle. Behind the castle was a waterfall and a channel of water, where a number of swans swam. There was a fountain whose waters rose so high that the top of its plume was lost from sight in the clouds."

I cannot imagine a fountain of such amazing altitude, even though the spume from our dragon near the Neptune basin climbs to a stupendous height. "How young were you when you saw it?"

"In fact, I was quite young and had little experience in viewing grand sights."

"But now, with your success," I say, teasing her, "they are commonplace, and it would require a great deal to impress you."

"The beauty of the simple rose that you hold in your hand and the way that you hold it, as though you knew its fragile value, quite take my breath."

"Ah," I say.

I believe that there is no one I would rather talk to than this artist. She tells the truth. She is without pretension, and all her experiences in the Parisian world of art and music interest me.

"I think I shall paint pearl bracelets almost the color of your skin around each of your wrists. Three strands of pearls, near the wrist, to suggest the curve toward the hand and to bind the lighted top part of the wrist with the shadowy underside."

"Shall I send for such bracelets? I can have them made exactly as you wish, for another sitting."

While her brush busily plies the canvas, she does not look up but replies, "There is no need, Your Majesty, for I see them with my imaginative eye and exactly how they serve my composition. I take the cue from the pearls of your necklace, though these need to be smaller to harmonize with the wrist instead of the neck."

Sometimes she lays down her brush, and we stroll about. When I seat myself at the harpsichord, she sings the songs of Grétry with me, and her voice is pure and true—more so than my own.

When we resume our session, she speaks again of Marly-le-Roi.

"It was later at Marly-le-Roi," she says conversationally, "that I first saw Your Majesty. Your Majesty was walking in the park with ladies from the court, but you were all wearing white dresses. I thought everyone so young and pretty that I must be dreaming a vision. I was walking with my mother, and I felt shy and not wishing to intrude, so I took her hand to lead her down another path, when the Queen stopped me. Your Majesty guessed my intent, to make myself unobtrusive, and Your Majesty invited me to continue in whatever direction I might prefer and to take no account of herself or her ladies, that I should enjoy the park uninhibited."

Although I try to bring the scene to mind, I cannot remember it, yet I easily envision it through Madame Vigée-Lebrun's picturesque words.

"To think," she adds, "that I should ever be invited to this apartment in the heart of the Château de Versailles to paint Her Majesty among her intimate furnishings."

ONLY ONCE, DURING the many sittings required to complete the portrait, do I see trouble pass over the brow of my artistic friend as she paints. When I ask her what perturbs her, she stands straight up, dropping both arms to her sides, one hand holding the brush. Yes, she is exasperated.

"It is your skin," she says. "Majesty, I do not flatter you when I say it is the most brilliant in the world. It is so transparent that it bears not a trace of umber. But I lack the colors, the delicate tints, to paint such freshness. I could not capture it before, and I cannot capture it now. I have never seen such a complexion as yours on any other woman." She raises her brush again to continue with her work. "Though I am delighted to paint you, your beauty challenges my art."

As she speaks, she slightly tilts her head first to one side, then to the other, as though to make the light enter the pupil of her eye at slightly different angles. Resuming her work, now with a contented air, she remarks, "Never mind, though. You are delectable, and my painting shows you thus."

At such praise, I feel a radiance bloom beneath my skin, particularly throughout my breasts. Almost, I am tempted to lift them with my breath until they emerge above the lacy neckline of my dress. She has filled me with pride, justified pride: I am a mother who has nursed her own first babe, and I am left more beautiful for it, more pleased by the bountifulness of life, by the abundance of love and beauty, by the fulfillment in such colors as pink and blue.

Impulsively, I confide in her, "My skin always improves in radiance when I am with child. But don't mention it to anyone yet."

"I am so very happy for both Your Majesty and the King. No one could love their daughters more than you and I love ours, but my prayer is that you carry a second boy and for the future of France."

Yes, I would more rather talk with the frank and sensitive Elisabeth Vigée-Lebrun than with anyone.

IN A FEW DAYS, the King announces to the world that once again I am with child.

THEATER, 1785

I have asked for my friend and advisor Count Mercy to visit my private apartment and to listen to my reasoning about a certain decision. As always he lends distinction to any interior that he inhabits, though I cannot help but notice that he prepares to take his seat carefully, and I fear that I have inconvenienced him in asking for his presence at a time when his condition may be delicate.

"My dear friend," I say quickly, "would you be so kind as to make use of this new pillow of mine?"

"Her Majesty is ever gracious," he replies courteously.

"Then allow me to place it in the seat of your chair."

"It delights me that we are to have another royal child." For a moment my old friend and I merely gaze at each other. We are both thinking of the Empress. Soon he continues the conversation. "I understand that François Blanchard has been the first balloonist to cross the Channel."

"The King keeps me informed on all things scientific. The English have more reason than ever to make amends with us. Their Channel shall become as outmoded a defense as a medieval moat."

I recall that the King has shown me some of their newspaper cartoons depicting a full-scale invasion of the French, by balloon, but these outlandish fancies are less interesting to me than another matter of a theatrical nature.

I ask the count what he thought of Beaumarchais's play *The Marriage of Figaro*.

"All that to-do last spring!" he exclaims. "Still, the play presented such a debauched image of the nobility that it made the populace quite ready to believe the worst about our morals." He adjusts himself to sit more comfortably. "I see now what I did not see before—that the play encourages the insubordination and rebellion of the lower classes and shows them most clever and resourceful in the face of their masters."

"I found it very amusing. The audience went wild with joy at the performance. I regret that the King was put in the position of feeling that he had to suppress any further performances. It is not Beaumarchais's fault. I am planning for my friends and me to stage *The Barber of Seville* at Versailles."

"And what role shall Your Majesty assume?"

"Rosine, the young girl whose old guardian wishes to marry her."

"But not in the near future, I think."

"Next summer we will begin rehearsals. When I am quite recovered from the delivery of the new child. The idea of performing in the play will give me something pleasant to anticipate when the labor pains are upon me."

The count carefully stands to make his exit. "I thank Her Majesty for the cushion. I would recommend one of even greater plumpness, goose down, instead of mere feathers. I'll send you one of mine from my apartment."

He carefully makes his way toward the door, and for the first time I realize that he is growing old. I myself will soon be thirty.

"Yes, another play," he says, pausing at the door. "I recall being told that when the mayor of Paris made an extremely well-phrased speech against *Figaro*, everyone applauded enthusiastically. Then they consulted their watches so that they would not be late for the performance."

The Birth of Louis Charles

I am so large, even I myself believe that I may produce twins. In fact, they have prepared two blue ribbons representing the Order of Saint-Ésprit should I give birth to two princes. My size has caused my husband to address me, with gentle humor, as his "Balloon." It is still dark on Easter Sunday when my labor begins.

My dear Duchesse de Polignac has reduced even more the number of people who will be allowed in the audience for this event. I am not long at my labor till the babe issues forth.

A boy! Not twins, but a child like his sister Marie Thérèse, of exceptional vigor and abounding health. He comes to us at seven-thirty in the morning, 27 March 1785, named Louis of course, as all my sons shall be, and his second name is Charles for his godmother Queen Maria Carolina of Naples, my beloved Charlotte. The babe is given into the arms of my jubilant Yolande, now royal governess to the children of France, but for a moment her knees give way and she sways, gasping, "The weight of my joy is almost too much for me," so that I almost giggle, and the deputy governess hastens to her assistance.

Ah, to give birth laughing with joy. I feel blessed beyond measure, now the mother of two boys. My good spirits seem to heal my body to such an extent that as the day passes, I decide to invite the Princesse de Lamballe to have supper with me. I sit up in my big bed, and trays are brought for us both, a hot chicken consommé made savory with celery and carrots, and some *pâté de foie gras* spread on toast. I would like very much to ask for some chocolate, but I fear it might sour my milk, and I would like to nurse this child for a day or two before giving him over to the professionals.

The princess is quick to tell me how lovely I look, quite youthful. She is a few years older than I, and I notice for the first time that she is no longer in the bloom of youth, though her alabaster complexion and lovely golden curls will always mark her as a charming beauty. She, of course, has never had a child, so her delight in Louis Charles has a special wonder to it.

"How is it possible?" she says over and over. "How amazing to create new life!"

"I shall call him my *chou d'amour*," I say, in response to her girlish enthusiasm. "His lovely face is as round as a healthy cabbage."

"No child could be more robust than this one."

I give him my finger and exclaim, "What an extraordinary grip he has!"

I HAVE NEVER felt closer to the King. His delight in the new child is extreme, and he has been pleased to buy the estate of Saint-Cloud for me, and another property as well, but Saint-Cloud, like Trianon, is titled in my own name, which means that I may dispose of it as I like. It has a lovely setting; the garden extends downhill all the way to the Seine, and it is easy for me to imagine our children running happily down that incline. Of course some people think it a great impropriety for the Queen to own property in her own name, but I have always ignored such petty criticism.

Nonetheless, when the jeweler Boehmer tries once more to persuade the King to buy me a famous and magnificent diamond necklace, whose stones form a letter *M* large enough to cover the entire chest and valued at nearly two million livres, I decline again. I very much want a simple life. Indeed, I have already declined the necklace twice before, even when Monsieur Boehmer got down on his knees and begged me to buy it, lest he be ruined having invested so much money in the extravagant item. I remind the King it would be better to spend the money on a warship.

MY JOY IS COMPOUNDED when Count von Fersen returns and accompanies the royal party to the official christening of Louis Charles in May.

Strange to say, when my carriage enters Paris there are no outpourings of joy among the people. Indeed, it is a cold reception. The King's face remains impassive as we roll through the streets, but I notice that the count looks melancholy. Because the finances of the people, as well as of the state, are an increasing cause of concern, they look for someone to blame. Who better than a foreigner such as myself?

I only regret that the Cardinal de Rohan, whose bad behavior when in Vienna caused such scandal, manages to officiate again at the christening ceremony. I am sure he leads a dissolute life, for all his clerical robes. An odious creature—I hate for him to hold my new child in his arms for even a moment.

A Fall from a Great Height

A lovely morning in June, I sit up in my bed and enjoy my coffee, with slices of oranges and a crisp ginger biscuit. The hangings around the bed and against the windows are covered with flowers—tulips, roses, lilacs, pansies, apple boughs—arranged in sprays and bouquets. The room is a flowery kingdom. My attendants buzz around me like so many cheerful bees, and I feel like a lily myself in my white gown with gold embroidery. On a whim, I ask that my lily-scented perfume be brought to me, and I decide that I shall pretend to be a different flower each morning I wake up in June.

To my surprise, the King suddenly enters, unannounced. All curtsy. From under his arm he takes a newspaper, which he waves at my companions, dismissing them. As soon as they exit, he says, "I have the gravest tragedy to report."

I am sure I turn pale as the whitest lily.

"News from the Channel. You recall the young physician Pilâtre de Rozier, the amateur balloonist?"

I nod, and a great dread seizes my heart.

"It's all here—in the newspaper account. The balloon exploded, even before it began to cross the water. Before the very eyes of the spectators watching from the cliff, Rozier and his companion fell fifteen hundred feet to the rocks below."

"Then he was killed?"

"One foot was entirely severed from his leg. They say he fell into a pool of his own blood. His body was shattered."

The wonder of the disaster overwhelms me. "We are so used to good news about the balloons," I say.

"Gravity has claimed its first victims from the sky."

He pinches his nose between the eyes. I am touched by the sincerity of this mundane gesture of grief, and I reach out my hand to him.

He sighs a mighty heave of sorrow. "I will have a medal struck in their honor."

I WONDER IN what state of mind were Rozier and his companion as they fell and fell from the sky. Were they filled with terror? Did their courage sustain them to the end?

Midsummer

After the terrible accident, many of us have nightmares of falling. Sometimes I dream that I am aloft in a balloon with my three children; a dark cloud pursues us, and our basket begins to rock in the wind. I look to gather them about me, but little Louis Joseph is gone. The basket tips, and my infant Louis Charles tumbles out headfirst—I awake screaming. I have had variations on this dream more than once.

Every day, Louis Charles seems stronger and displays more baby smiles and winsome expressions. Everyone remarks how far beyond other babies of his age he has progressed. His big sister likes to teach him games, though of course he is still in his crib. Still, she earnestly explains life to him.

One day I am shocked to hear her call Louis Joseph to stand beside the crib. She looks back and forth between the faces of her two brothers. Louis Joseph looks as transparent as a little angel, his big eyes focused trustingly on his sister.

"Now," she says, "I am deciding which of you will someday be King of France. Do you have an opinion?"

Louis Joseph looks over his sister's shoulder at me and speaks in a firm, clear voice. "That is a matter for God to decide."

Following his gaze, she turns and sees me. "It was just a guessing game," she says.

I am troubled by her lack of frankness. "But the answer is the one your brother has given. You should pursue other entertainments, those more likely to be fun."

MY DAUGHTER'S GROWTH in body causes me no concern, but sometimes I worry about the growth of her spirit. She is haughty, and she does not understand that all people are God's children, regardless of their station in life.

Once I heard Elisabeth Vigée-Lebrun say to her, "I admire your mother the Queen so much. She never loses an opportunity to make any person in her presence happier than they were."

I have invited a peasant girl to play with my daughter and to grow up with her, but Marie Thérèse does not want to wait on the other little girl, or take fair turns, and speaks to her ungraciously. Seeing my anxiety about my daughter, Elisabeth tries to reassure me. "She is still very young. As she sees more examples of kindness about her, she will gradually learn to consider the feelings of others. When I was a child, I was told, 'You catch more flies with honey than with vinegar.' It made all the difference in my attitude."

"And did you have a happy childhood, Elisabeth?"

"All day long I made little pictures. I drew with charcoal on slates, and with a stick in mud. Eventually I was given colored chalk and then paints. I was happy every minute I was at my art, and thoughts of art filled my hours."

"I enjoyed music and dancing, theatricals," I replied. "But I did not fill all my time that way."

"Your Majesty had many brothers and sisters to be happy with."

"Yes. We were very happy. My mother took care of everything."

BECAUSE I KNOW that the theatrical world offers a refuge from the world I must live in, I begin to learn my lines for the ingenue Rosine in *The Barber of Seville*. In the midst of focusing my attention on my part, I am given a note from the jeweler Boehmer, which I tuck away till later.

In my room I read it aloud to Madame Campan:

"'Madame, We are at the summit of happiness . . . The latest arrangements proposed . . . New proof of our devotion to . . . Your Majesty. The most beautiful set of diamonds . . . The greatest and best of Queens.'"

"What is this about?" I ask my First Lady of the Bedchamber. "You are adept at solving newspaper riddles in the *Mercure de France*."

"This letter makes no sense to me." Madame Campan sounds weary.

Because this note also makes no sense to me, I twist the paper into a spill and thrust it into the flame of my candle and drop the ashes onto a plate. Instead of asking Madame Campan to read me to sleep, I decide to lie in bed considering my role in the play.

Is Rosine at all attracted to her would-be seducer? Suddenly I remember the old King, Louis XV, and his special kindness to me. I was always able to speak with him in a manner that he found charming, but in many ways I was uncomfortable in his presence. I have always thought my lack of ease with him arose from my knowledge of his morals in regard to women—that I was powerless in ending his scandalous relationship to the du Barry.

But at the same time, no female could not be attracted to his luminous eye, the charm of being in his favor.

I know now that he kept something like a harem of young prostitutes, just the age I was then.

Lines from Beaumarchais's *Figaro* come to mind: "Nobility, fortune, rank, position make a lord so proud! What have you done to deserve these advantages? You were born—that is all."

My husband swore that the fortress-prison of the Bastille would have to be razed before he would allow the performance of such subversive lines. Then the Polignacs had the effrontery to tell the King he was acting like a despot. Next, Beaumarchais said he would excise the objectionable parts. Assuming he was as good as his word, I never bothered to read the revision, but only a few of the promised changes were made. I trusted where perhaps I should not have done so—but the play was so clever and funny!

The Barber of Seville was performed ten years ago. It is merely light and frothy—no one has ever found its ideas objectionable.

A Hoax in Diamonds

I have never seen Madame Campan so distressed! Upon returning from a walk in the gardens, I was about to settle at the harp, when a servant reported that Monsieur Boehmer, the jeweler, wished to see me, here at Trianon! How irritating to be bothered at a place where everyone knows admission is only by special invitation! I waved my hand in the negative, then I casually asked Madame Campan if she had any idea why Boehmer was being persistent in his attentions.

All in a moment, her face becomes stricken. "Majesty, you recall the mysterious note two or three weeks ago?" Not waiting for my reply, she rushes on. "Last night, at my home in the country, the jeweler Boehmer came to me and spoke as though he had lost his mind. He said that Your Majesty had contracted to buy the diamond necklace, through the Cardinal de Rohan, that the necklace is in your possession, and a payment of four hundred thousand livres is now due."

"Impossible. I despise the Cardinal de Rohan. I would never use him as an intermediary. And I have no new diamond necklace, as you well know."

Madame Campan is not a woman given to hysterics, and she remained calm now.

"I said as much to Monsieur Boehmer. And I asked him what made him think you had given any such commission. He said that he possessed notes signed by the Queen to the cardinal."

"If he does have such notes," I say as calmly as I can, "they are forgeries. Certainly, I have no necklace from Boehmer or the cardinal." That last idea makes me shudder.

"Boehmer was distraught," Madame Campan explains. "He told me there are bankers involved, who lent him money on the strength of the letters to the cardinal said to bear your signature."

My signature! I am speechless.

Madame Campan continues. "I told Monsieur Boehmer to consult Breteuil, since he is the minister of the royal household. Instead the jeweler has gone straight to the cardinal."

Immediately I think of turning to Count Mercy for advice, but I know that his hemorrhoid condition has become exceedingly painful. "I must turn to Breteuil myself," I tell Madame Campan, "but also to the King."

"THE CARDINAL IS either a knave or a fool," the King thunders, when I tell him of my supposed purchase of an extravagant necklace.

For all of its over 670 diamonds, I never even thought the necklace beautiful. It hung like a halter around my neck, the one time I consented to try it on, years ago.

"I think he is both," I reply.

"As crown jeweler, Boehmer is a sworn officer of this court. His duty is to consult Breteuil or myself before such an outrageous purchase."

Trying to be fair to the jeweler, I add meekly, "I suppose if the cardinal, as a member of the House of Rohan, showed him a letter with my signature, he felt he had received assurances enough."

I do not believe I have ever seen the King so angry, and I remind myself again of his goodness and loyalty to me.

A MONTH HAS PASSED slowly, as not even rehearsals drive from my mind my anxiety about this diamond necklace affair. The King has investigated the missing necklace to the extent possible and discussed matters with Breteuil and with our trusted advisor Abbé Vermond, both of whom hate the cardinal as much as I do. I am very glad the King includes Vermond, who has served first as my tutor, then as my spiritual advisor ever since I came to France.

At times, Vermond and Breteuil speak with glee about this necklace affair's being an opportunity to destroy Rohan, and I admit I would also like to do so sometimes. I am grateful that I am utterly innocent in the affair. Because I feel anxious, I do not care, really, if they destroy Cardinal de Rohan, whom I too have disliked for years; I only want my reputation to be untarnished. Yet of course I have been the subject of lying pamphlets for years. I do not know to what extent people may have believed such fabrications. I have considered them beneath my notice.

This is 15 August, the Feast of the Assumption of the Virgin Mary, for whom my mother, all my sisters, and I are named. Today, as he makes his way in his red robes—I suppose his stockings are cardinal too—to celebrate the Mass, the cardinal will be summoned to appear before the King and his minister to give an accounting of this sordid business. Surely I can take the coincidence of the date as a good omen—that today the name of Marie Antoinette will be cleared of any vile association with this mystery of the diamond necklace. No one seems to know where it is.

It is Breteuil who conceived the idea of summoning the cardinal so publicly, in all his splendor, so as to cause the most embarrassment. Breteuil, I explain to Madame Campan, does not forget that when the cardinal was recalled from Vienna, Breteuil was sent in his place. But Breteuil's work as ambassador was then ruined by the cardinal, who spitefully cut off the connections Breteuil needed in Vienna to help him serve effectively.

Madame Campan responds that perhaps those insults in Vienna are best left to lie in the past.

I reply, "Because the Cardinal de Rohan helped to depose Choiseul, to whom I owe the happiness of my marriage, I, like Breteuil, have an old grudge to settle with him." I do not mention that his behavior has long offended me.

It is not without satisfaction, though I greatly dread the confrontation about to occur, that I consider how, as the defender of my good name, the King will also be able to disgrace and totally discredit the cardinal. It is a sign of the King's complete trust in me that he insists I be present—"That way you will always be perfectly easy about my role in this affair and about what has been said," he tells me. I can see the sorrow in his eyes that I am to be worried by such unpleasantness. It is noon, and we fall silent as we sit in the King's inner chamber, expecting any moment to hear the sound of the cardinal approaching the room.

When he enters the room, the splendor of his garments, the richness of the fabric and of the lace at his throat, impresses me so much that I quail inside and am grateful that it is the King himself who conducts the interrogation. He shows all royal firmness and majesty in every syllable as he upbraids Rohan for the purchase of diamonds and then demands to know where they are. All of the time I am looking at the needlepoint of the cardinal's alb, which seems too beautiful for human fingers to touch.

"It is my impression," the cardinal replies, not without his own clerical dignity, "that the diamonds were delivered to the Queen."

"By what agent were they to be delivered?"

"A lady named the Comtesse de La Motte-Valois held the commission."

At this news—the name of someone with a reputation for many careless affairs, though personally quite unknown to all of us—we cannot suppress a gasp. Comtesse Jeanne La Motte!

The cardinal continues. "I believed I was pleasing Her Majesty because I received a letter from Her Majesty commissioning me to undertake the purchase."

"How could you ever have imagined, sir, that *I* would ask *you* to do such a thing?" I cannot mask either my indignation or my anger. "I have not spoken to you in eight years! Not since you returned, rejected, from Vienna have I said a single word to you. In fact, I treat you with nothing but coldness, and despite your stubborn requests, I have never granted you an audience. I would never select as a mediator such a person as the one you name." I am close to crying, but I gather all my dignity and glare at him hotly instead.

"Witnessing the agitation of Her Majesty," the cardinal says simply, "I now see quite clearly. Unmistakably, I have been duped. My ardent wish to be of service to Your Majesty blinded me."

To our amazement, he has come to this meeting somewhat prepared. From his sleeve, he produces a note. With false humility, he inclines his head and holds up the piece of paper. Immediately the King takes it from him and begins to read. My heart drums with astonishing rapidity against my chest.

With full severity, the King pronounces, "This letter was neither written by nor signed by the Queen. Are you, sir, of the House of Rohan? Are you the Grand Almoner? How could you possibly imagine that the Queen would sign herself as 'Marie Antoinette de France'?" The Queen never deigns to present herself so crudely. Her Christian name, alone, always represents the Queen. Everyone knows who she is. There has never been a single occasion on which she appends the phrase 'de France.' What need does 'Marie Antoinette,' the Queen, have for 'de France'? Furthermore, *all* queens and kings merely sign their documents with their baptismal names. Surely you and your family are aware of the convention! The letter is an obvious forgery, and I can only ask how could you be such a villain?"

The King orders the cardinal to retire to an adjacent room to write out his account of the matter. As soon as he leaves the room, I burst into tears for a moment. Quickly I regain my composure, and we all chatter at once about the stupidity of forging a letter ending in the signature "Marie Antoinette de France." The King tells us his intention to have the cardinal arrested, no matter what explanation he offers. When the keeper of the seals asks if it is wise to arrest the cardinal while he is wearing his scarlet robes, the King replies, "The name of the Queen is precious to me and it has been compromised." As soon as the cardinal reappears in the room, now looking rather frightened, the King places Breteuil, the cardinal's enemy, in charge. I see the prelate blanch as he hears Breteuil's name pronounced as the person who shall conduct the investigation.

When the King tells the cardinal that he shall shortly be arrested, the cardinal pleads for "the reputation of my family name."

The King responds in a sharp, ironic tone that he will try to shelter the cardinal's relatives from the disgrace. "I do what I must do, as a King and as a husband."

He then orders the cardinal to leave and subsequently arranges for the arrest to occur as the cardinal traverses the Hall of Mirrors, where all the court will be gathered. The cardinal is to be conducted straightaway to the Bastille. Breteuil is to arrange for the sealing of the cardinal's residence and all his papers there.

My heart overflows with gratitude for the King's defense of my name, and for his firm decisiveness.

Thus, I am vindicated in a single afternoon by my champion, the King.

IT IS A GREAT PLEASURE to throw myself into the role of Rosine. Even while I am acting the part onstage, a part of my mind is saying, "You are not the maligned Queen; you are the young and simple maid Rosine." Then I feel her emotions, her gaiety, her alarm, her vibrancy a thousand times more intensely. Artois is splendid as Count Almaviva. Vaudreuil could have played Almaviva just as well, but he is adorable in *The Barber of Seville* as Figaro. He brings his high spirits to the role, and it amuses Yolande no end to see him as a barber.

I make the very most of my role. Those privileged to see the performance universally exclaim that I play the role as well as any real actress. The King is delighted with my acting, and the tiny theater a few minutes' walk from Trianon has never been more charming.

Because it is blue inside, I think of the blue interior of the balloon with Montauciel the sheep aboard. In my theater, I feel as though I have entered the balloon and here live in an enchanted world where all turns out well.

Sad Days

I am happy to be with the King these days, for I continue to be as grateful as I was the moment when he spoke in my behalf as a husband and as a king. I give him a warmer warmth when he comes to me, and I am more determined than I ever have been that he will take pleasure in our bed. Although I know that I am utterly innocent in the imbroglio involving the cardinal, I feel guilty—perhaps for past extravagances. It gives me a sort of wicked pleasure to feel when the King and I are together that I am doing my duty, as a good wife should, be she queen or peasant or shopkeeper's spouse.

As soon as the performance of *The Barber of Seville* is over, we leave for Saint-Cloud. As September with its change of season comes on again, I am outdoors a great deal, riding in the open carriage with the Comte d'Artois, whose mischievous and naughty tongue makes me laugh and laugh and forget his ambitious side.

Sometimes I ride in the Bois de Boulogne. I have had the large painting made in 1783 of me riding in the hunt with the King brought to Saint-Cloud. It is not in the tender style of Vigée-Lebrun, this painter being Louis-Auguste Brun, but Elisabeth does not paint horses. Actually I look as though I am about to fall from the horse, but the posture displays my gray riding habit and tall plumed hat to great advantage. My horse is painted in the very act of leaping a ditch. Under the arch of his forelegs one sees in the distance a miniature line of other riders. It is really quite charming, but I suppose it is a sign of my age that I now prefer to look at the painting and derive vicarious enjoyment instead of actually riding at such a clip.

Occasionally I hear gossip or actual information that adds to the increasingly scandalous tale of the diamond necklace. Some people, as is only to be expected, believe that the cardinal actually gave me the necklace in exchange for certain favors of the flesh. Such a preposterous notion almost makes me laugh, but then I find my eyes full of tears at the outrage of the idea. The King told me that he gave the cardinal a choice of trial by the Parlement of Paris, or a royal verdict and sentence, and the cardinal has chosen the trial.

Someone said that at the time of his arrest, Rohan was able to slip a note to his valet directing that his papers, in a certain red valise, be destroyed at once. In any case, Breteuil's investigators found little left at the cardinal's residence to merit its sealing.

Here at Saint-Cloud, I allow people who come out from Paris to stroll around the grounds and to gawk at the royal family. It's quite different, in that way, from life at my Trianon. Cafés have actually sprung up along the way to feed the people on their Sunday outings. They seem so delighted to see me with the Dauphin or my other children that I feel loved again by the populace.

I indulge a whim to have a yacht built for myself, and in October I very much enjoy gliding down the Seine to Fountainebleau. When we pass the Invalides, cannon go off in a fine salute, as they did when I first entered Paris. But we do not stop at Paris.

Fontainebleau is always a sparkling setting for concerts and entertainments, but I prefer to stay in my own chambers there. Often I find myself half–lying down doing nothing, not even my beloved needlework. A great lassitude comes over me. Until this scandal is settled, I seem disengaged from myself and my life.

THE STORY HAS IT that I was impersonated in the gardens of Versailles, that the cardinal was sent a forged letter by Jeanne La Motte, pretending to be me, calling for a rendezvous with the cardinal. She actually hired a prostitute, a woman named Oliva, who bore an uncanny resemblance to me, to speak with him. Their meeting was brief, and she was heavily veiled in black, they say, but he was certain it was I.

At the trial, I feel sure, people will see this trollop, and those who know me will remark the resemblance. I myself will not be there, and the King has promised that my name will be pronounced as little as possible.

HERE IS THE KING, all sweaty and dusty from hunting in the woods of Fontainebleau. He says he has come in early, that he had a premonition that I might be in some despair. He has come to comfort me. I hold out my arms to him.

The silk counterpane is ruined when he comes to me half-clothed, but there are many others like it in the storage closets. The careful matching and shading of colors in the room will not be disrupted.

After his bath, the King and I sit together with a small round table between us. "People are saying," the King remarks, "that the cardinal is more fool than knave, that he was quite deceived by Jeanne La Motte, who was his mistress. He was not her accomplice, perhaps, but her victim."

Neither he nor I can grant any credence to this account.

FOR CHRISTMAS, I ask the factory at Sèvres to prepare settings of porcelain with inset jewels. They will be the most expensive I have ever ordered, but when I hold one of the sample cups in my hand, the large ruby on the cup catches the light in just such a way as to make me feel that I am about to drink liquid light. The fancy pleases me. "Ah, this cup takes me to fairyland," I say to the King, who always leaves the holiday selection of porcelain entirely up to me.

"Then you must have plates and dishes galore," he says.

"Some with topaz stones," I suggest, "some with emeralds."

Neither of us mentions diamonds. Indeed, the stone itself with its hardness and sharp edges has come to seem to me both evil and ugly.

I would hesitate to make a purchase of bejeweled dishes, but the porcelain industry depends on our annual endorsement. The silk industry accused me of trying to ruin them when I began to wear muslin.

IT IS CHRISTMASTIME, and I am feeling that I have put on too much flesh. In the morning, all too often, I experience a nausea. I believe that it is all due to my anxiety about the developing story surrounding the cardinal. People love to hear details of his debauched and stupid life. We learn about his liaison with Jeanne La Motte but also about a scoundrel who pretends to mystical powers as a reincarnation of an ancient Egyptian, the Count de Costilgiano, who has pulled the wool over the cardinal's gullible eyes. Someone has said that the cardinal will believe in almost anything—except God.

While the stories make great sport of him, they hardly make less so of me.

Not even the carols of the season, sung in German, can raise my spirits.

I write to Charlotte, and she answers always that I must be brave and believe in my innocence. I *am* innocent. Belief is not the issue.

Not even Count von Fersen can cheer me through these dreary winter months.

FEBRUARY. I CAN no longer deny the truth: I am pregnant again. I feel that I have had enough children. I do not wish for more.

Every sight and sound reminds me of something doleful.

Out my window, I saw hunters, and the sight caused me to remember when I took a bad fall from a horse. Later, when my daughter saw me, someone told her that I had fallen and could have been killed. She said she did not care. My friend did not believe that my daughter understood what she was saying, but little Marie Thérèse averred that she did: if one were dead, she went away and never came back. My daughter said she would be glad if I suffered such a fate. She said that I did not love her, that when we went to visit the aunts, I never looked back to see if she were behind me or quite lost, though her Papa always took her hand and cared about her.

Somehow I fear that this story will come out at the trial of Rohan, and the jurors will decide I am not a person worthy of respect or love, though at the time, I merely inflicted some mild punishment on the child for her saucy tongue and soon forgot the matter.

She is not a beautiful child, though Elisabeth paints her so, and I fear sometimes that her inner being, which is so much more important, may also be less attractive than one would hope.

Although the Empress felt it her duty to impress on me that I am not beautiful—despite the flattery of the world—I will never hold up a harsh mirror before my daughter.

They say that the Comtesse La Motte sent the dismantled necklace to London, with her husband or her new lover—the three have something of a triangular arrangement—and that the recovery of the necklace is unlikely. It makes me furious to think how Rohan's schemes have made poor, foolish Boehmer suffer. I have heard that he has applied to the du Barry, who is also one of his customers, for help.

Sometimes I wonder if her fate has not been more fortunate than my own. Everyone says she is like a queen in her château in the village of Louveciennes, that she is much loved, and that no one lives in poverty there. The populace of France as a whole is far too large for anyone to work such miracles of rehabilitation. I wonder if Zamore, her little black page boy, still attends her. Sometimes she dressed him as a hussar in boots and with a darling saber, sometimes as a sailor lad. So, now I am burdened with another pregnancy. Only the King can maintain his good cheer in my company. The others mirror my own long face.

THIS MARCH 1786, the trial brief of the prostitute Nicole d'Oliva who impersonated me has sold 20,000 copies, so keen is the public's appetite for rotten scandal.

SPRING COMES ON slowly but my girth increases rapidly. I must now write down my own version of what happened concerning the necklace. I have nightmares of the scene between d'Oliva and Rohan in the Grove of Venus. How cunning La Motte was to arrange a meeting in such a secluded bosquet, and one with such a suggestive name! They say La Motte wrote him dozens of love letters, pretending to be me, and these are the papers that were destroyed before the seal was set on his house. Thank goodness he ordered them destroyed. In my dreams, I begin to write a respectable letter to Fersen, but it turns out I have written the name Rohan instead.

When I insisted that Fersen tell me how the scandal was received in the courts of Sweden, he looked grieved and then spoke truly: everyone thinks the King has been fooled.

No one who knows me can look at me without pity. And yet it is all undeserved! I did nothing. I knew nothing. I did not even think the July note from the jeweler worth keeping but burned it with my candle for making seals. All my preoccupation was with Rosine, an imaginary figure!

It does give me some pleasure to think that the performance of the play was a success. I had no idea that the necklace affair would drag on and on. Still, when I think of my enchanting little theater a small smile teases the corners of my mouth.

Now I have no energy for theatricals or for dancing. I would rather play backgammon or other table games. Artois is so kind to try always to bring me out of my depression.

The Verdict of the Trial of Cardinal de Rohan, etc.

31 May 1786

The question before the jurors is whether Rohan was an accomplice in a swindle or whether he was duped, as he claims to be.

Nicole d'Oliva, who played the role of the queen, did so unwittingly, they decide, and she is acquitted with a reprimand. (Surely she knew of our resemblance, and it was for that resemblance that she was paid to meet someone in the Grove of Venus. But it is pitiful to read that she thought she was serving me in some way, that she was performing before the eyes of a hidden Queen. I look at her and remember the girl who haunted Versailles many years ago who resembled me. Could this be she? I don't wish to inquire.) She wore a simple white muslin dress with a ruffled neckline, like the one I have been painted in by Elisabeth Vigée-Lebrun. Like the one declared indecent—underwear—by those who saw it in the salon exhibition. That most innocent and unpretentious of frocks!

The man who forged my letters—he admitted to having written hundreds of love letters in my name to the cardinal—was banished, and all his belongings became forfeit. They were not much. I suppose they meant a great deal to him. And how much had he enjoyed pretending to be me when he took up his vile pen?

The La Mottes, man and wife? The man is sentenced in absentia, for he is safely in England (selling diamonds), to flogging, branding, and life imprisonment. Jeanne La Motte, the instigator of all this misery, has been stripped naked, then beaten by the public executioner. Next she was branded, screaming and fighting so hard that the red-hot letter *V*, for *voleuse*, to mark her as the thief she is, is burned into her breast instead of her shoulder. It saddens me to think of her pain, though she has been hateful in besmirching my name. She was taken to the women's prison at Salpêtrière, where she will spend the rest of her life.

And the Cardinal de Rohan. He entered the session of the Parlement de Paris in his purple robes, which is the color a cardinal may wear to express mourning. His entire powerful family, dressed in black, attended the trial. In addition, all of Europe, figuratively speaking, was watching him. As Frederick the Great said, "The Cardinal de Rohan will be obliged to use all the resources of his considerable intellect to convince his judges that he is a fool." The cardinal's own lawyer, a man named Target, argued that the cardinal was the victim of deceit. The forger having already confessed; the impersonator in the Grove of Venus, Mademoiselle d'Oliva, having admitted she played the part of the Queen; the cardinal himself having urged the two jewelers to go and thank the Queen on the very day the contract was made— "With all these facts established," the attorney argued, "it can be convincingly proved that the Cardinal is a fool" and has already received his disgrace.

After imposing certain requirements, the court acquitted my tormentor, and he is to remain free.

The court requires that the cardinal apologize for criminal temerity in believing he had had a rendezvous at night with the Queen of France, and he is to seek pardon from the monarchs. He must give up his position as Grand Almoner, donate alms to the poor (from his own coffers, not the King's), and be banished from court.

Despite these requirements for the cardinal, he is to be thought of as an innocent and free man. The judges were applauded. The King's direction through the *procureur général* had been that the cardinal should admit that he acted in a "malignant" fashion and that he knew the Queen's signature was a forgery by means of which he might deceive the jewelers. Neither of these directions in favor of the Queen's position were accepted or acted upon. Nor was the King shown respect.

What does all this mean about me, the Queen in question? She whose reputation was on trial, though she was not present? It means that they believe the cardinal was justified in assuming that I am such a woman as one who would agree to meet him in the dark of the Grove of Venus. They believe I am such a person who might be expected to do anything necessary to acquire a diamond necklace for myself, and that it is reasonable, given the context of my history, for a prince of the Church to believe that I might write a hundred letters describing my lust for his body, though no one has actually read any such letters, even in their forged state. It means that the honor of a prince of the House of Rohan is taken more seriously than that of the Queen of France.

The verdict means the spirit and the heart of the Queen, who has done nothing to the people of France and who has worked for their peace and prosperity, is broken and trampled upon.

The people do not remember that in coming here from Austria to marry the Dauphin I gave my existence for the Alliance that yet protects the peace of Europe. They forget that I protected them from the additional tax that was my legal due after the marriage. They forget or do not know of a hundred other times I have remembered their burdens, as has the King, whose authority they now flout.

In my inner chamber I ask only to see Madame Campan, who has known from the beginning of my innocence and of my struggle under the weight of such growing suppositions. "There is no justice in France," I say to her, and she does not know how to reply.

After he asks to be admitted to my chamber, the King says quietly that the Parlement de Paris was determined to see only the robes of a prince of the Church, when in fact he was just a greedy man who needed money. The King feels certain Rohan has stolen the necklace from the jewelers.

I find my mind has become a dense, opaque cloud of confusion. And what has become of the part of me that I mean when I say "I"? I am lost in a fog. I have little sense of who I am. But I know I am not what they imply.

Portrait in Red

She has not yet painted me with my children, and it is with them, we agree, that I will reestablish my reputation—as the fecund mother-queen. The dress is red velvet, trimmed in dark fur, with a matching plumed hat. With my feet on a tasseled cushion, I am seated beside a large crib, wherein my new child will be placed. The Dauphin will point toward the crib with one hand and with his other hand toward his little brother, Louis Charles, my "love cabbage," dressed all in white, who will sit plump and happy on my lap. On the other side of me, when she is brought in for her sitting, leaning against me, nuzzled against my side in an attitude of adoration, will be my daughter.

"Do not idealize my faults or make me too beautiful, Elisabeth. I don't wish to incite envy."

"Dignity, maternity," she echoes. "A little fullness under the chin?"

"No necklace. Of any kind."

"I hear the King has gone to Cherbourg and the seaports to review the naval installation."

"And Count von Fersen, following the trial, left for England and then to his regiment."

"Your sister is expected to visit next month?"

"Marie Christine, born on my mother's birthday. When I was a child, she always tried to make me feel small and unimportant. The Duchesse de Polignac is in England too. She writes me that the English refer to Count von Fersen as 'the Picture,' because of his handsomeness. I should like to see the English gardens for myself someday."

"I'm painting a garden of roses at your feet in this portrait. In the carpet. So, we bring the outdoors to the inside, with a rich golden background for the roses and the greenery."

"The carpet as garden will be my favorite part of the portrait. What color will my daughter's dress be?"

"Madame Royale wears deep claret, darker than your true red dress. Claret with a good bit of black in it."

BECAUSE THOSE DEAREST to me are away, I feel that I have been somewhat abandoned. But as I sit for a new portrait, a new image, with Elisabeth Vigée-Lebrun, I feel that I begin to heal from my humiliation. To be envisioned by her, to sit before her as she works, loving her work, gives me peace. Once I almost say to her, "Your brush—as it creates me anew on the canvas, I feel almost that I am being licked, cared for, as a kitten would be by the mother cat."

I do not need to say this to her. She, like Fersen, intuits my feelings and I do not have to represent them with words. She is such a keen observer that she notices that as she paints me, I relax, feel at home within myself, that my eyes and skin come alive and glow.

"I like very much," she says, "the new needlepoint you are making. You paint the flowers with your thread."

I tell her that it is for a waistcoat for the King. "I noticed the fine needlework adorning the cardinal, when the King summoned him to his inner chamber. I would like the King to have something even finer. The colors are those of Trianon, pale greens and blues, pink and lavender flowers. Pastels and spring colors. When he wears it, he will remember that he has a refuge when he visits me in my little palace that he so kindly gave me to hold in my own name."

When the King returns from the seacoast, he is a very happy man.

All three of the children and I wait for him on the balcony of the château, above the Marble Courtyard. We watch his coach approach with great excitement, as it grows larger as it comes closer. He passes the outer grille and the wide courtyard where we watched Montgolfier's balloon ascend, past the bronze equestrian statue of Louis XIV—I cannot help but recall the first day I came here, not yet fifteen, and how each courtyard became smaller, and the arms of the buildings enclosed me ever more closely. Perhaps he sees us standing here—the Queen with her three children—waving to him. When the coach stops, all three of the children cry out "Papa! Papa!" He flings himself out of the carriage to run up to us, puffing and panting, embracing all three of our happy children—Madame Royale, the Dauphin, the Duc de Normandie—and myself as well.

Ten days have passed since the King's return. Having viewed the sea for the first time, Louis tries valiantly to describe its *sublime* effect to me. Although I would like to see the ocean sometime, I know that things of vast size—the starry sky, for example—often frighten me with their natural magnificence.

"For me, gardens are the reminders of paradise," I say with a smile.

"You are a medievalist at heart," he teases. "You must see the tapestries of Cluny, the lady in her enclosed garden, with her unicorn and lion. She is a devotee of the five senses, even as you are."

"While I truly enjoy tapestries, I do not require an enclosed garden," I reply in a bantering fashion. "The gardens at Trianon stretch on and on."

"Yes," he says, "once you have been admitted. Actually, the whole estate of Versailles is enclosed. The walls are just too far away for you to take much notice of them."

When I congratulate him again on the success of his visit to coastal Normandie, he replies, "The love from my people touches the deepest springs of my heart. You must judge for yourself if I am not the happiest king in the world."

I FEEL THE BEGINNINGS of my labor, but I choose to ignore them so that I may first attend Mass. Since my humiliation, it is a part of my healing to enter the Royal Chapel, to enjoy the space between the colorful splendor of the marble floor and the high painted ceiling, where I was so innocently wed, and to be succored by taking the holy communion. As the organ of Couperin begins to play the gritty, deep notes from pipes as big as my waist, the sound always makes my heart swell, and I gladly give thanks for the goodness of the Creator. The very words of the liturgy give me a sense of connection as I renew my beliefs: "God the Father, Almighty, Maker of Heaven and Earth . . ."

I smile at Mesdames Tantes during chapel and remember how they welcomed me when I was fifteen; I have forgiven them for how they tried to use me to lever apart the old King and his mistress. I am happy to have pleased them by suggesting that if the new child is a girl she shall be named Sophie, after the one of their number who has died. I do not signal my secret: that my labor has already begun, for to do so would only increase the length of their anxiety for me.

I return to my chamber to conduct my labor. Three hours after the official ministers are summoned to witness the royal birth, at seven-thirty when it is not yet dark on this July night, 1786, I give birth to another daughter.

I like the message sent by the Spanish ambassador to the King: "Though Your Majesty must keep his Princes at his side, with his daughters he has the means of bestowing gifts on the rest of Europe." Still, I remember how I myself was once a gift to be bestowed on France in the name of an Alliance and the peace of Europe.

I do not particularly enjoy the visit, just three weeks after the birth of Sophie, of my sister Marie Christine, whom our mother allowed to marry for love. Count Mercy—always avid for stronger ties between me and anyone Austrian—has urged me to give up old ideas about her. I suspect that it was she who kept the Empress so very well informed of everything concerning my life. I know that she has sent my brother the Emperor some of the disgraceful pamphlets circulated to destroy my reputation. She considers herself quite superior to me, and I plan not to invite her to Trianon. She and her Albert will return to the Netherlands without having any opportunity to judge my private, tender life.

Would that she were Maria Carolina, my Charlotte! I would show *her* all my favorite roses and trees at Trianon. Skipping, I would take her across the bridges to visit the Temple of Love. We would eat berries together on the balcony of my retreat at the *Hameau*, and we would feed bread to the fish in the pond. I would even show her the secret cave and grotto close to the Belvedere, and everything would be illuminated magically at night for her, followed by an extravaganza of fireworks.

After Christine and her mere Prince of Saxony have left Versailles, I rather saucily ask Count Mercy if he deemed the visit a success.

Truthfully and too seriously, he replies, "The renewal of acquaintance between the two august sisters has not been without its clouds."

"Then let me be 'the Queen of Clouds,'" I reply. Though the words are haughty, I smile at him when I pronounce them, for he has been my constant friend these many years, and I love him. He returns the smile. I know he prefers me to my sister.

Matters Grave and Financial

Very troubled, the King enters my private chambers where I rest in the afternoon and gravely tells me the finance minister, Calonne, believes no bank will extend loans to us. "We are on the verge of national bankruptcy."

Though the King has never before said such a startling thing to me, I am surprised at my calm suggestion. "Then surely Calonne has some plan that will avert such a disaster." My private apartment seems too intimate to hold a discourse of such moment to the nation. Rising from my small blue daybed so cunningly tucked in its alcove, I suggest that we retire to his study.

The King has recovered his composure before we begin to pass through the more public rooms. As we walk, he says, "In fact Calonne has given me a document produced over the summer by himself and his assistant Talleyrand."

"And its title?" I inquire.

"Appropriately enough, *Un Plan pour l'amélioration des finances.*"

As we reach his study, the King rolls back the sliding cover of his large and beautiful desk, one created with all the marquetry of Riesener. Almost as a reflection of my own calm manner, the King now appears quite in control. He lifts the document up to its reading position, dismisses the servants, and begins to share with me some of the features of Calonne's plan for our salvation.

"It is a bold proposal, and its chief focus is taxation. All landowners, without exception, are to pay at a fair and uniform rate. Not the poor, though."

"Is the Church to be taxed?"

"For its landholdings, yes. And the nobility will no longer be exempt from tax on their obvious signs of wealth. Those most able to pay—the Church, the nobility—will have to contribute more toward the revenues of the nation. For the first time."

"How can such an idea be implemented?" I am truly startled now, more by the proposed remedy to the impending disaster than by the disaster itself. Vaguely, I recall that Louis XV had had a plan, constructed with Malesherbes, to tax the nobility.

"Calonne says that we must create an Assembly of Notables—"

"I have never heard of such a convocation."

"None has occurred for some hundred and sixty years, not since the time of Louis XIII. It was a maneuver instigated by Cardinal Richelieu. The Notables will be as carefully selected as possible. After they approve the reforms, they will be passed on to the various Parlements. I register the reforms as *lit de justice*, laws that I institute from my private chamber."

"And who selects the Notables?"

"I do."

Now it is time for the King to calm my nerves. "Reform is necessary," he replies. "I am not against a reasonable adjustment in our society. It is the nobles who will prove the most resistant to change."

22 February 1787

I spend this day on my knees in the Royal Chapel, praying for the King as he opens the Assembly of Notables. I picture him, dressed in purple velvet, flanked by his two brothers. But also I pray for the Notables themselves because I can understand their reluctance to let go of their privileges and their exemptions. Their support and loyalty to the King is predicated in part on his protection of their assets and their family wealth.

When I have supper with the King, he is downcast. He tells me that the Notables are in a disobedient mood. They wish to spend a great deal of time debating and discussing the issues. Already the idea of having representation from the Parlements and possibly even convening an Estates General has been mentioned.

The King explains, "The Assembly of the Notables is quite different from the Estates General. The Estates General has not been convened for an even longer period of time. Not since 1614, some one hundred and seventy years ago. The three estates represented in the general assembly are the nobility, the clergy, and the commoners. For that assembly, each estate chooses its own representatives."

I feel a shudder pass through my body. I do not know the history of Austria so many years ago, but I am quite sure that no such precedent was being set whereby peasants participated in ruling the empire by choosing their own representatives.

"But there is no need now for an Estates General," I say. "Perhaps they prolong the arguments merely for the sake of deferring decisions unfavorable to themselves."

The King's reply is that it is the people—such as those at Cherbourg—who truly love us, and we must work for their good as much as for the good of the nobility.

"I have always worked for the good of the people of France," I reply. My sentence sounds like an echo from the distant past. Yes, I made such a vow long ago, when I was young, and the new King met the unrest of the Flour Wars with such unexpected firmness.

With sorrow, the King mentions the death of Vergennes, the minister upon whom he has depended for advice for the last three years. Now it is necessary to appoint a new foreign minister, and the King has proposed his boyhood friend Montmorin, who has served as the ambassador to Spain. I know that Mercy wishes otherwise. He has instructed me to advocate the appointment of the Comte de Saint-Priest, who is favorable to Austria, and, as it turns out, a good friend to Axel von Fersen.

When my old friend Count Mercy importuned my intervention, I said to him something I have never said before. "It is not proper that the Court of Vienna should dictate who the ministers of the Court of France are to be." My heart is with the King in these difficult times, and I feel that it is my place to offer him my quiet support. My children need to inherit a prosperous and well-governed country from their father. The King falls into fits of despondency, and I must try to keep my own wits about me, without so much influence from Austria. All too sadly learned has been the lesson of the diamond necklace: in France one must fight for justice.

I worry too for the King's health. He is very heavy. In the evening when I drink my mineral water, he takes a good deal of wine. Sometimes he is so weary, especially after a hard day of hunting, which becomes more and more an obsession, that he staggers and loses his balance.

On April 8, Easter Sunday, the King finds it necessary to dismiss Calonne, who is a friend of the Duchesse de Polignac. The Minister Calonne has speculated in land and dealt unwisely with the syndicate under contract to provide water to Paris. The King has discovered that Calonne has misrepresented the national deficit as some thirty-two million less than he reported. He has circulated an inflammatory statement demanding that more taxes must be paid: "By whom? Solely by those privileged classes who have not paid enough. Would it be better to tax the underprivileged, the People of France?" With such public language, Calonne drives a wedge between us and the Notables. He has behaved in a way recklessly dangerous, without solving the financial crisis. We hear that he has purchased with public funds a thousand bottles of wine to be housed for private use in a monastery near his home.

Because she is angry with us for not protecting her friend and keeping him in his position, the Duchesse de Polignac has turned the education of the Dauphin over to a governor, and she has gone to England again. Her coolness has much hurt the King, who has always appreciated her charming manners and friendliness. To try to smooth things, he has agreed to pay the debts of her sister-in-law, Comtesse Diane de Polignac—some 400,000 livres—under the false flag that the money was spent for my entertainment.

I am amazed at the number of our friends among the nobility who bitterly resent our attempt to economize. Besenval, deprived of some of his income, has said, "That kind of dispossession used only to happen in Turkey." The Assembly of Notables is disbanded. When I appear at the Opera, I am hissed. At the theater, it has long been the custom of the audience to respond to some accidental line in the script as though it were intended to apply to the world beyond the stage. When a line from Racine—"Confound this cruel Queen"—was pronounced, the audience cheered and applauded ferociously. Yet I have done nothing to them. I have cut the positions in my household by 173 people in an attempt to economize.

Still, they call me Madame Déficite.

Of the national budget, 41 percent is allocated simply to pay the interest on the national debt. The new minister of finance, Brienne, whose appointment I very much favored, for he is an old friend of the Abbé de Vermond, who taught me when I was a child, consoles me by pointing out that the expenditure of the entire court is only 6 percent of the annual budget.

WHEN I BEG my friend Count von Fersen to describe truthfully to me my own position and that of the King as others see it, he asks me, with utmost kindness in his eyes, to withdraw my request, but I insist.

"If you will have it so," he answers, and he extends his hand to me as he speaks, as though by this means, he offers consolation. "It profoundly grieves me to report that the Queen is quite universally detested. Every evil is attributed to her, and she is given no credit for anything good. People claim that the King is weak and suspicious; the only person he trusts is the Queen. People say that in these days, the Queen must do and is doing everything."

I know that my loyal friend—his eyes filled with sadness—has spoken truthfully about our miserable reputations. "Promise me," I say to him, "that you will never repeat those words to the King."

Sophie

Though she was born a big baby, my daughter has not thrived. She has grown very little, and between worrying about her, and the health of the Dauphin, and the deficit, my mood has become pessimistic. I recall how my believing in his future health has often helped Louis Joseph to make amazing recoveries, and I try to do the same for Sophie.

I sit beside her crib and tell her over and over—she is only nine months old this June—she is beautiful and good. I tell her that I love her, and when she grows older I will play tea set with her and teach her to play the harp, but she is too young to understand these promises.

From restlessness and fever, she progresses to convulsions.

Her death is the saddest moment of my life.

Madame Elisabeth stands beside me to view her little corpse at the Grand Trianon and calls her "my little angel." They say that it was the emergence of three tiny teeth that caused her to suffer convulsions.

"She would have been my friend," I murmur.

I SEE THAT Madame Royale has learned the bitter lesson of death. Her sympathy with my loss moves me to more tears. The child looks lost—as though she had never thought the world capable of such cruelty as the death of an infant. I tell her that in such matters we can do nothing but submit to the will of God, whose wisdom far exceeds our own. We cannot know his reasons.

LATER, AFTER CONFERRING with the King, I instruct my friend to paint Sophie out of the red velvet portrait with my children. In the painting, the crib now appears to be empty. The Dauphin still points at it, as though to remind whoever might gaze at the painting of our poignant loss.

However, when the time comes in August to exhibit the Vigée-Lebrun picture, I am advised by the chief of police not to appear in Paris. The hatred for me has grown more virulent because Jeanne La Motte has escaped from the Salpêtrière prison and fled to England, from which she has authored and autographed a description of her "Sapphic" relationship with none other than the Queen. *Was I ever in her presence at all?* Furthermore, she reinforces the rumors that as a tribade I have also made love to the Princesse de Lamballe and the Duchesse de Polignac.

In the empty place where my portrait should have appeared, someone has displayed a note which reads "Behold the Deficit!"

IN THE WAKE of the failure to receive the approval of the Parlement for the financial reform, the King has simply made the age-old pronouncement "I ordain registration." Thus, the new law imposing financial reform is legitimately registered. It has long been the right of monarchs to declare from their bedrooms, if need be, what will become the law.

Our cousin Philippe, Duc d'Orléans, has protested the legitimacy of such an utterance. Flouting tradition, he claims that because votes were not counted in the Assembly of Notables, the new law is invalid. The King has been forced to send his cousin into exile.

To the reconvened assembly, the King declared in a fury, "It is the law because I wish it to be."

A terrifying silence followed.

I hear my own sigh as I write of these troubling events to my brother

Joseph II. I take up my pen and add: "I am upset that these repressive measures have had to be taken; unhappily, they have become necessary here in France." I am ready to drip wax onto my letter and to press my seal into the hot wax, when I remember the most dreadful and dreaded piece of news. I unfold the paper to write again that the King has hoped to quiet the unrest we witness through France and especially in Paris by calling within a time period of not more than five years a meeting of the Estates General.

On the Fate of Charles I, of England

5 October 1788

Knowing that the fall season will soon turn to winter, I have taken the opportunity to sit for a while beside the fountain of Ceres. When a messenger brings a request for an audience at the château with the Abbé de Véri, I gather my warm woolen shawl about me and send word that I will meet him in the Peace room. I am glad that I have come into the gardens in an enclosed sedan chair, and I am happy to enter its cozy little space and to have the door closed behind me. Here the fall breeze cannot reach me.

As we progress back toward the château, I wonder what has brought the abbé to call. He is a friend of the King's, and they often have scholarly conversations together about the course of history. I have never had much reason to converse with him. These are sad days, so it is nice that someone from outside the walls of Versailles has sought out my company.

When the Abbé de Véri enters the room, I note that he is carrying a large leather-bound journal, stamped with the year 1788 in gold, and that his countenance bears the mark of serious thought.

His complexion is sallow, caused no doubt by his long hours away from the healthy effects of the outdoors. He has a rather knobby nose, but his blue eyes have a straight and piercing gaze. At this moment, he opens the book that I have taken to be a journal and asks if I would like to read something that he has written therein. "Or would Her Majesty prefer that I read aloud to her?"

Noting that his handwriting is tiny and crabbed—the better not to waste paper, I suppose—I invite him to read to me.

"It was intended just as a note to myself," he says in a humble way, "but as I wrote it, a vision of Her Majesty came to my mind, and I felt that I was being led, perhaps simply through my own imagination, to share my thoughts with Her Majesty."

"Please be so kind as to read to me," I repeat encouragingly, but suddenly I have an almost violent craving for chocolate, which I ignore.

"'The current of opinions tends toward some sort of revolution.'" He pauses to see my response, but I merely nod for him to continue. "'It is a torrent which is steadily increasing and is beginning to burst the embankments.'"

"I wonder if there is something in particular that you have observed?" I ask.

"It is not so much observation as scholarship that has given me pause," he answers. "I have also recorded in my journal a conversation that I overheard earlier today between your husband, His Majesty Louis XVI, and his minister Malesherbes. If you will allow me to continue, then your ears will be present, even as mine were."

"Please do continue," I say. His tone of voice is so gently coaxing that I do not want in any way to be impolite in the face of his concern for his King. At one time, I would have had grave reservations about Malesherbes because, in the eyes of Louis XV, he wished to weaken the monarchy. But my husband has admired Malesherbes's willingness to use compromise as a means of preserving the monarchy.

"Malesherbes began by saying, 'You are a great reader, Sire, and you are more knowledgeable than you are thought to be. But reading counts for nothing if it is not accompanied by reflection. I have recently reread in David Hume's *History of England* his passage on Charles I.'"

"Yes." I interrupt the good, eavesdropping abbé with some enthusiasm, for I recognize the reference. "When I first came to France, a girl of fourteen, the Dauphin confided in me his interest in the thought of Hume, whom he had actually met."

"Yes," the abbé replied and then continued peering through his lens and reading aloud. "'Your positions have much in common. That Prince was mild, virtuous, devoted to the law, never insensitive, never taking the initiative, just and beneficent; he died, however, at the hand of the executioner upon the scaffold. He became king at a time when argument was arising about the prerogative of the crown as against those of his subjects, and you are in a similar position. The question has arisen here in France, as it did in England in the last century, between the usual practices of authority and the complaints of the citizens. An important difference is that here in France there is no religious element in the dispute.'

"'Ah! Yes, very happily,' the King responded at this point to Malesherbes, even placing his royal hand upon his minister's arm. 'There will not be the same atrocities committed in France.'

"'And besides,' replied Malesherbes, 'our gentler manners will set your mind at rest about the bloody excesses of those days. But they *will* strip you by degrees of your prerogatives unless you make a definite plan as to what concessions you can make and on what matters you should never yield. Only your own resoluteness can preserve the monarchy. I would be willing to swear that the unrest will not go so far as taking Your Majesty to the fate of Charles I, but I cannot reassure you that there would not be other excesses.'"

The abbé closes his journal.

"I think it is the matter of resoluteness that has brought me to Her Majesty. Others may have a different opinion of Your Majesty, but I know you are the daughter of Maria Theresa, of Austria. I know that you must have witnessed that august person exercising a certain resoluteness of will, when the occasion called for such measures.

"You know that I am not speaking of any need to strengthen the ties between France and Austria as we now live. But I am asking Your Majesty in the days ahead to embody the spirit of her mother, to remember her courage, her compassion, and her resourcefulness."

"So it is," I replied with soft gravity. "Just as Malesherbes would remind my husband of the fate of Charles I of England on the scaffold, so would you remind me of the strength of the Empress of Austria."

"Just so, Your Majesty." The Abbé de Véri stood, bowed, and began to take his leave. "And may your gracious Majesty remember that she is always in my prayers."

In the Town of Versailles, May 1789

From the parish church named Notre Dame, here in the town of Versailles, at the head of the Procession of the Deputies of the Estates General, the King and I follow the canopy hovering over the Blessed Sacrament. The members of the three estates—nobility, clergy, and commoners—each walk with their own groups. Slowly, we cross the Place d'Armes. The King and I turn our heads toward the window in one of the royal stables for the Dauphin to see us pass. Yes! There he is, his tiny, frail body propped up on a great pile of cushions. How bravely he smiles at us, his parents, as we pass by below! He is a noble child. Tears try to flood my eyes, but I must be as brave as he is, only age eight. It is his spirit that is noble, a fact of much greater importance than any social position can convey.

If these people aspire to nobility, let them practice courage and compassion. A little child could lead them.

Having passed his station, I fasten my eyes again on the sacrament as it leads the way from the local church of Notre Dame to the Church of Saint-Louis. Every window is filled with spectators and lining the streets are vast crowds, who sometimes cheer. Often, when they see me, a dark silence falls. I lift my head higher. It is a dazzlingly sunny day. No one here has ever witnessed such an historic event: the Estates General will convene tomorrow, here in the town of Versailles. We are right to entreat God's guidance—all of us, today. Some of these deputies have disavowed God or renamed him simply as the Supreme Being, who cares little for the fate of humans. I do not believe that.

EARLIER WE SAT for a moment with the Dauphin, who sometimes struggles to breathe. His spine has become quite crooked, and he can hardly stand erect. Some of the vertebrae jut out. He has become embarrassed by his hunchback appearance and does not like to be seen unless he can trust in the love of his visitor.

"Your dress is very beautiful," the Dauphin said to me quietly, and I was glad that he took pleasure in the splendor of my wide court dress, made of silver cloth all ashimmer wherever the light touches it. The King is dressed in cloth of gold studded with brilliants; he sparkles all over, as though touched by a magic wand, with diamond buttons and shoe buckles, carrying a diamond sword, and decorated by the order of the Golden Fleece and the Order of Saint-Ésprit. He wears the enormous diamond known as the Regent, and my hair is ornamented with the flawless and starlike diamond named the Sancy.

"My papa must be the King of Enchantment as well as of France," the Dauphin said.

Then he began to cough, and I could see a flush of feverish red cross his face. Gallantly, he calmed his heaving and managed to ask, "Is light more silvery or gold?"

I gasped and said, "My darling, I asked the same question when I rode many days across Europe inside the regal coaches to meet your father."

AS I WALK forward in the procession, someone steps before me and shouts in my face, "*Vive le Duc d'Orléans!*" The insult causes me to stumble, such an insult, almost an assault on my dignity. I regain my balance.

Yes, to ingratiate himself with the people, the King's cousin opposes the compromises the King would institute between the old regime and the new demands of the citizens. I am sorry that the whole branch of the family has not been consigned to and kept in exile. D'Orléans does not march in his proper place as a Prince of the Blood but establishes his preference for those who lack nobility by walking with them. Should there be a revolt, d'Orléans wants the people to count him as a friend. The cries of the people make me feel as though I may faint, but I lift my chin.

AT THE CHURCH of Saint-Louis, the bishop sermonizes about the riches of the nobility in contrast to the poverty of the people. I watch the eyelids of the King half-hood his eyes. Then they completely close. So it is with him. He escapes into sleep, when he cannot hunt in the countryside. I can only hope that he does not snore.

At the end of the sermon, the King is awakened by the applause. In the old days, we were taught it was disrespectful to applaud when the Blessed Sacrament was uncovered. These are a people lacking in manners, cruel and wild.

Here in the Church of Saint-Louis I vow, always, to treat the people of France with civility, in the hope that it will be returned to me and my family. Perhaps such a hope is to be pitied.

AT THE OPENING of the assembly of the Estates, 4 May, the King stands in his majestic robes, sparkling with jewels. He invites me to be seated, but I curtsy and continue to stand. From his high throne, just as he begins to speak, a shaft of sunlight enters through a gap in the curtains and shines on his face like the approval of God. I wish the Dauphin were well enough to see his father so blessed by heaven.

When the noblemen are seated, they don their hats, as is their habit to do in the presence of the king, as a sign of their own privileges; it has been so from ancient times. All of the plumes sweeping up together make me wonder if they are not like the cresting foam of an ocean wave, as the King has described to me. I wish my children could visit the ocean, where they say the salt breezes are restorative to the lungs.

Standing on the royal dais, splendid in my clothes, violet and white, I know that I cannot help but look sad: I fear the Dauphin is dying. I am glad that we have moved him to Meudon, overlooking the Seine river from the highlands not far from Sèvres, where the air is noted for its purity. As a boy, the King was once taken to Meudon to recover, but the health of the Dauphin does not improve.

The King's speech goes well, after having been rehearsed last night over and over. He speaks of the financial crises as mainly a result of our expenditure in the American war of independence from England. He calls it "an exorbitant but honorable war." And now it has been won. His voice is firm.

I but half listen to the interminable speech of Necker, even though it is through my own advice that he has been restored as minister of finance. My alarm grows as it becomes clear that he has nothing of substance to say, not even on the issue of how the Estates will be allowed to vote.

My thoughts drift to the Dauphin. I think of my young son's great tenderness to me, and how when he asked me to eat my favorite dinner with him in his room, I swallowed more tears than bread. For all his frail condition, I rejoice to have given birth to such a child.

I recall how when he wanted to be carried out into the garden—so like his mother—he asked not to be carried by a certain valet, "for he always hurts me." When someone told him that the valet does all he can to ease him and that his feelings would be hurt if his services were declined, the Dauphin replied, "Ring at once, then; I would rather suffer a little than cause any pain to this worthy man."

Mature beyond his years, the child is a saint of patience, and as I sit in this public place listening to political speeches, I swallow and swallow the tears that run down the inside of my throat, for I will not let them see me weep, lest they think they have some power over me.

GRIEF

It is after midnight, and my child has just died. I look at his tortured body and am glad his spirit is with God. 4 June 1789.

At the same time, my heart is broken.

I run to the window, throw it open to the darkness, look down into the neglected garden. The redolent aroma of honeysuckle, roses, jasmine, all in decay, floods into the room.

The Revolution of 1789

17 June

I am told that the Third Estate, representing, they claim, 96 percent of the nation, has broken off from the Estates General to form a new group, the National Assembly, the voice of the commoners. Each time an advisory body is formed and dissolved—the Assembly of Notables, the Estates General, the National Assembly—we lose power.

Who has the power? It is a man once named Comte Mirabeau, now known usually as Mirabeau. Though he is said to be anything but beautiful, his presence represents a kind of miracle. Gigantic in size, he became an outcast from his own noble family. He was a seducer of countless women, despite his hideous pockmarked face, and his own father had him imprisoned for three years for having run off with a woman. When the famines and hardships came to Provence, he made himself a spokesman for the common folk of the Third Estate and was elected their representative. "Woe to the privileged orders," he is quoted as saying, "for privileges will cease, but the People are eternal." He both inflames the people and pacifies them. He claims to respect the monarchy while moving France toward the republicanism of England. His hair towers above his steep forehead like a thundercloud, and on his back the great snarl of hair is caught up in a black bag, they say.

Mirabeau himself is said to be the author of his own promotional pamphlet, which the King gave me to read:

> *The good citizen* [meaning himself] *is the greatest orator of his time; his mighty voice dominates any public meeting as thunder subjugates the roaring sound of the sea; his courage astonishes all who hear him, and his strength affirms that no human power could cause him to abandon his ideals or principles.*

We tremble at the name of Mirabeau. With their tears, the women and children of France bathe his hands, his clothing, even the footprints he leaves in the dirt.

He is not only feared, but loved. But so are we—still loved—to some extent.

20 June

Locked out of their meeting room, the commoners meet on the tennis courts of Versailles and swear an oath to their cause. I wish I'd ordered the courts plowed up and planted in roses.

We have choices: to stand against them or to capitulate.

After I consider how to rouse the King, I take my two children—two, only two are left us—by their hands to speak to their father. I find the King in his chamber.

"Hold him in your arms," I say, pushing the new Dauphin in all his robust health into his father's arms.

"Embrace your father," I say to Marie Thérèse.

"Protect her," I tell him. "Do not allow the monarchy to become the ghost of itself. Your brothers and the nobles will stand by you."

The King kisses his children, and he opens his arms to me.

"Never doubt my love for my family," he says. "But I must decide the best course, and that course is not clear. Necker advises us to compromise with the Third Estate. Take the children away now, my dear. Necker thinks that at bottom, the Third Estate loves us. They will support us in reforms that will control the irresponsibility of the nobility and the clergy. We must not be hasty. I will consider the future."

I do as I am bid, but I have witnessed the vascillation of the King too many times. I have little hope.

24 June

A majority of the clergy have gone over to the position of the Third Estate, calling for a new constitution to be drawn up. Mirabeau has spread the word that the wealthy clergy, unless they leave their station to join the people, do not represent the humble pastors who do serve the people; instead, like the nobility, the privileged clergy are parasites. Such clergymen must become civil servants, agents of literacy for the poor. They must nurse the sick and shelter the dying.

25 June

Many of the nobility have agreed to support the Third Estate; among them is the King's cousin the Duc d'Orléans. They betray their own social class but even more the monarchy by giving these rowdies their support.

I would like for us to leave Versailles, to go to Compiègne, but we would not be safe on the roads. And if we left, we might be leaving all our power behind. Count Mercy says that we have all lost our heads, while the danger of famine, bankruptcy, and civil war is imminent.

27 June

There are still good hearts in France. To be loyal to the King and to the royal family is to be loyal to the country they love. When they see that we are a family, even as they too are members of a family, then their hearts are touched. Though I can no longer command their love as an enchanting princess, they can love me as the mother of France, just as my mother, with her fifteen births, became the mother of Austria. Are these ideas true?

Yes, the King is truly the embodiment of the people. When I showed him his children, he became a man again, firm in his manhood. When the deputies came to call upon me, I greeted them as I held the hand of the new Dauphin. They were charmed, and their hearts filled with loyalty. Louis Charles represents their children and the future of their children.

Surely it was because they loved him that the representatives of the Third Estate insisted they be allowed to sprinkle holy water on the little silver coffin of Louis Joseph. When they stood around the coffin, some of them remarked on the presence of a great, bright light; others felt that they had glimpsed in their little leader the radiance of God.

"We will stand with you on the balcony," I tell my husband, "so that the people will see you with your family. At the same time you might wish to affirm that concessions *à la* Necker will be made. Because this is a new era, perhaps you should say you will allow all three of the Estates to meet together. We do not hold any longer to the traditions of 1614."

I tell myself before we step out on the balcony, our stage, that we must make the entrance as though we will all live forever. Though he is not so tall as Mirabeau, they say, the size of the King will help to establish his grandeur. The innocence of the children and their utter vulnerability will make the people feel that they are our lawful protectors, not our adversaries. I will show my joy that they have come to visit us.

"These are our people, whom we love," I say and smile at my family.

Yes, the King goes first, and the crowd roars with approval: their King is yet among them: they have not lost their souls by questioning our authority. Quickly, holding the hands of the children, we step beside him, and I radiate love as they cheer us. These are the commoners, the people whom Louis XV identified as united with the person of the monarch. But sometimes they hate us. Spontaneously, I bend and lift my son into my arms. I hold him up so that they may see him better, above the railing of the balcony. Here is the future! *We have no fear in showing our only remaining son to the people. We trust in your love. We show you what love is like: we share ourselves, even our most precious and innocent member, with you because we are one with you.*

Their demonstrations of affection—applause, shouting, cheering—continue and continue. They are at a visual feast, and we cannot deny them the pleasure of looking at us, on the balcony of Versailles, our official home, and the seat of their government, the locus of the glory of the nation, from the time of Louis XIV to this day. Our authority is that of a loving father.

If there is a scale whose swinging arm represents the favor of the people, Mirabeau, that gigantic count who left his origins to lead the commoners, stands in one pan of the scale. He is weighty; people say his clothing must strain to cover his great bulk; he has an enormous head, and hair that stands all around like the mane of a lion. People never tire of painting his portrait in words. Some say his face resembles the snarl of a tiger. Mirabeau, the defector from the nobility, speaks endlessly, without notes, in a stentorian voice. Germaine de Staël, the daughter of our Necker, has said that it is impossible not to be entranced by Mirabeau's eloquence; she pays him this tribute even while he vilifies her father, Necker, our minister of finance.

But the eye is mightier than the ear.

The memory of what is viewed outlasts the memory of what is heard. And here in this courtyard and on beyond to the larger one, and even beyond to the widest courtyard stand far more people, enraptured, than those who listen to debates of the Third Estate and the speeches of Mirabeau.

In the other pan of the scales that weigh the loyalty of the people stand we, the royal family, the emblem of the people, a family that is the archetype of all families: a powerful husband, a charming wife, a son, a daughter. Together, as a family and the emblem of the very identity of France, we stand on the balcony of Versailles for a length of time greater than when Mirabeau enthralled their representatives by advocating actions that presage revolution.

Sometimes I put down the Dauphin, and then when I lift him aloft again, again the people roar with pleasure. Like music, I create a rhythm to their enthusiasm by setting him down and lifting him up again. Mirabeau only spoke to their representatives; we are viewed and approved by the people themselves.

Finally, finally, we wave good-bye.

Now they understand better who we are.

Now they have demonstrated their own goodwill.

Yet, tomorrow I know they may wish to imprison us, or worse. Their addiction is to intensity, be it love or hate.

WE COME INSIDE. I kiss my children and thank them for playing their parts so well.

"Your beauty, your charm, your smiles and pleasantness," I tell them, "have contributed to the peace and future happiness of France. Always, always, you must show the people that your hearts are full of love. Even though you are small, in their own minds, they are your children. If you forever show them the trust and the abundance of your affection, then, like a mirror, they will reflect it back to you."

Now for the King, I must show no fatigue, no weakness, no vacillation in my deepest principles. "Now we have said what we had to say"—I smile—"without uttering a word." I reassure him. He gazes at me with loving gratitude. He is reliving the cheers of the people as we stood on the balcony together over the Marble Courtyard. "They were packed so close together," I observe, "that I could not see the light and dark squares of the marble below their feet."

No sooner have I spoken than I am shocked at my statement. Of what use is the fleeting visual picture of feet obscuring a pattern of marble? I have let down my guard. Quickly, I add, "Now having presented the vision they wished and needed to see, we must act in the way that we need to act."

The King nods.

"And the Maréchal de Broglie?" I ask him. Our new minister of war is very old.

"Even in his advanced age, he shows a spirit of resolve, and of great resourcefulness."

"Yes." I pause and smile at my husband. "And how many troops does he promise?"

"Thirty thousand."

"And where will they be located?" I smile again.

"On the outskirts of Paris."

I reach out my hand to the King. I want him to feel the warmth of my small hand in his large one, and the trust that I have in him. "And by what date will the troops be in place?" I ask.

"His promise is for July thirteenth."

ALTHOUGH THE KING and I are convinced that a show of force is necessary, I continue to exhibit a relaxed and cheerful mien. I believe in our strength, and that we will show the people that the age of aristocracy is not over. We are not the British, nor the Americans, though Lafayette would offer them a constitution on the American model. As God is the King of the Universe, so it is that Kings assure the order of their countries. As the angels are arranged in ranks around the throne of God, so must the sectors of society be arranged by their rank. It is a divine plan, and it is our sacred duty to uphold it, lest the chaos of hell spread over the land.

One evening as we sip chocolate with our friends—they are all here—Fersen, Saint-Priest, the Princesse de Lamballe, the Polignacs, Artois, and the Comte de Provence, and their wives (I have heard that the Comtesse de Provence is, in fact, having a passionate love affair with another woman), I suddenly say, "The very beauty of the palace and gardens of Versailles testify to the rightness of the rule of kings, just as the beauty of the earth reflects the glory of God." In response, they all applaud.

Later I confide to everyone how much I have always admired the painting of the Princesse de Lamballe in the bosom of her husband's family, all of them enjoying a cup of chocolate with the little pet dogs about. "I thought it the essence of our century," I say.

Everyone looks at me curiously. "All elegance and refinement," I add.

"Anyone who hoped to capture the essence of our time would have to paint Her Gracious Majesty into the picture," Fersen says gallantly.

The King attempts to raise his cup to toast Fersen's compliment, but his fingers are too pudgy to fit the delicate handle. He lifts the cup, nonetheless, by embracing the circumference of its lip. "From the moment of your arrival, France has been blessed and graced by your presence," my husband says, and they all raise their cups in a sweet salute.

I cannot help but blush with pleasure, yet almost as though there were voices outside, I seem to hear the disdainful appellation *L'Austrichienne!* I actually cannot resist rising and going to the window to look out. Only a few groundskeepers are moving about the pedestals of the classical statues.

The King quickly says, "It may be dangerous to stand in front of the window."

Obediently, I turn away from the glass. Now, if anyone saw a woman standing in the lighted palace window, they would think her just a woman, not the hated Queen. Or do they love me? They loved me when I stood with the King on the balcony with our children. I have always loved the French people; it was I who would not allow the royal hunting parties to gallop across their fields. It was I who supported the tax reforms offered by the King. It was I who gave alms and last winter had the King build fires at the crossroads to warm any who had to be about in the fierce winds. Turning now to look at my friends in the mellow candlelight surrounded by the sparkling chandeliers, I say, "If our friend Elisabeth Vigée-Lebrun were with us, I would ask her to paint this scene, so that we could have it always. She could do a new series of paintings by candlelight, and the corners would be dens of darkness."

The King rises and comes to stand beside me. He holds up both his hands so that the thumbs form a square angle from the fingers. He is improvising a frame for the scene, and we both look through it at our friends.

For a moment, no one stirs.

I cannot resist seeking out the eyes of Fersen, and for one quick moment he gives back the gaze to me, his soul flickers like an ember through his eyes.

Ours is a cozy sadness. We are living through the end of an era, but we are together.

1 July

The so-called National Assembly has voted itself a new name: Constituent National Assembly with a license to create new laws.

Saint-Priest, our minister of the household, reports that the people are made nervous by the amassing of soldiers near the edges of the city, and he warns that if the military resorts to violence, such violence might be the spark to ignite a conflagration.

9 July

To appease the nobles (whose support we must win to survive), the King has made a firm decision, backed by myself and by his brothers, to dismiss Necker as minister of finance. The nobles reject Necker's efforts to abridge their privileges in any way. Necker is to leave France as quietly as possible. Artois has been particularly firm about refusing compromise in his effort to conserve what people have begun calling the *Ancien Régime.*

The King's decisiveness about the minister makes me glow with happiness, and my soul sings as I walk through the Hall of Mirrors. I feel as immaterial and powerful as sunlight streaming through the windows and bouncing off the mirrors, filling the corridor with itself.

I do not know if this state of being is power or the illusion of power, but it has a wonderful and frightening ability to satisfy the soul.

12 July

The rioting in Paris, at the news of Necker's dismissal, has caused the closing of the theaters and the opera. Seeking arms, the rioters were furious when they discovered that the swords and axes used dramatically onstage are nothing but cardboard. Yelling "These are real," they picked up stones from the street and flung them at the Royal German Regiment. The Prince de Lambesc's troops drew their real swords and retaliated.

When the prince was accused of excessive brutality, I privately took his side with both the King and Count Mercy: "How wrong that anyone should be punished for being loyal to the King and obeying orders!" The prince was acquitted.

14 July

When I see that new troops have arrived here at Versailles, I decide that we should make them welcome with wine and song, and I enlist my friends to help me. What fresh-faced young men they are. Soon they begin to toast us for our hospitality: *"Vive la Reine! Vive la Duchesse de Polignac! Vive le Comte d'Artois!"* Blessed words! My appreciation and gratitude are very easy to express.

When I go to sleep, they are singing under my windows. With such loyal good fellows, surely we shall prevail. I drift to sleep on a cloud of hope. An afternoon well spent!

BEFORE DAWN HAS COME, the King is speaking softly to me, but I am loath to give up my dreams.

After some moments, I hear what he is saying:

I am hearing that there has been an attack on the Bastille. How strange to hear the disembodied voice of my husband speaking new realities in the darkness.

"I was awakened at two in the morning by the Duc de Liancourt who gave me the news. When I said, 'But this is revolt,' he answered, 'No, it is a revolution.' I think I must prepare to go to Paris."

I dress as quickly as I can and then see the King off to speak to the National Assembly. When he walks across the Marble Courtyard, he is accompanied only by his two brothers, and I experience the greatest anxiety for his safety. Quickly as the three pass below me, I memorize their dear and familiar faces, for I may never see them again: corpulent Provence of the square, well-cornered jaw; slender Artois, who wanted to race me when I first came here, with his narrow, sensitive face and luminous eyes like his grandfather's; Louis Auguste, my husband, with a body and head like two boulders—solid in his affection, his eyelids always half lowered. He turns back and glances up over his shoulder, as though he too would memorize me.

I hurry to the chapel, which is empty, and hasten down the aisle, where I walked as a bride. I kneel at the golden altar and look at the long recumbent form of Christ crucified, how he died for us. With bowed head and closed eyes, I spend the hour on my knees, praying for my husband's safety and that of my children. Long ago, my mother told me that I would find comfort in Jesus, when I turned to Him.

The King has said that the Bastille is destroyed, but it is an enormous fortress, and I do not see how that really could be possible.

FINALLY, I HEAR his footsteps on the marble floor. He has come to find me. I rise from the altar and fly to him, his arms open for me.

He tells me that he appealed to the group for their support. "For the first time," he says sadly, "I addressed them as the National Assembly. I said, 'Help me to ensure the salvation of the state. I expect as much from the National Assembly.'"

"But what has happened in Paris?"

We begin our walk to his apartments.

I ring for the King's breakfast to be brought to him, and as he eats, he tells me what he has heard, that the populace went to the Invalides looking for arms. "The people of Paris are filled with inflammable gas, like a balloon lighter than air." They were met, of course, by troops under Besenval. Besenval, my old friend, who entertained me at Trianon when I had the measles and my breasts were painful with unsucked milk, dared not order the charge because many of the troops were joining the populace, who helped themselves to forty thousand guns and cannons. Then they lacked only gunpowder, which they believed to be stored in the ancient fortress and prison, the Bastille.

The Bastille was attacked at the expense of one hundred lives. While the liberators found only seven prisoners incarcerated in the whole of the vast structure, the mob went wild with glee.

They took the gunpowder they found. They cut off the head of the governor of the Bastille, the Marquis de Launay, with a knife, as they did to the heads of several others who tried to stand against the mob. Their heads were mounted on pikes and paraded through the streets amid a terrible celebration in the name of liberty.

The Bastille was dismantled till not one stone lay atop another.

As the King tells me the horrifying story, I feel all the light in the room grow dim. In a terrifying grip, ice encases my heart. What can I do to save us? I remember the pleasant afternoon—only yesterday, July 14—with the young troops. Finally, the King says, "Perhaps you should gather your jewels and pack your trunks."

"Where shall we go?"

"We will convene our advisors and generals and discuss the decision."

AS THE DAY PASSES, I sometimes listen to the debate, but again and again I envision the head of the Marquis de Launay being pulled backward and his throat exposed to the edge of a knife. Perhaps they will kill us if we stay—our own heads brutally taken from our bodies. Would our absence from Versailles not signal our defeat? While I supervise the packing, I wonder if it is wise to leave. Surely at least the King and Queen should remain. And I could not bear to be parted from my children.

But I do not want my friends to endanger themselves. Yolande is almost as hated as I am, because of her love for me. I consult with the King about our friends, and we decide they should be asked to leave. None of them wish to desert us. Finally the King makes it his command to Artois to leave.

I ask if we might flee to Metz, still in France but comfortingly close to the Netherlands controlled by Austria, the territory governed by my sister Marie Christine and her husband. The faithful Maréchal de Broglie hesitates; it has cost him much of his pride to have to admit that his troops could not be trusted to try to recapture Paris. Finally, he looks up; his eyes are red, and he seems to have aged another ten years, his face is so wrinkled. "Yes," he replies, "we could get to Metz. But what will we do once we have arrived?"

I take Yolande aside and regard her with all the force of my affection. "I am terrified of what may come." While her gaze mirrors my own, she reaches out to touch my shoulder, but I continue: "Now is the time for you to escape the wrath of those who hate me."

The King, who is almost as fond of Yolande as I am, tells her that if she does not agree to leave, he will order her to do so, as he has with his younger brother.

Finally the King calls for a vote of the ministers present as to what we should do. The vote goes for the royal family to remain at Versailles.

By midnight, I am too exhausted to remain upright. I sit at my *secrétaire*, close to my bed, and write a few lines of farewell to my dearest friend. The word *Adieu* is a terrible word to write, and almost, the point of my pen trips over itself. But finally, fearing that I may never see her again, I pen the word and thus commit her to the care of God: *Adieu*. And I make her a gift of five hundred louis.

I shall not be able to help her anymore, my Yolande, fresh and sweet as a berry.

Then I stand up and straighten my back. I will face my fate here in France, though I will not consign my friends to the unspeakable possibilities. I envision the head of Launay upon a pike.

They say a bounty has been set on my head, and on that of Artois and the Polignacs. At least they will be safe in Switzerland. I will keep my place beside the King.

When the coaches roll away in the morning, toward Belgium, I note that all my friends wear disguises so that they will not be recognized by the grandeur of their clothes. Yolande is dressed to resemble a serving girl. It seems a strange thing to do. How can I play my role—that is to say—how can one maintain her identity, without the proper costume?

17 July

I beg the King not to go into Paris.

He merely says that it is required: he himself must tell the people of Paris that Necker will be restored to his position as minister of finance. He must display his loyalty to their cause, that of the Third Estate.

"If you are to die in Paris," I say, "let me accompany you."

He gently denies my request and reminds me that I must guard the children.

Again, I go to the chapel; I pray all morning, and then I request a chair so that I may sit comfortably with my head tilted back and contemplate the image of God the Father who flies across the ceiling with his white beard, his bare foot penetrating a cloud.

Sometimes I think of my friends on the road and wonder how they are, in their disguises, traveling and traveling inside their coaches. And what of my husband this day, in Paris?

In the middle of the afternoon, I return to kneel before the altar. I know that the King has his own courage; he has never been a coward. Still, I pray that his heart will be strengthened.

At one point, I hear the voice of my son. He is running, and his dear valet Hüe is chasing him. Both of them are completely merry, and the cheeks of Louis Charles are pink from the summer heat. I think of the golden frieze of playing children that encircles the King's anteroom, the Oeil-de-Boeuf. Some of the games of the gilded cherubs are peaceful; but some of the boys are playing at war. Suddenly I desire to see the room again and that largely peaceable kingdom of childhood that it depicts. I want to see the seesaw. The children are displayed against a garden lattice of gold, and it reminds me of the playrooms at Schönbrunn, with their tropical and colorful pictures of vegetation and birds. To my surprise, I find that I am thinking in the German language.

It is in his antechamber, where we waited together those long hours when Louis XV was dying, that the King finds me. I have not heard his horses arrive. Since my friends left the court, there is a stillness at Versailles. I do not run to him but glide as silently to him as a ghost.

"So you have returned. It is you."

The King gives a startled laugh. "Ah, that will be for you to judge—whether it is yet I."

"You have something colorful in your hand." I can see the colors blue and white, and then red.

"It is the tricolor cockade. Mayor Bailly, whom I installed, says it is the emblem of the French nation. I think that we would consider it the emblem of the revolution that has now taken place."

I CANNOT BELIEVE that the King is correct in thinking that a revolution has occurred. I had not thought it possible that the people would want to revolt against a good king—kind, moral, rational—such as my husband. The insane George III of England and the American colonies were quite another matter. The physical barrier of the ocean between the two countries made it much more logical that they should exist as separate states.

Yet in the last century, even within the boundaries of England, the church was challenged and the countryside erupted in bloody revolution. We had thought ourselves much more civilized, in this more advanced century, than the seventeenth-century English.

When I write to inquire of Count Mercy, fled now to the country and protected by guards, he confirms my husband's words. Written in his own elegant handwriting, Count Mercy's reply to me reads, "Most certainly there has been such a diminution of the power of the crown that one must acknowledge a revolution has occurred, however unbelievable that may appear."

WHEN THE RUSSIAN MINISTER in Paris comes out to visit us, I hear him remark in a very respectful fashion that "the Revolution in France has been carried out, and the royal authority annihilated. I mean of course in the form to which we are accustomed."

"And so the worst is over?" I inquire. I feel both resigned and hopeful.

"I could not go so far as to assure Your Majesties of that idea," he replies.

Then the King asks, "You would not go so far, if you were I, to advise our friends or the Comte d'Artois to return?"

"No, Your Majesty, I would not," he replies, taking a pinch of snuff.

"The palace seems haunted now," I remark. "Haunted with quietness. I have always adored the company of my friends, but now their faces and presence seem more to be valued than words can express."

The King regards me very sympathetically. "It is necessary to appoint a new governess for the children, since our dear Duchesse de Polignac has arrived in Switzerland."

I delight in thinking of my dear friend's safety.

"Yes. The new governess shall be the Marquise de Tourzel. I have already given the matter much thought. She is the mother of five and a paragon of virtue. She will bring her daughter Pauline, who is eighteen, with her."

THE LAST MONTH of the summer of 1789 continues to pass in a very quiet fashion. Since I no longer have my adult friends, I give myself more fully than ever to the Dauphin and Madame Royale, and to their education. I shall not neglect my daughter's education the way my own education was neglected, nor do I want the Dauphin to receive more than his share of Madame Tourzel's instructional attention at the expense of Marie Thérèse. Already my daughter likes to read better than I do. Sometimes she reads aloud to me as I do my needlework.

The Dauphin adores his sister, and he is full of mischief. He has a lively imagination and makes up his own stories—even about us!—while his older sister must be transported by the words of others to any world that is not directly before her eyes.

There are aspects about the characters of both my children that trouble me. Like her father, Marie Thérèse is not so warm or winning as I could wish for her. Certainly, at age nine, she has become less selfish as she has grown older, but she still has a haughtiness about her at times. But I know she would not be indifferent to my death. She loves her family; I am one of her possessions, and she would not want to lose me.

The Dauphin's sensibility is entirely suitable for his age, but he needs to learn to distinguish between fact and fiction. He lacks tact and discretion, though that too is partly a matter of being still less than five years old. Indeed, the world I knew at his age has almost evaporated from my memory, it was so insubstantial. His nerves are not so steady as I would like. He prefers cats to dogs, especially if they are sizable or if they bark loudly. The dogs themselves seem somewhat nervous these days, however.

Ah, I remember my mother saying how she preferred calm, wise dogs to nervous, yippy ones, no matter how cute. I remember using some of the big dogs of Schönbrunn almost like cushions.

Summer has yielded to fall, but it is still warm enough to enjoy being outdoors in the gardens of my Petit Trianon. Count von Fersen writes me that he will return just as September turns into October.

5 October

Ah, he comes to me in the château and he comes to me here at the Petit Trianon, he the most innately noble, the most handsome, the most kind and good and loving—ah, yes, above all, loving—man in the world.

He has made this most terrible year into one of bliss. I call those moments "islands of timelessness," for when he is with me, we are out of time and space and into a realm that surely partakes of eternity. In his company, there is no world but the loving nonmaterial tissue of love itself; perhaps it is like being unborn when the world is perfect and all needs are satisfied, yet I feel no sense of enclosure or confinement.

Today I return to the very best of nests: to the moss-lined grotto. I can see my Petit Trianon from here and imagine the simple elegance of its interior. Perhaps my own house is inside me as much as I dwell in it. But here within the rocks, where a waterfall falls more naturally than any fountain, where the moss is the best of mattresses, where the space defined is so perfectly artificial that it is the very essence of nature—here, today, I will dream of the bliss of the days that have come before.

It is almost the noon hour, and even the time of day pleases me: the morning is swooping toward its apex, when it kisses the sun both hello and farewell, and begins its descent. It is the crest of the wave, the peak of time, and for me the time to daydream, to remember and savor. To be so loved—surely nothing in the material world can compare to the idea of knowing the beloved and being just as fully understood by the beloved. Who can want more?

Not I, not I, not I. I am so content, my being dissolves into a boundarylessness. I am nothing and everything, I am every place and no place. What other word than *bliss* can describe the conjunction of like minds?

Égalité is one of their words, but *they* know only its bitter meaning, only the *lack* of it, and never its perfect realization, which is only to be experienced privately away from the appraising world. *Liberté?* The heart is always at liberty—the sudden spark of feeling, the quick jet of passion, the mellow glow of satiated love. In all these states, the heart has its independence and will not be governed. The great secret is that all the conventions of society can be satisfied, and *still* the heart is at liberty. The heart knows what it knows, and it knows when it is *met* in a rapture of recognition.

And what else do they demand? *Fraternité.* No. *Amour*. Surely everyone knows that. I sink my fingernails into the cool moss and feel silly. Never mind *fraternité*—it is so ignorant of *sororité*! Sisterhood is all-helping, all-vanquishing of domination. Fraternity? They might as well go hunting. As they do go.

Only this I do not understand of Fersen—why he wishes to be a soldier. Why he has been willing to risk his life and our happiness in order to impose the masculine will on whatever it sees. But he does not impose his will on me, any more than I on him. We come and go as we please. And when he is absent, the moment of my awareness of him is just the same as when he is present. We are the perfect friends.

This transcendence of separation is what I learned from our letters to each other. The marks on the page that bring his *mind* into the habitat of my mind represent his mood and his being in a truthful way, one that is always affirmed when he himself appears. Is there anything so luxurious as long conversations? They are the true hallmark of friendship. Almost, through the words of my own thoughts, I can imagine him into being now—just as he recently was. I can envision him standing in a shaft of light that enters this grotto through a crevice in the rocks.

Now I look out—for this slit was made exactly for this purpose—to see while not being seen.

And I see someone approaching. A messenger from the outside world.

WHEN I ARRIVE at the château, I learn a messenger has been sent on a fast horse to find the King, who is hunting. Here are the Comte and Comtesse de Provence, and Madame Elisabeth, and the emissary of the minister of the household, all speaking at once: the people of Paris are marching on Versailles.

Why?

They fear a bread famine now, because the old harvest is used up and the new one not yet ready. They fear a counterrevolution led by the King, using the new troops that have come to Versailles, and they wish to put us in Paris where they can supervise us.

Who leads the people?

It is the market women.

I recall their leather skins, how they pumped their arms obscenely, how they tried to shame me for not producing an heir.

"But now there is yet a Dauphin," I exclaim.

Elisabeth says, "They protest the high cost of bread."

The Comte de Provence says, "They wish the King to remedy the condition of lack of work."

I learn that these women are armed with sickles, pikes, and guns and that it is *myself* whom they blame for the financial crises, for the famine last winter, for the fact that the weather was colder than in any year of the last seventy-five. It is I, and not the American War, who have emptied the treasury, and I who have enacted the thousands of pornographic deeds depicted in the pamphlets, and I, most heinously of all, who have seduced the King into activities that have left the people destitute. Not even I hold myself blameless, but I am not a harpy and I have lived the life dealt to me with as much kindness as I could.

Their appellation for me is *L'Austrichienne*, and they clamor for my head as they march, but really what they want is a "scapegoat"—someone upon whom to heap all their suffering and misfortune and disappointment and anger. Yes, if I alone am responsible and they dispatch me, they tell themselves, all will be well. They are to be pitied.

They have no more reason than a troupe of insane children burning with rage.

Some of the ministers say we should flee to Rambouillet, some all the way to Normandie. I will go nowhere till the King returns.

AT THREE IN THE AFTERNOON, the King and his hunting party ride up to the château. They come like a whirlwind, like knights of old, their horses and themselves covered with sweat and dust. But once they have arrived, I know well what will follow.

Talk.

The indecision of the King reigns supreme. The time passes while more and more people arrive from Paris.

But they have stopped in the courtyards. They do not enter the château—yet.

At eight o'clock at night people still arrive and begin to camp in the vast Place d'Armes. Torrents of rain descend on the crowd; still they keep little fires burning. We hear that they are butchering and roasting horses, and I can smell the meat of the animals, bloody raw, cooking, and burnt.

In a flurry of confusion, first I tell the ladies to prepare the children to leave. Then I tell the ladies that the King and I and the children will not be going after all. Next, I tell them the carriages are now prepared. "Pack what you can! Hurry."

We hear that when our horses and carriages emerge from the royal stables, they are surrounded by the mob. The harnesses are cut to bits, and the horses are stolen. They disappear into the sea of people on foot. Perhaps the horses are slaughtered and eaten.

Yes, we could yet go to other carriages—they have been offered by Saint-Priest and by La Tour du Pin, their very own carriages waiting beyond the Orangerie. The King and I look at each other. We have lost heart for flight, if we cannot go in our own carriages—I do not understand my own sense of identity. Besides, it is raining so steadily, surely the rain will drive them away, will drench their spirits.

I see our inability to impose our wills on this situation. We must wait and see what will happen.

SOMETHING DOES HAPPEN. At midnight arrives the Marquis de Lafayette, commander of the new National Guard, which marches with the populace. Because Lafayette reassures the King, and the King trusts him, my husband agrees: it is time to go to bed. Here before me stands his valet, repeating with his young and trembling lips the words of the King: "Your Majesty may set her mind at ease concerning the events that have just transpired. The King requests that Her Majesty retire to bed, as His Majesty himself is doing at this moment."

IS IT TWO IN THE MORNING? I hear unnatural sounds, struggle, fighting.

"Save the Queen!"

It is the voice of a bodyguard stationed in the guardroom. From the sounds of desperate fighting, I learn my guards are being slaughtered, their heads severed from their bodies. I leap from the bed, pull on a skirt, something falls softly around my shoulders, and run for the secret door cut in the wall beside my bed. My two ladies are behind me, and I run through the inner rooms toward the inner entrance of the Oeil-de-Boeuf.

The door is locked! I hear my own voice shrieking that the door be opened, that my friends come to my aid, and suddenly! the door opens. A bailiff stands before me. Running past him, I enter the King's bedchamber and find his bed is vacant, but now there are people to help, kind people who speak of safety in the King's dining room.

And just in a moment, here is the King with our son in his arms. And Madame Royale?

There is an interior stair leading to her room. I descend it with wings, then pause, and say with utmost calm that we must quickly leave. I take my daughter's hand—how slender and helpless it is—and guide her back to the others. Here with their coiffures askew are Mesdames Tantes, and I am very glad to see them and embrace them warmly.

I hear desperate fighting in the Oeil-de-Boeuf. But the Dauphin has fetched a chair, and he stands on it, so he can better reach the top of his sister's head. He twines his baby fingers into her hair. He is in a rapture of touching, gently touching, her hair, sliding the strands through his fingers, curling them around a stubby pointing finger. He has no idea that men are fighting and dying outside the door.

Suddenly the Dauphin says, and repeats, "Maman, I'm so hungry."

Outside, in the courtyard, the people are congregating and shouting.

"You must appear on the balcony over the Marble Courtyard," Lafayette says to my husband, who merely nods in agreement.

First Lafayette steps out to face the crowd. They fall silent, as though before a god. "You have sworn loyalty to the King," he yells in a terrible voice. "Swear again!"

"We swear it." What a sound! Is it hundreds, or thousands, or hundreds of thousands, speaking in unison, as though a mountain had spoken. Almost, I faint.

Hold on tight, Marie Antoinette.

I remember. I remember who I am.

Now the King and I and our children are on the balcony beside the hero, but my husband cannot speak. Some of the people begin to cry at the sight of us. I can see their faces melting in awe and an astonishing mixture of terror, love, pity.

Lafayette promises, speaking in the King's name, that the people will have better and cheaper bread, lumber to repair their homes. But the people are no longer silent. They have begun to chant, louder and louder, and then to shriek their demand: "To Paris!"

Quickly, while Lafayette tries to continue his speech about the condition of the country, the King, the children, and I step back inside. Soon I can no longer hear Lafayette's words, though I can see the side of his face, and the force with which he shouts. But they are shouting too. "The Queen. Let us see the Queen again!"

The children begin to cry. I take their hands—all those around me beg me not to go out—"I will appear to them." And I step out onto the balcony, with the children, into the damp, outdoor air.

"No children!"

Ah, so they may wish to kill me. Better I am alone. My hands first turn the shoulders of Marie Thérèse, then gently push in the middle of the Dauphin's back, and they are inside. Now I turn and merely face the people. I am full of sadness, but I face them. Fear leaves me. I bow my head. Then I bow my body in the deepest of curtsies. Across my heart, I fold my wrists. My strong dancer's legs hold hold hold the curtsy.

"Long live the Queen."

It is more than I dared hope for. The cry is repeated. Over and over till the courtyard rings with it. But there is another cry too: "To Paris. To Paris."

The people wish to possess their King and Queen.

Slowly, with dignity, I stand and nod my head, to left, to center, to right, so that no group, regardless of where they stand, has been ignored. Then I reenter the bedchamber of the King of France, and of the King before him, and of the one before him.

First, I hold my son in my arms and wash him with my tears. Then I whisper to Madame Necker what I know will be our fate: they will take us to Paris, preceded by the heads of our bodyguards on pikes.

Outside, the people roar and roar till we know we must address them again.

This time the King speaks forcefully in a confident and clear voice: "My friends, I am going to Paris with my wife and children. They are far more precious to me than my own life, and I entrust them to you, my loyal subjects, believing in your love and your goodness."

We return inside. In my own apartment, I quickly put my diamonds in a chest to take with me, and I make gifts of other pieces of jewelry to those who have served me. I notice an odd shining on a ruby pin, and then I see that the sun is rising and a shaft of light has passed through a slit in the curtains to strike the heart of the ruby and make it glow.

"The sun is rising," I say gently to my daughter. "Go see." And then I remember, and the remembrance is bitter as gall on my tongue, that the calumny about me began when I innocently wished to see the sun rise. That was one of the first of the pamphlets that dragged my reputation into the mud and began to prepare my image as one to be hated and reviled.

THE JOURNEY OVER the mere twelve miles between Versailles and Paris takes seven hours, such masses of people jam the road. During the trip my husband is utterly silent. I sit as though turned to stone. But I can hear the chants beyond the carriage: "We're bringing back the baker, the baker's wife, and the baker's little boy."

The Dauphin, half asleep on my lap, mumbles in a baby voice, "Bake me a cake."

When we reach the gates of the city, we see that Paris has turned out to greet us. Now in the love phase of their paroxysm of hate-and-love, their worn and crusty faces beam at us. Their faces are pink, and tan, some pale, some sallow—what varieties of complexion flesh can assume! I see a black face and remember the little black page boy of Madame du Barry. For the first time, I wonder without malice as to what her life may be like. Are these happy, careworn people those who marched out to Versailles, or are they some other, more benign, citizens?

Mayor Bailly, who is also a man of science, an astronomer, comes forward. For an awful moment, I think he is bearing the black head of Louis XV.

No. It is a dark velvet cushion, and on it, in the rays of the afternoon sun, glint the silver Keys to the City.

Holding the pillow and its keys in outstretched arms, Mayor Bailly pronounces with utmost sincerity: "What a beautiful day, Sire, on which the Parisians welcome Your Majesty and his family to come into their city."

"Long live the King!" they shout.

Mayor Bailly turns to the King and in a private voice says, "His Majesty's illustrious ancestor Henri IV, acting as general, once conquered Paris. Now it is the challenge of the city to conquer Louis XVI with our hearts."

I suspect that the mayor is trying to exhibit his knowledge of history, as well as his affable wit. To me, his words drip bitter irony.

The King replies loudly, with astonishing warmth. "It is always with great pleasure and happy confidence that I find myself amid the worthy citizens of my good city of Paris."

So well does my husband act the part of a king who delights in his subjects and their deeds that I almost believe he has convinced himself we are glad to be here, safe among loyal subjects.

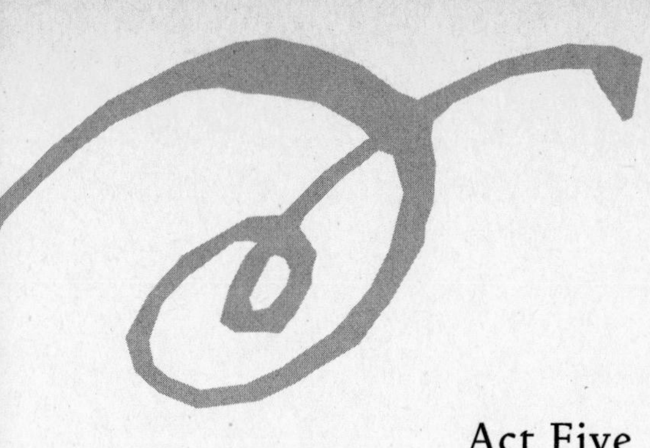

Act Five

THE TUILERIES, PARIS;
FALL AND WINTER 1789

In the morning I am awakened by a soprano soloist on one hand and by a choir of singers on the other, in a sort of antiphonal arrangement. Yes, I know where I am. I am at the Palace of the Tuileries, in Paris, where I keep a pied-à-terre, though the kings of France have not made this place their home for almost two hundred years. I breathe deeply and smell the ancient dust of the place. Louis XIV left Paris to create Versailles.

The soloist is not a singer; it is the piping voice of my son, the Dauphin, and he is saying over and over in a singsong voice, "Mama, could today still be yesterday? Is today the same as yesterday? It's ugly here, Mama, and dirty. Is this more of yesterday?"

I open my eyes fully and hold out my arm to him while I yet lie in bed. He comes into the circle of my embrace and stamps his foot. "Make it be a different tomorrow, Mama!"

"We are at the Tuileries Palace, an accommodation that we will never criticize in any way, my son. It was good enough for Louis XIV, and we must not be more particular than he was."

Then I hear coming from the terrace not a choir of altos, but the angry murmur of coarse female voices. Ah, I must watch this tendency to transform devils into angels, or I shall not have the wits to survive. As quickly as possible, I dress, put on my hat, open the glass doors that separate us from the terrace, and step outside.

Into the faces of anger, I smile and bid the market women assembled on the terrace a good morning.

A few of them suddenly freeze in whatever attitude they happened to have assumed before my appearance. Awestruck in the presence of royalty, they are like statues. Others become more excited and call for explanations.

"Please tell me," I say pleasantly, "exactly what you wish me to explain. It is my honor and pleasure to address your questions."

"Why do you have servants, as though we are not all equals, and you are privileged?"

"It has not been my choice to have servants. I like to dress myself and my children, even as you do. Attendants have been customary for so long at court that people have forgotten life can be conducted otherwise. But I intend, every day, to do more and more tasks for myself. If I were to dismiss my servants immediately they would have no livelihood. Surely you can imagine what it would be like to be suddenly deprived of one's living wage."

They are satisfied with the humanity of my answer, and I call for any other questions they might choose to ask.

In a furious tone, I am asked why we had planned to besiege their city on 14 July.

"It is true," I say, "that soldiers were gathering on the perimeter of Paris, but that was because a violent element had been detected in certain quarters of the city. The presence of the soldiers was to protect the good citizens of Paris. Please remember that the soldiers did not fire on the citizens when they wished to enter the Invalides. It was the defenders of the Bastille who were already present in the fortress who tried to defend it, unfortunately resulting in deaths. Our soldiers did not nor would they ever have attacked the good people of Paris. My heart is full of sadness at the shedding of any French blood. It is not what I wish. The King and I always work for peace and reconciliation."

It amazes me that I am able to speak the exact truth within the context of giving them answers that are meant to be reassuring. It amazes me that by using my stage voice, I am able to project my words clearly so that they can hear me, and at the same time, my voice loses nothing of its sweetness.

"It would be criminal for the King to flee to the frontiers. Why do you encourage an illegal flight of our sovereign?"

Now I explain that the King has no wish to leave, that we are at our new home at the Tuileries, and it is always and always will be my duty and honor to live at the side of the King. I see that they believe in my devotion to the King, and hence to them, for they identify with the person of the King in a way that is a part of their religious faith. They believe in my loyalty to the King, for I believe in it myself.

"Is it true that you have nursed your own children, even as we do?"

"It is true," I reply simply.

And suddenly our conversation is about caring for our children, and education, and *their* difficulties in affording adequate food and clothing for their families.

Before I go back inside, those closest ask if they may have a flower or a ribbon from my hat as a souvenir of our meeting. "With pleasure," I reply, reaching up to remove a blue cornflower from the satin ribbon encircling my hat.

When I reenter the room, I am surprised to see my husband and Count von Fersen standing there.

"Her Majesty has soothed the savage beasts," Count von Fersen remarks.

"I only spoke with them," I reply modestly. My heart is racing with the success of my encounter, a success in which it is difficult to believe. Still the faces of the women are before my eyes, as their features modulated from hostility to friendliness.

"Simply the speaking voice of Her Majesty is like music," the count continues, bowing his head toward me.

"I knew that you would wish to thank the count," the King says, smiling at me, "as I have already done, for being among those who made it a point to be here at the Tuileries when we arrived last night, so that we might be greeted by friendly and familiar faces."

Count von Fersen explains to us both that he is arranging to sell his horses and his house in the town of Versailles and to arrange to borrow an abode close by, in Paris, but I am reliving the horror of our journey, the bloody heads on pikes, the cries of pain as our bodyguard was cut down, the terrifying faces presented to me just now as I stepped out onto the terrace.

"My dear, you are trembling," the King says.

"It is my intention to appear calm at every moment," I reply, "but I cannot control this shaking." And then I begin to sob.

The King takes me tenderly in his arms while Count von Fersen, his face stiffening in sympathy, courteously turns his back on the scene. *Ah, my chevalier!*

WHEN MY HAND is no longer shaking, I pen a note, using as my address the Tuileries, Paris, to Count Mercy: "*I'm fine. You mustn't worry.*"

Soon the King and I take a tour of the palace, begun so long ago in the sixteenth century by Queen Catherine de Médicis and completed by Louis XIV, before his departure to Versailles. Because there are nearly four hundred rooms here, we do not attempt to see them all. They must remain *terra incognita*, the King remarks, as was true of certain areas on the old maps. He chooses three rooms on the ground floor opening onto the gardens for his study, where he will contemplate geography. The apartment immediately adjacent has been redecorated by the Comtesse de La Marck, and I ask the King to buy her furnishings for me, and I request that some of the furniture made by Riesener be transported here from Versailles, particularly my little mechanical dressing table that I enjoy so much.

In an act that seems to partake of the dreamworld, I hear the courtiers referring to some of the rooms here by the names of rooms that served these functions at Versailles: here too there is the antechamber called the Oeil-de-Boeuf, in spite of the fact that this antechamber does not have an oval window that resembles the eye of a bull.

As is demanded by protocol, all the foreign ministers pay a formal call upon us in our new residency so that business may resume. Each time one of them speaks to me sympathetically, I can hardly restrain my tears. When the Spanish ambassador asks me how the King is feeling, I cannot restrain the truth: "Like a captive King."

IN THE DAYS THAT FOLLOW, I resume my needlepoint work, among my ladies, and I supervise the education of my children, along with the Marquise de Tourzel. The Princesse de Lamballe, who has been ill, takes up residence in the Tuileries, as she is still my superintendent of the household.

I rush to take her in my arms, and I call her over and over "my dear friend." She is a bit pale—from her illness, she explains—but she is as lovely as ever, with her bright hair framing her kind, widely spaced eyes.

And here is Madame Campan, who has answered my summons, and who looks at me with great approval. "No matter where Her Majesty lives," she says, "she shows to everyone around her the same charm and consideration. Everyone in the room with her wishes to draw closer and to warm his hands at the glow of her kindness."

When she asks me privately how we feel, I reply into her private and discreet ear, "Kings who become prisoners are not far from death."

It is impossible to express to them how dear I hold their presence, and also that of Madame Elisabeth, who has been my friend since she was a little girl watching me opening the drawers of the great coffin of my wedding jewels. I am sorry that Elisabeth seems to take up the standard of the émigrés, led by her brother Artois, who demand that royalty make no compromise with the revolutionaries.

The King and I, who live among them, know that the only hope of maintaining any kind of monarchy in France is to compromise. For this reason I plan to make friends with the radicalized Comte Mirabeau, who despite his noble origins is, in fact, a spokesperson for the National Assembly. I have for him a great aversion, almost physical in nature, as I did for the Comtesse du Barry.

Madame Campan summons me to the window to see what the Dauphin is doing this moment, under the watchful eye of his guard. A small crowd of visiting Bretons has assembled behind the grille to watch him play, and he is endearing himself to them by giving them flowers from the late gardens—bronze chrysanthemums. But suddenly, he has plucked them all, and still people smile at him, waiting. Quickly, he improvises. He plucks the leaves from a lilac shrub, carefully tears a leaf into little green pieces, and presents them to those who reach their hands through the bars. His childish courtesy moves some of them to tears and his mother as well.

IT SEEMS STRANGE that we import to the Tuileries the customs of Versailles, including the official rising from bed in the morning and retiring to bed in the evening, surrounded by courtiers who hand to us or take from us various items of our dress in the ritual of changing our garb. The elaborate processes of the *lever* every morning and the *coucher* before retiring to our beds are more tedious and pointless than ever.

But these ceremonies mark the days as they pass, and as autumn turns to winter.

For as long as possible—until the great chill sets in—I encourage the Dauphin to play outside in the courtyard, for the sake of his health. Now that I spend more time with my children and less with the court, my own health improves. The dear Dauphin at play has become in his own little person something of a scenic attraction in Paris. People adore him and come to watch him sail his little boats in the basins we have had constructed. Sometimes he stands, mesmerized, in front of the aviary in the courtyard and watches the birds flutter. Occasionally, he flutters his little hands and fingers as if he too would fly.

Because we have taught him to respond to any remark, friendly or hostile, with royal graciousness and because he is still not yet five years old, after he has uttered a felicitous remark to someone, he runs to us and whispers in our ears, rather loudly, "Is that good?" or "Did I speak nicely?"

In the evenings, I write letters to friends who cannot be with me—to Count von Fersen, when he is away as an emissary of Gustavus III, or to the Duchesse de Polignac. I do not yet know if she will ever return. As long as Fersen has life in his body, I do not doubt that I will have the joy of seeing him again.

To Yolande, I write:

The King and I live in the same apartment with the children, who are nearly always with me. They are my consolation. Le chou d'amour *is charming, and I love him madly. Without embarrassment, he returns my love, in his own way. He is well, grows stronger, and has no more temper tantrums. Every day he walks or plays in the courtyard. Behind a holly tree or sitting on the other side of a yew shrub in the garden, I station myself discreetly—almost out of sight, but close at hand. That way I feel more comfortable about his safety before the unpredictable public of Paris.*

Once the Dauphin was asked whether he liked better to live in Paris or in Versailles. Like a small diplomat, he replied, "Paris, because I see so much more of Papa and Mama."

I dread the approach of winter, the last one having been among the most cruel in modern history. Even though they have captured us now and keep us in our cage in the heart of Paris, though we do go out for carriage rides and for walks, sometimes for Mass, if the winter is harsh, they are sure to blame us. We live within the allotment they have made us. You will be glad that I see Rose Bertin from time to time, though my expenditure for wardrobe is cut to one third.

24 December 1789

I get ready for bed alone this evening because it is the happiest day of my life.

"By myself," I tell my attendants. "There will be no interminable *coucher* this evening. Hurry to those who wait for you." My smile for them is shy. "This small release from convention is yet another gift."

It is the evening of the birth of the Christ Child, and I have been to Mass and thought of the miracles of God. *I bend to remove my shoes, their squat, deeply curved heels once more remind me of a tiny teapot.* My most treasured miracle is the gift of my own son—Louis Charles—and I have prayed to God to keep him in health and to help him grow in the ways that win favor with God and Man. *Off with the overskirt, all stiff and ceremonial, and then the soft chemise to puddle with it on the floor.* During Mass, the odor of incense filled our nostrils like a benediction as we knelt and prayed and gave thanks for the Advent of the Christ Child.

On with the nightgown, held over my head for a moment like a cloud ready to descend. And I asked that Holy Child to kiss—oh most tenderly—the cheek of my older boy, Louis Joseph, who has already gone to live with them. I cannot think his name without weeping.

Here is a handkerchief from the pocket of my nightgown. Here is a bit of soft lawn trimmed with lace almost as wide as the tiny white square of cloth in its center with which I wipe my nose and cheeks. Here in my hand, this small white handkerchief is an emblem of the things of this world. Beautiful perhaps—at least to my eye—and totally inadequate for what they are asked to perform. A handkerchief is meant to wipe away tears. But what of sorrow?

Ah, the Christmas music, sung so angelically by the little boys in their robes.

The Dauphin pulled at my sleeve and said, "May I also sing, Mama?"

I smiled and said, "Later," and then, over the head of my son, caught the fatherly eye of my husband, and just beyond him, the eye that holds all understanding in its warm gleam, that of Count von Fersen. For all their differences, their faces were the same: happy for my happiness.

How peaceful it all was! What quiet and holy joy contained on Christmas Eve in the cathedral.

And why has this 24 December been the happiest day of my life? Count von Fersen spent the entire day with me. When he rose to leave, he asked me to guess what he would write to his sister, to whom he confides everything about our bond. Though I have never met his Sophie, I love her with all my heart because she loves Axel as I do. She is my twin.

Then we pronounced the very words simultaneously: "Imagine my joy."

THOUGH A WARMING PAN has been passed between these sheets, my own body, as I slide between the linens, is yet warmer. I pull the covers up to my nose. I remember the candle-brightened cathedral, and I hear again the echoing songs from medieval times that sing "Noel" and that continue to do so to this day.

I tell myself that this cruel year, 1789, will soon be over.

And I squeeze my eyes tight shut and vow to touch the beads of my rosary till I fall asleep, praying that the year of terrible change is over.

The New Year,
the Tuileries, 1790

4 February 1790

A day of speeches.

The King makes his to the National Assembly, and in the speech he refers to himself as "at the head of the Revolution."

At the Tuileries, deputies appear on the terrace and I go outside to speak to them. I begin with a gesture. "Messieurs, behold my son." I know they wish some expression from *L'Austrichienne* of her loyalty to France, and so I speak of "the nation I had the glory to adopt as my own when I became united with the King."

27 March 1790

The birthday of the Dauphin! He is five years old.

After he has received his gifts—nothing bejeweled this year—I remind him of our recent visit to a Foundling Hospital. I whisper to him again, "Don't forget what you have seen. Someday you must extend your protection to just such unfortunate children."

Easter Week, 1790

That my husband is yet King and that I am yet Queen and that we are privileged to be able to wash the feet of the poor, as is the ancient custom of kings and queens of France, fills my heart with humble joy. Every moment I am on my knees before the twelve of them is a blessed moment.

I see the tears on the cheeks of the King, as he scoops water and flings it on the naked right foot of each of these poor men and women, here dressed in new clothing. Humble and modest, I see his thick lips move: "May the Lord bless you and keep you." I follow behind, and taking the napkin provided to each pauper for this purpose, I pass it in solemn ritual over the wet foot, drying where the King has washed.

Truth to tell, someone else has already thoroughly scrubbed their feet and removed the dirt from under their toenails, at least for the exposed right foot.

There is something of reality about nakedness, whether it is myself as a naked girl leaving home, the painted bare foot of God the Father on the ceiling of the Royal Chapel, or the foot of a Parisian pauper. I cannot help but remember the extreme cleanliness of my cows, at the *Hameau*, when I would say that I wished to milk them. And the bucket! Made of finest porcelain. What fun it was to give a tug or two on the cows' teats, rather like long, clean toes, though I never squeezed out a single drop. Quickly, a true farm girl would strip away the milk. With a flared gold-edged cup, I would bring the frothy milk to my lips for a warm sip.

Almost afraid that they will be swept up into heaven itself, these twelve poor quickly thrust their feet back into their shoes. Now they feel like themselves again and safe on the familiar earth. I can see it on their frightened faces.

They hurry to the wooden boxes stocked with the things they need to take back to their families.

8 April 1790

Today is the First Communion for Marie Thérèse.

This sacred event is not celebrated as it would have been before the revolution. The King will not attend the service, and I will do so only incognito.

But we have our little private ceremony before the one in the church.

Speaking most tenderly to his daughter, the King explains that she cannot be given the usual diamonds that have marked such a holy day. "You are too sensible to worry about jewels," he tells her. "And you are too sensitive to want such items when the people still need bread."

Her father places his hand on her head to say a prayer of blessing, and he invites me to place my hand there, as well.

"Most Gracious King of Heaven, bless my beloved daughter whose destiny remains unknown, whether she continues her maturation in France or in another kingdom. Give her, I humbly pray, the grace to please and fulfill the needs of my other 'children,' the people of France over whom You have given me dominion."

ON 12 MAY, Mayor Bailly of Paris gives the King a gold medal and gives me a silver one, with a bronze one for the Dauphin. All our medals bear this motto: "Henceforth I shall make this place my official residence." Perhaps these medals are lucky passports. For the summer, in order to escape the heat of the city, most miraculously the National Assembly allows us all to move to Saint-Cloud. Just outside Paris, Saint-Cloud was bought for me by the King, after the birth of the Dauphin. I remember how convenient it was to stay there and to come in for the operas and the balls in Paris, before our popularity dwindled.

As we drive to Saint-Cloud, I remind the children that the grand jet rises ninety feet into the air because its reservoir is located high on the bluff above the gardens. The King supplies the scientific explanation that water will seek its original level. "And the Grand Cascade," I chime in, "is so beautiful—do you remember?—that even the great Italian sculptor Bernini, who often disdained anything French, exclaimed when he saw it, '*É bella! É bella!*'" As we journey toward Saint-Cloud, I am as happy as I was in childhood when we left the Hofburg in Vienna to spend the summer away from the city, at Schönbrunn.

To my own amazement, one day at Saint-Cloud I notice that I am laughing! Soon, I find that I have abandoned the dull, ugly dresses of Paris. I am wearing the light clothing recently made stylish. While I have lost the calluses on my fingers that make playing the harp a pleasure, I can nonetheless touch the ivory and wooden keys of the harpsichord without pain, and soon, why, I am singing as I play!

Every evening I am visited by Count von Fersen, who has borrowed Comte Esterhazy's house close by.

Poor Saint-Priest, he has cautioned me of rampant gossip that a guard discovered the count at three in the morning on the grounds and almost arrested him. "Ah, you must tell the count to be more discreet, if you are worried," I replied. "For myself, I left my regard for gossip at Versailles."

My friend's words whisper to me in the night, even when he has left my presence: *You are the most perfect creature I know.... It is your courage that thrills my soul, and your gentle goodness.... You are an angel.... You are so wonderful to me, I owe you everything.... I live to serve you.... My only unhappiness is not being able to fully console you.... You deserve a fuller consolation than I can offer.*

Never was a man more chivalrous. Never has a woman's happiness been guarded so completely. His sensibility is one of strength and bravery and, at the same time, of utmost tenderness. With all modesty, he conceals from others the position he occupies in my regard.

You are an angel. It is the fulfillment of the charge the Empress laid upon me as I left Austria. *Do so much good to the French people that they can say that I have sent them an angel.*

They do not regard me so. But I have tried my best.

STRANGELY, I FORM another alliance. On 3 July, the former nobleman Mirabeau of the lion's mane hair comes to visit. I was wrong to count him a traitor cut from the same cloth as the Duc d'Orléans. Yes, he consorts with the commoners, but he is also as ardent a royalist as is Fersen. It is the nobility but not the monarchy that he would check for the sake of the people. Mirabeau believes, as do the King and I, that we must compromise with those here in France and not conspire with the émigrés in colluding with foreign powers for a counterrevolution. While he has written letters expressing these ideas to the King and me in the past, listening to him speak is a far more convincing experience. He is passionate and utterly sincere. His rough, pockmarked face glows with his ardor for France.

Despite his history as a dissolute person, I find myself drawn to him as he speaks. His eye is not so much luminous as a burning coal in his head. He is all roughness whereas Louis XV was all elegance, but the compelling power of both men is undeniable.

And Mirabeau expresses enormous respect for me.

He thinks that we may need to leave Paris, but only to go to some other part of France, where there is greater loyalty to the crown. Here I bow my head a moment, remembering Fersen's pleas that we all should flee. Certainly, I want to fly, but the King is uncertain. Yes, it will be difficult to return to Paris, after the freedom at Saint-Cloud.

14 July

This day we must leave Saint-Cloud in order to attend the Fête de la Fédération, a new Parisian holiday in honor of the destruction of the Bastille.

They have created an enormous amphitheater to celebrate this enormous atrocity. The Champ-de-Mars, extended, can hold 400,000 people. They have erected something very like a pagan temple, with an altar and incense, to do homage to the Goddess of Liberty. I did not know that she thrived on blood.

Even though the day is pouring rain, as though the heavens were weeping for this obscene spectacle, we must participate. The women of Paris wear white dresses with the blue-white-red cockades in their hair and tricolor ribbons ornamenting their dresses. They are gay with triumph, cocky and impudent. When those who possess umbrellas try to raise them against the deluge, the mob shouts out "No umbrellas!" for umbrellas would block the view to which they feel entitled.

Led by Talleyrand, the Bishop of Autun, they pretend to celebrate Mass, but they have forgotten their Christian principles, the commandments to obey and not to kill.

Now they require their King to take an oath of loyalty to the new constitution and its laws.

As they cheer, I lift up our son to show them the future. I lift him as high as I can so that his sweet face will float like a small balloon above their heads.

Now they shout in a rapture, "Long live the Queen! Long live the Dauphin!"

I am glad to hear such joyful noise, but my heart is cynical.

Then I notice that the Dauphin is getting very wet, and the rainwater streams off the matted strands of his hair onto his tender neck. Instinctively, I take my shawl and place it over him.

Now they are truly wild with love. Why, I am a mother, like themselves! I protect my child as best I can, whatever the circumstance.

Almost, their cheers warm my spirit.

In a whisper, Fersen rails against this convocation of the people. "It is nothing but intoxication and noise," he says. "The ceremony is ridiculous and indecent." With great contempt he labels their celebration as nothing but "orgies and bacchanalia."

The word *orgies* cuts me, for just so have the pamphleteers often labeled my innocent outings.

During the course of the many speeches, a friend comes and whispers in my ear. "Mirabeau believes that your courage will save the monarchy," the voice says.

"Truly?" I question. I am quite surprised to learn of the impression I have made on the fiery orator.

"He says the King has only one man with him—his wife. Her safety lies only in the restoration of royal authority. Mirabeau tells himself that the Queen would not want to live without her crown, for she is true royalty. Mirabeau is even more certain that she cannot preserve her own life without her crown. Mirabeau says the time will come, and soon, when the world will see what a woman and a child can accomplish, when they rule."

I turn to see who speaks this way into my ear, for her voice is familiar. It is Jeanne, the little seamstress who sometimes accompanied Rose Bertin when she measured me for finery. My memory races backward down the corridor of time: it is Jeanne who used to lurk, sometimes, within the draperies of the Château de Versailles.

"Did someone send you to me?" I ask.

"Yes."

She stops, but I ask her to tell me who. She begins to stutter. "I think you will not want to hear the name. She said for me to avoid saying her name."

"But now you are with me, and you must do as I say. I command you to tell me."

"Madame du Barry, Your Majesty."

"The du Barry! And what else did she tell you to tell me besides the words of Mirabeau?"

"She said that if you forced me to reveal her name that I must add another sentence."

"Please say it."

"Truly, I would rather not."

"My heart will leap out of my chest if you do not tell me."

"She said, 'Say *Now we are both the whores of France.*'"

Strangely, I find a smile curling at the edge of my mouth. Do I, in fact, in my present degradation, begin to feel some sisterhood with my old enemy, the du Barry? There is a certain sardonic pleasure in the thought. After all, what power or protection is left me? Is not that the position of a whore? Even of a respectable woman who is poor?

I refuse to succumb to such thoughts. I am myself, and I will act my own part and not that of another.

Jeanne has disappeared back into the crowds of citizens, or was it Nicole d'Oliva—certainly a prostitute—the woman who also has been said to resemble me, according to the Cardinal de Rohan?

MY BROTHER Joseph II of Austria has died.

His successor, my brother Leopold, has become Emperor of Austria, and he has recalled Count Mercy as ambassador to France and reassigned him to Brussels.

I am in despair and double despair.

WITHOUT COUNT MERCY, I do not know how to advise the King, and I know full well that I am capable of grievous errors concerning what course of action, if any, we should take. More than ever, I depend on Count von Fersen and on his belief in my goodness and that my instincts are good ones. Perhaps I can learn to believe in them myself.

There is the issue of the oath that the state demands the French clergy take. They must swear allegiance to the new revolutionary state, but the pope has forbidden them to do so. The clergy is put in the position of having to decide which authority to obey, though the King has begged the pope to allow the clergy to take the oath. I see the clergy losing the allegiance of the people, if they will not swear.

Of the three estates, the nobility has lost its power, and now the clergy is losing its power as well. There remains only the populace, all-powerful, and their leaders who are full of cruelty and defiance for its own sake. Like adolescent boys, they want all the power for themselves and if it is exercised in an arbitrary, unlawful manner, then they are all the more assured that their control is absolute. It is time to leave.

In August, we hear that the Marquis de Bouillé has put down a disturbance in the northwest, at Nancy, and we rejoice in the idea that the rule of law can still dominate. The marquis is a great friend of Count von Fersen, who has spoken to me many times about the possibility that we should leave Paris. Bouillé might well be the general to make that possible, as he is a person of courage, and his German regiment has great confidence in him. They consider him to be attended by good luck. At Saint-Cloud, we celebrate.

In Paris, however, we hear that demonstrators congregate outside the Tuileries, and we fear that they may march out to Saint-Cloud, for they know that the Marquis de Bouillé is our loyal advocate—a royalist who favors the adoption of a constitution. Some of our advisors, including Mirabeau, feel that civil war will result in the bloodletting necessary to purge the country of revolution. Even the King's sister Elisabeth thinks so.

The King and I agree that it would be madness to provoke civil war.

Yet I can feel the mounting anger of the populace against us. People like

Mirabeau and Bouillé would support the monarchy while giving the people more voice through a constitution created in a lawful manner. Because we have been so brought up, the King and I feel it is our Christian duty to maintain the power of the throne, insomuch as that is possible, given the thirst of the French for a new kind of liberty. The divine right of kings to rule should not be abridged by mere men. And yet compromise is surely a practical necessity.

NO SOONER DO WE return to the Tuileries at the end of October than Edmund Burke publishes in England his treatise *Reflections on the Revolution in France.* Soon there is a French translation, and people become resentful of the sympathetic portrait he offers of myself.

For me, there is solace (as well as danger) in what he has written. How fondly he describes me as the Dauphine and brings to mind again those glory days when the people could not express enough love for me: "And surely never lighted on this orb, which she barely seemed to touch, a more delightful vision. I saw her just above the horizon . . . glittering like the morning star, full of life, and splendor, and joy."

The tears fill my eyes, and I savor his description, hardly wanting to read on. Yes, as a young person I came to France full of life and warmth and innocence. The joy of life touched me every moment. And what could have preserved that mood? It was like a soap bubble too fragile and tremulous to last, even had it been protected. *Ah, but it was beautiful.*

I read on in Burke's book: "Little did I dream that I should have lived to see disaster fallen upon her in a nation of gallant men, in a nation of men of honor and of cavaliers. I thought ten thousand swords must have leaped from their scabbards to avenge even a look that threatened her with insult. But the age of chivalry is gone."

No, not quite. There is still one sword that will always leap to my defense, and he is a man who protects and nourishes my spirit, not only my person. He has established a secret code with his friend Bouillé so that they can communicate about the state of the nation and about their plans—for escape?—that need to be made.

18 April 1791

It is Holy Week again, and we are prepared to go to Saint-Cloud for the week. My spirits rise on wings of happiness—a week in the country away from this dreadful city, where the carriages splash my skirts on purpose if I am recognized while going for a walk.

All during Mass, I think of nothing but our imminent departure to Saint-Cloud. We are into the carriage, and I cannot repress a smile so wide that my family laughs to look at me.

Yet, there is some problem. The King looks out the coach window and says that the men of the National Guard have taken hold of the horses. We have been given permission for this trip; we have gone to Saint-Cloud—the estate isn't far from Paris—and returned in the past, but these men will not allow us to go forward.

Finally the King thrusts his head out the window and says, "It is astonishing that, having given liberty to the nation, I should not be free myself."

Lafayette, as the commander of the troops, cannot make them obey. He is humiliated and offers the King the use of force.

We are detained for some two hours, and many threats and vile curses are said in the hearing of the children. Worst of all, someone shouts, "If there is a single shot fired, the next will be for this fat pig in the coach and he will be torn into shreds."

At that point, I ask the King to abandon the attempt to go to Saint-Cloud.

He replies, "If we yield, then we must realize that we are going back to what can only be called prison, for after this outrage there can be no other name for the palace."

Thus, we return to the Tuileries.

TWO DAYS HAVE PASSED, and still my nerves are so unhinged that I can scarcely sleep at night. Just now the King shows me a sealed letter. He speaks quietly so that only I can hear. "At last," he says, "I am writing to

Count von Fersen to begin to implement the plans of which he has long spoken and often urged."

This news fills me with hope. My eyes grow moist, as do the palms of my hands. Count von Fersen and the Marquis de Bouillé may have completed their plans for our removal from this dangerous city—and the King agrees to those plans.

Escape from Paris

20 June 1791

"Then we're acting in a play," the little Dauphin says to me. He is surprised to be awakened so soon after he has gone to bed.

"There will be soldiers and fortifications when we get there," I reply. "For now, allow yourself to be dressed as a girl and make no noise. No one must know we are leaving."

"But I want to wear my armor, and my saber," he replies and sticks out his lower lip.

"It is only the bravest of boys who dares to dress as a girl," I explain. "It is a noble part that you are to play in our drama."

I have not told the Dauphin that we are fleeing under the protection and plan of Count von Fersen.

"Is Papa going?" he suddenly asks anxiously.

"Of course. I would not leave without him. We will all meet in the big coach, the berlin. But we get in at separate times."

My daughter whispers, "I remember our walk in the public gardens this afternoon, Mama. I remember you said not to be upset if strange things happen. But this dress? It's goose-turd green."

"It is to make you look ordinary, and when we get in the coach I will tell you both your pretend names, should anyone try to stop us. My pretend name will be Rosalie. I'll play the role of your nurse."

"I said we were acting in a play," my son replies.

"Now take my hands," I tell my children. My son's little six-year-old face is bright with adventure.

Like ghosts, we cross through the empty rooms of an abandoned apartment. We carry no lights, but the light coming in through the windows illumines our shadowy way. I see a figure, the outline of a coachman, standing close to a glass door. He appears to hear us coming, as he opens the door, and it is Count von Fersen, exactly as we have planned.

The Dauphin is amazed to see his noble friend dressed in coachman clothes, but Marie Thérèse says shyly, "I hoped that might be you."

My Fersen takes my son's hand and winks at him, while Madame de Tourzel guides my daughter forward. I watch the children enter the coach. Fersen climbs up and sits on the box, for he himself will be our driver. Like an ordinary coachman, he begins to whistle to pass the time.

QUICKLY I RETURN, noiselessly gliding through the empty rooms till I rejoin the King, with the Comte and Comtesse de Provence. They are off to Brussels, but we shall stay in France, stopping at Montmédy, where a house has been engaged for us and we will live among a mass of loyal soldiers. Still, Montmédy is near the border, and foreign help or farther escape would surely be available there. After our customary supper together, the Comte and Comtesse de Provence leave for their home at the Luxembourg Palace, while we endure the long rituals of our *couchers.* The King will have to appear to take his time, as both Mayor Bailly and Lafayette will attend the ceremony of his bedding.

I shall make my exit from the Tuileries after the King; in the event that I am captured, he will have already made his escape. After I have been undressed, washed with a sponge, and dressed in my nightgown and nightcap, I lie quietly in my bed, listening to the night noises of the great palace. I imagine that perhaps now the King is putting on his black wig, now the green-brown overcoat that resembles the one worn by the Chevalier de

Coigny, who for two weeks has visited the King, then left the premises through a particular door to the outside of the palace. To exit his room, the King is stepping into a large, mahogany wardrobe, in the back of which is a secret door, leading to a small staircase. He is careful to make no noise. Now he is on the ground floor, walking at the rear of the people who participated in his own *coucher.* But they suspect nothing. I pray God they suspect nothing. It is our hope that the King will be mistaken for the chevalier, for they are both large and portly and have beaked noses.

Now I arise and put on a gray dress and large hat with an impenetrable veil.

I expect to cross through the empty apartment, but! A guardsman stands before the front door of the apartment. I can hardly breathe, but I try to take my breaths quietly. I must wait and watch.

Ah, like a good guardsman he knows that it is less tiring to walk than it is to stand in one place. He begins his pacing. I count the seconds to see how long his back is turned to the apartment door. I calculate the number of steps it will take me to cross the hall and slip into the door, which I pray God is yet unlocked. Three times I rehearse my exit in my mind, then go!

My hand is on the knob. I have made no sound. Unlocked. And I am inside. Never has that much-praised noiseless step been used to such advantage as now, without admirers, when I steal my way through the dusky rooms toward freedom.

Here is the glass door, and Monsieur de Malden, my escort, standing just beyond in the courtyard. But hold, there stands Lafayette, waiting for his own coach. It is clearly his face and sandy hair illumined by the torchlight.

Now he is inside his coach.

Now he rides past, and I step forward, leaning on the arm of my escort, for my legs are still weak with fright.

Only a short walk, and I see the carriage, and the King is opening wide his arms to me and saying over and over "How glad I am to see you!" In a wink, we are in the coach, all of us together, and with a crack of the whip, the carriage begins to move forward. The children's faces shine with excitement and Elisabeth is radiant with hope.

Is it possible? Is it possible that we are actually going to escape this city of hate? We had all agreed beforehand that the most dangerous part of the journey was leaving the palace. And that has been accomplished! We are all here in our strange disguises, but it is us, inside, and we are rolling through Paris.

The King begins to tell me of the letter he has left behind in which he explains the necessity of our leaving the city. "Foremost are the events of 18 April, and the outrage perpetrated on my family when our progress to our estate of Saint-Cloud was prevented," he recounts. "And I expressed my disgust that they would require the clergy to take an oath that reduces them to the status of civil servants, and my anger that the passage of Mesdames Tantes to Rome was delayed." I can see that it has given the King a great deal of relief to enumerate and express clearly his frustration and criticism of the new regime.

After waiting patiently for his father to finish the account of his escape, the Dauphin asks where we are going now. I explain to him that first of all, we will find a second conveyance, the berlin of which I have spoken. "It's most comfortable," I say, "set on springs and upholstered in white velvet. The seats are covered with soft green morocco leather, and it has some surprises in it. When one of the cushions is removed, there is a commode built in for our convenience."

Not once do I look out the window at Paris, which I half hope never to see again. I listen to the clatter of the horses' hooves on the cobblestones and imagine the stops to come in our journey when we replace the horses. With every passing moment, I feel lighter and more confident that our plan will succeed. I feast as I gaze at the happy faces of my husband and my children, the Dauphin looking so much like a little girl with his long flaxen curls that I know anyone else would believe he was one.

We practice calling them Amélie and Aglaé, and they elbow each other and softly giggle. I am their governess, Madame Rochet, and the King is to be treated as a mere steward named Durand. He wears the hat of a lackey.

We have yet ahead of us to pass through the custom gate of Saint-Martin at the perimeter of the city. "It is two in the morning," the King says, "they will be tired. We will encounter no protest." I wish to feel reassured, but who can say what will happen next on this journey?

When we come to the gate, we find its keepers are eating and making merry. As my husband foresaw, they pay no attention to us. Thus, with a casual wave, we pass through. Only a little distance away, out of their sight, is the magnificent berlin, a little green house on yellow wheels. It amazes me to think that such a commodious structure can actually be pulled by horses, and for just a moment I wish that we had agreed to a fast, light vehicle such as good Bouillé advised.

The children are quite sleepy now, but they too are amazed by our conveyance. As we get in, the King says that there is a cooker within for reheating soup or sliced meat, and that if we raise the floor, which is double, then we shall have a table to eat on. Everything about the berlin is sparkling new, for it has only been delivered to Fersen's residence in Paris on June 18. Again, he takes the reins, and we are off, with the horses trotting very rapidly. In his seat above as coachman, Fersen does not spare the whip.

THE NEXT STOP is at the relay station, at Bondy, where we will change horses. It is also where Fersen will leave us, for the agreement is that he will ride horseback from this point to Brussels. He carries letters to Count Mercy, and money as well, and we hope to see Fersen himself again in two or three days. Fersen is an experienced campaigner, a man of decision and action, and we will part with him at Bondy, as the King has arranged, but I wish this plan of splitting up could be revised.

Now I begin to glance out the window, but I see only the black and melancholy night. The houses along the way are dark with sleep. Now the Dauphin is curled up on the floor of the berlin, sheltered under the ample skirts of Madame de Tourzel. Occasionally she and I exchange glances, sometimes of anxiety, sometimes of encouragement, but we do not speak.

At Bondy, the King and I get down from the coach to stretch our legs while the new horses are being harnessed. Fersen comes back to speak to us, and to my surprise, he all but begs the King to allow him to continue to be a part of our party and to drive us until we are safe. I think of his vast experience, his courage and decisiveness in the face of danger or of the unexpected, and I wish that the King would accommodate his request.

But the King does not hesitate. He insists that Fersen go to Brussels, but he speaks sincerely, with great gratitude to the count for all that he has done to save us. I add my own thanks to that of the King.

I drink in my friend with my eyes, praying we will meet again.

Fersen replies that it is his greatest happiness and privilege to serve us, but I can see the misery in his face. He is afraid—but only for us.

We bid Count von Fersen a hasty farewell. He rides his horse once around the carriage, then shouts out, "*Adieu*, Madame de Korff," which is the name Madame de Tourzel has assumed. I listen hard for the sound of his retreating hoofbeats, but I hear only the turning of our own wheels. In my imagination, his brave voice rings out, "*Adieu!*"

If we are captured, it is better for him, of course, that he not be in our company. If we are captured, it is better for us that he remain free so that he can continue to work on our behalf.

As we drive away, the King seems in better spirits than ever. I try to hide, then banish, my tears. Already, we have succeeded at so many crucial junctures. I am apprehensive about the time, as we are several hours behind schedule, due to the length of our *couchers*, but the King is not concerned. Now we are pulled by eight horses, instead of four, and our speed is improved. I believe that I will feel truly safe when we begin to meet the armed escorts along the way. Count von Fersen has arranged that we meet first a mounted escort commanded by the young Duc de Choiseul, the son of the man who arranged my marriage. But we are some two hours behind schedule. Close to Montmédy, our destination near the border, it is the Marquis de Bouillé who will take us under his strong wings.

The King says quietly but jubilantly to Elisabeth, Madame de Tourzel, and myself, "My joy at being clear of Paris, where I have drunk so deeply of the cup of bitterness, fills every fiber of my being. You can be sure, my dears, that once I feel my arse on a saddle again I shall be a different man from what you have seen of me recently." Indeed, already, still in the confines of the berlin, I can see that he is changing. He spoke to Fersen with unusual and resolute firmness. But of what merit is firmness if it represents a wrong choice?

It has been a nightmare for me, these months during which my instinctual impulse to fly has been pitted against my loyalty to the King. But I will not think of those times: we move ever forward, and Paris recedes in the distance. Surely they have noted our absence; surely they have sent men on fast horses in pursuit. But how could they know our direction? Perhaps the riders explode from Paris down roads leading in all directions.

At this moment, one of the carriage horses stumbles and falls. The carriage rocks precariously, and it is clear another horse has fallen. When we come to a stop, we are told that the harness has broken.

It can be repaired, but it must be sewn back together. We travel with the tools to do this heavy leather work, but it takes time to mend the harness. I grow increasingly worried about the delay, but there is nothing to be done but to try to remain cheerful and hopeful. Full of trust, the children are asleep and remain quite unaware of our mishap. Trying to find some benefit in what is surely an unfortunate occurrence, the King and I stand beside the carriage to stretch our bodies. We do not speak, but each of us stares into the darkness. Gradually the sky begins to lighten, and each of us takes a few steps—pacing, really—back and forth along the side of the coach. Once, the King walks all the way around the carriage and horses. When he returns to my side he says, without looking at me, "All is well."

As soon as a postilion appears before us, bows, and reports that we may resume our journey, the King and I hurriedly get back into the carriage. There are the faces of our children in their repose. My daughter's head is thrown back, and she breathes with her mouth slightly open. I look at the thin edges of her teeth and wonder if one day she shall have to have wires put on them, as I did before I left Vienna.

As we begin to move, I think of my journey into France, how I rode sometimes in the blue coach, sometimes in the red. At no time did a horse fall or a harness break. The whole trip, in memory, seems to have been taken in a rain of applause.

AT SIX O'CLOCK, we refresh ourselves with the delicious breakfast that Fersen has had packed for us. The beef and bread renew hope as well as strength. Even I doze a bit, after eating. What bliss it is to awaken to the morning light and to know that we are still traveling. When we have been on our way for more than an hour, the King takes out his watch. He remarks that it is now eight o'clock in the morning and adds, with a bit of boyish satisfaction, that Lafayette is probably very much embarrassed to discover we are gone. I try to take comfort in the many hours that we have traveled and the many miles that we have passed. The sun is up now, and people stare curiously at this gigantic carriage making its rapid passage through the countryside.

As the day brightens, so do my spirits, and those of Elisabeth as well. When we stop for the change of horses before Chalons, I say to Valory, one of our guards who have accompanied us on horseback, "François, it looks as if all is going well. If we were going to be stopped, surely we should have been by now." The night itself seems to have put a barrier between us and those who might wish to pursue.

He answers me reassuringly, "There is no longer anything to fear. There is no suspicion anywhere. Courage, Madame! All will go well."

I believe him. The King sends Valory ahead to let the young Duc de Choiseul know that though we are late, we are making good progress toward the relay station and our rendezvous at Somme-Vesle, which is next after Chalons. Inside the coach, the summer heat begins to raise the temperature to an unpleasant level, but we are too happy to make any complaint.

"At Somme-Vesle," the King says, "when we meet the first detachment of troops, our transit will be assured."

While the horses struggle to pull the berlin up a hill, the King decides to stretch his legs by walking beside the vehicle. "I will lighten the load," he says happily. Because of the rising heat, the hides of the horses are dark with sweat and foam. No doubt they are grateful, in their animal way, for the benevolence of their king. My husband glows with happiness.

As the King walks, he calls out to a peasant in the field and inquires about the crops. His voice is full of good feeling and paternal concern. Yes, surely we are safe. We are among the good country folk whose chief preoccupations are the weather and their grain.

"The heat is good for the harvest," the King calls out confidently.

"But in a few days, rain would be good," comes the answer.

At the crest of the hill, the King reenters the carriage, his happy face wet with perspiration from climbing a hill in late June.

WHEN WE FIND NO TROOPS at Somme-Vesle, we simply decide to drive on. But what has gone wrong? We are afraid to inquire if troops have been here, as we do not want to call attention to ourselves. Something has gone wrong. What has happened to the young Duc de Choiseul? I begin to feel uneasy. Aside from the delay in starting and then the breaking of the traces, everything has gone so well. But did the young Duc de Choiseul become impatient? Or was he afraid? I remind myself that it seemed fitting to all of us that he should be the one to help us in our flight, for it was his father who arranged the famous Alliance between Austria and France. Fersen trusted in Choiseul, despite his youth. Can good plans be so quickly dismantled? Has the Alliance itself crumbled? Perhaps someone should have repaired and maintained an alliance between the monarchy and the people, within France.

Today we talk less, but each of our faces is full of anticipation—and a certain anxiety. With every minute, I think it would be too cruel to be allowed to come so far and yet to fail in our mission. As I sit facing forward, my feet press against the floor, as if this relentless pressure would assist our speed. Always, we watch for supporting soldiers, for some sign of Choiseul. The Dauphin chatters in spurts; he would like to take off his girl's dress, and really I see little harm in his change of clothes, but the King claps him on the shoulder and tells him to be patient: it's best to wait.

The heat of the day is less now, for it is six-thirty in the evening. But as the sky begins to darken so does my mood. Where are the soldiers? Still, we have met no resistance. Perhaps we can simply drive all the way to Montmédy without escort? Perhaps de Brouillé will send his troops down the road to meet us. Plowed land with growing wheat, gardens of vegetables, small houses, barefoot peasants, chickens—we pass it all, over and over. I see a lone apple tree leaning toward the setting sun and loaded with nascent pippins. It is disconcerting for the plan to go awry in any way.

At Orbeval, we find no troops. As we leave the town behind, I seem to hear bells ringing, but the sound is faint, and Orbeval is already behind us. The noise of the berlin replaces the sound of village bells.

At Sainte-Menehould, seeing no troops, we begin to experience a great deal of anxiety. Suddenly a lone soldier approaches and says, "The arrangements have been made badly. I arouse suspicion even by talking with you. Travel on."

We have now been on the road for some eighteen hours, but I could not be more eager to resume our travel. I wish that I myself could urge on the horses, but instead I sit quietly on the padded seat and take shallow breaths.

At Clermont, we encounter the Comte de Damas, who is the colonel under the dragoons of the Comte de Provence. A bolt of hope runs through my body, but I look at his face and read there chagrin rather than purpose. To our despair, he informs us that he received a message from Leonard, my hairdresser, who traveled with another party, that we would not be arriving. I do not doubt Leonard's loyalty in the slightest, but this miscommunication suggests that there is confusion about our plans, when we need all clarity, all intelligence, and cunning. If only Fersen were with us to assist in the decisions we must make. In his steely, quietly professional way, Fersen would assess the situation, give orders to the soldiers, reorganize whatever is going wrong.

Damas has already allowed his men to unsaddle their horses and to retire for the evening. We are advised to go on to Varennes. Our horses are very tired. I hear their labored breathing.

When we reach this next tiny town, Varennes, we find the place to be totally dark. The King worries that we will be unable to find any fresh horses here, but we cross the bridge—Varennes is cut into two parts by the river

Aire—and the King himself goes to knock on cottage doors to get advice about the horses. The bodyguards are also seeking horses. It is not so very far to Montmédy, and I am about to urge that we move forward, even if the exhausted horses must walk. We can all walk beside them, all the adults.

Suddenly the town fire alarm is sounded, and with that sound, I feel with great dread that suspicions have been aroused about us. The sound rips my brain into two parts. A weary, meek, and dry little man who identifies himself as Monsieur Sauce appears and asks to see our passports.

Madame de Tourzel produces the documents, and they are found to be in good order. How right the King was to maintain the Dauphin's identity as a girl! I bless him for his prudence and myself for my obedience to his casual wisdom.

Monsieur Sauce is about to wave us on when a man steps forward who calls himself Drouet, from Sainte-Menehould.

With no preliminary, Drouet shouts at Sauce: "I am sure that the carriage carries the King and Queen! If you allow them to pass into a foreign country, you will be guilty of treason."

All my hope and happiness crumble inside me. By what authority does this Drouet dare to denounce us! I search the dark, hoping to see or hear some sign of an armed escort.

In his own worried, humble manner, Monsieur Sauce insists that we must not leave. Then he prevails on us to come to his house to rest until morning, and the King acquiesces.

We are shown to an upper room in the back of the house. At my request, clean sheets are spread on the bed for the children, who immediately fall asleep. When I glance out the window, I see that peasants are gathering below.

All the time, my heart is raging: *We must go on, we must go on.* But I know it is of utmost importance to remain calm. My terror runs like fire through my veins, but what can we do? What can I do?

The King says, "Now that the children are asleep, with good Madame de Tourzel to watch over them, we must go downstairs and converse with this Monsieur Sauce." He smiles at me encouragingly, and now I know my role. It is for me to charm this country grocer, a member of this provincial town council, to speak to his wife, to help them see that we are but a family, under duress, as they themselves must be from time to time.

Madame Sauce seats us in her best chairs amid the barrels of flour and salt pork. The crops have not yet come in, but there is a slatted box with a few withered potatoes in it, left over from last winter. A net bag of onions sits on the counter. Straps of green have sprouted at the tops of the marooned onions. Madame Sauce explains, apologizing, that her husband has gone to fetch a neighbor.

"Once," she says, "our neighbor lived at Versailles." Then she adds, "For five years."

The King and I exchange a glance. Anyone who has lived in the town of Versailles for so long has surely seen us. But, I think, hopefully, we are much changed.

When Monsieur Sauce enters with his neighbor and a small group of men, the neighbor bows to his King. The former citizen of Versailles is clearly flustered and very much afraid; his eyes dart wildly about. He falls to one knee.

Another man from the group steps forward. "Majesty," he says, not without rustic dignity, "we are the town council of Varennes. Are you our King?"

The King rises from the kitchen chair. He extends both hands to the frightened morsel of humanity who cowers before him and raises his subject to his feet. He embraces the man. Next he steps back and addresses the group. "Yes, I am your King," and he steps forward to embrace them all, in turn.

The sobs gush out of me, like water from a struck rock. I can find no language. My face distorts in my grief and my body trembles. The King stands beside me and places his hand on my shoulder, but his touch brings me no comfort.

"We have left Paris," the King tells them, "because the lives of my family were under threat every day." His voice is calm and has in it a note that bespeaks—I recognize for the first time—*fraternité.* Hysterically, in the interstices of the moment, I hear the sweet, wise voice of Louis Joseph, my dying boy, speaking—*"Papa would not say 'we' if he meant only himself; he speaks for me as well; he means us both, when he says 'we.'"* I gasp at the clarity in my mind of the voice of my firstborn son, for he was like a sacrificial lamb offered up to Fortunata when the Estates General began the meetings that began this revolution. He was the sacrifice, and now we must be let free.

The King speaks on, explaining his position to these simple village folk. "I could no longer bear to live in the midst of bayonets and knives of those who would assassinate us." He speaks simply, as a man, a lone man appealing to each of them, also alone for all their awkward standing in a group. "I have come to seek asylum, for myself and for my most dear family, among my loyal subjects."

The King stops. I wish him to go on speaking, to become Mirabeau, to thunder. But he chooses otherwise. In his new dignity, he will not play the politician. He will not make a speech; he will only speak—a man conversing with other men, strangers, but men like himself.

I cannot but try to help. Carefully, even shyly, I take the hand of Madame Sauce who stands beside me. I tug ever so gently till she looks down at me, looking up, still seated in her chair. I must clear my throat to speak.

"You too are a mother and a wife," I say. "Would you not appeal to your husband to allow us to continue our journey?"

The men are conversing among themselves. Both she and I can see by their faces that they are moved by our plight and by the words of the King. He is huge before them. He stands without nervousness, calmly waiting, but withdrawn into himself. We see compassion and hear it in their tone of voice, but there is also fear.

I hear Madame Sauce's reply. "My husband would be risking his life, should he allow His Majesty to pass. I value my husband's life more than that of the King." I hear anger in her words, which are also full of wonder that she is in a position to formulate such a thought at such a moment as this. Yet she has used her intelligence. I would have said the same.

"Come back upstairs with me," says the King. "See my children, and my younger sister who accompanies us. Watch us while we quietly gather up our things, so as not to wake the children. We will all go on together to Montmédy. You will accompany us. You will see that it is not our intention to flee the country, but to remain in France, to govern from a safe place among peaceful people, and from there to prepare for a new order in the capital, one that will maintain the order imposed by the monarchy, an order that is necessary for the advent of the long overdue justice due the people. Come go upstairs with me, and let us talk quietly there."

Without waiting for their answer, or permission, the King leads the group up the spiral staircase to our room. When we reach the top of the stairs, we hear a cry from outside.

"The hussars are here!"

My heart leaps up with hope. Choiseul's hussars! Our escort!

The King says with supreme calm, "Let their leader be taken here, to this room, to talk with us. We will all confer together. I am in no hurry until you good people are reassured of my intentions."

The number of people gathering outside has increased, and we hear the threads of a dialogue developing: sometimes the phrase *Vive le Roi!* Sometimes the phrase *À Paris!*

It is the young Duc de Choiseul who enters the room, his uniform covered with dirt. He collects himself, bows to the King, and states that he awaits his orders. With incredible tact and courtesy, the members of the town council withdraw.

Yes, young Choiseul tells the King, he is arrived with forty men. Some of his troops he can unseat from their horses. Then the King can ride with the Dauphin before him, and I with Madame Royale before me. The hussars will surround us and protect us as we ride for the border.

"Will your men be in danger?" the King asks.

"We will fight to the death," Choiseul replies.

The King hesitates. I see the terrible goodness in his countenance. "It has never been my wish that any blood be shed or the death of any Frenchman occur for my personal protection."

Stunned, Choiseul clicks his heels together and bows in submission. He is too young to try to reason with his King. He has been trained to obey. Would that Fersen were with us!

"Perhaps the town council will decide to let us pass," the King says hopefully. He instructs Choiseul to tell the council members to return.

"We will stay and await your orders," Choiseul replies. The whites of his eyes are reddened with fatigue, and his lips are cracked from heat and dust.

As soon as he has gone, I burst into tears afresh, as does Elisabeth. Sitting beside my children in their bed, Madame de Tourzel covers her face with her hands.

With renewed patience and with the confidence only a just man who has taken the course dictated by conscience can assume, the King speaks with the government—the butcher, the baker, the candlestick maker—of this tiny, miserable town.

It is not long before Madame Sauce reappears at the door, with a very old woman. In no way ugly, *plain* is the best way to describe Madame Sauce. Her dark hair is parted to both sides by a straight line through the middle of her head. Her face is oval.

Madame Sauce begins to speak with her head bowed, then she raises her eyes to me. "May I present the grandmother of Monsieur Sauce. Our grandmother is now past her eightieth year. Before she dies, she would like to see her King and Queen and their children."

I straighten my body, as does the King, so that we may look our parts. I merely nod permission.

With only a quick and frightened glance at us, the bent old woman creeps toward the bed where the Dauphin and Madame Royale lie asleep. She goes to them like an iron filing drawn toward a magnet. *Ah, children!* For the better part of a century children have stirred her aging heart with hope and love. I see them through her eyes. Never have there been such beautiful children, asleep in their innocence like angels.

The old woman falls to her knees beside their bed, looks first at the King and then at me—as their mother—and humbly asks permission to kiss their hands.

I smile at her. "It would be their honor to be blessed by your kisses."

Clasping her twisted fingers together, the old woman prays beside my children. Then she opens her eyes. Very reverently she lifts their hands—she knows well how to touch a child without waking him—and brings her old cracked lips to brush their tender skin.

As she struggles to her feet, Madame Sauce assists her on one side, and suddenly the King is there too, with his strong hand under the other elbow. She looks at him in disbelief, and his kind eyes meet hers. Tears well up in her eyes, overflow, and course down her old cheeks.

With bowed head, weeping profusely, she hobbles away.

The King has only begun to confer again with those about him when we hear running footsteps on the spiral stairs. A delegation from Paris has found us here, in Varennes. Our fate is no longer a matter for these isolated townfolk to decide. In his desire for a peaceful passage, the King has tarried too long.

The envoy's hair is in great disorder, and his tunic has been hastily mis-buttoned. He pants and speaks with difficulty in a voice vibrating with emotion. "Sire, in Paris, they are cutting each other's throats. . . . It is a massacre. . . . Our wives and our children will die. . . . Without you, there is not nor can there be any order. . . . Sire, we beg you to go no farther. . . . For the welfare of the state, Sire. . . ."

"What is it that you really desire to say?" the King asks.

"Sire, I present to you the decree of the National Assembly."

The King quickly reads the paper handed to him, then he tosses it on the bed where our children lie sleeping.

To me, he says bitterly, "There is no longer a King in France." Then he whispers to me, "Choiseul has sent a message to General Bouillé. Perhaps he will arrive with a much larger force, if we can delay our departure sufficiently."

I approach the young Choiseul and ask without subterfuge, "Would you be so kind as to tell me, if you know, is Count von Fersen safe in Brussels?"

"Majesty, he is."

For that information I bless the young man, though he failed to meet us at the appointed place, Somme-Vesle.

Fersen

The Marquis de Bouillé with his troops does not arrive. Now we are prisoners and helpless.

Surrounded by villains and moving very slowly, the berlin has not conveyed us very far down the road back to Paris when, as we pass through the countryside, a nobleman, the Comte de Dampierre, whose lands are adjacent to the highway, tries to approach our carriage. He wishes to show his respect by greeting us. As we watch him coming toward us, he is taken down by the mob and killed.

I have no more tears, it seems. I turn my face away so that my eyes look out the other side of the carriage.

THE FEET OF THE HORSES and people who travel with us raise such an intolerable cloud of dust that we can hardly get our breath. In addition, the heat becomes intense, and we move at such a slow pace that not the slightest breeze enters the coach. We are obliged to keep the window blinds open so that everyone who wishes may see us.

Hours pass, and with the passing of each hour, the people along the route become more hostile. I determine to use the time as best I can, talking with one of our captors who has chosen to place himself on the seat of the carriage beside me. His name is Barnave, a member of the National Assembly. He is young and willing to be charmed by the conversation of one who passes for the Queen. I do my best to convince him of our humanity and of our concern for the welfare of France.

WHEN WE REACH the Tuileries, the King stumbles from the carriage but walks unaccosted by the howling mob up the stairs. When I step out, several people lunge at me—I watch their approach with the equanimity of exhaustion. Behold, members of the National Guard step between me and my would-be assailants. A gigantic guardsman takes the Dauphin in his arms and rushes inside.

I am covered by the gray dust of the road. When Madame Campan greets me at the door of my apartment, I take off my cap to show her my hair, which has turned completely white. I ask for scissors and snip off a lock, which I intend to send later to the dear Princesse de Lamballe, whose own escape, I pray, has been accomplished. I shall simply explain that my hair has been blanched by sorrow. Now I ask for a bath.

The King is taken away to offer explanation to the National Assembly for our flight. "Just remember," I say softly into his ear, my lips so dry with dust that I can hardly form any words, "we never had any intention of deserting France."

But I worry about the accusations and complaints my husband has so injudiciously left behind in his farewell letter, for all to read, before our flight.

AS SOON AS POSSIBLE, I take up my pen to write to Axel von Fersen:

Put your mind at ease, for we are alive. Yes, I exist, but I cannot begin to express how anxious I have been about you. To know how you have suffered for lack of word from us has doubled my own suffering.

Do not write to me—I know your thoughts and feelings already—and a letter might incriminate us further in some way.

Above all, do not come to Paris under any pretext. It is well known that you planned and helped us to leave, and everything would be lost if you came here.

Although I am watched every minute, both night and day, I do not let that bother me. Do not be anxious, as it is already clear that the Assembly wishes to deal with us in a kindly fashion. They wish to pretend that we were abducted and not ourselves responsible for our absence.

Farewell. I cannot write any more, only to say I love you and indeed that is all I have time to say. Tell me to whom I can send my letters to you because I could not live without being able to write you. Farewell most beloved of men and the most loving of men. With all my heart, I embrace you and only you.

My most dear friend, Princesse de Lamballe,

No, don't come back, my dear heart, no, don't throw yourself into the mouth of the tiger. It would only add to my distress and my deep and constant anxiety about my husband and my poor little children. By all means, do not come. My chou d'amour *will now sign his name in his own little hand, and you must obey me and your future king.*

The princess replies to me, in mid-November, from the home of her father-in-law, the Duc de Penthièvre, that she wishes to return as "a patriotic act." The winter is coming on, and my dear friend will no longer allow me to remain alone and cold. It seems I am unable to prevent her return, so the good Barnave has persuaded the National Assembly to let her live in an apartment close to me within the Tuileries and to resume her post as the superintendent of the queen's household.

I SPEND MY DAYS writing to the crowned heads of Europe, imploring them to come to our assistance. I write to Fersen, my champion, who travels from Brussels to Vienna to speak with my brother Leopold, the Emperor, and to speak with his own King Gustavus, who wants to help us. Day in, day out, I weary myself, trying to be convincing, trying to avoid saying anything stupid.

I tell my friends that the tigers who surround me grow more fierce and hungry every day.

With great secrecy and only in whispers to each other, the King and I speak of Count von Fersen and how he hopes to arouse support for our position among the monarchs of Europe. Surely they would rather put down rebellion in France than face it in their own countries. But the King always worries that any force from outside our borders might then try to *occupy* France.

ON NEW YEAR'S DAY, 1792, I don a new court dress, with wide panniers in the grand old style. If Barnave were still here, he would glory in such a dress, but he has been sent away as too moderate a voice in the Assembly. His party, termed the Feuillants, is being displaced by those called the Jacobins, and the Girondins also struggle for power.

The dress is blue satin and will remind the people of the portrait in blue that Vigée-Lebrun painted of me holding a pink rose, which everyone loved. This dress, however, is more elaborate, and the satin is embroidered all over.

I think there may be civil war; nothing is more horrible in the King's mind than the idea of Frenchmen fighting against Frenchmen, spilling fraternal blood on the soil of France.

THOUGH STILL BITTERLY COLD, February has come and with it, in disguise and using a false passport, my Fersen! How can I be unhappy when he is here? My joy makes me numb to his danger.

We are full of gaiety at seeing each other again, both of us as splendidly dressed as of old, but he is risking his life to see us. After staying here this evening, he will confer with the King tomorrow, bringing news from the King of Sweden. As soon as it is possible, we embrace, and I remark that it is like embracing a man made of ice.

He tells me that it is so cold outside that his carriage wheels make exactly the same crunching sound that they make in the extreme cold of Sweden as they pass through the snow.

Then he tells me that despite the chill that lingers in his clothing, his heart within is a glowing ember, eternally. Simply to look at him again fills me with the most exquisite pleasure, and I know that it is the same for him. What friends we are!

We speak of that last day at my beloved Trianon. I tell him that I had returned to the mossy grotto among the rocks to remember our intimacy when I saw the messenger coming with the news that the market women were marching from Paris.

"Ah, I had not known that it was in that most hidden and delightful spot that you were lingering when the world changed. To think, we have not had time till now for you to share that moment with me."

He takes both my hands in his, then slowly with that combination of passion and elegance that he evokes, he bends to kiss my knuckles, then steps backward, our hands still joined, to view me at exactly the distance spanned by our two arms, outstretched. "I am memorizing you," he says. "Just so."

"And I you."

I think that we both have a premonition that we will never see each other again. But it is our disposition and determination to forbid the occasion to be sad. No, every moment that we are together has always been and is to be filled with joy, just as the bee perpetually fills the honeycomb.

"What nectar," I say to him, smiling.

He knows exactly what I mean.

"It has always been so," he replies.

With exquisite grace, he draws me a step forward and meets me in a holy kiss.

THE TOWER, 1792

1 September

With a great deal of irony, I think of us this way: *One afternoon during the Reign of Terror—that is, on 1 September 1792—the King and the Queen of France sat in the Tower, built as part of the palace of the old Knights Templar, in Paris, playing a game of backgammon.*

Taking turns, we each scoop up the dice from the playing board, rattle the spotted cubes in their leather-covered cups, and toss the dice out among the triangular shapes painted on the game board, which have something of the appearance, at least to me, of a dragon's mouth full of opposing, pointed teeth.

According to the numbers we have rolled, we move our pieces, his chocolate brown, mine cream, in opposite directions so that each little group of pieces has to face and pass through the defenses of the other in order to get home. Usually when we play, I try to keep each of my pieces safe from capture, while the King takes more risks to set up blocks in order to impede the movement of the Queen's creamy troop.

We are playing for the sake of the children, for Marie Thérèse and Louis Charles, the Dauphin, so that they may think the Temple, as this palace and its towers are known, seems homelike and safe instead of like the prison it actually is. Because the Knights of Malta left a collection of some fifteen hundred books in the Tower, the King has a library here. He would rather have retired upstairs to read in the turret-study adjacent to his bedroom than to play backgammon. I muse and wonder for a moment about how the King has always been a man who enjoys the company of books, while I prefer active conversation with real minds. I wonder if my life would have been different had I liked to read, or his, if he had liked to converse.

In his turret, my husband reads twice a day, after breakfast and after dinner, for two or three hours at each sitting. Lately he has been studying an account of the English king Charles I, who left his head on the chopping block in the century before. Really, the King has studied this story since he was fifteen, and even before I came to France. Perhaps it has always been a cautionary tale for him.

The French, or rather Dr. Guillotine, have recently introduced a more humane means of execution than the hand-held, shoulder-swung ax of the seventeenth century. A high sharp blade is hoisted between two grooved struts that make the device resemble the skeleton of a tall door, with a slant of steel, something like a butcher's meat cleaver, but more triangular and without a handle, positioned at the top. If the execution occurs on a bright day, I am told, the glint of the sun on the polished steel can be seen by even those far back in the crowd. Near the base and at a right angle to the upright business, on something like a wooden sled, the criminal is made to lie face-down with hands tied together behind his or her back. The sled with its human cargo is shoved forward so that the head of the person is positioned just beyond the open door, and the blade rattles down the grooved frame to fall straight down upon the neck, lopping off the criminal's head, which falls neatly into a waiting basket. I suppose there must be a great deal of blood. Spectators have said, I am told, it all happens very quickly, mechanically, and one can hardly believe how brief that moment is between a living body . . . and what is left, that is, between life and death.

Because my hand starts to tremble, I quickly take up my dice cup and rattle it furiously, throwing out the "bones" onto the board. I rest my hand, hunched, on the table. The King is not deceived. He places his hand over mine for a moment, making a little shelter for me.

I breathe deeply, a long pull of air into my lungs, and resume my courage. "Your turn," I say, and smile.

As we play, both of us recall, though we speak nothing of it, that only a couple of weeks before this game of backgammon there was a great deal of brutal killing by revolutionaries at the Tuileries. They hoped to kill us, I believe, but the Swiss Guard stood between us and the mob, and the loyal guardsmen were massacred.

After the carnage, the Tuileries was uninhabitable, and we were to be moved to the Convent of the Feuillants. The mob left the Tuileries smeared with blood and littered not only with shredded pieces of clothing—velvet and brocade—but also pieces of human flesh. It required only two carriages to carry away those of us of the court of Louis XVI who remained alive, including my most precious friend the Princesse de Lamballe. I have almost forgotten my other friends, such as the Duchesse de Polignac, who have fled, although I hear from Fersen that he had a touching reunion with her, someplace in Europe.

If I could, I would like to have a sensible conversation with the painter Elisabeth Vigée-Lebrun, but I do not know where she is, and if she is alive or dead. I wonder if the violence of the times we live in has affected her artistic style. I hope that she has lived to paint the royalty of some other more fortunate country.

As the carriage rolled away from the Tuileries, I remember thinking how beautiful and strangely calm was the face of the Princesse de Lamballe. We have never been lovers, not in the sense of the obscene pamphlets, but my love for her knows no bounds. Of all my friends at court who successfully fled the country at the beginning of the revolution, when flight was relatively easy, only the Princesse de Lamballe, upon learning that I was alone, returned to France. In the past her sensitivity was so extreme that she sometimes burst into tears for fear of a mouse or over the touching beauty of a rose, but her love for me has given her the courage to return to a country increasingly dangerous for any aristocrat.

As the carriages transported us across Paris, from the blood-drenched Tuileries to the Convent of the Feuillants, she never flinched. The air in which we moved was filled with the snarl of snare drums and the thud of huge tympani, along with the ominous tolling of bells, not to mention the shouts of the people of "No more King." She and I ignored those who called out as our carriage rattled over the humped stones shaped like loaves of bread. They shouted that Louis XVI is nothing but a fat porpoise. Through the coach window, I saw the huge heart of an ox, with a cuckold's horns attached to it, displayed and labeled as that of the monarch. Placards and little models with dolls showed an image of a Queen being hung from a lantern post.

Once at the convent, all of us were happy to inhabit only four rooms, and those rooms had humble brick floors and whitewashed walls for the most part. We had plenty of food.

Despite the stress of the times, the King slept well and ate a dinner of eight appetizers balanced by eight desserts with four roasts in between. I could not eat at all, and my friend the Princesse de Lamballe joined me in my abstinence. Clothing being scarce at the convent, my fastidious friend the Princesse de Lamballe, who had not worn fresh underwear for two days, sent a note to a friend to borrow a chemise.

"WE STAYED IN the convent for only a few days," I suddenly remark to my husband. He is about to win in this Tower game of backgammon, unless the dice go very much against him. Our eyes follow the dice and the movement of the tokens of the game, while our thoughts wander in the past.

EACH OF THE CARRIAGES bound from the convent for the Temple was pulled by only two horses. Though we left the convent at six-thirty in the evening, it was nearly nine o'clock before the horses succeeded in pulling their heavy loads the short distance between these two locations within Paris. On the way, we passed our former abode, the Tuileries palace, where someone had placed a For Rent sign. We also passed through the old Place de Louis XV, where the people had pulled down the statue of the grandfather of Louis XVI. The mob not only had smashed its face and broken off the statue's arms and legs but also had battered flat the head of the bronze horse he had been riding.

Inside the carriage the procurator-general of the Commune pointed to the mutilated statue and informed us, "That is how the people deal with kings."

Not lacking in a sense of humor, Louis XVI replied, "How pleasant for us that their rage is focused on inanimate objects."

I smile now to think of his wit and glance at him, but he is lost in his own thoughts.

As we approached the walls of the Temple, people were chanting, "Madame goes up into her Tower / When will she come down again?"

When we were taken to eat dinner into the portion of the Temple that remains a palace, I allowed myself to hope that perhaps we would remain there. The taller tower was not ready for us—I trembled only when I heard our keepers consider separating the King from the rest of the family—but in the long run, we went together to the small tower attached to the wall surrounding the palace.

THOUGH CLOTHING has remained scarce, and there is a great deal of climbing up and down stairs, food is still plentiful in the Tower, and the King enjoys fare with which he is familiar—savory soups, fowls, and the pastries he loved so well when he was a big boy of fifteen and sixteen. He has Champagne and Bordeaux and sometimes a single sweet and potent after-dinner drink. Despite ugly rumors and many pamphlets blackening my reputation as one who often participated in drunken orgies, I never drink liquors or wine at all, not even now.

I do not know if there is any virtue in my abstinence. I enjoy the clarity of my thought, and I wish to respond to reality unclouded by alcohol. The princess Elisabeth sometimes takes a glass of wine with her brother.

After only a week in the small Tower, we are informed by the Commune that the Princesse de Lamballe is to be taken away to the prison known as La Force. We embrace, we weep, we part. My heart goes numb.

More indirectly, from the town criers outside the walls of the Temple, we hear that Lafayette, who fought for American independence and was considered a hero by the populace of France, has fled France and its mockery of the rule of law in the name of liberty. This revolution in France has not ushered in a better order; it has opened the gates of chaos and anarchy.

Terror, Fury, and Horror Seize the Earthly Powers

By 2 September, some four hundred throats on the other side of the wall surrounding the Tower are chanting "Strangle the little cubs and the fat pig" and "She shall dance from the lantern." If my friend the princess were still here, we would pretend together that we do not hear these voices.

A letter blessedly arrives, delivered by one of our keepers, from the King's aging aunts, who have escaped to Rome and are leading devout lives there as daughters of the Church. Both the King and Queen—my husband and myself—read it over and over, silently and then aloud to each other as reassurance that there are quiet, safe places in the world where people do not behave more cruelly than rabid animals.

THE ROYAL FAMILY—I mean ourselves—are exercising within the garden walls on 3 September when suddenly their guards escort them inside. Drums sound, and they hear shouts and a confusing din in the distance. When a cannon is fired nearby, Marie Antoinette—called Toinette by her friends, but none of them are left and she does not know even what has become of the last of them, the beautiful princess Lamballe—cries out, "Save my husband!" As to what is going on in Paris, no one tells them.

Once inside the Tower again, the royal family dine, and then the King and Queen settle down to their board game upstairs, watched as always by four municipal officers, one of whom pities the royals and treats them with consideration. Madame Elisabeth (who is she, really? the younger sister of the King) reads aloud one of Aesop's fables—possibly a cautionary tale—to the children. More like a picture than a mirror, the scene is one that the Queen views from a safe distance. There is perhaps some confusion about time in her mind—so great is her anxiety about the future of her children—for it seems that the King and Queen have been playing backgammon forever, and the game does not progress.

Suddenly the gruff and impassive keeper downstairs—Madame Tison—shrieks! A sound like a bright pick into the convolutions of the brain.

I hear savage cries from the streets surrounding the Tower: "Kiss the lips, kiss the lips!" Upstairs, the municipal officers hurry to close our shutters. We hear the sound of footsteps running up the stairs, and four unarmed revolutionaries burst in demanding that the King and Queen stand at the window.

"You must *not* go to the window," one of their municipal guards, his young face radiant with anxiety, tells me, but the mob spokesman who has burst into our domain insists more vehemently that the King and Queen of the Tower expose themselves to the crowd by standing in a narrow window just yonder. We have done as much in the past—faced them.

"Why should we not address the people?" the King stoutly asks our familiar guard.

"If you must know," the guard replies, "they only want to show you the head of the Princesse de Lamballe."

The cry from below rings out, "Kiss the lips you've kissed before!"

The cry hits me with concussive force. I wilt into a chair, my mind vague as a cloud.

"The people have attacked the prisons, killing the aristocrats," another guard explains.

Opening the shutter a crack, the hairdresser Cléry looks out and recoils in horror. He gasps, "The head of the Princesse de Lamballe is on a pike." He begins to vomit, burying his mouth in the crook of his arm.

Another guard replaces him at the open window. He takes a step backward, while the cry below becomes a chant: *The Queen! The Queen! The Queen—must—see!*

"Her Majesty must not see," the guard insists.

"Tell me what you have seen, monsieur." There is nothing between our world and theirs, except height. The window is open, and the air moves back and forth between the inside and the outside. I can hear them very clearly. From my seat, I see a narrow blue rectangle of sky. I ask, "What is out there, on the street?"

"On a second pike, is a dripping heart." He begins to sob, for he has often been in this room with the princess. "On a third, her entrails."

"Enough!" the King thunders. He goes to another unopened window, stands a step away from it, but peers through the latticework. "The men holding up these trophies are yelling with glee and fury. Not yet having obtained their goal," the King says grimly, "they are carrying stones and boards to pile against the side of the tower."

Numbly, I know their thoughts. They want the Queen to kiss the dead lips of her lover. It is to be the culminating act for their pornographic feast. I think of hunting dogs leaping against the side of a tree where their prey has taken refuge.

"They are trying to construct a means of raising the head higher," I explain. "They wish to make Marie Antoinette kiss the lips of the gory head of her dearest friend." Yes, I know they carry rubble to place against the wall of the Tower so that they might climb higher and raise the head of the princess up to the next level in the Tower, where they believe the Queen to be. They want to make the eyes of my dead friend appear at my window to look in at me.

"Jackals! Jackals!" the King mutters, his eyes wet with grief. "Is it certainly the princess?" he asks Cléry.

His face streaming with tears, holding his soiled arm out from his body, Cléry says, "Her golden curls float around her face as though she were alive. Someone has dressed her hair."

With terrifying glee the men who have invaded our rooms recount that, indeed, the head had been taken to a hairdresser and also to an apprentice wax modeler, Marie Grosholz. At her name, I am startled into reality, for in earlier days this girl came to the palace to instruct Madame Elisabeth in art. She would surely have recognized the princess.

One of the rough boys from the mob adds, "She didn't want to touch it, but we made her hold the head between her knees and cover it with molding wax. For an impression."

AS THE FURY and frustration of the mob mounts, they call not just for the grisly kiss but for the head of the Queen "to parade beside the tribade Lamballe."

One of our commissioners goes downstairs to confront the rioters. I can hear him shouting at them.

"You shall not have the head of Antoinette," he yells. "I hold up the tricolor ribbon. See it! I speak with the authority of the revolution. The head of the Antoinette does not belong to you."

I expect to hear the rush of their feet mounting the steps. I fix my eyes on my son and rise so as to move as far from him as possible.

But the room below falls only into muttering. When we hear movement, it is for them to go outside again, among their own constituents.

The King takes me by the hand to lead me higher in the Tower. Among the books, he puts me on a small sofa in the turret. Here there is a heavy velvet curtain, and he draws it across the only window. As he moves the curtain, its brass rings rattle.

Rigid with sorrow, I lie awake all night, thinking of the soft, kind body of my friend, my first real friend in France, the Princesse de Lamballe. I recall the day when we, with Elisabeth, still a little girl, sat beside the fountain of the dragon and watched the spume from its mouth tower into the sky. My sobs, like a child's, are automatic convulsions I cannot end.

Sitting beside me, the King says with calm sadness, "The fiends have finished with us, for tonight." All around the Tower is the silence of ordinary noises.

"Did others die?" I ask. "In the prison." We would have known many of the people in La Force.

"After they broke into La Force, they stormed the prisons of Salpêtrière and Bicêtre—"

"At the Bastille, at least they liberated the prisoners. There were only seven."

"These prisons, Salpêtrière and Bicêtre, were full of beggars, pauper children, prostitutes. They all have been raped and murdered, even the young children, though God knows what crimes against the people they were supposed to have committed."

Despite my sobs, I feel I must speak. "Then they only want"—yes, I will say the simple truth, despite the horror of it—"to drink blood. These revolutionaries."

"They have no concern about guilt or innocence. They feel only rage and the need to release their rage."

Far below, the wheels of a cart are turning slowly and carefully over the cobblestones.

For a moment, I lie so still and silent that the King fears I may have died. My sobs have suddenly ceased.

"The princess was not alive," he murmurs, "when they mutilated her body. The blow of a hammer had already killed her."

Slowly, with many tears of his own, my husband tells her story: "When the Princesse de Lamballe was brought before the revolutionary court, she was asked to denounce us as conspirators against the happiness of France. 'I have nothing to say,' she answered. And to show she would not be intimidated by their threats, she added, 'Dying a little earlier or a little later makes no difference to me.'"

The King pauses in his narrative. "Locked here in the Tower," he muses, "just think—we knew nothing of her brave refusal to incriminate us.

"They told her to go through a certain door, one that led to the courtyard where the mob waited. They fell upon anyone who came through the door. One of that number stood beside the door to deliver a blow to the head with his giant hammer as soon as a person emerged. The princess fell dead to the cobblestones."

I begin to breathe; I jerk the air slowly into my nostrils, and then heartbroken words squeeze out. "All the same—they did those things—*to her.*"

Making no effort to lift my hand to wipe my eyes, the sobs break out of me again, till dawn.

In a quiet moment, the King picks up a pen and tears a blank page from one of his library books upon which to write. "I will fashion a dignified and official statement," he says.

At dawn, I sit up, my eyes so swollen that I can see only through a narrow slit.

He reads to me, "The loyalty and devotion the Princesse de Lamballe has shown to us during our misfortunes validates many times over the Queen's initial choice of her as a close friend."

End of the Monarchy

Today, 21 September, we hear from the town criers, who are paid by our friends to shout the news particularly loudly as they pass by the Tower, that monarchy in France no longer exists.

The King does not raise his eyes from his book. He turns a page, and his eyes begin their ceaseless travel from left to right. I detect no change in his large impassive face. Slowly, I rise from my chair and make my way to my bed. All strength has gone from me. I cannot even sit up. In bed I lie on my back so that both ears will be open as I listen to the details of the news proclaimed loudly from the street below.

France is to be ruled by a National Convention, the members of which are to be elected.

As for the royal family, our name is now Capet; my husband is Louis Capet, the name of ancestors who ruled France until the year 1328.

This year is no longer 1792; it is the Year One, heralded into being by the blowing of trumpets all over Paris.

The sound of trumpets has a certain brightness to it; for some trumpets the sound is silvery, for others it has the mellow fullness of gold. I prefer any musical sound to that of human voices growling their hatred.

France has its borders to look to now. The European powers see this country as weak; they would like to defeat this new regime—not to rescue us—but to bite off pieces of France for which they have long hungered.

And what is to be our fate? They take the King away from us, to the Great Tower.

The children and I are devastated; we make no attempt to stanch the flow of tears and our words of supplication to those who control our destiny. Elisabeth throws herself onto her knees. To our surprise and great joy, they are moved: they allow us to take our meals together under the condition that we speak in loud, clear French.

Nonetheless, sometimes I can send my husband a more private message—*we pray for you*—in a hollow cut into a peach or in a cavity concealed inside a macaroon. We continue to eat very well, off silver, and the King has wine. At the end of October, the children and I join the King in the Great Tower, with newly decorated rooms, including a toilet made in the English style, flushed with water.

11 December 1792

The sound of snare drums rolls over my heart. Something of enormous importance is about to occur. We can hear the regular footsteps of soldiers approaching us, ascending the stairs. The volley of the drums becomes louder and louder till they fling open the door to our rooms.

Pétion stands before us to read a decree to Louis Capet. It is a lengthy, grinding denunciation for treason asserting that Louis "left France as a fugitive with the intention of returning as a conqueror."

"Capet is not my name," my husband replies mildly. "That detail is inaccurate, as are many others."

Pétion says, "These children cannot remain under the influence of both their parents. One of you will be taken from them. Which one?"

Stricken to the core, I can only gasp and look at my husband. He gazes at me fondly, even with the slightest of smiles, and says, "Of course our children must remain under the care and protection of their noble mother."

He sees my gratitude; I am sure he does. Nonetheless, I cannot prevent myself from collapsing into sobs.

"Go to her now," he says gently to the children, who obey as though winged. Louis Charles jumps into my lap, turns to his father, and says, "We will care for her well, Papa."

Marie Thérèse leans lovingly against my shoulder.

Only after the King has said farewell and walked from the room in perfect dignity do I realize that we three have assumed the pose in which we were last painted by Vigée-Lebrun, when I wore red velvet and a floral carpet swirled beneath the cushion for my footstool. Only my son is now a little boy and not a chubby baby, and my daughter is growing into a young woman, soon to be fourteen.

19 December 1792

Today is my daughter's birthday, and our good and faithful hairdresser, Cléry, has brought her a present from her father, an almanac for the coming year.

"Your father sends you this gift with his blessing," I improvise. "May the coming year bring you safety, peace, and joy, and each year following even greater joy toward a long and happy life."

Later in the day, I ask Cléry to arrange my hair again, and that of my daughter, in case their kindness should extend to allowing the King to visit his daughter for supper on her birthday.

It is one of the few pleasures remaining to me—the gentle and caring touch of my hairdresser, as he combs and braids or pins my hair. It is my rule, in order to make both him and myself more happy, always to compliment him on the very latest creation and to find, for myself, some curl or lift that pleases me in particular.

I try to train my daughter in this courteous habit and always ask her, when Cléry has finished, what it is she likes best about her new coif.

At the end of the day, I say, "Though your dear papa was not allowed to visit, you can be sure, as you fall asleep, that he is thinking of you and blessing you."

THERE IS A NEW COMMISSIONER—Lepître—who pities us. Because the harpsichord in the Tower is in such miserable condition that playing it only makes us sad, he has ordered a new one from an artisan I have always used in the past.

Lepître himself comes with the instrument, and we greet it and him with genuine expressions of gratitude. As I open the case, he exclaims, "What's this?" for it is a sheaf of music.

Reverently, I examine the sheets.

"It is one of Haydn's symphonies—from the mid-1780s," I remark, trying very hard to control my emotion.

"Which one?" our benefactor asks curiously.

I know that I will collapse as soon as I give the title, but I make myself speak steadily till the words are out. "It is my favorite, which the composer dedicated to me, *La Reine de France.*"

Lepître weeps with us.

Christmas Day, 1792

I am told that the King's trial begins tomorrow, and he is spending this sacred day writing his will. I am told that he refers to himself as Louis XVI, King of France, not as Louis Capet, and that the date is given in the Christian calendar, not the atheist revolutionary one. I am told that he advocates Christian forgiveness, and he expressly says to the Dauphin that if he should be so unfortunate as to become King, he should dedicate his entire life to his people's happiness; on no account should he seek revenge on his father's behalf.

So it is, the great and good Louis XVI tries to pave a safe road for his only son.

I am told by Cléry, who has memorized the language in his effort to serve as our conduit, that the King begs his wife's forgiveness! Mine! "For all the ills she has suffered for my sake and for any grief that I may have caused her in the course of our marriage and she may be certain that I hold nothing against her."

ROBESPIERRE, I hear from the crier beneath my window, asserts that Louis Capet's actions warrant his death. There is little need for a trial. Of all the leaders of the revolution, Robespierre is the most cruel and bloodthirsty.

Thomas Paine, a revolutionary hero of America, begs that Louis be exiled to that far country across the ocean.

Marat ridicules Paine for his Quaker softheartedness and automatic abhorrence of death as a punishment. *Oh, let the Quaker rule us all!*

Danton agrees with Marat: revolutions are made with blood, not rosewater. *Only a barbarous nation claims execution is justice.*

Philippe Égalité, the King's cousin, formerly called the Duc d'Orléans, votes for the death penalty.

From the criers standing under our windows on the pavement below, we hear the news. My husband is sentenced to death. Tomorrow, the execution by guillotine.

WE WILL SEE HIM to say good-bye, I assure the children and Elisabeth. We will tell him of our love for him. That is all that is left. And our bottomless sorrow.

And here is the King, standing before us, a huge man, his eyes full of sadness and regret. Immediately, he speaks to his son about the necessity of forgiveness of one's enemies. "I do not hate them, and you must never hate them."

He knows that he is beloved of his children, that his love for them is of the most tender and sincere kind. But I see he is suffering terribly at the necessity of leaving us. We cling together, all of us, and weep.

I beg that he spend this last night with us, but the King himself says that he needs to be alone to prepare his soul. There are promises to say good-bye again in the early morning, but we withhold nothing now of our love and our grief.

When morning breaks, someone arrives for a prayer book, but the King does not come to us again. We are told he is being taken in a closed carriage to the place of execution.

Very far away, very faintly, after waiting and praying, we hear drumming. It is half past ten in the morning of 20 January.

That shout, that awful joyful shout, so far away—it must mean the King is dead.

Elisabeth explodes with hatred. "The monsters! They are satisfied."

To the Conciergerie

25 January 1793

When my daughter cuts her foot by accident, the color of her blood is what calls me back to my senses. The crimson gash cries out with red lips that my daughter is yet alive and she needs my help. It is I who need to procure clean rags to bind it up, and it is I who must arrange for an appropriate physician.

I hear of the courage of Malesherbes, minister to both Louis XV and Louis XVI. He volunteered to defend my husband. The tribunal asked the aged minister from whence he drew the courage to serve Louis Capet. Malesherbes answered, "Contempt for you and contempt for death."

7 February 1793

Now my daughter's foot is almost well again. For some days she has been practicing the harpsichord in preparation for a little musical performance with her brother. I hear him humming from time to time, or softly singing in his sister's ear.

Since the death of the King, the guards watch us far less carefully. We are allowed to amuse ourselves and to speak softly with one another. Lepître has been allowed to write down some words for a song and to help our little King to memorize them. The concentration in his face as he reads the words almost makes me smile. Perhaps like his father, he will become the kind of reader who gives his soul to written words.

Because my daughter wants to surprise me, she practices the music only in short phrases, saving the composition as a whole for its performance. She has written out little invitations to our municipal guards to join us for a brief musicale today. The music is original, composed to fit Lepître's words by Madame Cléry, who is an accomplished amateur.

My daughter looks quite the young lady as she leads her brother out into the area around the harpsichord—their stage. We all clap our hands in greeting—Elisabeth and I, the municipal officers. My daughter seats herself on the little bench before the keyboard, and the little King stands in front of the instrument. She announces that they will sing a lament for the death of their father. My whole being swells with love for my family; it is almost as though we are all present. As the soloist, it is my son's privilege to nod to his accompanist that he is ready to begin. After her short keyboard introduction, played with aplomb, he opens his precious lips and sings in an angelic voice:

All joy is ended for me on this earth,
But I am yet beside my mother.

Nothing could be more affecting. Yes. Of course, I live for my children, who love me and who need me. Together, joining their feelings and talents, they seek to comfort me, and I must respond.

There is a second verse, sung to Elisabeth, whom they hail as a dear second mother.

How can these children have known how badly Elisabeth and I needed solace? The eyes of the guards are glazed with tears at the purity of the children, and so are those of myself and Elisabeth. With enthusiastic applause, we transform our sorrow into appreciation. We request an encore, and the little King sings his lament ever more confidently in his charming voice.

This night I keep the image of my children and the sound of their music alive in my consciousness till I fall asleep.

MY HEALTH IS NOT GOOD: when the Générale pays her visit at intervals of a mere three weeks, the bleeding is very extreme, and as a result, I see a shockingly pale face whenever I look into the mirror. The Pole Kucharski comes to make my portrait, in my black widow's dress, and he does not fail to represent me as pale as death. But my expression is serene, and I am grateful for that. I pray continually so that my soul will be at peace, no matter what shall come. My pious sister Elisabeth is a great help in leading me along the way of devotion.

I do not know what shall come, but it is possible I will be allowed to go back to Austria. In my original marriage contract, Count Mercy wrote in the stipulation that my location was to be my choice, should my husband die before me. Also, because revolutionary France is at war now with Prussia, with England, Spain, and Holland, they might wish to arrange for my release or for my ransom.

When Monsieur Moëlle, a member of the Paris Commune as well as a commissioner here at the former palace of the Knights Templar, escorts me to the top of the Tower to breathe the more healthy air there, I ask him what I might expect. Because my daughter is with us, I hesitate to ask so blunt a question, but the opportunity for frankness seems one that I should not allow to pass.

Monsieur Moëlle thinks I may be spoken for and claimed by my nephew, Francis II, now the new Emperor of Austria. He reassures me that further bloodshed (meaning my own execution—I was grateful for his circumlocution) would be considered "a gratuitous horror," which is against the precepts of the revolution. At this point, my daughter gives a little gasp of hope, and we cannot resist exchanging a reassuring glance. Ah, I remember how it was when she was born that I said she would become my friend!

THROUGH LETTERS to the brothers of my late husband, I try to form a connection, with the hope that they who are safely out of France will confer with foreign powers, led by the King of Sweden, for our release. When the

King rode to his death, he sent me his collection of hair from his family and also his wedding ring. He had managed to keep these precious items with him. I send the first of these sacred mementos to the Comte de Provence and the second to the Comte d'Artois. In a postscript, the children and Elisabeth also add their signatures and a few loving phrases.

Through my secretary, I send the briefest of notes to Count von Fersen with an impression of my seal and its motto, which means "All things lead me toward you." I can only hope that my message goes before me and that someday I shall be reunited with him.

In these quiet days, my thoughts turn often, especially when I listen to my daughter practice the harpsichord, to what Fersen has meant in my life. He has often been absent from me, in the physical sense, but he has always been present in the inner chambers of my soul. After he came back from the American War—partly because of our correspondence during this period—it became impossible for him to ever become fully absent from me again, no matter where he traveled. He has been the mirror, not of my soul, but of what has been best in me. He has been the reassuring reflection of all that I aspired to be. He has believed in my goodness, that I was not trivial, that I made every effort to add to the happiness of those around me. In the hard days, he saw that I had some capacity for courage, and, again, his belief in me made me fear nothing for myself, even when my anxiety for my family has been overwhelming. Still, within me was a calmness, a faith that I could never be violated—not in my essence, for it was known by this beloved and esteemed man.

I used to think that if Axel von Fersen held my hand on my deathbed that I would have no fear of the moment of death. His touch would ease even that passage. Now I know that I do not have actually to hold his hand. The thought of him and the perfection with which our souls fit together is enough, both now and at the hour of my death, howsoever it should come.

3 July

I worry for the health of my son. In May he had a persistent fever; in June he asked me to feel his groin, and there my fingertips found a swelling that thoroughly alarmed me. Upon summoning a physician, the diagnosis of a hernia was made, and an expert truss-maker was called in to fit the leather and steel harness to his small body. Also, the dear little King spoke of an accident with his hobbyhorse whereby he bruised a testicle.

At this news, I look at Elisabeth with some alarm, for we both have found the boy masturbating from time to time, and I fear that he may have done injury to himself that way, rather than in play. We have spoken to him firmly about not abusing his body, but I cannot believe that we have cured him of this habit. I wish that I could ask a man to speak to him about the body and its proper care.

But he is the dearest of children, and I feel confident that just as he outgrew his temper tantrums, he will also be able to practice self-control in other areas. Although I enjoy his fanciful imaginings, I am careful to try to train him in the difference between fancy and fact.

THOUGH IT IS NIGHT, and we are all tired, I suddenly hear a commotion on the stairs, steps of great determination and loud voices.

Through our door come a handful of commissioners, with a decree. In the candlelight and its dancing shadows, their faces quickly take on the distorted countenance of demons. They read that whereas there have been reports of possible plots to abduct the "young King," he is now to be removed from his family and taken up to the most secure compartment in the higher Tower.

Understanding everything, my little boy throws himself into my arms, in which I enclose him with a wild strength that I have never felt before.

"Never," I shout. "You shall never take him from me!"

He sobs and presses his face into my thin chest.

They demand, they threaten, but I am adamant. For an hour we display our wills and our steadfast determination.

"We shall kill you, if you do not release him. We shall cut off your arms at the shoulders, if we must."

"Never. Never!"

They are amazed at my power. They step back a little to whisper among themselves. Then one of them takes my daughter by her wrist while another announces, "We will kill this girl, if you do not release the boy to us."

Another says, "What we do is for his own safekeeping and protection. You must reassure him, instead of defying us."

"And we will kill the girl, if we must."

I look at my daughter and see no fear in her eyes. It is her courage, her fearlessness so like my own, that somehow convinces me. Whispering to Louis Charles, "They mean you no harm," I drop my arms to my sides. Quickly, he is pulled into their group.

"He is in his nightgown," Elisabeth says. "Allow us to dress him properly."

I have no strength left in my hands and arms with which to clothe my son. His sister and his aunt bring his clothing and help his arms into his shirt and his small legs into his pants. His sister kneels before him to place his shoes upon his feet.

As they lead him away, he does not scream but he sobs.

Far into the night, I listen to his sobs, for they echo throughout the stone tower. I send him all the love in my heart whispering over and over, "You are not alone," until finally his sobs subside into what must be blessed sleep.

NOW MY DAYS PASS entirely in trying to find positions from which I can catch a glimpse of my son as they take him into the courtyard for exercise. Sometimes I see him. How my heart runs toward him then, and I crucify myself, both hoping that he will glance my way and hoping that he does not, lest they take him farther away from me.

He is placed in the care of a rough cobbler, Simon. They say they must make him forget his rank. They teach him to swear. To please them, I can hear him saying vile things about his sister, his aunt, and me. He does not know what he is saying, but his keepers laugh with glee. Sometimes I stop up my ears with my fingers, but to do that is to deprive myself of the sound of his voice. *Mon chou d'amour.*

1 August

I have heard that subsequent to disastrous military defeats of the French, a member of the Committee of Public Safety raises this idea: the enemies of the nation have believed the French to be weak, and that false belief has given them the courage to achieve amazing victories in battle. Why have the enemies thought the French weak? Because the nation has an "over-long forgetfulness of the crimes of *L'Austrichienne,*" who, like her husband, must be brought before the bar of justice.

I HAD HOPED that they would not come for me at night, but it is the dead of night—two o'clock in the morning—when we are awakened. They allow me no privacy for changing into a dress, but watch me. I am allowed to take a few items with me, including a handkerchief. I gather these meager things with an outward calm, but my heart is crying for my children and for my dear sister, who must now try to care for them by herself.

In answer to my sister's urgent inquiry, they say that I am to be taken to the ancient prison called the Conciergerie, on the Île de la Cité, in the midst of the Seine river. I ask nothing. I feel nothing, but I will my numb hands and feet to do what they must do and to go where they must go in their little circuit around my chamber.

They allow little time to say farewell, but what opportunity I have I use to tell my daughter, my Marie Thérèse, to obey her aunt, to look upon her as a second mother, to help her brother. I recall the lines to his aunt of my son's song—when he sang a verse, accompanied by the harpsichord—but I do not refer to them. With the lips of my most tender love, I kiss them each farewell. I know that my sister will be a rock of strength and that she will instruct my daughter to open her heart to God. My little son—I dare not even think his name.

They lead me downstairs, and I strike my head, it seems.

"Are you injured?" someone asks.

In my mind, I hear the sound my skull must have just made against a low wooden beam, but I feel nothing.

"No," I reply to the guard's question. "Nothing can hurt me now."

WE LEAVE THE TOWER and begin to traverse the dark and silent Temple gardens to the palace. Those surrounding me carry guns, swords, and daggers, and I feel that I move inside a beast made of metal with many legs and arms. We pass into and through the palace, and I remember the dinner there before we were taken up into the Tower, when the Princesse de Lamballe was yet with me.

We pass into the street, where several hackney carriages wait along with a large group of soldiers. The city is utterly quiet, and the sounds of the carriage wheels, the hooves of the horses, and the boots of the soldiers on the cobblestones sound a somber cadence. The twin towers of the Cathédrale de Notre-Dame rise high above us, in their square, unfinished state, and I think of times when I have worshipped within that sanctuary and given thanks for my newborn children, how once I turned and saw the light streaming in the gigantic round window with a glory that made me want to fall on my knees again. The resplendent window serves as the manifest intermediary between God and man. Now we are at the bridge, and I recall that I used always to thrill at crossing a bridge—the slight danger that it might fall, the hope that one was crossing over into a newness of being.

Ah, over the bridge and rolling onto the Île de la Cité, where Paris was born, where barbarians congregated, protected from enemies by the arms of the Seine, whose waters are behind me and also ahead of me. On this island, the Roman soldiers of Caesar found the beginnings of the Frankish culture. I remember that other small island, that neutral place around which rushed the waters of the Rhine when I gave up my Austrian name and became French. *Maria Antonia—Antoine,* they called me, those who loved me. I have not thought of myself by my German name for very many years.

I have seen a most exquisite depiction of this place, this Conciergerie, in a facsimile of a medieval book once given me by the King, in the highly illuminated *Très Riches Heures du Duc de Berry.* Yes, I can picture that small and charming page and let it replace the blackness of this brutal night. The tiny painted building is proud, noble, and royal in its structure, but its setting is rustic. The peasants, wielding scythes, are making hay in the foreground, and women are raking the hay into tentlike shocks beside a stream where willows grow, for what surrounded the Conciergerie and is now the city of Paris was once a meadow. It is a lovely day, one of order and beauty. I too have known very rich hours—not of opulence but of the spirit.

Here among the jumbled Parisian buildings, we move forward in the dark of night, a secret from the city. Beyond the roofs, I make out the shape of the upper story of the Gothic Sainte-Chapelle, the jewel box. Once I saw it on a snowy night, the lights within shining out through the rich color of the windows onto the snow. Though it is summer, I shiver; it is the blackness itself that wraps me with chill air. I too am dressed in black, a widow.

We pass through wicker gates, where the turnkey waits. And suddenly, my forehead is bathed in sweat, and the oppression of the summer heat envelops me. Is it cold or hot? I scarcely know who I am.

"What is your name?" the registrar asks, and I can only reply, "Look at me," in the hope that he will recognize me and know who I am, though I have forgotten the words for myself.

I am prisoner #280.

Ah, my handkerchief is here to help me. I wipe my forehead. We move forward through the gates and corridors.

The Death of Marie Antoinette

Here is the end. My cell. The floor is brick, and I can smell the dampness coming up from the dark clay. Two chairs and a table wait for occupants. One chair is surely for me. I can imagine myself sitting here perhaps to read, or, if I am allowed needles and yarn, I might ply that art while sitting in one of those chairs; certainly, I will sit here to eat. I bless the chair, for I shall know it intimately. On the table is a cracked china basin where I shall wash my face. There is a cot with two mattresses on it, a lone pillow to elevate my head. The coverlet is of light weight, but we are in August now, the hottest month. Beside the bed is a bucket. Really, little more is needed.

Two women enter, the younger of them carrying a stool. Their faces are kind. Madame Richard of the more lined face introduces herself and tells me that she and Monsieur Richard are the concierges of the prison. The candlelight casts a warm glow on her somewhat worn face.

I glance at my gold watch. "I must apologize for the lateness of the hour," I say. "It's just now three o'clock in the morning. I know I have disturbed your rest."

The younger woman, holding the stool in her hands between us, looks exceedingly sleepy. Suddenly I realize her face is strikingly familiar. Where have I seen her before? "What is your name, my dear."

"Rosalie, Your Majesty." She and the stool make a slight curtsy. In her other hand, her candle bobs. *I* was to be known as *Rosalie* during our escape.

"Here," I say, "we will not speak of royalty. We live here in equality, though my freedom is perhaps more in doubt than yours." I smile reassuringly at her. "Please put down the stool, my child."

I see that a row of lace edges the pillowcase, which is clean and recently ironed.

"You have carefully prepared this room for me," I say to them. "What well-pressed lace."

Madame Richard replies, "I wanted you to see something—a little pretty, when you came in. We meant to be here to greet you. We heard you pass through the corridor."

"Madame Richard was awake and listening for you, but she let me sleep. She shook my arm just now and said, 'Hurry, hurry, wake up, Rosalie.'"

"And you brought your stool with you," I add. The girl is quite befuddled.

"Yes. I don't know why."

"I see a nail on the wall," I say. "If I stand on your stool, I will be just tall enough to reach it, and there I will hang my watch."

She places the stool next to the wall, and with as much agility as any girl could muster, I scamper up its rung and stand on the little pedestal. Still I must rise up on tiptoe to reach high enough, but the stool is steady, and there! There, my watch dangles from the nail against the wall. I come down, a bit more cautiously than I ascended.

"Well done, Madame," Madame Richard says and smiles at me.

I return the smile, and for a moment, the three of us regard one another. We feel very much contained in this space, defined as much by the presence of the furniture and of ourselves, as by the walls. Illumined in shifting patches and undulating strokes of candlelight, we are yet ourselves in spite of everything. I know that I am blessed in my keepers, one perhaps a few years younger than myself, the other really a very young woman. I am the matriarch of the group. "We should all retire to our beds," I say, and I immediately begin to unbutton my clothes.

"May I not assist you, Madame?" Rosalie asks in a clear, bell-like voice edged with fear.

"Thank you, my child. For some time now I have had no one with me to help with undressing or dressing. I do it myself. Here too I will look after myself."

They glance at each other, then Madame Richard nods, licks her thumb and forefinger, and pinches the wick of her candle. Rosalie follows suit, but before she leaves, she bends to turn back the coverlet of my bed. Madame Richard is already at the door. Standing between them, I can hear Rosalie mutter, "It is unworthy," but I do not know if Madame Richard hears her. As the wife of the current concierge of the prison, Madame Richard knows that to obey with alacrity is to show respect.

Soon enough, they both leave. Because they are heavily shod, the two women make a clatter when they move over the bricks. Clodhoppers, my mother would have called their shoes. Again, in the semidarkness—the dawn is beginning to gray the blackness—my fingers find my buttons, familiar little sentinels. I pray for my children and for Elisabeth, in the Tower, for they are now beyond my help.

SOON ENOUGH, I am awake again, for the Conciergerie is full of people coming and going. Lawyers, magistrates, prisoners—like so many ants they scurry around in this vast nest. The Revolutionary Tribunal itself is in this building, but at some distance. It is a place where, without doubt, I myself will be taken. This cell that I would call mine is only a holding pen.

As the days pass, many curious people are taken here to see me, for I, in my cage, am a spectacle for which they can charge admission. Still it is not a cage, but merely a brick-floored, stone-walled room with bars here and there instead of curtains. The King used to say that I always fell in love with my possessions, that I was grateful to them for their mere proximity, and though it takes some time, I find, ruefully, that I become rather fond of the things here. I like one of the chairs better than the other. Rosalie does not reclaim her stool, and while the guards sometimes find it convenient to sit there, I always identify the sturdy stool with Rosalie, even when she is not present, and with her kindness. Because there is no other piece of furniture like it in this cell, the stool seems somewhat enigmatic.

To pass the time with motion, I slide my diamond rings up and down my thin fingers.

I cannot recall where I have seen Rosalie before, though the impression persists. Except for the guards, we are all women here, awaiting our trials. A barred window looks out on a paved courtyard, and sometimes I watch the women walking there for exercise.

At first, they seem remote to me, but the second afternoon a woman who is a nun kneels before this window and stretches her arms toward it. I step back in surprise. Then I realize she has heard who prisoner #280 is, and she is praying for me. I step closer to the window, so she can see my features beyond the bars.

What I like most to see is the patch of sky that hovers like a blue lid above the courtyard. The sky has always seemed the boundary of our world to me, even when it covered my gardens around the Trianon. I remember those flowers with great fondness. Sometimes I imagine myself walking those paths in various months of the year, for I know that each month had its mood, expressed in particular flowers.

Assisted by Rosalie, the Richards serve my meals, breakfast at nine, dinner a bit after two o'clock. At first the girl stays shyly by the door, but I call to her, "Come on in, Rosalie. Don't be afraid."

With great fascination she watches me use my knife to separate the meat of the baked chicken from its bone. At one point, almost in spite of herself, she murmurs, "You must have practiced many hours and very often to do it so well," as though eating daintily were the necessary hallmark of royalty.

Suddenly, I hear the sound of harp music, and my hands freeze in the air, holding the silver knife and fork.

"What is it, Madame? What is the matter?" Rosalie asks.

"Does one of the prisoners play the harp?" I reply.

"It is the daughter of the glazier. She plays for her father while he works, replacing broken glass in the windows."

"I have spent many hours with my harp," I tell her. "It was always a good friend to me. I always leaned it close to me with great affection, my fingers eager to pluck its strings."

"I think that angels in heaven often play the harp," Rosalie says.

"There are many depictions of them with harps," I reply. "Or blowing trumpets."

"If you like books," the girl says, "I know where some are."

Because she is so eager, I reply with all graciousness, "I should very much like to read some books."

When she smiles at me, her face becomes the most youthfully beautiful face I have ever seen.

FROM BEYOND these thick walls, a package arrives, and in it a white dress, several chemises, more handkerchiefs, black silk stockings, a petticoat made from cotton of India, and for my shoulders two fichus, one of crepe and one of muslin, and ribbons—ribbons to tie back my thin, white hair. All of this has been folded and wrapped so lovingly that I exclaim, "I detect the hand of my sister Elisabeth in this kind work."

Now I have a few possessions, a wardrobe, and each item is treasured. They can be combined in countless ways.

"I believe that I could dress Madame's hair now," Rosalie says. "People say I have a hand with hair." Indeed, her own chestnut hair is arranged differently every day, sometimes parted here, sometimes there, sometimes hanging loosely, sometimes tied back with a short scarf.

"I would be most grateful," I reply. "Do you suppose," I ask Madame Richard, "that I could have a box to keep my things in?"

Madame Richard regretfully bows her head. "I dare not, Madame. They would think I favored you in a special way that would be dangerous to us both."

"I have a cardboard box," Rosalie says. "Might I have permission to bring it here?"

Keeping her eyes on the floor, Madame Richard mumbles, "Yes."

One of the guards says, "I could remove the rust from the heels of your shoes, Madame, with my knife."

Without hesitation I sit on the edge of my bed and hand him first one and then the other of my plum-colored slippers. A sort of brown moss has grown up from the damp floor to coat the little scooped heels, but he carefully scrapes them clean for me again, and their graceful curve emerges from what had become an unsightly clump under my foot.

In return, I give him my sincere thanks and bow my head.

The good gendarme is so moved that he must leave the cell to hide his tears.

That night, waiting for sleep, I picture Elisabeth, how she has gathered ribbons and yarn for me. I wonder how my children are passing the time since I have been away, and I ache to think of their concern for me. "I am all right," I whisper. "There are many reasons to hope."

I hardly notice anymore the crowds of people who pay admission to gawk at me. Perhaps captive animals do not see beyond the grilles of their menageries.

ONE EVENING ROSALIE startles me. She is standing in the very dim light near the door, watching me, but the light catches only her skirt, how it hangs in folds, and though it is a very plain skirt, the way it drapes reminds me of the curtains hanging beside the windows of the château at Versailles. Fearing mental displacement, I jump at the moment of mistaken recognition.

"Please pardon me," Rosalie says in her sweetest, clearest voice, soft as a vesper bell. "I have brought you some tea with herbs in it. For your nerves, so that you can sleep better."

My guard is asleep. Noiselessly, she crosses the floor, and I see that she is in her bare feet on the clammy stones. Quickly, I drink the tea and hand her back the cup, indicating with my eyes that she is to leave as rapidly as possible, taking the saucerless cup. In handing the cup to her, its last drop splashes onto the brick floor.

She smiles at me, and even in the dark, I can see how her face is shining.

She is gone.

Then tears come to my eyes. I stoop and with a swoop of my index finger wipe up that drop, lest its presence in some way signal an unsanctioned visitation.

Ah yes, there are many lessons learned at the Conciergerie, this one of the overwhelming beauty of simple goodness. It is not the deeds themselves but the spirit in which they are done—the slightest glance of understanding—that comforts me. How is it that she, a simple girl, understands so perfectly how I feel and how to offer companionship?

I return to my bed, opposite the window, so I can lie looking at the window, though now it is only a black square. The taste and temperature of the warm tea linger in my mouth.

With her presence, Rosalie makes of the moment something less lonely. I remember how it was when I was a child, after Charlotte left Austria to be married, a girl named Lynn was brought to play with me. Simply to see her made me glad. And Fersen, the friend of my heart. Yes, this Rosalie, little Lynn, and he—the quality of their attention, that is what distinguishes them, no matter the occasion.

Then I remember one night, how the draperies at the château moved, and a young girl had stepped out from their folds. The way Rosalie's skirt swayed reminded me of that movement, and yes, Rosalie somewhat resembles that girl, though Rosalie is younger than that maid could be now. Yet, in the eyes of both these girls there is a haunting, a knowledge of human vulnerability and our need, regardless of our station.

THROUGHOUT THE USELESS DAYS, my memory is full of places and the dear people who were once with me are recalled to inhabit those places. I remember the lattice-surrounded fountain of the fallen Titan Enceladus and of course the bosquets of Ceres and her daughter Flora. I think of my little bedroom in the Trianon, where the cornflowers are embroidered into the white wool that upholsters the chairs. I recall my daybed in the room called the Méridienne, in my private chamber deep within the château, and the mirror that covers the wall beside the little bed. I remember the Bernini bust of Louis XIV, and how I stood before it with Papa-Roi, Louis XV, when I was not yet fifteen. I remember lying in my wedding bed, holding the hand of the young Dauphin, and how we galloped on horseback during the hunt, leaping the ditches in graceful arcs. I remember my mother, always at her desk, always working. I never don my black dress without thinking of her, and her good round face. And sometimes I dream of dancing, to her delight, on the stage, dressed as a shepherdess. I am so slender and lithe my feet barely skim the boards of the stage. Always I am aware as I dance of how the great velvet curtains, like rivers, stream down at the sides of the stage.

In the first week of incarceration, I tried not to picture such scenes or my loved ones—their absence made me too sad, even imagining their clothing broke my heart—but now I do not try to discipline my memory. I invite all who come to mind. Even my old enemy, the lovely Madame du Barry, and I recall how taken I myself was by her appearance when I first saw her and did not know of her relationship to the King. I wanted to know her. In some ways, I wanted to be her, with her beautiful bust, instead of myself with my skinny chest as straight as a shield. In some ways, perhaps, the Princesse de Lamballe, also blond, was a replacement for the du Barry, though not so fetching and a great deal more wholesome and pure.

HERE, BY THE MONTH of September, I have established the reign of courtesy, and both the Richards, husband and wife, treat me with as much consideration as they dare. Rosalie extends a degree of affection which the Richards tacitly sanction by ignoring or casting their eyes discreetly elsewhere when the young woman's face is lit by pity or love.

All of them together conspire to bring me a priest of the old type, whose allegiance is to Rome and not the republic, and I receive much comfort from confession and communion. I learn that the wars are not going well for France, and the priest holds out some hope that the republic will be crushed and the old regime reinstated. I do not think that the foreign armies will reach me in time, and if they do arrive at the gates of Paris, I will be promptly butchered—still my only hope is for foreign rescue, and I know for this cause Fersen is working night and day.

I whisper, "Father, is it not ironic that in my greatest hope also lies my greatest danger?"

"The human condition is defined by irony," he murmurs. "From that prison, there is no escape except through faith in the ultimate goodness of God."

He tells me the Comtesse du Barry was arrested over the summer, denounced by Zamore, her former page. Because she received, however, the unanimous support of the inhabitants of Louveciennes, the Committee for General Safety exonerated her, saying, "There is no accusation that can be made legitimately against the citizeness du Barry."

For a moment I think bitterly that even now she is better loved than I was, but that thought is sweetened by another: her essential goodness and beauty have inspired the magistrates to practice justice.

SEEING HOW MUCH good this visit has done me, all of them together again conspire to let Hüe, who was once my son's valet, visit me.

"You appear to me more glorious than the angel Raphael," I tell him.

"I come to speak of your children," he says quickly, lest he be snatched away before his precious words can be uttered. "They are well. Madame Elisabeth cares for your daughter as though she were her own mother. And the little King—oh, he is very clever; he knows how to fool his jailers and make them think that he is one of them. But once or twice his sister exchanged a glance with him, and she declared that he is not at all changed, not in his loving heart, only a little taller now and very quick in his movements."

I watch the happiness in his eyes, his gladness to see me, his joy that we can speak together of those we love. He never runs out of scenes but describes one after another—what they were wearing, their very words, the quality of their glances—till Madame Richard finally says that to her regret the safe time for a visit is passing.

Immediately, I rise from my chair. "Go at once, with all my blessings and love." I fight back my emotion. I curtsy low, low to him and gain control of my features in that moment of bowing. When I rise, there is only a blankness where he stood. But he was real.

My children are alive. They live!

A FEW HOURS after he has left, Rosalie comes to me with a cup of the soothing herbal tea. Under the cup is a saucer decorated with a painted rose.

"Monsieur Hüe wished to speak only of your dear family while he was here. But as I took him to the wicker gate, he whispered another story, a frightful one, to me."

"Whom does the story concern?" I ask her.

"The Comtesse du Barry." She bows her head as she pronounces her name so as to avoid, most tactfully, whatever expression may cross my face.

"I think of her from time to time. I have come to wish her well."

Taking my reply as encouragement, Rosalie tells me that the lover of Madame du Barry, the Duc de Brissac, was massacred as he was taken from one jail to another. Within an hour, the mob had carried his head on a pike to Louveciennes. They broke a window and threw his head inside, to land at the feet of Madame du Barry.

Now my teacup chatters on its saucer, and I squeeze my eyelids shut with all my might so that the guards will not know by my tears that I have received the most distressing news. In my mind, I turn to God, thanking Him for sparing me the sight of the severed head of my dearest and most loyal friend, the Princesse de Lamballe.

That night I lie on my cot unable to sleep. If I could, I would fold the du Barry into my arms with every tenderness. In the dark I seek the scenes of friendship in my memory. Again and again, I picture myself chatting behind our fans with Yolande de Polignac, exchanging a knowing glance over the gaming tables with the Duchess of Devonshire, sitting among the mythic fountains of Versailles with the Princesse de Lamballe. Finally, when the square of my cell window begins to pinken, I recall that dawn when the princess sat with me on the grass and watched the glory of the sunrise. No clouds of rose and gold appear this dawn, but I remember their astonishing beauty.

I think of my children, then, and the stories that Hüe told that made me picture them anew.

ONE DAY WHEN both guards are so bored with their game that they fall asleep with fans of cards in their hands, Madame Richard comes to me and sits down at the table.

"What do you knit?" she asks.

"A pair of stockings with a rosy ladder up the side. They are for you."

She is overcome, presses her fingers against her throat. "My stockings have always been plain," she replies. She lifts her skirt and thrusts out a black leg.

I nod and continue the work of my fingers.

"Once I heard a story," she says. "Perhaps it was a fairy tale, not really about you and the King at all."

"A story?"

"A pretty story."

"Then I would like to hear it."

"In your old country, where there were mountains, you loved to ride sleds?"

"Yes," I say, "and to go sleigh riding behind a swift horse. The King and I enjoyed sleigh riding here many times."

"But one time, it being summer, there was no snow, but you wanted to go sleigh riding. You confided so, to the King, one hot evening.

"In the night, he had the street of your little play village covered with sugar, and when you woke up you looked out, and all was sparkling white. Your windowsill was heaped with it.

"You kissed the King and said, 'With your magic wand, you have made snow in July!'

"He said, 'Your sleigh awaits.'

"You looked out and there it was, snow piled everywhere, and a white horse bedecked with silver bells. You ran out and climbed in and put a red robe trimmed in ermine fur around your shoulders, and with the King beside you, holding the reins, you took a sleigh ride, as though it were frosty winter.

"Is it true?"

"Perhaps not in every part," I say, because I can see the pleasure she takes in imagining the pictures.

"Is it true that you were loved—so splendidly?"

Suddenly I see the image of Fersen, sitting on the high box of the berlin, with the straps of leather, the reins, hanging loosely in his gloved hands. And I envision the King beside him, ready to play the role of coachman for my sake.

"Yes," I say. "I was loved so splendidly."

AMID A CROWD of the usual sightseers, here is someone I know, carrying two red carnations: Alexandre de Rougeville. He drops the flowers at my feet. Immediately I bend to pick them up. I turn my back for a moment on this crowd of visitors, my fingers seeking and finding a tiny note, and in a flash it is read. *Escape?* it reads.

In a terrifying moment, these people visiting my cell coincidentally begin to discuss how attempts at organizing my escape have been hatched by people outside, plans of which I have known nothing. The Wigmakers, I learn from this casual chatter, formulated a plan, and the former pastry cooks at the château tried to join the plot before it was discovered. The terrible danger such people are in fills me with horror. I pluck a pin from my dress and try, with shaking hand to prick out *Non* onto the scrap of paper, but someone not in on the plan calls attention to my unfinished pricking. A guard is called, then two or three; hurriedly the visitors leave while I conceal the note in my sleeve.

When I see that Rougeville has escaped, I say yes there was a note but I have dropped it. All of us together get on the floor and look for it. I find it only when enough time has passed for the visitors to have reached the outside. Bearing away the little note (*Escape?* with a few holes pricked in it: *No*), the guards stomp away. There is great menace in their determined feet, but I try to calm myself.

Holding the pretty red flowers with their fringy petals in my hands, I say, "I once had a passion for such flowers." Without saying a word, the brave Rosalie improvises a vase for them from a brown jug.

The Carnation Plot is not without repercussions, for that night they come to interrogate me in my cell. They leave, only to come again, determined to squeeze some truth from my words.

I am questioned for sixteen hours, but a lovely calm has come upon me. I no longer fear that I will make mistakes or say something stupid or dangerous. Within this calm, I find that I am quite as intelligent and cunning as the lawyers. I have practiced tact all my life; now I use it to confound them.

They want to know if I take an interest in the military victories of the enemies of France.

After glancing around the walls of this impenetrable cell, I reply that my only interest is in the success of the nation to which my son belongs.

"And to which nation does he give allegiance?"

"Isn't he French?" I reply, as though puzzled.

Surrounding me, they have the faces of wolves. But I do not falter. I will not fall. I think of the words of the brave Princesse de Lamballe: *It matters little to me whether I die now or later, for it is the fate of all of us to die.*

"When you were in the Tower, after the execution of the King, did you not give your son, who bore the empty title of king, a special place at the head of the table—eh, Madame? And special privileges to instill in him the idea of his innate superiority?"

"My only desire is to see France powerful and happy," I reply.

"You cannot deny that you wish to see a king on the throne of France."

"If France is content to have a king, I would like that king to be my son, but I am just as happy, as is he, if France is content to be without a king."

"Can you deny that you support the enemies of France through your emissaries and by secret communications?"

"I regard as my enemies any who would bring harm to my children."

"What do you mean by harm? What do you regard as harmful, Madame?" His voice is sharp as a razor.

I blunt my reply. I repeat myself. "Any kind of harm . . . Whatever might be harmful."

My words meander vaguely. Yes, I have been trained to act a role. My mind is as keen as his, and, fundamentally, I have truth on my side, for I have always desired the happiness of France.

ALAS, THE GOOD Richards are arrested!

My diamond rings and the golden watch that hung on its nail like a lucky charm are taken away. That night I cannot control my sobs. I cry into my pillow like the girl I was when the watch first came into my hands, from the hands of my mother. I position Rosalie's stool beside my bed and pretend it is that sympathetic girl.

With my thumb I stroke the blank finger where I wore my loose rings, as I lie in bed. They would gladly have *stripped* them from my fingers. "Wait," I commanded. Then I took the rings off myself and placed them into the outstretched palm of the guard. I noticed the palm was yellow and calloused with work, as though it were turning into some hornlike substance. He closed his big fingers over my little silver circles.

Today, Monsieur Bault, the new concierge, takes away the stool.

13 October

Two lawyers appear in my cell. They have only been appointed recently, and they wish me to write, asking for an extension of time so that they may prepare my defense.

"When is my trial to commence?" I inquire.

"Tomorrow," they say in duet, with expressions of the most extreme anxiety and urgency defining their faces.

"I do not wish to ask them for any mercy or consideration," I reply. "They have no authority either to judge me or to respond to my petition."

Monsieur Chauveau-Lagarde says that he wishes to preserve my life. "For your own sake, Madame, of course, but even more so that your children will not be left motherless."

I look at this man more carefully. His hair is pulled back from his keen, birdlike face. He is fearless. I see something of myself in him. "You are willing to defend a helpless woman?"

"I have defended Charlotte Corday, tried for the murder of Marat, as he sat in his bathtub."

"Marat the extremist is killed?" Marat spoke against the proposal that we should be exiled in America.

"As he sat in his tub," the other lawyer adds. His name is Tronson Doucoudray.

"And what was her fate—Charlotte Corday?" When I try to imagine her, I see Jeanne d'Arc.

Chauveau-Lagarde does not answer, but Tronson Doucoudray says, with intentional irony, "She met the swift, humane death offered by the guillotine."

"You are brave men to agree to defend me."

Now Chauveau-Lagarde smiles. "Not so very brave. As I passed through the wicket-gates and through the labyrinth of corridors, I felt I was descending into hell. My knees trembled. But we must make this effort, Madame, for your children."

"For the sanity of France," his partner adds.

"For your children," Chauveau-Lagarde reiterates. "We defend in your person, the widow of Louis XVI, the mother of the King's children."

I pick up my pen and ask for three days' delay, so that the numerous documents pertinent to my situation may be examined by those appointed to conduct my defense. With wan satisfaction, the three of us smile at the reasonableness of our request.

Before they leave, my lawyers regretfully prepare me for the fact that my son's keepers have extracted from him statements resulting in documents claiming that I and his aunt caused him to lie between us in bed and to have intercourse with us of a sexual nature.

"There are documents from interviews with his sister and from his aunt contradicting the charges."

"The villains have trumped up this charge in its entirety," I say boldly, but my heart is stricken. How they must have manipulated my son to make him say such things. How they have sullied him and stolen away his innocence.

They wish to try me not as a human being, but as a monster. In their filthy pamphlets I have been depicted that way: a harpy wearing my face, a devil woman with talons of steel.

THE PETITION for postponement is ignored, and today, 14 October, the guards come to conduct me to a far part of this enormous fortress, where I am to be tried before the tribunal of the National Convention.

As I walk the corridors to their court, my resolve is only to preserve my dignity. How strange it is to move one foot in front of the other. In a few days, I have no doubt, these feet will have no life in them, and I will lie under the earth. Such ideas lack vividness in my mind, yet I believe them to be true. Only my shoes are vivid, their plum-colored toes occasionally emerging from under the hem of my black dress, appropriate for a widow, as I walk through the hallway.

Sometimes I feel the blood of my womanhood gush from my body, but Rosalie has tied me up into cloths very securely in that region, using her own chemises for the purpose. How strange it was to stand before her, her gentle fingers sometimes brushing my old flesh, making me as secure as possible.

When I enter their court, I lift my head, for I am the daughter of Maria Theresa, Empress of Austria, and the mother of Marie Thérèse, the dearest girl in Christendom, my friend. And I am the friend of Rosalie, who has come to be my hidden daughter. It is I who represent the seamstresses, laundresses, and painters, the mothers and sisters of France, and not these rabid men. I look the man named Robespierre in the eye. Just once, I will show him my spirit. After this glance, he is beneath my regard.

There are some forty witnesses to be called, and my lawyers whisper that we will not finish today. Ah, I am to live an extra day. It does not matter to me.

I am sworn in as Marie Antoinette of Lorraine and Austria, widow of the King of France, born in Vienna, age almost thirty-eight, but I am always referred to in their discourse as the Woman Capet.

It matters little to me. I make the shortest possible replies to their preposterous accusations: that I sent great sums of money to my brother Joseph II through the Polignacs, that I manipulated the King and gave him evil counsel, that I plotted to have the representatives of the people murdered with bayonets, that I made the guards drunk with wine, that I have slept with my young son.

All witnesses against me lie. All is hearsay. They produce no documents, only assert that they could do so. From time to time I see that my hands are moving over the table as though they were playing the harpsichord. I do not know exactly what notes I finger. I think it is a piece of that form called a fantasia, one that is by its nature formless. It follows the thoughts of the composer as they float along, like clouds in a reverie.

I once heard such a piece for pianoforte, composed by Mozart, whom I knew as a child, but he has been dead several years. They say he died a pauper, of neglect. And yet I am sure he had talent. He was a glittering child. As I have done throughout my life, I recall the child's question. "Now do you love me?" he asked my mother, sitting in her lap.

Suddenly I think of the immense talent of my friend the painter Elisabeth Vigée-Lebrun. With all my heart, I hope she and her brushes have escaped this tiger nation.

From my lawyers I have learned that the du Barry was denounced again by a fellow servant of the little Nubian page, now grown up and become her footman. They coveted her wealth. Like myself, she is imprisoned and may await that swift and humane death invented by the enlightened French. But the lawyers know nothing of my friend the painter.

I believe that the court will finish with all the witnesses today. Perhaps I shall be marched straight to the guillotine, but no, there is to be a second day among them. For me, it is all one. Not so important as to be an ordeal, this event leaves me greatly fatigued, and I have bled so much that I fear the back of my dress may be besmirched.

THIS NIGHT, ROSALIE comes to me. She brings fresh cloths and takes the soiled ones away to wash. "I will heat the flatiron and iron them till they are dry," she whispers. "Now try to eat a bit." She mothers me.

The second day is much the same till they circle back to the question of my son.

"Citizen President," one of the jurors insists, "I ask you to request of the accused that she respond to the facts concerning what occurred between her and her son."

I am roused. I stand. My royal composure leaves me, and I speak with all the ardor of my outrage. "If I have not replied, it is because Nature itself refuses to respond to such a charge against a mother." The courtroom stirs in response. Some women, the market women, cry out that this proceeding is unfair, that the court is an insult to all women, that the trial must be stopped.

"I appeal to all mothers who may be present," I add, and then I sit down.

The murmurs subside. The market women are too curious to see what will happen next; they wish to be entertained. Today it is not their mood to change the course of human events.

Close to panting, I try to subdue my impulse to gulp the air. Chauveau-Lagarde puts his hand over mine in a kindly fashion. It is finished.

"Did I do well?" I ask him. I am flushed with the success of my appeal, how I have admitted nothing.

"Madame, be yourself and you will always be perfect," he replies.

THERE IS A BREAK in the proceedings. I see Rosalie approaching, bearing no doubt some of the consommé of which she is so proud. A wife of one of the jurors stands in the girl's way and insists that she will be the one to serve the deposed Queen of France. She is a careless woman, and I watch her spill a good deal of the soup onto the shoulder of another woman.

I have eaten nothing since morning.

It does not matter.

Yes, there is a little left, and I spoon it to my mouth, seeking the eyes of Rosalie, to thank her only with a steadfast gaze. Nothing in my public expression can ever be construed as cause for her arrest.

When I am asked if I wish to speak before the jury retires, I stand and say very simply, "No one has substantiated any claim against me. I conclude by remarking that I was the wife of Louis XVI. It was always my duty to obey him and to submit to his will."

Chauveau-Lagarde reminds the jury that I was never mentioned during the trial of Louis XVI as having influenced the King in any way. He has a graceful silver tongue with all the strength of iron. Then he argues against the charge that I conspired with foreign powers. There has been no proof. Chauveau-Lagarde speaks not only with conviction, but with ardor. Doucoudray argues that I have not conspired with enemies of the state within its borders. There has been no proof of conspiracies on my part, only empty allegations, he insists.

When they have finished, I thank them with utmost warmth and gratitude. To my brave defenders I say, "Your elegance and honesty manifest themselves in every syllable. Forgive me, my own words are inadequate ever to thank you sufficiently." Looking into Chauveau-Lagarde's sympathetic eyes, I say, "Please know the inexpressible gratitude that I will feel to you, even until my last moments."

The man blushes, and bows. He has said all that he can say.

I wait an hour. I imagine that I will be deported, for it is my due. I hope for that outcome, but I do not have faith in their justice.

They summon me now.

The verdict is that I am guilty of high treason and sentenced to death.

I feel nothing. I feel my chin tilt up—ah, yes, the royal habit. I am pleased that my body remembers the gestures typical of my life.

IN MY CELL, I am given pen and paper and I write to Madame Elisabeth:

> *I have been sentenced, not to a shameful death, for it is shameful only for criminals, but to join your brother. Innocent like him, I hope to show the firmness he showed in these last moments.*
>
> *I deeply regret having to abandon my poor children. You know that I lived only for them and for you, my good and loving sister.*

For a moment, I think of Elisabeth as a small child, coming to help me unpack the great coffin of wedding jewels, how she handed me a pink rose. I loved her then, and I love her now. She has truly become my sister.

You who have out of friendship sacrificed everything to be with us in all our troubles....

May my son never forget his father's last words, which I expressly repeat, that he is never to avenge our deaths. In regard to the great distress this child must have caused you, forgive him, my dear sister. Remember his age and how easy it is to make a child of only eight years say anything, even things he does not understand....

I die in the Catholic, Apostolic and Roman religion, the religion of my fathers, the one in which I was brought up and which I have always professed....

I forgive all my enemies the harm they have done me. I here bid farewell to my aunts and to all my brothers and sisters, my companions of many years.

I had friends. The thought of being separated from them forever and their sorrow is among my greatest regrets in dying; may they know, at least, that I thought of them up to the very last.

Farewell! Farewell.

Now I lie in bed and think of my life here in the Conciergerie. In its own way, it was a new beginning, bereft as I was of all those whom I loved and for whom all my efforts were made—my family. As a single soul, I have had to become acquainted with my starkest self. And yet I lived, though I suffered deeply. I saw the birth of some new affections. I explored the world of memory, that strange realm where nothing is real but thinking makes it seem so. I never imagined a future. I wish that I had tried to do so.

I wish that I had laid aside my youthful self-righteousness and been kinder to the Comtesse du Barry. I wish her peace. I wish that I had chosen to have less so that the people of France might have had more. I wish them happiness.

With my fingertips, I touch my own body. I am telling it good-bye—the protuberances of my wrist bones, my curving ribs. I touch an ear and feel the mobile cartilage within that gives it shape. I tug on the lobe of my ear. Finally, I place one hand on my head and the other on my body. My head is to be severed from my body tomorrow. I touch my throat, and then my fingers seek for vertebrae in the back of the neck. It is here that the blade will fall. It will have no difficulty, falling as it does from a height, parting this column of small bones. Will I think a last thought, perhaps even as the blood drains from my brain? If I must, I will. If not, then a blankness, perhaps a bit like this blank moment.

A bell tolls. I am yet in this world. I move my feet, flex my toes. I am cold, but they said I could not have an extra blanket. I pray, but always there is a numbness. I can will myself to go through certain motions—holding up my face, looking at the sky, watching for dawn. I cannot will myself to feel. It is better not to feel the pain of separation from those I hold so dear. It is true: here I have come to know myself in a way I have not done before.

Rosalie is here.

Reaching into my cardboard box, she tells me that they will not allow me to go to the scaffold in my widow's black, lest it stir the sympathy of the populace. She helps me change into the white dress, and she tries to stand between me and the guards, whom I would not like to see either my nakedness nor my bloody cloths. I speak to the young man, as gently as I can, for he is too young to have learned much about the need for gentleness among human beings.

"In the name of decency, monsieur, allow me to change my undergarments without witnesses."

"I cannot give my consent for your privacy," he answers.

Rosalie shields me, as she helps me. My new chemise is the white piqué, with a mild waffle texture. In the dark, I have already kissed Rosalie goodbye, explaining that I must not do so in front of our jailers, lest she, like the Richards, should be arrested for excess sympathy.

I told her also, to kiss me, as a daughter would.

"And again," I say, "as a son would do. You are their proxy, but I love you, too, for your own dear self."

Between us, we contrive to stuff my bloody cloths into a crevice in the stone wall beside my bed.

I hear bells toll perhaps ten times. It is morning, and they crowd in, to read to me again the indictment, and that occupies its time and is over.

Here is the executioner, saying, "Hold out your hands."

"Must my hands be bound?" Hopefully, I remind them, "The hands of Louis XVI were not bound."

Executioner Sanson hesitates.

"Do your duty," the judges say, and with ostentatious roughness, he obeys.

He removes my little bonnet to shear my hair. The blade passes against the nape of my neck, and in a single grainy slice, my hair is gone. I raise my head and have an odd urge to smile. There is that strange lightness one always feels after her hair is cut.

In the courtyard waits the small cart with two large wooden wheels. It is an open cart, and no one who loves me is to ride with me. They order me to sit with my back to the horses, but before I turn around, I notice their powerful tan haunches. They are draft horses, very heavily muscled. I have always admired the huge haunches of such horses. I will be a light burden for them.

When they start to move forward over the courtyard, I am jolted off balance and almost fall from my bench. Because my hands are bound behind me, I must sit on the edge of the plank, and I cannot steady myself with my hands, but I quickly extend a foot and regain my balance and my upright posture. I glance down at my plum shoes. They have lasted well, and I have always liked their shape and color, battered now though they are.

For a moment, I wonder what cobbler's hand fashioned my shoes, little suspecting that I would wear them now. I smile a little at the whimsy of my thought.

I know that we move very slowly through a great throng of people, through the streets of Paris. What a crowd that day at Versailles when Montgolfier's balloon ascended! That day, a sheep was made to fly. Montauciel did rise to the heavens. I hear the jeers and cries of derision, but my eyes and my ears are turned inward. Let them see a sacrificial lamb on its way to slaughter. Now is the time to think of those I have loved. Now is the time to meditate on God's love for me and my faith in his mercy.

There it stands, in the center of the vast circle now known as the Place de la Révolution . . . crowded with soldiers and spectators: their guillotine is a framework like an open door, with the shiny blade overhead. Is light more silvery or gold? It is misty today, and no sunshine gleams off the blade.

All my body feels full of air. I seem to weigh nothing, and I move with great ease, almost as though I were dancing. I step down the little stair placed at the end of the cart. My balance is sure, and I forget that my hands are bound. I do not need them. Weightless, I mount the scaffold stairs. But on the platform, I tread upon a fleshy lump. I have stepped on the toe of Sanson, the executioner. Quickly, I beg pardon.

"I did not do it on purpose," I say with simple sincerity.

One of their priests sanctioned by the revolution speaks to me, but I have not and will not turn to him for consolation. "This is the moment, Madame, to arm yourself with courage."

Ah, he does not know my mother armed me with courage when I was a child at her knee. Thousands of eyes regard me.

"Courage!" I exclaim. "The moment when my ills are going to end is not the moment when courage is going to fail me."

I kneel in order to lie upon their board, and they help my body to lie straight. So lay my noble husband nine months ago; I but follow. Through a crack between the planks—a man squats beneath on the balls of his feet. He has the dirty, upturned face of madness. Ah, he is waiting to bathe in my blood. I meet his wild eye. The sled slides forward—the basket—no need to hold on—I open my hands resting on the small of my back—the basket—I had friends, loving friends (I am not afraid)

Afterword

For readers interested in the historical fates of those dear to the heart of Marie Antoinette, perhaps a few facts will suffice. Her young son Louis Charles (Louis XVII) died in prison on 8 June 1795, probably of tuberculosis, as had his older brother Louis Joseph. Her daughter Marie Thérèse was released from prison in an exchange of prisoners with Austria in 1795, when she was seventeen. She eventually married her cousin, the Duc d'Angoulême, the son of Artois. The unhappy marriage was not consummated, and she died in 1851, at the age of seventy-three.

Both of the ambitious brothers of Louis XVI became kings of France. The Comte de Provence became Louis XVIII in 1814 and died in 1824. The Comte d'Artois became Charles X and abdicated in 1830.

Tried on trumped-up charges as a British spy, the Comtesse du Barry was executed during the Terror, December 1793. Like Marie Antoinette, she was conveyed in a cart to the Place de la Révolution. In spite of her sobs, pleas, and resistance, she was carried up the steps to the guillotine.

Count Axel von Fersen died 20 June 1810, torn apart by an angry Swedish mob who believed he had poisoned the heir to the Swedish throne, Christian.

By abandoning her belongings and disguising herself and her young daughter, Julie, as commoners, Elisabeth Vigée-Lebrun, Marie Antoinette's friend and portrait painter, escaped the French Revolution. Resuming her work as an artist, Vigée-Lebrun traveled throughout Europe and reestablished herself as a painter in Turin, Florence, Rome, Vienna, St. Petersburg (where she painted Catherine II), Berlin, and London, eventually returning to Paris and settling in a pleasant home in Louveciennes, where she lived until she was almost eighty-seven.

Acknowledgments

The friendship, encouragement, and guiding wisdom of both Joy Harris, my literary agent, and Marjorie Braman, my editor, make possible my work as a writer.

Abundance, A Novel of Marie Antoinette is dedicated to my daughter Flora, who has given me much joy and inspiration. John C. Morrison, my husband, translated material concerning Axel von Fersen from the Swedish; both John and Flora continually supported me with their loving encouragement throughout the writing of this novel. To my family and friends who traveled with me on research trips to France, Austria, and Sweden, I owe a happy debt of gratitude: John Morrison, Flora Naslund, Amanda Jeter, John Sims Jeter, Derelene Jeter, Lynn Greenberg, Nancy Brooks Moore, and Marcia Woodruff Dalton. I offer profound thanks to those writer-friends/family who read the typescript of this novel and generously gave me their professional advice: Nancy Bowden, Julie Brickman, Lucinda Dixon Sullivan, John Morrison, John Sims Jeter, Marcia Woodruff Dalton, Katy Yocom, and Karen Mann. I thank Kelly Creagh, graduate assistant in the Spalding University MFA in Writing, for help with typescript preparation.

To other friends and family who gave me their invaluable heartfelt support—Ralph d'Neville-Raby, Frank Richmond, Nana Lampton, Kay Callaghan, Mary Welp, Alan Naslund, Robin Lippincott, Neela Vaswani,

Thelma Wyland, Pam Cox, Debbie Grubbs, Pam and Bob Sexton, Deborah and David Stewart, Suzette Henke and Jim Rooney, Annette Allen and Osgood Wiggins, Patricia and Charles Gaines, Elaine and Bobby Hughes, Loretta and Bill Cobb, Norman and Joan MacMillan, Sandra and John Lott; David Morrison, Marvin "Bubba" Jeter and Charlotte Copeland, Sara, Michael, and Ashley MacQuilling—a very special thank-you. I thank Leslie Townsend for an illuminating conversation on the concept of *abundance.*

FOR A NOVEL based on the published research of others, I need to acknowledge, with admiration and gratitude, particular nonfiction authors and their works that provided the foundation for my imaginative re-creation of Marie Antoinette and her times: Antonia Fraser, *Marie Antoinette: The Journey* (2001); Evelyne Lever, translated from the French by Catherine Temerson, *Marie Antoinette, The Last Queen of France* (2000); Ian Dunlop, *Marie-Antoinette, A Portrait* (1993); Stefan Zweig, translated from the German by Eden and Cedar Paul, *Marie Antoinette: The Portrait of an Average Woman* (1933); Olivier Bernier, *The Secrets of Marie Antoinette* (1985); Olivier Bernier, *The Eighteenth-Century Woman* (1982); Chantal Thomas, translated from the French by Julie Rose, *The Wicked Queen: The Origins of the Myth of Marie-Antoinette* (2001); Madame Campan, *Memoirs of the Court of Marie Antoinette, Queen of France;* Elisabeth Vigée-Lebrun, translated from the French by Lionel Strachey, *Memoirs of Madame Vigée Lebrun* (1903); Mary D. Sheriff, *The Exceptional Woman: Elisabeth Vigée-Lebrun and the Cultural Politics of Art* (1996); Gita May, *Elisabeth Vigée LeBrun: The Odyssey of an Artist in an Age of Revolution* (2005); Amanda Foreman, *Georgiana, Duchess of Devonshire* (1998); Simon Schama, *Citizens: A Chronicle of the French Revolution* (1989).

For their administrative support of me as Writer in Residence at the University of Louisville, I express my profound gratitude to James Ramsey, president, and to Blaine Hudson, dean of the College of Arts and Sciences, and to my colleagues of the Departments of English, Humanities, and Modern Languages; I thank as well President Jo Ann Rooney and Vice Presidents L. Randy Strickland and Tori Murden McClure of Spalding Univer-